Other books by William Heffernan:

*BRODERICK*

*CAGING THE RAVEN*

*THE CORSICAN*

*ACTS OF CONTRITION*

*RITUAL*

# WILLIAM
# HEFFERNAN

A DUTTON BOOK

DUTTON
Published by the Penguin Group
Penguin Books USA Inc., 375 Hudson Street,
New York, New York 10014, U.S.A.
Penguin Books Ltd, 27 Wrights Lane,
London W8 5TZ, England
Penguin Books Australia Ltd, Ringwood,
Victoria, Australia
Penguin Books Canada Ltd, 2801 John Street,
Markham, Ontario, Canada L3R 1B4
Penguin Books (N.Z.) Ltd, 182–190 Wairau Road,
Auckland 10, New Zealand

Penguin Books Ltd, Registered Offices:
Harmondsworth, Middlesex, England

First published by Dutton, an imprint of New American Library, a division of
Penguin Books USA Inc.
Distributed in Canada by McClelland & Stewart Inc.

First Printing, March, 1991
10  9  8  7  6  5  4  3  2  1

 REGISTERED TRADEMARK—MARCA REGISTRADA

LIBRARY OF CONGRESS CATALOGING IN PUBLICATION DATA
Heffernan, William, 1940–
    Blood rose / William Heffernan.
        p.   cm.
    I. Title.
    PS3558.E4143B57   1991
    813′.54—dc20                                          90–46463
    0-525-24962-1                                         CIP

Printed in the United States of America
Set in Melior
Designed by Leonard Telesca

*For Stacie,*
*who brings love and laughter*
*and delight to each day.*

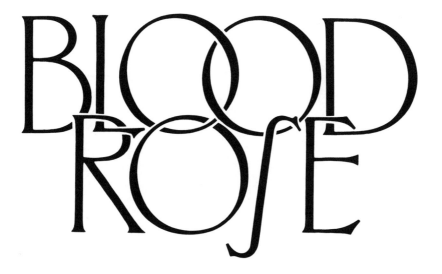

# PROLOGUE

The bed was soft and warm and luxurious, and the woman lay there content, her thick blond hair fanned out across the oversized down pillow, the trace of a smile playing lightly on her lips. The man had left her bed only an hour ago after again filling her with himself, and she could still feel the lingering after-rush of the orgasm that had sent her writhing about the bed; had nearly overwhelmed her with pleasure as close to pain as she could bear.

She glanced toward the curtained window. Dawn was only now beginning to pierce the night, sending its faint, filtered light into the room. She had beaten the clock again, she told herself. Gotten her latest lover out before his presence in her bed could no longer be denied. Her eyes moved to the opposite wall, beyond which her child slept, awaiting her call that would signal the start of another school day. The small smile slipped from her lips. She had dismissed earlier questions about the sounds coming from her room as the product of bad dreams. And the questions had stopped. But the look on the child's face some mornings had not disappeared, and she often found those eyes staring at her, appraising her—condemning her? she wondered—then quickly looking away when she confronted it.

She turned on her side, hugging herself, her eyes now falling on the photograph of her husband that sat on the bedside table. Next to it lay the single red rose her lover had brought her. She felt a sudden surge of guilt and dismissed it. What was she to do with the hours, the days her husband spent away from her? She was still young enough to be wanted, to be told she was beautiful; to have a man come to her with that special hunger in his eyes, a hunger only her body could satisfy. She needed that, needed it like she needed air to breathe.

And the child had no right to question her, judge her. It was something that would be understood someday. Something that time itself would explain. She had given the child life, through nine long, hard months. And she had given years since then. Years that had consumed her day and night, day and night, one after the other until they blended into one endless stretch of time. Now if she wanted to fill the emptiness that burned in her belly, she would do it.

Her eyes fell on her husband's picture again. But what if he's told? What if he's told about the sounds that come from her room when the child's supposed to be sleeping? What if he's told about the other men, not just this one, but the others who have made her cry out with so much pleasure. She can deny the sounds, but not the men, not so many of them. And this morning those sounds were bad. But she couldn't help it. What this one had done to her had been so good, so very good. But the men hadn't been seen. Not one of them. Not ever. She was sure of that. She'd been so careful about it. Always, so very, very careful. But the child was so sly. So strange and sly. How could she be sure of anything?

She turned to the sound of the bedroom door opening. The child stood there, staring at her with those blank, empty eyes. God, it almost made her shudder, looking into those eyes. It was as though everything had been blocked out; beaten back and hidden. And among the things hidden was she, herself. It was as though the child looked at her but didn't really see her. Her own child. The one she had given life to. She sat up slightly, drawing up the sheet to cover her nakedness.

"Hi. You're up early. You can sleep for another hour if you want." Why no answer? Why just that blank, horrible look?

Always such a difficult child. So distant, so impossible to reach, so cruel in some ways. "Did you hear me?" A nod of the head. "Then answer me!" The words sharper than intended.

The child nodded again, then began to walk toward the bed, hands behind the back, the feet almost shuffling, all of it making the movement seem awkward, almost jerky. The eyes stared at the picture on the bedside table, the single rose next to it. "When will Poppa be coming back?"

"Not for another few days. He went off hunting with some friends. You know that." God. Ten years old, and still calling him Poppa. And in that singsong, baby-talk voice. "Maybe he'll bring you something. He usually does."

The child looked away from the photograph, the rose, the eyes now fixed on the woman's face—the look cold and empty again, the eyes unblinking, very much like those of a mannequin in a store window.

"Are they going to keep coming here every night?"

The woman flinched, as though prodded by something sharp. "What are you talking about? Is who going to keep coming here?"

"The men. The men who always come here when Poppa's away."

The woman stared at the child. Standing there. Rigid. Hands behind the back, almost like a block of stone. And the eyes. They still hadn't blinked. Not once.

"What are you talking about?" There was a tremor in the woman's voice, and she hoped the child didn't notice it.

"I hear them. I hear you. Through the wall."

A smile flashed to the woman's mouth, but it was weak, ineffective. "It's just those bad dreams again, that's all. Sometimes they seem very real."

The child continued to stare, eyes fixed. "No, I'm awake. The sounds wake me up."

The woman's mouth twitched; she forced the smile to remain in place. "Maybe you're hearing me have bad dreams," she said. "You know you're mommy's favorite. I don't need anyone else but you."

The child's head shook back and forth, the first sign of any movement, any animation. But the eyes remained blank, unblinking.

"Please don't let them come here anymore. Poppa wouldn't want them to come here."

Rage surged through the woman and she jumped forward on the bed, coming up to her hands and knees, the sheet falling away. She glared at the child, her mouth twisted and angry and vengeful. "When I tell you something's a dream, it's a dream. Don't you *ever* tell me it isn't. Don't you tell me something's happening, when I tell you it's not. Don't be so stupid. You always say such stupid things. Don't you dare tell *anyone* those things. Not ever. *Do you hear me!*"

The final words were shouted, but the child didn't move, or flinch, or blink. The woman reached out and grabbed the child's shoulders, squeezing them between her hands, the fingers pinching into the flesh.

"*Do you?*" she shouted again.

A hand came from behind the child's back, holding a kitchen knife, the glistening steel blade eight inches long. The second hand joined the first, clasping the handle.

"Why do you have that knife!" the woman demanded.

The child's eyes widened in fear. "It's the men. They scare me."

The woman's fingers dug into the child's shoulders. "You drop that knife right now." She began to shake the child, making its head flop back and forth like a lifeless doll.

The child's arms shot forward, driving the blade into the woman's stomach only inches above the pubic mound.

The woman's eyes widened in shock and her mouth gaped open as she let out a breathy grunt. Her hands tightened on the child's shoulders, and she tried to push its body back. But all strength had already left her arms and the child's body seemed firm and solid and unmovable. She stared at the child, watching as its body began to shake, to jerk in uncontrolled spasms, propelling its arms up, dragging the blade in erratic jolts through the abdomen, until it struck the sternum and lodged there.

The woman hunched forward, eyes already beginning to glaze, blood flowing from her still-open mouth. The blade stopped her forward movement, and her body began to fall back, dragging the knife down and finally out, bringing with it a slithering trail of intestine, the long, stringy organ slashed open and covered in blood and bile and excrement.

The child stared down at the twitching, shaking body on the bed, then turned and walked purposefully from the room, down a long, narrow hall and into the kitchen. There, almost somnambulistic in its movements, the child filled the sink with soapy, hot water and methodically scrubbed the blade clean, then dried it carefully and placed it in its proper drawer.

Turning, eyes still fixed and unblinking, the child walked slowly back to the bedroom, to the cluttered bedside table. A small hand picked up the rose, the fist closing, crushing the petals, then dropping the flower into a pool of spreading blood. Now the small body seemed frozen, rocklike at the side of the bed. The eyes stared down at the now still, lifeless, gutted body. Blank eyes, staring at blank eyes.

"Mommy's favorite," the small voice whispered.

Slowly, the hands rose to the sides of the head; the palms pressed firmly against the ears. The eyes widened, suddenly filled with fear and horror and recognition. The mouth snapped open and breaths came in sharp, jagged gasps. Then the child began to scream.

# CHAPTER
# 1

Leslie Adams scanned the grocery list, convinced she had forgotten something. It was typical these days; she knew it and it annoyed her.

"Damn it," she said, a hissing voice, almost inaudible.

Her light brown eyes moved from the list to the 12-year-old boy standing a few feet away. He was grinning at her, his eyes—duplicates of her own—dancing with a mischievous challenge.

"Say it and I'll clobber you," she warned.

The grin widened as he shrugged. "I'm not saying anything."

Leslie closed her eyes and ground her teeth. "Tell me what I forgot."

The boy took the list, read through it, and shrugged again. "I'm just your brother, not your keeper," he said, fighting back another smile.

"Robbie, don't do this. You're playing with a time bomb today." She watched his attempt to fake a serious pose. His mouth was a hard line, lips pressed together, making his slender, boyish face seem older than it was beneath the mop of brown hair that fanned his forehead. He pulled on his small, straight nose with an air of concentration, and she had to hold back her own laughter. God, how she loved him, had ever since they were forced back together three years ago when their father had died, leaving the boy homeless. It had been the only thing that had been good in those three years.

Robbie looked up from the list, his head raised to his full height now. He was five foot five, the same height as she. A bit short for his age at 12, where she was just average at 28. But his bones were large on a lanky frame, and she knew he would shoot up one of these days and tower over her.

"Just Coke," Robbie said. "It's the only thing I can see that's missing." He made a face, screwing up his nose, until the few freckles remaining from summer seemed to bunch together. "I suppose we'll *have* to get that diet, caffeine-free junk."

"That's right, unless you want a fat sister going around on your arm." She took the list back. "You sure that's all?"

"Yup," he said, hooking his thumbs in the loops of his jeans.

Robbie had begun mimicking local slang and mannerisms ever since he had moved to Vermont two weeks earlier, and he added to it now by shuffling his feet and bobbing his head, his tongue stuck in his cheek.

Leslie fought back her own grin. "Stop it," she whispered. "You'll get us thrown out of here."

After pulling a six-pack of caffeine-free diet Coke from a well-stocked cooler, she made her way to the counter of the country store, where her other purchases had been piled. The store was crowded with late Saturday afternoon shoppers, several of whom were local women—longtime residents, Leslie suspected—who followed her progress across the store with unmasked disapproval. But she was getting used to it. Ever since she had arrived in town she had had the uncomfortable feeling of being watched.

It's the way you're dressed she told herself. And the fact they already know there's no man living in your house. She offered a false, brave smile as she passed, silently vowing she wouldn't alter herself in *any way* to satisfy *anyone*.

But it wasn't just the women. A group of teenaged boys had been hanging out in front of the store when she and Robbie had arrived, and they had openly leered at her, showing only the good grace—or the timidity—to keep their mouths shut. She comforted herself with the thought that back home in Philadelphia it would have been worse. But damn it, there was nothing wrong with the way she was dressed. She glanced at herself in the glass-fronted case behind the counter. Okay, the jeans were tight, but the blue workman's shirt was loose, almost baggy, even if one button too many had been left undone. And she couldn't help it that her face was young and thin and pretty, or that her brown hair, with hints of red and blond, was long and—she had been told—sensual. And it sure as hell wasn't her fault she lived alone. What for Christsake did they want? That she bring the drunken, abusive bastard she had lived with for five years with her, just so she could put their minds at ease?

She pushed the thought of Jack away. He had taken up too much of her life already, and she wasn't going to give him another inch of it, another hour.

"I think this is it," Leslie said to the tall, droll-looking man behind the counter.

"I was next here." The words came from a heavy, frumpy woman of about 40 who had been standing talking to another who could have been her sister. They weren't directed at Leslie, but rather at the man behind the counter, almost as though she didn't exist.

"I'm sorry," Leslie said. "I didn't realize you were in line."

"Not standin' here waitin' for a bus." The words again directed to the man behind the counter.

"Won't get one, should ya," the man said. He offered Leslie a small smile as if telling her not to worry. She was grateful for the gesture.

Leslie waited, one foot tapping nervously, as the woman's purchases were bagged and paid for. But she didn't leave. She simply turned her back and continued talking with her friend/sister.

"Moved into the old Beebe place, I hear," the counterman said, as he began totaling Leslie's purchases on an old crank-operated adding machine.

"Yes, it's a lovely old house," Leslie said, thinking that everyone in town had probably known all about her, even before the first box had been taken off the U-Haul.

"Yup, old Lestina Beebe took good care of the place. Probably had the best vegetable garden in the county too. Took good care of the roof; know that for a fact." The man, whose name was Elson Gallup, but who answered to the name El, nodded approval of his own remarks as if bestowing some imprimatur to his opinions.

"It was very well cared for inside as well," Leslie said, immediately wondering if she was seeking some kind of approval or acceptance of herself with the remark.

"Folks take good care of things hereabouts." It was the other woman, the friend/sister this time, and she was looking at Robbie as she spoke, as if she found something uncared for about the green Philadelphia Eagles sweatshirt, or the well-worn jeans, or the battered Nikes that he wore.

Leslie offered the woman an "up yours" smile that would have been understood in Philadelphia but probably didn't mean shit from shinola here, she decided. She slipped her arm around Robbie's shoulders and gave him a hug he would probably hate, then turned her attention back to El, who was methodically cranking away on his adding machine.

Robbie stood quietly, hoping none of the kids outside would come in and see his sister hugging him that way, wondering why these old bats were being so mean to her, knowing they were being mean to him as well. Jesus, it's bad enough he had to be dragged off to live in the boonies. Now he had to deal with boonie people too.

He had liked his three years in Philadelphia. It had been neat. The kids, his school. Not living with Jack, of course. Nobody could like that. But Jack was history now, and it would have been nice if everything had stayed the same, especially the kids and school. He wondered what school would be like here. He had only gotten here three days ago. He had been with his grandmother in Philly, hiding out from Jack until Leslie found a safe place for them. But, Jesus, if this was what safe meant, a little danger didn't seem all that bad.

He glanced around the store. At least *it* was neat. He had never seen so much different stuff crammed into one small store. It was like the corner stores back in the city, but it had all kinds of stuff you'd never find there. A whole section with guns and hunting clothes and boots, and fishing stuff and traps for catching animals. He could have used some of those traps in his school back home. Put a couple in his locker so the creeps who were always breaking into it could lose a couple of fingers the next time they decided to rip him off. Robbie grinned at the idea, then wondered if there were rip-off artists up here too. Hell yes, he told himself. Probably a whole bunch of cattle rustlers. He had never seen so many stupid cows in his life. The whole place looked like the set of some spaghetti western with black and white cows.

His sister's words brought him back. She was asking the guy behind the counter if he knew anybody who could help her get some stuff squared away at the house.

"What type of work you need doin'?" El asked. "If it's 'lectric or plumbin' or just bangin' nails, it'da be a different fella for each."

Leslie bit her lower lip. Peripheral vision revealed the two "sisters" turning toward her, and she knew they were waiting to see what innocent local she was about to lure to her lair.

"It's mostly repair work on the outside of the house and some yard work." There was some work inside, especially the years of clutter that had to be cleared away, but she was damned if she was going to say it now.

"Well, let's see," El began. "Might you could ask—"

"Don't have to look much farther than right here, El." The words came from a tall, well-built young man who was approaching the counter from the rear of the store. There was a smile on his face, and like his pale blue eyes, it seemed somewhat smug, perhaps even a little cruel, Leslie thought.

She watched him approach. He was about 22 or 23, and he was dressed in a jacket and tie, which made his offer seem incongruous.

The young man seemed to read her mind; his smile broadened and he touched the lapel of his jacket with one hand. "Don't let the fancy clothes scare you off," he said. "Just been to a funeral this morning. I promise I won't show up for work dressed like this."

Leslie glanced at El and found him staring at the counter as though he had removed himself from the conversation. Even the two "sisters" had turned away. It was absurd, but it almost seemed as if the young man had somehow frightened them into being civil. But he certainly didn't seem frightening. He was smug, obviously a bit self-centered in the way attractive young men tended to be, but definitely not frightening. In fact

Leslie realized she hadn't even noticed him being in the store, and yet he had come from the back, so he must have been there.

Robbie was also staring at the young man. He had noticed him—noticed him staring at his sister, openly checking her out every time she bent over to retrieve something from a low shelf. He didn't know exactly why, but he knew he didn't want him at their house.

"Name's Billy Perot," the young man said, pronouncing his last name as the French would, with the *t* silent. "I heard what you said you needed and I didn't hear anything I couldn't handle."

There was something about the way this Billy Perot said it that gave her a nervous twinge, but she was sure it was nothing more than her old paranoia reasserting itself. And she'd be damned if she'd let the two "sisters," whose necks were craned to catch every word, see her appear even slightly timid. Instead she placed her hands on her hips and stared directly into the young man's cold blue eyes.

"I couldn't pay you very much," she said. She inclined her head in a gesture of resignation. "The fact is, I don't have very much right now." She smiled, a large, beautiful, friendly smile. "Except work that needs to be done."

Billy returned the smile; it too lacked any warmth. "Like to help you out with whatever you need. You're here awhile, you'll find a lotta folks feel that way." He glanced at the "sisters' " backs as though silently dismissing them, then looked briefly at El, who was still staring at the counter. When he turned his attention back to Leslie, he was smiling again. "I can start whenever you want. Tomorrow be okay?"

"Sure. Let me give you directions to the house."

"Oh, I know where it is." His smile broadened. "Word has a way of gettin' around pretty fast in a town like this. But I suspect you found that out already."

"Indeed I have," Leslie said, offering the "sisters' " backs her own look now. "How's ten o'clock sound?"

"Great. I'll be there."

Leslie turned back to the counter, paid her bill, and began gathering her groceries.

"Let me help," Billy said, relieving her of the load before she could object.

Outside, Billy loaded the groceries into the rear of Leslie's pickup truck, repeated the time he would arrive the next day, then watched as she climbed behind the wheel, the smile on his face changing to a leer. He glanced toward Robbie, who was still outside the truck, watching him. He winked at the boy.

Paul Devlin stood across the street taking in the spectacle of Billy Perot playing gentleman, noting, as he did, that two women had come to the window of El's store to watch it as well.

Devlin was tall and slender, and standing there, dressed in a gray tweed sports jacket over a red sweater and jeans, he looked more like a college instructor than a chief of police. But it was an image he fostered—not looking like a cop— something he had carried over from his years as a detective with the New York Police Department. Like his decision not to carry a gun. That too had come from New York, although it was something he never spoke about. Not to anyone.

Devlin reached in the driver's window of the Jeep Cherokee the town had given him and retrieved his zippered briefcase. He had just returned from the funeral of Eva Hyde, from doing the old cop standard of attending the burial of a murder victim on the off chance someone might say or do something suspicious. It had been a waste of time. But then, it had been a waste of time whenever he had done it in the past, and he had not expected it to be any different.

It had been a small funeral. Eva had had no relatives left alive. The main contingent, headed by Billy Perot, had been made up of regulars from the roadhouse where Eva had spent most of her idle hours. Then there was Jim McCloud, camera in hand, no doubt representing the local newspaper he ran; his assistant Electa Litchfield, who, years before, had been one of Eva's high school teachers; Orlando Quint, the town doctor, who had autopsied her body; Gunter Kline, owner of the restaurant where she had worked as a waitress; and Louis Ferris, a teacher at the local grammar school. Ferris was the only one who had struck a strident cord with Devlin. There had been no apparent tie with the woman. But then, he was single, and Eva had had a reputation of seeking out every single man she could find, along with a few who weren't. So much for the wonderful world of suspects, Devlin thought. Especially in a case everyone else had labeled an accident.

There was a small two-inch scar on Devlin's left cheek, reminiscent of the dueling scars once favored by European aristocrats. And in one sense it was similar. It was a gift of the last case he had worked in New York, a tangible sign of other scars better hidden. It also served as a warning to his moods, appearing to turn whiter when he was angry or tense or nervous. It was white now.

He ran one hand through his wavy black hair, already flecked with gray, despite his 32 years, and turned toward the basement entrance of the courthouse, where the police department was housed. Inside, the town's oldest patrolman, Fredom Sergeant, sat behind a gray metal desk guarding the telephones. Devlin stopped, picked up his messages and skimmed through them before turning his attention to the fat 60ish town cop, whose uniform looked as though it had been pressed with a steam roller.

"Any problems I should know about?" Devlin asked.

Fredom—known to his drinking buddies as Free, because they claimed it was what he always expected—fitted gold-rimmed spectacles to his fleshy red face and began scanning a legal pad next to the telephone. He scratched his thick white hair, sending a shower of dandruff to the desk top, then looked up and shrugged.

"Electa Litchfield had a prowler last night," he said.

"Electa always has a prowler," Devlin said.

"Well, that's about it. What happened at Eva Hyde's funeral?"

"They buried her," Devlin said. "Did Gaylord and Luther interview that list of friends I gave them last night?"

"Don't know," Free said. "Suspect they did. But they should be in soon. Don't really see why we should bother, though. Staties from BCI gonna do it anyways."

Devlin studied Free's blank, expressionless face—a man named Sergeant, who had never made that rank, and never would. But in a sense he was right. The State Police Bureau of Criminal Investigation would be assigned the case, as it was all unexplained deaths in rural areas not covered by a large, professional police department. And Devlin's department certainly didn't qualify as one. But Eva's death had already been ruled an accident by Quint, the town coroner, so any investigation would be perfunctory at best. Something in Devlin's gut told him more had to be done.

"We'll bother, because that's what we get paid to do," he said, turning toward his small private office. He stopped in the doorway and looked back. "And, Free, get that damned uniform pressed, will you?"

Devlin sat at his desk and reviewed the already growing file—photographs of the scene, the coroner's report, the interview with the farmhand who had discovered the body, and a list of almost nonexistent physical evidence.

There was still the possibility the coroner was right, that Eva Hyde's death had been an accident. But Devlin found himself unable to accept it. Eva had been 21 years old and had had the reputation of being the town pump. The locals fond of talking about such things were quick to point out that getting into Eva's knickers, or enjoying a blow job, or hand job in the back seat of a car on a first date, was equivalent to a goodnight kiss from most other young women. Devlin doubted the veracity of that claim, but he also didn't give a damn either way. The young woman, he knew, had come from a brutal environment, a broken home of two equally abusive parents, and she had sought love and comfort and affection wherever she could find them. And that had led her to bars and roadhouses, and to men who were quick to provide any substance that would make her pliable to their wants.

"Born to be fucked." That had been Free's idiotic comment when the body had been found. And indeed she had been, by many people, in many ways. But Free was too stupid to understand what that meant.

Devlin looked at the photographs again. Eva's body had been found in an uncultivated meadow outside of town by a farmhand looking for a lost heifer. A sharpened stake had been driven into her chest. But the stake had had dirt on its blunt end, and it was possible she had fallen on it. At least that's what the coroner thought. The theory was that she had been cutting across the field to escape an amorous misadventure, had stumbled and impaled herself. But Devlin couldn't buy that scenario. The body had been savaged by animals, the entrails scattered and partially eaten. But Devlin thought he had detected the remains of an incision, although the coroner disagreed, and the badly mauled state of the body made it impossible to be certain. And then there was the matter of Eva's missing heart. Animals or a madman? Devlin could not be sure. And the dried red rose found some distance from the body, the petals brittle with age, as though it had spent years pressed between the pages of a book. Had it been closer to the body before the animals finished their work? Left as some sort of totem?

The possibility sent shivers through him. His last case in New York had involved brutal mutilations, an ancient religious ritual performed by a madman—a madman who had been his friend and his partner. A man he had loved, and whom he had been forced to kill. No, worse than that, he told himself now.

He looked at the book that lay on his desk, the binding still rigid, the pages, yet to be turned, pressed together in a solid block of white. It had arrived in the morning's mail from New York's Strand Bookstore, ordered from their catalogue of arcane books—a catalogue that already had filled one bookcase in his home over the past two years and had made a fair start on a second.

Devlin stared at the title, emblazoned in gold across the book's solid black jacket. *The Psychology of Pleasure in Killing.* He reached out and picked up the book, tilting it forward, holding it at arm's length, almost as though it were some kind of talisman that would provide answers to impossible questions, but one that shouldn't be brought too close, too soon.

His former partner, Rolk, had been a student of murder, and after his . . . death . . . Devlin had taken over the subject, but with a subtle twist. Unlike Rolk, he had not wanted to learn why killers killed. He had wanted to understand why some enjoyed doing it so much.

Part of your endless study of self-understanding, he told himself, allowing the book to fall back to the desk.

He shook the thought away and turned back to the report on Eva Hyde. The suspicion—his suspicion—that her death might have involved deliberate mutilation had, like the crushed rose he had found, been kept from the public, or at least he thought it had. With the cops he had inherited it was impossible to tell.

But they feel the same way about you, Devlin told himself.

They resent where you came from and how you were brought in, and most of all that you're not one of them, and never were.

Yet he couldn't blame them. He had moved to Vermont to escape the past, to be alone with his 6-year-old daughter, and away from police work. Then the old chief had died, and town officials—aware of his past employment, as they seemed to be aware of everything about everyone—had come to him and had asked him to take over. He had agreed, in part for therapy, in part to escape the boredom that had begun to gnaw at him. And it had worked, and when his reappointment had come around the following year, he had gotten it, much to the displeasure of the men who worked for him.

Fuck 'em, he said to himself, as he had whenever the thought crossed his mind. Life sucks, and the sooner his deadhead cops learned that basic fact the better.

The outer office erupted with laughter, and Devlin knew that deadheads Gaylord French and Luther Barrabee had decided to honor him with their presence. He stood and went to his office door, knowing that Free would either not pass on the message that he wanted to see them or, if he did, it would simply be ignored until he pushed it.

The two patrolmen stood with their backs to Devlin's office. From that view they looked like twins, two large, rawboned, blond-haired farmboys. When they turned, Devlin knew, the differences would be apparent. Gaylord, at 30, was still trim. Luther, 10 years older, featured a paunch that hung over his Sam Browne gunbelt. Gaylord had a large, hooked nose and squinty eyes; Luther, the flattened nose of a prizefighter and eyes that seemed ready to bulge out of his head. Both were slightly less than bright.

"What did the interviews turn up?" Devlin asked, ignoring any false need for pleasantries. The two turned, confirming his earlier mental observations.

"Nothin' we already didn't know," Gaylord began. " 'Cept she was at Pearlie's roadhouse last time anybody saw her."

"She leave with anybody?"

"Nope. But she never did. Always arranged to meet up later, did she want to," Luther chimed in. "Guess she thought folks wouldn't know that way. 'Cept they always did."

"Who was there that night?"

"Usual crowd," Luther said.

Devlin stared at him, waiting for more, but Luther only blinked.

Devlin lowered his eyes and drew a deep breath, then looked back at Luther. "In case you haven't noticed, I don't drop in at Pearlie's every night. So could you just tell me who the fuck was there?"

Luther rolled his eyes toward Gaylord, silently stating that any good cop would know Pearlie's regulars. "Like I said, usual crowd," Luther continued, reinforcing his view. "Billy Perot and his buddies. You know that lot. Billy's daddy stopped by. And that teacher over the school, Louis Ferris was there. Seems he's been hangin' out there a lot lately. Only person who wasn't a regular was crazy ol' Jubal Duval. But even Eva wouldn'a gone off with him. She weren't *that* horny."

Gaylord and Free burst into laughter over Luther's unexpected wit, and Luther himself was so pleased he joined in as well. Devlin just shook his head and turned back toward his office.

"Type up the interviews and have them on my desk before you go back out on patrol," he said over his shoulder. In the glass front of his office Devlin could see Luther raising his middle finger to his back. He stopped and turned, the scar on his cheek a bright white line.

"Luther," he said, his voice calm and soft and cold, "if you ever toss the bird at my back again, I'm gonna fire you right then and there. Then I'm gonna grab you by the throat, drag your fat ass out of here, and kick it in front of this whole shitkicking town. You understand me?"

Luther stared at him, his face growing scarlet with a mixture of embarrassment and anger.

"The reports. Ten minutes. On my desk," Devlin said, then spun on his heel and returned to his office.

Back behind his desk Devlin jotted down the names Luther had given him. He underlined Louis Ferris, deciding he would speak to the teacher himself, then wrote "at funeral" next to his name. Ray Perot, Billy's father, would be another matter. There'd be no cooperation there. The rich, egotistical, womanizing bastard would be his usual patronizing self. He'd play his role as the man who employed most of the town, all the while letting Devlin know—without saying it—that his clout in the community meant he employed him as well. Then he'd answer what he wanted to answer, and nothing more. And the truth was he probably did employ Devlin. And Devlin knew it. He just didn't give a fuck. And Ray Perot didn't know that.

He stared at Billy's name again, and the sight of the woman and the boy climbing into the truck, with Billy watching, came back to him. He had heard about the woman; knew she lived only about a mile from his own house. He could make a point of speaking with her. Just let her know Billy wasn't the pussy-cat he made out to be. He thought about the woman again and wondered if that was the only reason he wanted to stop by. Devlin shook his head. Hell, she was a big girl from a big city. She didn't need him to hold her hand. And maybe she wanted a Billy Perot in her life. And if she did, so be it. If there was one thing he didn't have time for in his life, it was protecting people from themselves.

The eyes follow the woman as she moves toward the door. The subtle sway of hips. Dark hair tossed over a shoulder in that unconscious gesture that was practiced and studied in her youth, a way to draw attention to her beauty, her availability; something that would bring her the filth she wanted, leaving behind only one possible ending. *Just like mother.* An image fills the mind—hearts torn and bleeding; broken by pain; pierced; rived; impaled; suffering. Oh, yes, suffering.

The hands close into fists and a slight tic develops at the corner of one eye. The woman disappears through the door, a young boy following close behind. The sound of a beating heart fills the mind, a rhythmic pulsing, soft, steady, unrelenting. The head nods, not to the rhythm, but to another voice, silent, unheard, speaking of punishment already begun, easing other pain.

But still the pain returns, again and again and again. And it will keep coming until you stop them. The beating grows louder, but only in the mind.

"Stop the men from coming." The voice, almost a hiss, the words drawn out, then again. "Stop them."

The figure moves toward the door the woman has entered, then hesitates, uncertain. Louder, a steady, constant, thumping beat. Fists open and close, open and close, open and close.

"Now. Stop them now."

———

Leslie parked the truck in front of the local newspaper office and stared up at the sign. The Weekly Clarion—and all of it crammed into the single floor of an old storefront. She had written to the editor before she had moved; had explained she was a freelance artist and sent samples of her work. The editor, someone named Jim McCloud, had responded immediately and offered her work doing advertising layouts. The pay wouldn't be great, but it would cover grocery bills, and combined with the work she had been promised by several book publishers and small ad agencies in New York and Philadelphia, it might just be enough to get Robbie and her through the long winter ahead.

She turned toward Robbie and offered a wan smile. "Have to go in and talk to the man. Why don't you come with me. Who knows, maybe you can get a paper route. Then we might even be able to eat this winter."

Robbie grinned at her. "Who wants to eat," he said. "We're supposed to be starving artists. Just like in that opera you took me to."

"That's us," Leslie said. "La Boheme in Vermont."

She climbed out of the truck and immediately felt a chill run along her back, as the feeling of being watched returned again. She turned, her eyes roaming the street. Nothing. No one.

They went through the front door and were immediately confronted by a long counter, behind which sat a small cluster of paper-strewn desks. Only two of the desks were occupied, one by an older, bespectacled woman, dressed in a forest green dress; the other by a man of about 40, who Leslie thought quite attractive despite his florid face and uncombed hair.

The woman looked up at them, apparently decided they weren't worth the effort, and returned to whatever she had been doing. There was a large stuffed black bird on the edge of her desk, a hideous thing, Leslie thought, with piercing yellow eyes that seemed to stare at everything at once, and a beak frozen in a permanent scream.

"Excuse me," Leslie called, a bit louder than she had intended. "I was supposed to see Jim McCloud."

The man looked up, his face breaking into a boyish smile. He jabbed a finger in Leslie's direction. "Leslie Adams, right?" When Leslie nodded, he stood, came around his desk and started toward her. "I'm Jim McCloud. Welcome to our miniature madhouse."

Leslie watched him approach. He was slightly more than average height, about five foot ten, she guessed, and he was still reasonably trim, although a bit on the soft side. But the rest was quite pleasing. He had sandy hair and warm brown eyes, set in a pleasant, gentle face that lacked any predominant feature, and left him looking like somebody's uncle—anybody's uncle, really. His sleeves were rolled to the elbow, his necktie askew, suggesting a television stereotype of a newspaperman. Leslie thought it might be a very practiced look.

"Come around this silly thing," he said, waving her around the long, battered wooden counter. "So you're our new artist. Damn I can't tell you how much we need you. We've had to ship everything to Burlington and then pay through the nose to get it back on time. *If* we get it at all." He took Leslie's hand, shook it warmly, then seemed to notice Robbie for the first time. "And who's this?"

Leslie made the introductions, explaining that Robbie was 12 and would be starting in the local school's seventh grade on Monday. "Maybe you can tell him what the school is like," she suggested.

"I can do better than that," McCloud said, turning and shouting the name Tim toward a door at the back of the room.

When the door opened a boy slightly smaller than Robbie, but obviously about the same age, ambled toward them, an uncertain look on his face.

"This is Tim, my son," McCloud said, "and he just started seventh grade this year." He winked at the boy, then turned back to Leslie. "Jim and Tim," he said. "My late ex-wife had a fondness for things that rhymed. *Her* name was Kim, and I always wondered if that was the main reason she married me." He grinned at himself. "But, in any event, Tim can give Robbie all the poop on the new school while you and I talk business." He turned to his son. "Why don't you take Robbie out back and show him our self-destructive printing press, and I'll introduce Leslie to Electa."

The two boys made their way to the back room, while Jim guided Leslie to the older woman still seated at one of the overflowing desks.

"We had a rather tragic death in town," Jim said as they

approached the woman. "A young woman who grew up here—an old student of Electa's—who worked in one of the local restaurants. Possibly murdered, although our local police chief—who still thinks he's a bigshot New York City detective—won't give us any confirmation on that. So we've been a bit frantic trying to put together a story without squat to work with."

Leslie noticed the hint of an accent in Jim's voice. It seemed to emerge with his anger at the local police chief. "Boston?" she asked.

"Yeah. That's where I hail from. Fifteen years on *The Globe*. But I spent so much time overseas, I thought I'd lost most of the drawl."

"It's not strong, but it's still there," Leslie said.

"Anyway, I decided to chuck it and satisfy a longtime fantasy—own my own paper in a small New England town. Well, I did it. For five years now. And this sure as hell is a small New England town. And, as far as I'm concerned, all it needs now is a good psychiatric clinic."

"That bad, huh?"

"It has its moments. If you don't believe me, ask Mary, my wife. She grew up here. But it's mostly the paper. Although, in some ways, it's the town too."

Leslie was sure she knew what he meant, recalling her earlier experience at El's store, but she decided to keep silent. They had stopped before the older woman's desk, and she looked up now, checking Leslie from head to foot.

"This is Electa Litchfield, our copy editor, advertising coordinator, and majordomo. Without her everything I write would be littered with misspellings, grammatical errors, and lapses in syntax that would expose my lack of talent to about fifteen thousand readers each week. Luckily for me, Electa taught at the local school for thirty years, then was foolish enough to allow me to lure her out of retirement."

Leslie smiled at the woman, who had not yet finished appraising her. It was impossible to guess her age. She could be in her mid-50s or much, much older. Her gray hair was tightly bound in a severe bun, and the sharp angular features of her face were accented by heavy eyebrows and eyes that seemed to gleam with some inner madness. She seemed almost avian, like the hideous stuffed bird perched on her desk.

"By the way," Jim continued, seeming not to notice the woman's slightly wild look, "Electa lives in the house next to yours. So you'll not only be cohorts in this great journalistic effort, but neighbors as well."

Leslie groaned inwardly, pleased only by the realization that houses on her road were spread widely apart. "Well, I hope we'll become good friends, then," Leslie lied. "It's such a beautiful place."

Electa tilted her head so her long, pointed nose was fixed on Leslie like a dagger. "Pretty, it is, if ya don't mind prowlers. Got them comin' out of our ears up there," she said. "But our cityboy chief of police couldn't catch one unless I peppered his tail with birdshot and tied him to a tree."

Jim, outside Electa's field of vision, rolled his eyes and fought off a laugh. "Electa's had some problems," Jim said, with a quick wink. "And neither of us is too enamored with the chief right now. But I'm sure the chief'll get it cleared up. Why don't we sit at my desk and talk about the work you'll be doing?"

"That fool couldn't clear up acne," Electa said to their retreating backs. "Tells everybody he's a widower. But I bet his wife just ran off on him."

"So then the folded newspapers come out of here and get stacked for delivery," Tim said. He shrugged. "I guess it's pretty neat, but I've seen it so many times it doesn't seem like a big deal anymore."

"You deliver them?" Robbie asked.

"Naw. Pop Duval does that. He just delivers them to stores in the different towns. People just pick them up there. Nobody gets them delivered to their houses."

"Who's Pop Duval?"

"He's this old guy, who mostly hunts and fishes. He's supposed to be a really big hunter. People say he knows all the woods around here like it was his backyard or something."

"Sounds weird," Robbie said.

"Everybody's weird around here," Tim said.

"So how's the school?"

"Weird. Really, really weird."

"How come?"

"It's just the kids. At least some of them. If you don't come from this asshole place, they really give you a hard time. You know what I mean? It's like because I came from Boston, and didn't grow up with cow shit in my backyard, there's something wrong with me. They really get on your case if you don't know all about guns and hunting and fishing and farms and tractors and all kinds of stupid stuff like that."

"But you've been here a while now, haven't you?" Robbie asked.

"Naw, just a year," Tim said. "My father and stepmother have been here a while. But I lived in Boston with my mother. She and my dad got divorced a long time ago. I was only five then."

"So how come you came up here?"

"My mom died. So I had to."

Robbie stared at the floor and shuffled his feet nervously. "Sorry," he said.

Tim shrugged and looked away. His slender face seemed pinched together, lips pressed into a line, large, blue eyes narrow. He ran one finger under his small, flat nose, then brushed away a long strand of blond hair that had fallen across his forehead. "So how come you're here?" he asked.

"My mother died a long time ago—right after I was born— then my dad died three years ago, and I went to live with my sister and her husband. He was really a creep. He used to drink all the time, and then he'd get pissed about everything and he'd whack both of us around. So my sister split and decided to come here so he couldn't find us. I guess we're kinda hiding out from him, at least until she can get settled and get a divorce."

"So where'd you live before you came here?"

"Philadelphia."

"Then you're in trouble," Tim said.

"Why?" Robbie asked.

"No cow shit in the backyards in Philadelphia."

Both boys began to giggle.

"Maybe we can buy some and rub it on our shoes," Robbie suggested.

They started laughing again.

"I tried that. It doesn't work," Tim said.

"Why not?" Robbie asked, tears forming in his eyes now.

"They know the difference between Vermont shit and imported shit."

Robbie was laughing so hard now his stomach hurt. "So we'll buy some Vermont shit," he suggested.

"Can't," Tim said, barely able to get the word out.

"How come?" Robbie asked.

"They won't sell it. They give it to each other as Christmas presents," Tim said.

When Jim and Leslie opened the door to the back room they just stood and stared at the two hysterical boys. Jim turned to Leslie and grinned. "I guess we don't have to worry about them getting along, do we?" he said.

# CHAPTER
## 2

The old man walked along the ridge of the mountain, his right leg—lame for 20 years now—dragging slightly more with each step. He was 70 years old, but even with the bad leg he moved better than most men 20 or 30 years younger. He was following a deer track only three or four hours old, and there was an 8 mm rifle slung over his shoulder. All about him the autumn foliage of Vermont battled the sun, sending off a kaleidoscope of color—crimson, orange, yellow, and brown—and with it the lethal rustling of the already dead, or soon to be dead, leaves that spoke of the long cold that would soon engulf all who lived there.

But the old man didn't notice—he was used to it; it had been part of his life for more years than he cared to recall—and his attention remained fixed on the fresh track before him and in keeping the sling of his rifle fixed to his shoulder as he traversed the rocks and slides and outcroppings of the ridge.

The rifle, of course, had no real purpose, and he knew it. Deer season, in Vermont, would not begin for another six weeks, and the weapon he carried was too large and too powerful for deer. He carried it only on the off chance a black bear might cross his path. The season for bear began in early September, and there was always the chance he might see one. He had seen at least three dozen in the 54 years he had hunted. And he had shot one—although it was a killing he never spoke about. It had been a sow, something he had not known until it was too late, and as he had gutted her, he had seen her two cubs 100 yards off in the brush, watching, and he had known they would die that winter without her milk, and he had left the carcass and had gone home without the meat, and had never shot at a bear again. Yet he still carried the large-bore rifle, because it seemed inappropriate to go into the woods without it.

A deadfall, an old, rotted poplar, lay across the deer trail, and the old man used it gratefully to rest his leg. He straddled it, the rifle across his knees, and he removed his black and red checkered cap and mopped his forehead with the back of his sleeve. The memory of his wife intruded on his thoughts. It was a painful memory, one that had come less frequently as the years had passed. But in recent days it always seemed to be there, sitting on the edge of his consciousness, waiting to bring back pain he only wanted to forget. He took several deep breaths, pushing the memory away, knowing unconsciously it would not go far, then rubbed one hand over his heavily lined—almost gaunt—face. His hair was short and bristly and gray, far from the bright red it had once been, and his still-wiry six-foot frame could no longer do what it had done for so many years before. It was simply tired.

That's why they call you Pop, he told himself. It's why they've called you that for more'n ten years now.

He grunted at the thought, then smiled. Can still hunt 'n' track the shit outta all of 'em, he told himself, knowing without doubt he was right. Not tough as nails anymore, but can still outhunt, outtrack any of them sumbitches. He paused a moment. 'Cept maybe one, he added to himself.

Pop shook off the thought, stood, stretched, and started off again, his eyes fixed to the track of the large deer he had been following.

It was a truly big deer, 200 pounds or more, before being field dressed. Probably a buck, he told himself. Or a big ol' sumbitch of a doe. But he couldn't tell, not without checking above and below the ridge to see if it carried the tracks of "skippers" tracing their momma along the trail. But it really didn't matter. Come the snow, when the bucks went into rut, the same trails would be followed again and again. You only had to know where they were. Pop grinned at himself. And be there at the right time.

He walked another 200 yards before he saw the first sign of blood. It sent a chill through him; he knew if he went on he would find something he had hoped never to see again. He followed the trail, his steps slower now, anger and fear building together as the blood sign grew heavier. The large doe lay 30 yards down the ridge, body twisted obscenely, its long, gray tongue protruding from its mouth, eyes dead as wax. The shotgun blast had taken it in the shoulder, and the belly and chest had been slit. Pop dropped to one knee and opened the fold, already aware of what he would find. He closed his eyes and let out a long, weary breath, then stood and dragged the animal off the trail and covered it with brush. He didn't want another hunter, scouting the ridge, to find it; to see the stake driven into its chest, to open the body cavity and see that too. The coydogs and fox and ravens would find the carcass and do their work, and in a few days nothing but scattered bones would remain, and that was the way it had to be.

Pop retraced the trail obliterating the blood sign, then continued until he reached the high open meadow where he had entered the wood. The grass was tall and brown and he stopped to rest, looking down at the town spread out below in the fading daylight. To the right, along a steep hillside, lay the cemetery, and he could see the freshly covered grave. Pop thought about the young woman they had buried yesterday; about her mutilated body, found only a few days ago. The chill of fear and anger he had felt earlier returned, and he closed his eyes and made the sign of the cross for the young woman's soul. He opened his eyes and looked away.

"Damn you, Jubal," he whispered. "Damn you to hell. I've covered up for you for so many years. Don't make me kill you now."

The town of Blake, Vermont, was made up of three villages, East Blake, West Blake, and Blake's Bend. It was located in what Vermonters called the Northeast Kingdom, a geographical term coined by a long-dead governor that had been immediately adopted by local residents to give that sparsely populated area a much-needed sense of importance. Situated in the northeastern portion of the state, it was dominated by dense woods, rugged mountains, and glacial lakes, and sliced repeatedly by fast-running rivers that seemed to permeate every valley and provide the excuse to construct covered bridges that would eventually generate a constant flow of tourists to bolster a fragile economy.

But this boon to tourism had been truly unintentional. The people, like the region itself, were remote and insular, and tolerated intruders only to the degree that it served their needs. Yet the raw beauty of the wilderness and lakes, and the abundance of wildlife, brought them anyway—hunters, boaters, fishermen, skiers, and those who simply wanted to witness rare beauty not found in the crowds and chaos of their own environments.

The villages of East Blake, West Blake, and Blake's Bend were particular beneficiaries. They attracted a collection of writers and artists and craftsmen, seeking a place both inexpensive and beautiful in which to work. And, as is often the case, these were followed by youthful entrepreneurs who saw opportunity and profit in that combination of intellectual sophistication and rural solace, so much so that within a short span of years the villages found their streets dotted with quaint restaurants and shops that were largely ignored by locals who remained faithful to the country stores, cafés, and roadhouses they regarded exclusively their own.

Leslie and Robbie had chosen one of the restaurants not favored by the average native, a German restaurant called Wolfgang's, located in a former church, the exterior now strung with small white Christmas lights that seemed to cry out with a promise of warmth and comfort.

The interior, they found, made good on that promise, a mixture of polished brass and wood, with soft lighting and genteel appointments that seemed to transport them away from the rural wilderness that now dominated their lives.

And the food was excellent, even though they settled for the least expensive daily special, *kalbshaxe*, a veal shank with dumplings, covered in a rich sauce.

Feeling pampered and satiated, Leslie grinned across the table at Robbie, who had wolfed down his meal as though it might be his last.

"Full?" she asked, watching him nod, eyes bright with pleasure. "I wish we could afford dessert. They look incredible. Settle for some ice cream at home?"

"Sure. I'm surprised we could afford this."

"We couldn't. But we're celebrating my new part-time employment. We successful freelance artists have to let our hair down once in a while."

Robbie gave her an impish grin. "Hey, I'll help you do that anytime."

Leslie glanced about for their waitress, inadvertently catching the eye of a well-dressed man who was moving about the tables. He seemed 35ish, with a round, slightly florid face and longish blond hair, combed straight back. His body was stocky, but it was well hidden by an impeccably tailored blue suit that matched his eyes, and his full mouth seemed fixed in a permanent smile that made him look like the manager of some fine European hotel.

He approached their table, still smiling, and introduced himself as Gunter Kline, the restaurant's owner. His eyes seemed to fill with unexpected pleasure as he looked down at Leslie.

"Did you enjoy your meal?" he asked.

Leslie smiled back at him, immediately liking the man. It was like finding an unexpected touch of the city life she already missed.

"It was excellent," she said. "A delightful surprise."

"Are you just passing through?"

"No, we just recently moved here." Leslie went on to explain where their house was located, and Gunter nodded.

"I've often hunted near there. I saw you in town today— one doesn't see many beautiful women here outside of the ski season—so I assumed you were a tourist."

Leslie felt herself blush slightly at the compliment. She didn't feel beautiful. She felt more than a little raggedy in her workshirt and jeans, but the decision to stop had been made impulsively, and she hadn't had time to change. But she liked the compliment, and the man wasn't blatantly flirting with her, he was simply being gracious, something he seemed to do easily.

"You're very kind," she said. "I've been getting a lot of stares today. From the locals," she explained. "I was beginning to think I had violated some dress code."

Gunter gave a small laugh. "It's the way you carry yourself, not the way you dress. It speaks of the city, and that's a very unknown quantity here. Although the local people are sure they know exactly what that means."

Leslie thought she knew too. It meant loose and promiscuous, and everything the locals felt they were not.

"Believe me," Gunter continued, "if you dressed in gingham and bows you'd be viewed just the same." He smiled again. "Don't change," he said. "You give us a breath of fresh air."

Now he was flirting, Leslie thought, and she realized she liked it. She smiled up at him.

"And promise me you'll come back," Gunter continued. "Now that you've discovered us."

Leslie assured him they would, as the waitress arrived and took their check. On the way to their truck she found she was smiling to herself. It was nice to be appreciated, she thought. Very nice indeed.

Leslie Adams' house was located on a dirt road that wound along a mountain ridge on the outskirts of West Blake. It was a simple two-story red farmhouse with a surprisingly well maintained red barn 100 yards to its rear, which Leslie planned to use, in part, as a studio. The house itself was a cluster of small rooms, designed to retain the heat provided by a scattering of wood stoves on the lower level, with ceiling registers to carry hot air to the three small bedrooms on the second floor. The large country kitchen was antiquated, but adequate, with a harvest table set before a large multipaned window that looked out at the dense wood that bordered the property. It would be a serene spot for breakfast, Leslie had decided, with occasional glimpses of wildlife and regular visits from the hummingbirds that reportedly came to the outside feeder each morning.

Leslie moved about the kitchen now, putting away the groceries she had bought. She knew she had to start making more home-cooked meals for herself and Robbie—especially Robbie. They certainly couldn't regularly afford restaurants like Wolfgang's no matter how pleasant it, and its owner, had been. But at least it wasn't the quick pizza we would have settled for in Philadelphia, she told herself. At least you didn't play chef by telephone as was so often the case after you ran away from Jack. Ran away. She weighed the words, felt the unpleasant sensation they left in her stomach; knew if she spoke them they would leave an unpleasant taste in her mouth. And even if she had finally stopped running, she was still hiding. And that was almost as bad. But soon you'll have your act together and you'll file for divorce. You'll do it even if it means he'll know where you are; even if it means he'll come looking for you to try and stop you.

She slammed a package of pasta against the countertop and fought the panic she felt spreading through her body, almost as though anticipating the blow that would invariably come from Jack after a display of anger or emotion not to his liking. But he's not here, she told herself. And he never will be again. You'll kill him before you'll let that happen. Kill him before he kills you.

She looked down and found her hand gripping the edge of the counter with such force her fingers were cramping. She released her hand and took a deep breath, then turned and stared out the wide window. Outside, the light above the entrance to the barn illuminated a broad path to the rear of the house, leaving the sides in shadow and the wood beyond eerily dark. Above, she could hear Robbie moving about his bedroom, and she wondered if he too was looking out at the night, and if it left him with the same strange mixture of pleasure and foreboding.

Leslie turned back to her chore, then called out for Robbie to come down for the ice cream she had promised. Tomorrow it'll be a real dinner, she promised herself. And a well balanced one, topped off with a real dessert. And no matter what happens, no matter what comes up, you'll take the time to do it.

Robbie burst into the kitchen, his small, lank body seeming to fill the room with energy. "What's for breakfast tomorrow?" he asked, as he glided into his chair and started in on his ice cream.

"You're planning that meal already?"

"Sure. What are you planning to feed me?"

"Exotic eggs," Leslie said.

"Do the chickens know?" Robbie asked.

"Not yet. I put golf balls in the nest to confuse them."

"Stupid birds." Robbie paused, a spoonful of ice cream halfway to his mouth. "Say, maybe we should *really* get our own chickens. We could probably save a lot of money."

"You going to take care of them? Food? Water? A couple of times a day? Not to mention certain gluelike droppings that have to be scraped up and carted off every so often?"

Robbie squeezed his eyes shut. "Oh, barf, eighty-six the chickens."

"I thought you'd see it that way," Leslie said. "Things seem to lose their sense of romance when there's a shovel and a pile of smelly stuff attached. Now eat your ice cream, and try not to think about where your breakfast will come from."

"Oh, gross," Robbie said. "God, I wish this town had a McDonald's."

"The true mark of civilization," Leslie said. "And, here I am, forcing you to live in the third world. No Egg McMuffins. No greasy sausage—"

"No lox and cream cheese on a bagel from the local deli." The boy's eyes had widened in mock horror.

Leslie's watched him, unable to keep herself from laughing. She looked away, her eyes passing across the window. Her body stiffened. There was something out there, a shadow moving just outside the illuminated path between the house and barn. Moving, then stopping, as though watching them, then moving again.

"What is it?" Robbie asked, noting the change in Leslie's body attitude.

"Somebody's out there, prowling around; watching us."

Robbie stood and bent toward the window. "I wonder if it's the same guy old Electa was yapping about? Maybe you should call her. You said she wanted to blast his butt with birdshot."

Leslie continued to watch the moving figure. It seemed to be carrying something long and slender, like a stick, or a gun. She turned and went directly to the wall telephone.

"What are you doing?" Robbie asked.

"Calling the cops," Leslie said.

"Aw, Sis!" Robbie complained. "Call Electa. I want to see her come out blasting."

Devlin read the reports Luther and Gaylord had turned in that morning. He had put off reading them, knowing they would be what they were—absolute, useless drivel. He tossed the reports aside, wondering if he should bother assigning anything further to either of them. The answer was obvious.

He'd handle the Eva Hyde investigation himself, working with the state cops whenever necessary, and he'd leave Luther and Gaylord and the rest of his misfits out in their patrolcars doing whatever it was they did out there.

Devlin picked up his coat and moved into the outer office. Arlene Cheney, the night dispatcher, was already on duty, which meant that Buzzy Fowler, the night man, was out doing whatever the hell *he* did in his patrolcar each night. Devlin was sure he was happier not knowing.

"I'm headed home. Everything quiet?"

Arlene looked up from the magazine she was reading, her round, moonlike face looking even more so under the crown of curlers that encircled her head. Devlin hated the curlers, despised them being worn to work, but had learned early on to keep his mouth shut about them. Arlene kept the department running at night, and she was, he had discovered, a vindictive woman. If he didn't want petty phone calls at three in the morning, the curlers were to be ignored.

"Just had one call since I came on," Arlene said. "That Adams woman. New woman out your way," she added, unnecessarily. "Got a prowler out behind her house, she says. Probably just a deer, but I can't do nothin' about it 'til I can raise Buzzy. He's gone missin' again."

Devlin stared at his shoes. The entire office was hopeless. "I'll take the call on the way home," he said.

"Thought you would," Arlene said. "Want I should call Mattie? Tell her you'll be later?"

"Yeah, and tell Buzzy I want a written report, explaining why we couldn't raise him."

"He's just gonna say he forgot to turn on his radio again," Arlene said.

"Yeah, I know. But let's make him do it anyway. It'll give his brain some exercise. Besides, I always find it a comfort to get some proof he really can write his own name."

Leslie and Robbie ate their ice cream as they watched the prowler move about the rear yard. It was unnatural and unnerving, bringing all her earlier feelings about being watched rushing in on her, but Leslie had forced herself to sit there just to prove she wasn't intimidated, or frightened. But prove it to whom, she wondered. Herself, Robbie, the prowler, or all of them? Or was it Jack, the man who wasn't even there?

Robbie turned to his sister. Her eyes were glaring, fierce. It made him uneasy when she got that way. No, it was worse than that. She actually scared him.

Lights flashed across the ground, hit the edge of the barn and stopped. A car in the driveway. Leslie was out of her chair and through the back door before the car lights were killed. "He's out back, behind the barn, I think," she called out. "And he's got a stick, or a gun, or something."

The thought hit her as soon as the words were out. *If he has a gun, why the hell are you standing here.*

Devlin came around the corner of the house, nothing in his hand but an oversized flashlight. "I'm Paul Devlin, chief of the local P.D.," he said. "Can we go inside?" He placed a hand on Leslie's elbow and guided her toward the rear door. She found the gesture annoying and her eyes flashed at him.

"I can find the door," she said.

"Good. If someone *is* out there, and they *do* have a weapon, we're both better off inside."

Leslie wanted to scream *I know that, dammit.* But the words wouldn't come. Instead she looked for some flaw she could turn against him. "Where's *your* gun?" she asked.

"There's a shotgun in the car, if I need it," Devlin said.

"What about your pistol?" Leslie demanded.

"Don't carry one."

"What?" Incredulous.

Devlin offered a tired smile. "Ms. Adams, this might be nothing more than a raccoon hunter looking for his dog. Or a kid out prowling. Or it could be more serious. But, right now, I don't think it warrants me going out there with a gun." The smile became more friendly, and Leslie found herself liking the man despite what she had heard about him earlier in the day. "Besides," Devlin added, "I don't like guns very much."

How could she argue with someone who didn't like guns. They terrified her. The thing that had always made her feel uneasy around police officers was the presence of guns and nightsticks and handcuffs, physical things with no other purpose but to harm or restrain people.

Leslie nodded. "What do you want me to do?" she asked.

"Nothing," Devlin said. "I'll look around outside, then I'll be back." He seemed to notice Robbie for the first time. He winked at him. "If I don't come back, call for help," he told the boy.

The flashlight Devlin carried was long and heavy, standard issue for every patrolcar he had ever seen, and as much a weapon as it was a tool. It threw a wide beam, illuminating both the area ahead of him and the ground at his feet. But the ground was hard and dry, useless for revealing fresh footprints, and even if some could be found, it wouldn't necessarily mean a damn thing.

Devlin moved along the side of the barn, keeping well away from the building. But it was more a response to past training than any concern someone might attack him. It wasn't that he questioned what the woman had seen—there had been complaints from Electa Litchfield as well. He just doubted it was more than some prowling kid, or a raccoon hunter. He turned the corner of the barn, moving the flashlight beam in a wide arc. There was an old apple tree 30 yards to its rear, with broad boughs that spread out almost from its base, giving the tree a majestic expanse that almost seemed to intone its longevity, and its unwillingness to surrender it.

Devlin smiled at the thought, then stepped out to continue the circle of the barn. He stopped short, as a flash of color at the foot of the apple tree caught his eye. He turned and looked more closely. The area at the base of the tree was littered with rotting apples, their reddish-brown color heightened by the beam of the flashlight. But there was more, a larger mound of slightly brighter color, with a smattering of white. He moved closer, his steps careful, trying not to disturb any potential evidence. Devlin's stomach tightened as he knelt before the carcass of the fox. It had been cut from pelvis to sternum, and steam still rose from the recently opened wound. But it was the stake that made Devlin cringe. It had been driven into the animal's chest, and its blunt end—like the stake removed from Eva Hyde—was coated with dirt. He scanned the area for some sign of additional evidence. Some fallen apples had been crushed under foot and might provide some sole or heel markings. His breath caught. A withered red rose lay on the ground a few feet away. Devlin forced a deep breath. He wanted to examine the animal now, to see if its heart was also missing. But he knew he would have to wait until a proper crime scene was established by the state police mobile crime lab. He stood and turned away. It was almost as though Eva Hyde's killer was trying to end any confusion about her death. But why in hell leave that message here? That didn't make any sense at all.

"Did you find 'em this time?" Electa Litchfield's voice cut the cold night air with razor clarity, and as Devlin raised his flashlight he could see the same clear sharpness in her eyes. "Well?" she demanded.

Devlin moved to her, then slightly past, turning the woman back in the direction of the house. She was small and thin, and his six-foot-two-inch frame dwarfed her, as did the heavy twelve-guage, long-barreled shotgun she had cradled in her arms.

"Pretty big gun for you, isn't it, Electa?" Devlin asked, trying to divert her attention from the carcass under the tree.

"Not so big I can't get what I'm after. Which seems to be more'n you're doin' lately." Electa's heavy eyebrows and severely gathered hair seemed to intensify the rigidness of the stare she leveled at Devlin. "I suppose you'll havta call the state police in now." Devlin's head snapped around, and he caught the trace of a smile on her lips. "So they can take a look at that fox you didn't want me to see."

"I hope you can forget about seeing it," Devlin said.

"Man I work for might not like that. Especially since your new evidence was found in the backyard of another lady works for him. He might get the idea we don't take freedom of the press too seriously, even if it does put bread on our tables."

"I'll talk to Jim," Devlin said. "I hope he'll agree to keep it quiet for the sake of the investigation. And I hope you'll agree to keep it quiet outside the newspaper." Devlin glanced toward the house, wishing he could keep this information from the woman and the boy, knowing it would be unfair, perhaps even dangerous, to do so.

Electa seemed to read his thoughts. "Nice movin' in present, isn't it?"

"Yeah, real nice," Devlin said. "Welcome to quiet, safe, rural Vermont."

Electa, Leslie, and Robbie were gathered around the harvest table, Robbie talking excitedly to Electa about the fox, Leslie stunned into silence, still more curious than believing.

Devlin put down the telephone, the scar on his cheek glowing white. Eric Mooers, the detective sergeant in charge of the state police end of the investigation had been his usual condescending self. *Guess you big city boys didn't have much call to deal with foxes gettin' wasted*, he had said. *But up here we usually call in the game warden when it happens.* Devlin had barely contained himself. Mooers could either put his fat ass in gear and get his mobile crime lab on the road, Devlin had hissed, or wait for a call from an attorney general whose dinner had just been interrupted.

Now, as he walked back to the table, he had a grudging agreement that the BCI crime lab would be there in the morning, and the knowledge that Buzzy Fowler was already enroute to safeguard the scene until then. Great, he told himself. A fucking speed trap expert, who's read a few books on homicide, and a local yokel who can't make his patrolcar radio work. The fucking killer ought to be shaking in his boots. He drew a deep breath and looked down at Electa. "I suppose you'll have to give Jim a call," he said.

Electa glared at him, stood and went to the telephone, and Devlin took her place at the table. He fought for control, looked first at Leslie, then at the boy. "It would help—the investigation, I mean—if none of this gets out." He concentrated on Robbie. "I know that's hard. You'll be starting at a new school, and you'll have information that could really make you a big man with all the other guys." Devlin offered a small shrug. "But it also might make it harder for us to catch the person who's doing this. And, if I'm right, he's already hurt one person, so the sooner we get him the better."

Robbie glanced at his sister, noting for the first time the concern—the hint of fear—in her face. "But it's going to be in the newspaper, isn't it?" he asked, still looking at his sister.

"I'm hoping Jim McCloud will hold back on it," Devlin said. "But if he does, it won't do any good if the rest of us start talking. This is a real small town, Robbie. It takes all of about three minutes for a bit of news to get from one end to the other." Robbie's face screwed up with pained resignation, and he nodded reluctantly. Devlin reached out and squeezed his shoulder. "It'll all come out eventually. And it will still be pretty big news to all your new friends."

Electa came back to the table and stared down at Devlin, who thought that with her hair pulled back in a bun, and her already sharp features, she looked very much like an avenging angel. Or a hawk that had just seen a mouse. "Jim said he'll hold the story." She paused. "But not forever. Only as long as it looks like some progress is being made. That, and the promise that he gets the story before any of the big papers in Burlington, or Rutland."

"Agreed," Devlin said. "Tell him I'm grateful."

Electa snorted. "Should be. You wouldn'a gotten that from me. If it were up to me, I'd make sure you were doin' somethin' first. Like findin' out where Jubal was tonight."

The sharpness of the woman's voice snapped Leslie from her thoughts. She certainly didn't like this man. Or, perhaps, it was men in general she didn't like. Electa, she noticed, was again dressed entirely in dark green, although the clothes were different from the ones she had worn that afternoon. She wondered if she always wore the same color. No, that would be much too much, she told herself.

Devlin watched Electa turn and start for the door. "Good evening, Electa," he said to her retreating back.

"Evening," she said. She glanced back at Leslie and Robbie. "Call me if you need anything," she said. "I'm a lot closer, and a lot more dependable than some other folks you might have a mind to call."

Devlin winced, then caught Robbie smiling at him.

When the door had closed behind Electa, Robbie said, "She doesn't seem to like you too much." His grin had widened.

"That may be the understatement of your young life," Devlin said.

Leslie leaned forward, slightly bewildered now. "You seem to be taking this pretty lightly," she said to Devlin. Her eyes moved to Robbie. "And so do you. It makes me wonder why I'm scared to death. Maybe I'm nuts, but I thought I heard that some madman had left a mutilated animal in my backyard— an animal that was killed the same way some young woman was only a few days ago."

Leslie's voice had risen in pitch; it seemed partly fear, partly rage. Devlin studied her, again feeling the physical attraction he had noticed earlier, and something more as well. This was one strong lady, he told himself. Scared shitless, and angry that she was.

"I don't want you to take this lightly at all," Devlin said. "But I don't want you to overreact either." He glanced at the boy. "I don't know why your place was picked for this. Maybe whoever did it thought you'd call the cops if you saw a prowler, and we'd get to see what he wanted us to see." Devlin shrugged. "Or maybe somebody's just trying to scare you. I really don't know. But I do want you to call my office if you see anyone around. And I do want you to keep your doors and windows locked—at least for awhile. And that's not something most people feel they have to do around here." Leslie's jaw had tightened at his mention of locking doors and windows, and Devlin wondered if she was frightened by the idea, or just annoyed by the need to lock herself away.

Leslie sat back, her fists balled in her lap. "What about this Jubal person Electa mentioned?"

Devlin shook his head. "I don't know. Jubal *is* strange. And he does spend most of his time on this mountain." Devlin looked at Leslie, tried a smile and failed. "He had some bad experiences in the military, and he's never been quite the same since. But I don't think he's dangerous. At least not to people who leave him alone." Leslie started to speak but Devlin stopped her with a raised hand. "But I will speak to him. Tomorrow."

"I would appreciate it," Leslie said.

Devlin hesitated, then pushed on. "I did see you speaking to someone today that I would watch out for," he said.

Leslie's brow knitted. "Who was that?"

"Billy Perot."

"But that's ridiculous. He offered to help me do some chores, that's all. He's just trying to make some extra money."

Devlin stared at her, eyes hard and a bit too knowing, Leslie thought. "Billy doesn't need to earn extra money. His daddy owns the largest apple farm around here—maybe in the entire state—and he gives Billy everything he needs, whether he works for it or not."

A broad smile filled Robbie's lips. "I knew that guy was a creep," he said.

Leslie looked at each of them in turn. "I don't know what to say." She settled the matter by shaking her head.

By nine o'clock Devlin was gone and Buzzy Fowler was ensconced as protector of hoped-for evidence in and around the aging apple tree. Leslie made her way to the rear of the barn and found Buzzy standing there, doing little more than shuffling his feet, and adding to the small mound of cigarette butts growing around him. Just adding a little extra evidence, Leslie thought. Christ, even she knew better than to do that.

"I've got some fresh coffee in the kitchen," Leslie said. "You're welcome to come in and have some."

Buzzy shifted his feet and looked at her, thinking hard. He was only average height and very thin, and the large gun and gunbelt he wore looked oversized and heavy about his waist. He blinked several times, and together with his thin, hatchet face, curved nose and close-set eyes, it gave him a birdlike look that made Leslie wonder if "Buzzy" was a shortened nickname for Buzzard.

"Could sure use one, if you wouldn't mind bringin' it out." He puffed himself up, almost like a bird displaying its plumage for a potential mate, Leslie thought. "Gotta stay here with the evidence."

"Oh, that's too bad. See, I've got some cake too, but I don't think I could manage to get that out here." Leslie paused as if trying to deduce some solution. "But listen, I could stay here and watch, and then I could call you if anyone came by. Of course, I'm sure they won't, but if you left the back door open, you could hear me if I did call."

"Sounds real good to me," Buzzy said. "Course you wouldn't mention it to the chief, now."

"Of course not. He doesn't seem too sympathetic."

"Pain in the butt, city boy's what he is," Buzzy said. He grinned at her. "You say the cake and coffee's in the kitchen?"

"Right on the counter." She reached out as Buzzy started to go, touching his sleeve. "Maybe you should leave me your flashlight," she suggested.

"Yeah, I guess I should." He smiled at her again, showing uneven teeth. "The kitchen counter, you say."

"You can't miss it," Leslie assured him.

Leslie waited until she was sure Buzzy was inside the

kitchen, then she turned on the flashlight and moved carefully to the base of the apple tree, trying not to disturb anything, anyone might consider evidence—anything Buzzy had not already destroyed. She was almost on top of it before she recognized the butchered fox for what it was, and a gasp rose in her throat as she stared at its grotesque head, the blank, filmed eyes, teeth bared in a soundless snarl, tongue protruding from the side of its snout. She moved the flashlight down its body, her grip tightening when she reached the muddied stake driven into its chest, the long incision down the length of its belly, which offered a hint of viscera that Leslie didn't want to see.

She turned her head away, the beam of the flashlight falling on the withered rose a few feet to her left. She squatted, staring at it, wondering how it could have gotten there. A long forgotten memory of her mother's funeral came rushing back—a tall man in a gray mourning coat handing her a dark red rose to place atop her mother's casket. The distant snap of a branch forced the thought from her mind.

She stood abruptly, the flashlight rising jerkily, then settling on an area of wood off to her right. Leslie froze. Standing there, between two large trees, as if rooted to the spot, was a hooded figure, its chalk-white face staring back at her.

The flashlight fell from her hand and she scrambled after it. When she raised it to the woods again, the figure was gone. She scanned the line of trees to make sure she had the right spot. No one was there. The figure—man or woman—had simply disappeared.

# CHAPTER
## 3

You thought Eva was the one. HER. But now you know. Eva was only prelude, the one who awakened you. And you thought SHE was dead; buried; gone forever. But now you've seen the other, the new one, the one who is *everything* SHE was.

But maybe there are more than one. Those who awaken the feelings in you, make you remember the devious, evil cunning that was HER. The heart of a beast hidden in those eyes. A heart that beats with the pain it wants to give.

It *is* HER, this new one. So beautiful, so perfect. Long brown hair, so soft it seems to float about her head. Brown eyes, thoughtful and gentle, hiding the corruption that lies beneath.

She is so much like HER. So much more than Eva was; ever could be. She's changed the color of her hair, but that hasn't fooled you. Never could. Never, ever could.

And she's marked now with HER sign.

The eyes widen with fear. But they won't let you have her. They won't let you be her favorite. The eyes dart back and forth, narrowed again, lingering at the corners, watchful, cautious.

But you can make them!

Leslie dipped the spoon into the pot and raised it to her lips. The concern she had felt earlier vanished. The curry was just the way he liked it: "not too hot, but spicy enough to give your system a slight jolt." His way of describing things always amused her—the certitude he seemed to feel, or at least express, over even the smallest matters. It was as if he never expressed an opinion, but rather a decision, or, perhaps, a judgment. She had often wondered if that was what he had been taught in law school, the need to be decisive; to have his position on a subject—on any subject, be it right or wrong—prevail.

She felt disloyal even thinking that, and it sent a wave of uneasiness through her. Loyalty was essential to him—he had said so many times—something he prized more than anything else. But, then, there were other things he said he prized more than anything else, and it was confusing at times to determine which was the truly prized thing and which was merely preferred. She shook the thought away. It sent a chill through her, and even that chill felt somehow disloyal.

Quickly, Leslie tasted the curry again to reassure herself it was right. But now it wasn't curry anymore. Somehow it had changed. Now it was pea soup. Jack had been in court that afternoon and he would be elated and playful if it had gone well, or depressed and easily annoyed if it had not. Either way dinner would be crucial. God, she thought, I hope it went well. Jack hates pea soup. Oh, my God. Oh, my God.

"What the hell is this?"

Jack's voice bounced around the room, shaking walls, rattling dishes. She couldn't understand where he had come from. She hadn't heard him come in, hadn't even seen him pour his drink. But he was there, glass in hand, standing over the curry, screaming at her.

"Just taste it, Jack. It's good. It is. Believe me, it's just the way you like it. Not too hot, but spicy enough to—"

The blow caught her just above the cheekbone, almost directly on the temple, and sent her crashing into the table. She caught the edge and kept herself from falling to the floor. She knew he would kick her if she fell to the floor, and she couldn't stand the idea of being kicked—kicked like some animal—and she knew she might kill him if he ever kicked her again.

"You're a stupid cunt." She felt his breath on her face, the heavy smell of liquor. Not from one drink, or even two. But from heavy drinking, for several hours.

She tried to push herself up, but the back of his hand caught her other cheek, forcing her back. "Jack, I tried. I thought it was the way you liked it."

"You stupid bitch. You don't do anything the way I like it. You don't cook worth shit; you don't clean the fucking house worth shit; you don't even fuck worth shit." He reached out and took her by the front of her blouse and pulled her toward him. "But that all makes sense, doesn't it? Because you're not *worth* shit, are you? You're not worth anything. Not a God damned fucking thing."

Jack pulled her toward him again then released her quickly, sending her falling back to the floor. Leslie stared up at him, knowing what was coming, knowing she couldn't stand it if it happened.

"Don't kick me, Jack. Damn it, don't you kick me."

But now Jack's arms had turned into legs; the hands into feet, and the first blow caught her in the ribs, forcing the breath from her lungs. She fought to get to her feet, but the point of his shoeless hand/foot caught her upper thigh and sent numbing pain through her leg, and her body crashing back to the floor.

"You bastard, Jack. I'll kill you. This time I'll kill you."

Leslie sat up in bed, awake, her hand moving instinctively to the large kitchen knife on her bedside table. She had put it there last night, as she did every night. Her face glistened with sweat, and the words still raced in her mind, and silently across her lips. *This time I'll kill you.*

Jubal Duval dropped two sacks of dried beans on the counter, stared briefly at El, then turned and walked to the canned goods. El watched him, feeling the sweat gather in his palms, knowing he shouldn't feel that way, aware that Jubal had never harmed him, or anyone he knew of, save a fight or two at the roadhouse. Still, those had been bad fights, God awful fights, and the man made him feel he'd as soon kill him as look at him; so he couldn't help how he felt. He had known Jubal all his life, known him as a nice, quiet boy who liked to hunt and fish with Pop, a boy who kept things inside pretty much, but who never caused no harm, never stole nothin', never sassed or backtalked. Then they took him away in the army, and put him in that Green Beret trainin'. And then they did that thing nobody could understand and sent him home, sayin' he was too crazy to kill for 'em the way they trained him to do. And after that he was different. Real different. And now he scared hell outta most people, 'cept maybe Pop and Billy Perot, who was just as crazy as Jubal anyways.

El continued to watch him. God he was a big man. Not so tall, maybe. Only 'bout six two. But neck and shoulders like a bull, an' arms like the trunks of a young hardwood. Had a tattoo—Green Beret insignia somebody had said—on his left forearm. But it wasn't all that made him scary. It was those flat blue eyes, had no feelin' in 'em, maybe. Or that red hair cut so close you could hardly see it at all. Or maybe that jagged scar on his jaw, somethin' he'd brought home with him from Vietnam. No, it was those eyes, El decided. Damn, those eyes were scary. No feelin' in 'em. Not one little bit.

Jubal returned to the counter and laid out some Spam, some dried beef, and some Dinty Moore stew. He was dressed in an olive drab T-shirt and camouflage fatigues tucked into his hunting boots, and there was a hunting knife hanging from his belt.

"How much?" he asked, the voice surprisingly soft, not much more than a whisper.

El added the total quickly and told him, then watched as Jubal took a small change purse from a pocket in his fatigues and carefully counted out the money.

Makin' that government disability pension stretch as best he can, El thought, feeling a twinge of annoyance that a hulking man, not even 40, should be paid to go hunting all day, while everybody else worked. But it was none of his business, he told himself.

El watched him pick up his package and head for the door, already experiencing a sense of relief. Feel just like a cat movin' around a tethered dog, he thought. Wonderin' just how strong that rope really is. Damn, wish you'd take your loony money someplace else, he told himself, knowing he'd never say those words aloud. Not to Jubal, or nobody else might tell him, he thought.

Jubal came out on to the sidewalk, feeling the autumn sun

on his face, the chill morning air on his bare arms. It felt good and clean, and he knew it would feel even better in an hour when he was up in the mountain woods setting his traps, getting his new campsight set up. He started for his battered Chevy pickup truck, thinking how fast the color was leaving the mountain; how soon those leaves would begin to fall and the snow would come, and how he'd have to start protecting his mountain from the hunters who would arrive then. A faint smile came to his lips and disappeared. Won't nobody hunt there this year, he told himself. Won't nobody cross my perimeter, 'less they wanna find themselves gutted and hung from a tree. He dropped the package in the bed of the truck and started for the driver's door.

"Jubal, boy!"

He turned to the sound of his name and saw Billy Perot swaggering toward him. He liked the way Billy walked, kinda cocky-like. Didn't like Billy much, but he liked the way he walked and talked. Kinda slick like. Woulda made it in Special Forces, he thought. Had that way about him. Like he could chew up anybody who crossed him. But he went to college for a year instead. Till they threw him out, or leastways that's what people said. So he couldn't chew up nobody. Leastways nobody knew what he knew.

Jubal paused, waiting for Billy to reach him. There was a grin on his face that seemed to be saying something Billy never spoke about, and Jubal wondered what it might be.

Billy stopped before Jubal. They were about the same size, although Billy didn't have Jubal's bulk. But all similarity ended there. Billy ran one hand through his dark, slightly greasy hair, which hung down well over his ears and the collar of his denim jacket. His grin widened.

"You do what I asked you yesterday?" he asked.

Jubal nodded. "You owe me the twenty you said you'd pay."

"Sure. Sure," Billy said, pushing a hand into a pocket of the tight jeans he wore. "Did the woman see what you left?"

Jubal stared at him. "Musta. Called the chief. He saw it." He decided not to tell him what else he had seen.

Billy's face clouded momentarily, then the grin returned. "That don't matter," he said. "Just so the woman saw. You see her?"

Jubal continued to stare at him.

The grin widened. "Prime piece a goods, huh? I'm goin' over there today. Just to help her out a bit. She ought to be real skittery." The grin turned to a leer. "Who knows. Maybe she'll help me out a bit too."

Jubal took the money from Billy's hand, sneered at him, then turned back to the door of the truck.

"Listen up a minute," Billy said. "I just might need you again. You willin'?"

"You pay, an' I'm willin'," Jubal said, not bothering to turn back.

Billy stared at him for a moment, disliking his sullenness, wondering what it would be like to slap the big fellow down. A momentary sense of nervousness appeared, but he pushed it away. He had never found anyone he couldn't slap down. Not since his daddy had paid for those karate lessons over in St. Johnsbury when he was only 14, or so. Jubal was big, but so was he. And big didn't mean that much anyway.

"Anyway, you stay in touch," Billy said.

"I'll be around," Jubal said. "You want me, you'll find me."

"Yeah, well don't go disappearin' on the mountain. What the hell you do up there anyway?"

"I jus' take care of it," Jubal said.

Crazy fucker, Billy thought. "Yeah, well you sure do a good job of that. Ain't nobody stole it, anyway."

Jubal glared at him for a moment, then started his truck.

"Jubal!"

Billy and Jubal both turned to see Devlin headed toward them. A momentary panic seized Billy, and he wanted to tell Jubal to get moving before the smart-assed cop could question him. But he knew Jubal would only do the opposite of what he was told. A self-satisfied smile formed on his lips. "Better sit tight, Jubal," he said. "Looks like our big-city cop wants to jaw on your ass a bit."

Jubal's eyes darted toward Billy, then to Devlin, who was halfway across the street now. He let out a low grunt, then pushed the gear shift into first and eased out the clutch. Devlin stopped in the middle of the street and watched the truck move slowly away.

Oh, Billy boy, you're so fuckin' clever, Billy told himself. He turned his grin on Devlin, who had started toward him again. "I guess old Jubal just don't like you big-city cops," Billy said, the self-satisfied grin widening now.

Devlin returned the grin, but it was as cold as his eyes and carried all the dislike he felt for the man. "That's all right, Billy," he said. "Right now you'll do just fine. You were number two on my list anyway. And it seems you just made number one."

The two stood facing each other, Devlin's hard cop face, which he had learned so well in New York, in full force; Billy's smile fading, then reasserting itself with the cocky sense of immunity he had carried with him all his life.

"Why, that's just great, Devlin," Billy said. "You just tell me what I can do for you, and I'll do it. And if I can't, I'm sure my old man can."

"Oh, I won't need your daddy right now," Devlin said. "Not unless he was spending time with Eva Hyde like you were."

Billy stared off down the street and shook his head in mock disgust, as he fought off the uneasy tightness he felt in his stomach. "Shit, can't you and your cops talk about anything else." He turned back and grinned again. "And maybe you *should* put my old man on your list. Old Eva didn't miss many in town, from what I hear."

Devlin smiled again, his hard eyes never leaving Billy's face. He had seen the momentary nervousness there, and he wanted to push it as far as he could. "Maybe I'll just do that. Maybe I'll even tell him you suggested it." Devlin took a step closer, bringing his face only inches from Billy's. "But right now, you just tell me about the night Eva disappeared. Tell me what you said to her in the roadhouse. Tell me what she said. And tell me where you two went after that."

"Shit. We didn't go anyplace." Billy shifted his weight, trying to gain some physical advantage. He was slightly larger than Devlin, and instinctively wanted to intimidate him with the fact. He knew immediately it wouldn't work. He tried the smile again, a warmer one this time. "Look, I saw Eva that night. Hell, I saw her lots of nights. But so did lots of guys in town." Billy's smile turned to a one-man-to-another leer. "Shit, Devlin, Eva's legs were like elevator doors, they opened and closed so much." Billy winked at him. "Look, I saw her a little that night, then I went back to the bar. Hey, man, gettin' your cock worked on in the backseat of a car don't make you a killer, does it?''

Devlin's first instinct was to grab Billy by the throat. Two years ago, in New York, he would have done just that. But it wasn't two years ago, and it wasn't New York, and even if Eva was just one more of the many sad young women he had seen victimized by vultures like Billy, it wasn't a problem he could solve by slapping the shit out of him.

"Yeah, I heard all that," Devlin said, returning the man-to-man smile. "But, you know, you're the first person to suggest to me that maybe Eva might of been killed by somebody." Devlin's smile faded as quickly as it had appeared. "You know something I don't, Billy?"

Billy's eyes filled with hate, and he jabbed a finger toward Devlin's chest. "You better back off, Devlin, you know what's good for your ass."

Devlin stared at the finger, only inches from his chest now, then raised his eyes slowly to Billy's face. "You want that finger, asshole?" he asked. He watched Billy turn red with rage, and he silently prayed he'd do something foolish. "You do, you better put it in your pocket," he continued. "Otherwise, your daddy's gonna have a funny-looking son— a one-handed, apple-picking asshole, not just the regular run-of-the-mill asshole he has to deal with now." He stepped in even closer. "You understand me, you piece of shit?"

Billy took a step back, then seemed to catch himself. The smile returned. "You're pushing the wrong person, and you're gonna find that out," he said softly. "You're not some big-city cop now. You're just a pissy-assed, small-town chief of police, who does what the people who pay him want him to do. And if you wanna keep gettin' paid, you better do just that."

Devlin kept his face right in Billy's and started to laugh. "Oh, you got a problem, big shot. You see, I've got a nice, fat, tax-free disability pension, a house with a real low mortgage, and some bucks in the bank. So even your fat-assed daddy can't help you with me. And, if he tries, and gets my butt fired, there's one last thing I'm going to do." Devlin stepped in closer again. "First, I'm going to kick your ass up and down this street. Then, when I'm through, I'm going to lock what's left of it up for any God damned thing I can think of. You got that straight, clown?"

Billy refused to step back this time, although all his instincts pushed him to do just that. He wasn't used to being challenged, and it rattled and confused him. "Fuck you, Devlin," he snapped. "You just try it."

Devlin's smile grew wide and happy, but the eyes remained flat and cold. "Oh, I will Billy boy. But first, I'm going to find out just what happened between you and Eva Hyde. I'm going to make that my life's work right now. And I'm also going to watch for any other shit you might pull. Anything at all. And, you know, Billy, if there's one thing I've learned over the years, it's that clowns like you always step on their dicks sooner or later. And all I have to do is wait for it to happen."

Billy's entire face became a twisted snarl. "Then you just wait, Devlin. But you're not the only one who's gonna be waitin'. And you're playin' in my backyard now. And you're gonna find that out real quick. You just watch. Then we'll see who kicks whose ass." Billy stepped back, and the snarl changed back to the cocky, self-satisfied grin. "Now you just fuck off, 'cause I ain't got no more time for you."

Billy turned and started off.

Gotcha, Devlin thought, and his own smile moved from his mouth to his eyes. "I'll be seeing you, Billy boy," he called to the retreating back. "And a lot sooner than you think."

Billy just kept walking, and as Devlin turned to head back across the street, he saw El looking out his store window. He too was smiling.

Robbie and Tim stood alone in one corner of the school playground, waiting for the first bell that would summon them to their class. There was a battery of swing sets, slides, and jungle gyms in the playground's center, each dominated by children from the lower grades, each engulfed by raucous screams and squeals and laughter. At the far end, opposite Robbie and Tim, the older boys stood under a large maple tree, eyes darting curiously toward the newcomer, their manner a mixture of posturing and playfulness, as they punched each other relentlessly on the arms and competed in making rude sounds that would send the group into peels of laughter.

Tim nudged Robbie's arm. "See that big kid with the blond hair?" he asked.

Robbie scanned the group under the tree, spotting the boy easily. "Yeah, I see him," he said.

"That's Tommy Robatoy, and before the week's over he'll try to push you around. He thinks he owns this place." Tim snorted. "He thinks he owns the whole town."

Robbie shrugged, but said nothing. He had known his share of school bullies in Philadelphia, had often taken circuitous routes home to avoid them, and had learned, the hard way, that you didn't avoid bullies; they always found you eventually.

Tim nudged him again. "So what are you gonna do when he starts bugging you?"

Robbie shrugged again. "Maybe he won't."

"Oh, he will. He can't help it. He's got to prove to everybody how tough he is."

"*Is* he tough?"

Tim nodded. "And mean too. Just watch out for him." He looked at Robbie curiously. "Unless you can take him. Boy, would I like to see somebody do that."

Great, Robbie thought. Now I gotta be Mike Tyson to survive. Just like in Philly. "I'm not gonna fight with anybody," Robbie said. "I don't wanna start off school by getting in trouble." He could see the skepticism in Tim's eyes, and knew he didn't want that either, but he wasn't about to get his head beat in just to impress somebody, even if it was his only friend. "I just don't want any trouble," he added lamely.

"Well, if you can avoid it with Tommy, you're doing better than anybody else. Either you join his gang, and do what he says, or you get pushed around." Tim looked perplexed for a moment. "Even the guys who join his gang get pushed around," he added, secretly hoping Robbie would not try.

The school bell sounded before Robbie could respond, and Tim gave him a gentle push toward the rear entrance of the school. "Come on," he said. "Now you get to meet Loopy Louie."

"Who's that?" Robbie asked.

"Mr. Ferris, our teacher. His name's Louis, and the kids call him Loopy Louie, 'cause he's such a dip."

"Is he really a dip?" Robbie asked.

Tim shrugged again. "I guess," he said. "He is kinda goofy.

But at least he doesn't think everything in Vermont is made of gold."

"Even the cow shit?" Robbie asked.

"Especially the cow shit."

Both boys started to giggle.

Louis Ferris, who served both as seventh-grade homeroom and English teacher, was a tall, slender, 30ish man, who was rapidly losing his hair and whose large nose, and eyes—each of which seemed to look in a different direction—did give him a slightly strange, if not loopy, look. But he would be okay, Robbie decided, silently hoping his other teachers would be also. At least Ferris didn't seem overly strict or vindictive, and he did appear to like the kids in his class, unlike many of the teachers Robbie had experienced in Philadelphia.

But his opinion changed almost at once, as Ferris decided to formally introduce Robbie to the class, and asked him to tell where he had come from. At the mention of Philadelphia it got even worse, as Ferris went into a long dissertation about the City of Brotherly Love—which produced a round of giggles—and an even longer diatribe about it being the cradle of American liberty, which made it sound, to Robbie, as though he had just descended from heaven. But the worst came when Robbie explained that he had moved to West Blake with his sister, and, upon questioning from Ferris, was forced to reveal that his parents were dead, a revelation that ended in awkward silence and left Robbie with the sensation that hundreds of eyes were boring into the back of his head.

"Now," Ferris said, "before we get too caught up in socializing, let me announce that in two days—and that means Wednesday, for those of you who have difficulty counting," he paused for laughter that didn't come, "there will be an assignment of a story or a poem for our English class. Neatness will count, as always. And originality will count even more." He paused again, his misdirected eyes scanning the class. "And there will be no excuses for the paper not being ready to hand in Wednesday morning. Understood?"

A groan rose from the class.

"Good."

The other classes that morning—history and science—were

much the same, although, for Robbie, the introductions were blessedly shorter, stopping with his name and the city from which he had moved. Next was lunch, followed by gym and math, a two out of three on Robbie's pleasure scale, and a ratio of enjoyment to pain he knew he could live with.

The cafeteria, like the school itself was fairly new and modern and, to Robbie's surprise, lacked the stale, mass-produced food smells that had permeated his school in Philadelphia. He thought he might even try some of the food cooked there one day, and forgo the bagged lunch brought from home. No, he decided. I'll still bring a lunch. Just in case.

Robbie followed Tim to a table for four off to one side. Most other tables were grouped in sixes and eights, and as they seated themselves he glanced at Tim curiously.

"Why don't we sit at one of the bigger tables? Then I could get a chance to meet some of the other kids," Robbie suggested.

"It doesn't work that way here," Tim said. "At most schools—at *normal* schools—a new kid at school is a big deal, and everybody goes out of their way and tries to be friends with them. But in Vermont it doesn't work that way. Here he's an outsider, who doesn't really belong. Not until they decide he does. And then not really. It's like they're saying: okay, we'll deal with you. We decided you're all right. But it's too bad you weren't born here. Then you'd really be okay."

"Aw, come on," Robbie said. "It can't be that bad."

"Wait and see," Tim said.

Before Robbie could object again, a young girl, no more than 7, slid into a chair at the table, offered each of them a cheery "Hi" and began opening her Minnie Mouse lunchbox.

"You must be Robbie," the girl said. "I've heard all about you from my dad."

She had blond hair, tied back in a long ponytail, and bright blue eyes that seemed to jump from her face, and Robbie guessed she was in no more than second grade, and couldn't understand why she was joining older boys for lunch.

"This is Phillipa Devlin," Tim explained. "She's the police chief's daughter, so we have to be nice to her."

Phillipa made a face at Tim, then turned to Robbie. "The truth is, I'm the only person who'll eat lunch with him—except for you now, that is—so it's really me who's being nice."

"Truth is," Tim interjected, "that the bigger kids labeled her a *flatlander,* and all the kids in her second-grade class picked up on it, so she won't even try to eat with them."

"They're jerks," Phillipa said. "They think if you don't come from here, you're weird or something."

"Where'd you come from?" Robbie asked.

"New York City. Queens, really."

"Maybe you are weird, then," Robbie said.

Phillipa stuck her tongue out at him, then bit into a peanut butter and jelly sandwich.

"I'm only kidding," Robbie said. "How'd your father get to be chief, if you came from there?"

"The old chief died," Phillipa explained. "And they found out my dad used to be a detective on the NYPD, so they offered him the job. Then he got reappointed. I still can't believe that."

"What's the NYPD?" Robbie asked.

Phillipa looked at him as though he came from outer space. "New York Police Department," she said. "I thought everybody knew that."

"Sorry," Robbie said.

"What are you sorry about, asshole?"

All heads turned to the sound of the voice. Tommy Robatoy towered over them, three other boys behind him, all giggling. He was bigger and older, an eighth grader, for sure, Robbie thought, and he was playing "beat up on the smaller kids," a game Robbie knew all too well.

"You sorry you're an asshole orphan?" Tommy asked.

Robbie wondered how he knew that already, then looked behind Tommy and recognized one of the others as a kid from his class. He remained silent.

"Or maybe you brotherly love assholes are just sorry you were ever born. I bet that's why your parents kicked the bucket. They saw you and just died."

"At least he had parents," Phillipa said. "He didn't just crawl out from under a rock like some creeps we know."

"Shut your mouth, you little city bitch," Tommy growled. "Your big-shot father's not around to protect you, so you better watch your mouth."

"He knows where to find you, if he has to," Phillipa said, offering Tommy an angelic smile. "He's real good at looking under rocks."

Tommy jabbed a finger at her, appearing to forget all about

Robbie. "I'll get you. I'll get you good. You wait and see if I don't."

Phillipa pinched her nose with her thumb and index finger. "Go away," she said, drawing out each word. "And take a bath, please."

Tommy's face reddened, as Tim and Robbie began to laugh. He turned on them, his face filled with rage. "You two think she's funny? When I kick your asses we'll see how funny you think it is."

"Go away," Tim said. "And please," he drew out the word as Phillipa had, "do take a bath."

Robbie started laughing again, the initial fear he had felt for Tommy momentarily gone.

Tommy jabbed a finger into his back. "And I'll get you special," Tommy said. "You see if I don't, you fuckin' asshole."

"That language, Mr. Robatoy, will get you a two-hour detention after school."

The voice boomed over all of them, and when they turned they saw Loopy Louie Ferris bearing down on their table.

"I didn't say nothin'," Tommy howled. "Just ask anybody."

"He said a really filthy word," Phillipa piped up. She grinned at Tommy as he offered her his most threatening glare.

"March," Ferris commanded.

As Tommy started to move off he slammed the side of his arm into Robbie's shoulder to let him know he could expect more very soon. Robbie turned to Phillipa and shook his head. "You trying to get us killed?" he asked. "We don't have any cops in our families."

Phillipa shrugged. "That's life in the fast lane, guys," she said.

Tim started to laugh again, joined by Robbie seconds later. "Where do you get these lines?" Tim asked.

"I've got good writers," Phillipa said, breaking them up again.

Billy Perot had stripped to the waist as he loaded a pile of scrap wood into the back of his pickup truck. The pile, located along one side of Leslie's barn, offered him a clear view of the large kitchen window, and regular glimpses of Leslie working inside. And she, he knew, could see him as well, which was the true reason for the missing shirt.

He had been there for two hours now, and the bitch hadn't come out of the house. She had acted oddly when he had arrived, he thought, but it had passed when he'd seemed eager to get to work. The thing that puzzled him was that she hadn't seemed scared, even though the staties and their mobile lab were just pulling out when he got there. It made him wonder if Jubal had fucked up somehow, and if maybe he should have done the job himself. Shit, too risky, he told himself. Besides, you'd have to crawl through those dark, fuckin' woods, and only Jubal, and maybe his old man, could do that without breakin' a fuckin' leg.

Billy straightened as he heard the kitchen screen door slam. Leslie was coming toward him, a glass in her hand. Damn, she looked good enough to eat, Billy told himself. Dressed in those tight jeans and loose denim shirt, with her sweet little tits floppin' around inside. He could feel himself starting to grow inside his own tight jeans, and hoped she noticed. Have I got somethin' you're gonna like, he told himself, certain now she was looking at his body, knowing she would like what she saw.

"Thought you might need something to drink," Leslie said, as she stopped in front of him, extending the hand with the glass. "It's just lemonade." She tilted her head sideways, studying him, seeming mildly confused. "Aren't you cold without a shirt?" she asked. "It can't be more than sixty out here."

"Feel kinda warm myself," Billy said, grinning. "Don't you? Just a little?"

The message was so clear, so blatant, it stunned Leslie, and the red that came to her cheeks was more anger than embarrassment, anger with herself for not sensing the situation, especially after what Devlin had told her. She placed the glass on the tailgate of Billy's pickup and turned back toward the house. She needed to regroup.

Billy took her arm and turned her back toward him. Then he stepped in close, used one finger to tilt her chin up, and smiled.

"Don't rush off," he said. "We could have a little fun here. Do somethin' we'd both like."

Leslie stared into his face, her rage building. It was Jack all over again, the same way he would force himself on her after he had hit her; his way of making her forget that he had. He would be all over her, using his weight and strength, smiling at her, telling her how much he wanted her; how much he knew she wanted him.

Billy cupped a hand at the small of her back and began pressing her toward him, thrusting himself out as he did. "You're such a beautiful little thing. And I know just how to make you happy." Billy's voice was almost crooning now.

Leslie brought her knee up with every ounce of strength and anger she possessed, felt the softness of him yield until it was crushed against his pelvis; saw his eyes widen, first in surprise, then in pain, his expression of confident anticipation turn to one of pure, pale agony. His body lurched forward against her, then crumbled at her feet, the knees and shoulders drawn together in a fetal pose. He began to retch and gag, and the only thing she felt was a deep, primal desire to drive the point of her boot into his face over and over again. Instead, she screamed at him. "Get out of here you sonofabitch. Get out. Get out. Get out."

Billy lay there, gasping for breath that wouldn't come, momentarily unable to pull his body out of the ball into which it had drawn itself. The pain seemed to push through every limb then return to its center with a stabbing, knifelike force.

"Oh, you bitch. You filthy, fuckin' bitch," he groaned, the words barely audible. He heard her shouting at him, but the words sounded as though they were coming through water. Slowly, the pain in his limbs began to ease, and he drew himself up to his knees and remained there, still unable to unfold himself.

He swung one hand out, grabbing for her leg, missed, as she jumped back, then dropped his forehead to the ground again, fighting to gather his strength. She had crushed his balls. He knew she had. Had done him some permanent damage. He could feel it. He'd kill the bitch. Beat her so bad they'd never put her back together again. He drew a deep breath, sucking in the pain, and began to rise unsteadily.

"You cunt," he said, barely able to get the words out.

"Get out of here, you bastard."

Leslie stepped back, looking for another chance to kick him again, knowing she would have to, but seeing no opening in his hunched, self-protecting shell.

Billy staggered to his feet, still bent over in pain, and took a weak yet menacing step toward her.

Leslie stepped back, thinking she could run to the house; lock the door; get some weapon to defend herself. Instead, she lunged forward—not even understanding why she had, acting on pure instinct. She pushed him with all her strength, forcing him back several steps, then rushed past him and grabbed a heavy piece of two by four from the bed of the truck. She whirled and raised it, ready to strike.

"Get out of here, or I swear I'll kill you," she screamed.

Billy stared at her, stunned by the rage that seemed to pour off the woman. Then the anger returned and his face twisted into a snarl. "You better make sure you kill me with the first one. 'Cause, if you don't, I'm gonna tear you in half. Then I'm gonna fuck you until you bleed."

He took three steps toward her, still weak, but stronger than before. Leslie raised the makeshift club, turning her body as Billy began moving in a small half circle. You should have hit him when he was on the ground, she told herself. You should have smashed his brains in then. She kept her eyes on his face, which was covered with sweat produced by pain. Just a little closer, she told herself. Just another step.

Billy watched her. The club was held high over her right shoulder, ready to strike out, but her body was facing him, both feet forward, and he knew if he lunged to his own right, there would be no real force in her blow. Then he would have her. Stupid bitch.

He took two more steps to the side, continuing the circle, searching for just the right moment. He came to an abrupt stop. The old man stepped out of the woods and began to cross the lawn, moving up behind the woman. There was a rifle slung from his shoulder, and as he walked, ever so slowly, the rifle seemed to slip off and fall into the cradle of his arms.

"Better go home, Billy. Just like the lady says." Pop Duval's voice was soft, almost gentle, and because it was, it was even more threatening.

Billy stiffened, unsure what to do now. "Get out of here, old man," he growled. "You know what I'll do to you if you don't."

Pop Duval kept moving slowly toward them, and Billy watched his thumb slide to the rifle's safety. "I don't really wanna shoot ya, Billy. But then, I don't mind that much neither." Pop's eyes looked quiet and calm and passive, and Billy felt a chill move through him. He's walkin' over your grave, he thought.

Pop stopped, only ten feet away now, and the barrel of the rifle swung up and across, quartering Billy's chest. "Time to get, Billy," Pop said.

Billy felt frozen to the spot. He knew it was over, that he had lost, that the woman, and now the old man, had made a fool of him. But he wanted some saving gesture. He moved slowly to the bed of the pickup, and angrily grabbed up his shirt. Then he turned back to the old man and the woman.

"You know I'll get you, don't you, Pop? You know me; you know I mean what I say."

"Get, Billy." The old man's voice was little more than a whisper.

Billy's eyes flashed to Leslie. "And your ass belongs to me, bitch. You and that punk brother of yours are gonna wish you never came to this town."

Leslie glared at him. "I wish that already. And don't ever let me see you near me or my brother again."

The anger that radiated from the woman made Billy pause. It confused him; flustered him. "You just wait, bitch," he said, fighting to regain control he had never had.

"Get, Billy." Pop's voice was still soft, but sharper now, and he had taken one step forward.

Billy took a step back, raising one hand. He nodded slowly, the anger in his face changing slowly to a wicked smile. Then he turned abruptly, climbed into his truck, started the engine, and gunned it, leaving a spray of grass and dirt in his wake.

Leslie watched him go, then she lowered the two by four and turned to the old man.

"Seems like you got some work 'round here," Pop said. "Be pleased to do it, if ya have a mind."

Leslie stared at him in disbelief.

Electa Litchfield sat in the window of her workroom, watching Leslie and Pop Duval. She had seen the confrontation between Billy and Leslie, and her face still radiated the dark rage she felt burning inside.

She was dressed in a dark green sweater and green slacks—forest green, the only color she ever wore—and behind her, on the long workbench that dominated most of the room, lay the skinned carcass of a bobcat she was preparing to mount.

She had learned taxidermy from her father when she had been a young girl, and had used it ever since as a hobby to occupy her spare time. And there had been much of that, especially as she had grown older, as she had turned from an awkward young girl to a homely young woman, in whom young men had found little to interest them.

Electa turned from the window and picked up a long, slender skinning knife from the bench and absentmindedly tested its edge with her thumb. Billy was scum, she told herself. Another man whose mind was filled with women's bodies. But it wasn't all his fault. The way that woman had been dressed had lured him to it; had brought out the lust that all men had hidden deep inside them. And some women knew that and used it. Some didn't want to attract them with their minds, their goodness. Some were just bitches in heat, who didn't even possess those qualities. Just had bodies they could use to get what they wanted. And this new one was one of them. Claimed to be an artist, but didn't use her talent or her mind. Dressed to show her body instead.

She jabbed the knife into the table, the blade sticking and vibrating as she released it. Sluts and whores, she told herself. All of them.

She raised her eyes and looked around the room. The walls were covered with animals and birds she had mounted over the years, their eyes collectively gathering in the room; seeing everything, just as she saw everything. She looked down at the raccoon pelt that Jubal had brought to her three days ago. It was good and clean and natural, the way things were supposed to be. She ran a hand over the fur, feeling its deep softness. It was too bad it had to die. But sometimes death was necessary, she knew. If just to preserve the purity and beauty of things. She smiled at the idea. It was something her father had told her; something she had never forgotten.

Robbie sat next to the window, watching the meadows and woodland roll past as the bus rumbled along the rutted dirt road. It was so different here, he thought. It looked so quiet and beautiful compared to the city streets and suburbs he was used to. Yet, somehow, it seemed even more threatening. It was as though he didn't know what to expect from it all; didn't know what might be out there that he had never been forced to deal with before. He thought he should go out in the woods behind his house. Just learn what was out there; learn how to deal with it. But he knew he wouldn't go too far, if he did. He wouldn't risk losing his way and making a fool of himself by not being able to find his way back. Everyone would hear about that, and they'd never let him forget it.

Tim sat next to him, reading a comic book, and Phillipa was one seat in front, doing whatever 7-year-old girls did. He was glad they all took the same bus, even happier that Tommy Robatoy didn't, and more pleased still that Tommy's two-hour detention had let him escape without the promised confrontation. Still, it would come. Bullies like Tommy never forgot things like that.

Robbie continued to stare at the woods. They seemed thicker here, darker and more forbidding. He glanced at Tim, trying to decide how to phrase the question he wanted to ask.

He gave up and blurted the question out, a little louder than he had intended. "You ever go into the woods much?" He caught himself. "You know, I mean to look around and stuff?"

Tim lowered his comic book and shrugged. "A little, I guess. Not for any long hikes, or anything." Tim seemed to recognize the answer might be perceived as unmanly, and quickly modified it. "I mean I'd like to. I guess I just never had the chance."

Robbie nodded. "You know anything about hunting, or tracking animals, or anything like that?"

Before Tim could answer, a boy in the seat behind them started to giggle. "You better be careful. You city boys might get et by a rabbit or somethin'."

Some other boys joined the laughter. One added, " 'Specially it hears how funny you both talk." The second boy tried to imitate Tim's Boston accent and failed, Robbie thought. But it was enough to send half a dozen others into near hysterics.

Robbie gave Tim an apologetic look. "Sorry," he said.

"It's not your fault." It was Phillipa. She had turned around and was kneeling on her seat, facing them. "You see, they don't have enough buses in this town, so we have to ride with the retarded kids."

The boy who had attempted the imitation raised his middle finger, but Phillipa just smiled sweetly in reply.

She looked back at Robbie. "But it's really fun," she added innocently. "You get to watch them wipe the drool off their chins."

Tim and Phillipa got off the bus at Robbie's house. Leslie had suggested that morning that he bring anyone he wanted home and had promised to provide any needed rides. The three filed into the kitchen, Tim already comfortable, having met Leslie at the newspaper; Phillipa at total ease, as she seemed to be under any circumstance.

Leslie served milk and cookies, and immediately found herself charmed by Phillipa. She had long wanted a child—a little girl, specifically—and Phillipa appeared to possess every attribute she had ever fantasized about. But it was more than that. She had found herself attracted to Devlin—the first such feeling she had experienced since fleeing Jack—but she had been put off by her own stereotyped idea of cops, and cop mentalities. Now she found herself questioning that concept—at least as far as Devlin was concerned. Certainly, no macho misfit could produce a child like this.

The children sat at the harvest table, jabbering about the school, the teachers, the kids, the town itself, with Phillipa seeming to have the final word on each subject, as though providing some juvenile imprimatur that all were expected to accept. It was amazing how effortlessly she dominated the older boys, Leslie thought. And when they tried to tease her, she seemed to dismiss it—and them—with an aplomb and sophistication far beyond her years.

Robbie seemed slightly baffled by Phillipa, Leslie thought; Tim less so. But then Tim had been exposed to her longer. Poor Robbie, she told herself. You have some difficult days ahead where the opposite sex is concerned. But that was as it should be, she knew. Male confusion was one of the few advantages women had. Providing they knew what to do with it. She was sure Phillipa would.

Robbie was chattering away about Loopy Louie when he suddenly stopped in midsentence. A truck had just pulled in and was backing up to the scrap woodpile. Through the large kitchen window he watched an old man get out and lower the tailgate.

"Who's that?" he asked, turning toward his sister.

"His name's Pop Duval," Leslie said. "He's going to do some work for us."

"What happened to bigshot Billy?" Robbie asked.

"He was found wanting, so I sent him packing," Leslie said, deciding not to get into the gory details with her 12-year-old brother.

"Pop's crazy Jubal's father," Tim piped up. "He's the guy I told you about. Supposed to be El Supremo hunter and tracker."

Jubal's name rang immediately with Leslie, and she began to wonder if she had fallen into yet another trap. Tim's next words eased her concern.

"He's a really neat old guy," Tim continued. "His son's crazy as a bedbug, but that's supposed to have something to do with him being in the army. According to my dad, even Pop stays away from him. He says Jubal stays in the woods most of the time, barking at the moon."

"I think Jubal's kind of sad," Phillipa said. "But he is kinda scary too. I think it's because he's so big and he never says anything to anybody. He just kind of stares at you." She gave a small shake of her shoulders as if fighting off a shiver.

"I'd really like to meet Pop," Robbie said.

"Well, let's do that," Leslie said. "All of us."

Pop was throwing lumber into the back of his truck with the ease and energy of a man half his age. He stopped as Leslie and the children approached and nodded to them, looking at each in turn.

"The kids wanted to meet you, Mr. Duval," Leslie said.

"Folks call me Pop," the old man said. "Even the younguns."

"Tim says you're really a great hunter," Robbie said, not wasting any time. He watched as the old man simply nodded. "You think you could teach us?"

"Wait a minute," Leslie interjected. "I'm not so sure about hunting. Guns and kids together don't exactly thrill me."

"Gotta learn sometime," Pop said. He looked back at the children. " 'Course ya don't need 'em ta hunt. Only need 'em if you're a mind to take somethin' for food. Huntin's just the findin' 'em part."

Robbie glanced at the rear window of the pickup where Pop's rifle hung on a rack.

Pop followed his gaze. "Like ta keep 'em handy, though," he said as way of explanation.

"Awe, come on, Sis," Robbie pleaded.

Leslie shuffled her feet; screwed up her face, then let out a sigh. "Okay. But no guns. Not for the children, anyway." She felt a twinge of regret as she watched Pop nod his head in agreement.

"Give 'er a try tomorrow, after school, if ya like," he said.

"All right!" Robbie said, looking at the other kids. They all wore grins, matching his own.

Devlin stood in the field, staring at the place where Eva Hyde's body had been found. He looked about him, wondering what had brought him back there. All evidence had been collected and removed. There was no point or purpose in coming back. Unless he was trying to get a sense of what the killer had felt. Or did he know that already?

It was as though a curtain had been drawn across his mind, hiding something, keeping it from view. He stared at the ground. The killer had known pleasure here, pleasure in the power of what he had done. Devlin's hands began to tremble. He understood that feeling, understood it too well. And he understood that the monster inside this man would make him kill again. He sank to his knees, locking his trembling hands under opposite arms, forcing the shaking to stop. His mind clouded, driving away conscious acceptance of his thoughts. Deep inside he knew he too would kill again soon. And that was much more than he was prepared to accept.

# CHAPTER
## 4

Still and dark and quiet. The only time there's safety is in the stillness. In the quiet.

On the table, in the plastic bag—the heart. Eva's heart. Frozen now. Hard as stone. Just as it was in life.

The body suddenly tenses. But you can hear it beating. Beating in the dark, in the stillness, the sound loud enough to move the air, make it vibrate, make it shudder with a steady pulse.

Hands rise to the head, cupping the ears, closing out the sound. Quiet, so quiet.

The hands drop and the beating starts again. The eyes stare at the plastic bag that holds the heart. It pulses, making the bag swell and fall, barely visible in the dim light of the room. But there. There.

Hands resting now in the lap, trembling. The body rigid in the chair.

No. It's not Eva's heart. That's dead and still and quiet. You made sure of that. It's HER heart, the one you never took, never stopped. Never used the stake to pin her body to the earth. And SHE's back now. You knew it the day you saw her driving through town. And you knew then you had to stop her—and all those who are her servants—stop her stone-cold, beating heart. Stop all their hearts. And then it can be quiet again. Then you can be her favorite again.

But not while the men keep coming like yesterday. She tried to make believe she didn't want him there, but you saw her, you knew what she felt, what she wanted. Just like you always know.

And you also know how to stop it. Stop the noise. Stop the pain. So much pain. For so long now.

The beating starts again and the hands close into fists, then open and close, again and again. Keeping pace with the rhythm. Softly. Softly. But soon you'll make it quiet again. Very, very soon. Tomorrow. Yes, maybe tomorrow.

The woods were calm, quiet; everything silent in a way it seldom was. No breezes moved through the branches of the trees. No animal or bird could be heard. It was as if the forest had turned in upon itself, and now sat feeding on its own stillness.

Jubal listened, his back resting against the trunk of a thick oak. He knew this quiet was rare; knew it would last only seconds, and he wanted to enjoy it, savor it. There, it was gone. A gust of wind moved through the trees, and a bird sang out.

Jubal thought about the bird as the normal sounds of the forest returned. Had the bird been silent because it viewed the stillness as a threat? He wondered if it had thought the world was ending, and had sat there, rigid with fear; finally singing out in joy when the wind had returned. Or had it, along with the other animals, merely taken advantage of the quiet, to listen for other threats, moving toward it through the wood?

Jubal himself remained still. The camouflage clothing he wore blended well with the bark of the oak, and he stood there, allowing only his eyes to move until he was certain he had seen everything within his 180-degree range of vision.

He smiled at his own perfection at becoming one with the forest. It was something he had practiced long and hard; something that went beyond even the training he had received. He stepped away from the oak and turned slowly, taking in that portion of the forest he had been unable to see. Off to his left a doe stood next to a stand of brush, certain its own stillness and camouflage left it invisible to his eyes. He smiled at the animal's foolishness. Nothing in these woods was invisible to him.

Jubal moved off slowly, each step carefully taken, designed to make as little sound as possible. It was the second week of October and the autumn color on the mountain had begun to decline. Already fallen leaves laid a multicolored carpet on the forest floor, and the previous night's rain had left them damp and soft, adding to the silence of Jubal's movements. It was warm this afternoon, but there was a hint of crispness in the air, and Jubal breathed it in, allowing the sharpness to fill his lungs, invigorate him with its own clear strength. The mountain was his; would be as long as he chose it to be, and he would allow no intrusion.

If asked, he could not put the words in any order that would be understood. He was not an intelligent man. But he could emit the words from his very being, and he left no doubt that those who crossed his path unwanted would pay a price far worse than would be reasonably expected.

Jubal stopped near the base of a large maple, squatted, and examined the snare he had set the previous day. It had not been tripped and no one had disarmed it. No man or animal had passed this way in more than 26 hours. But soon, he knew, more and more hunters would intrude on his mountain, and he would have to begin digging the punji traps that would punish them for their trespass. The stakes had already been sharpened and stored away, awaiting use. The punishment would be meted out, and they would quickly learn to stay away.

Jubal rose, circled the snare, and struck off up a small incline that led to the cave where he stored his weapons. The cave was hidden by a stand of tall cedars, and when he reached them, Jubal pushed his way through and lit the Coleman lantern he kept near the entrance.

The cave was only 12 feet deep, and just high enough to accommodate Jubal's six feet two inches. Against one wall three rifles hung on a rack affixed to the rock, one equipped with a powerful telescopic sight. Just below, boxes of ammunition were stacked according to caliber, and next to them lay a supply of wire and rope, and two long-bladed hunting knives. In a nearby corner, the sharpened stakes were propped

up against the wall. Above the stakes, a mounted goshawk—
its blue-gray wings spread in a simulated attack—sat perched
on an outcropping, its killing eyes taking in every corner of
the cave.

Jubal studied the hawk, as he always did, then surveyed his
cache, assuring himself nothing had been removed. Turning,
he allowed his eyes to slowly roam the remainder of the cave.
His gaze stopped, as always, on the opposite wall. There, pictures of carnage in Vietnam were intermingled with newspaper
and magazine photographs of Vietcong warriors, some barely
in their teens. The photos were cracked and yellowed with
age, and beneath some were captions written in Jubal's hand
that warned of the dangers of this sworn enemy.

"They never should have sent me home," Jubal muttered,
his voice loud enough to echo in some deep corner of the cave.
He walked to the wall of photos and squatted before a large
footlocker set before them. He stroked the footlocker with his
hand, allowing his fingers to linger over his name and rank,
stenciled on its top. He glanced at the rear wall. A calendar
hung there, a date, two weeks off, circled in red. It marked his
coming birthday, the day on which he would be 40 years old.

Jubal looked back at the wall of photographs. One, hanging
just above the footlocker, showed a group of Saigon whores
plying their trade outside a sleazy, neon-spattered bar. He
closed his eyes, and his brow knitted into rows of furrowed
lines. He was Eva Hyde now. He had become her in his mind;
saw through her eyes; felt through her body.

Eva Hyde laughed her raucous, brittle laugh, as she climbed
out of Billy Perot's pickup truck. The truck was parked on a
turnaround on an isolated dirt road, and Eva walked away a
few feet, then turned back to look at Billy, who sat behind the
wheel, illuminated by the interior light.

"I told you I was just goin' for a ride with you; that I wasn't
doin' nothin' else. So you just zip them jeans up, an' put that
thing of yours away."

Billy slid over and climbed out of the open passenger door.
He walked slowly to Eva, then gently took her arm, two fingers
of his other hand softly tracing the line of her jaw.

"You just think you can do me one day, then decide the
next it ain't gonna happen no more." He smiled down at her,
but the smile didn't carry to his eyes. "Think again, girl."

Eva twisted her body, pulling her arm free. She took several steps back. "I do what *I* wanna do, Billy. Don't you, or nobody else, tell me what I haveta do."

"It's my daddy, isn't it? He told you to stay away, 'cause he wants your ass all to himself."

Eva sneered at him, her face twisting with contempt. "I told you, what I say's the only thing that counts. But if I was gonna listen to somebody, it sure as shit wouldn't be some little boy who's scared shitless of his own daddy."

Billy took two quick steps forward and slapped her full in the face. The blow sent Eva back, and she stumbled and fell into a low pile of brush.

"You do what *I* say; not that limp dick old man of mine," Billy snarled.

"You sonofabitch," Eva screamed. She pulled herself up and glared at him. "You wait until your daddy hears what you called him. Then we'll see how tough you are."

Billy started toward her again, both hands balled into fists, but Eva turned and bolted through the brush and out into the dark, unplowed field.

Billy started after her, then stopped, losing sight of her in the darkness. "Get back here, you cunt," he screamed, then waited for her reply so he could get a fix on her. When no reply came, he crossed into the field, then stopped again, searching for some flash of movement. There was sweat on his face now, and his hands opened and closed involuntarily. "You tell my old man anything and I'll kill your fucking ass," he screamed into the night.

Eva Hyde fell, cried out in pain, then rolled on to her back and lay there, fighting to catch her breath. After a moment she pulled herself up and sat, staring at the scrapes on the palms of her hands. Shit, she told herself. Now she'd have to walk back to town to get her car, and if anybody saw her they'd be out talkin' the next day, how she was wanderin' around covered with dirt. And if Ray Perot heard, he'd not only kick Billy's ass, he'd kick hers too. She fumbled in her jacket pocket, searching for her compact so she could check her makeup. She stopped, telling herself it was a stupid idea. Can't see shit out here, and you're lookin' to check yourself out, she told herself.

"Oh, fuck," she said aloud. Better start walkin', she added

to herself. But better wait a bit too, just to make sure that asshole has headed back. Don't need to get the shit kicked out of you on top of everythin' else.

She started to rise, then fell back gasping in fright. A shadow filled the area before her, and she began to scuttle back on the seat of her pants. She gasped again as she saw the sharpened stake rise in the air above her.

"No!" she screamed. "I'll do anything you want. Please, don't."

The stake plunged down, striking her just above her right breast, driving her back against the ground.

Eva's eyes bulged as she stared at the stake rising up from her body. She tried to reach for it, but the hand fell away weakly. Words formed on her lips but were drowned by the blood bubbling from her mouth. The figure knelt beside her, and the blade of a hunting knife flashed.

Eva's arms and legs gave a final shudder as the blade slid into her abdomen and started up the length of her body. The figure with the knife smiled with satisfaction and continued to cut.

Jubal opened his eyes, again staring at the photo of the whores. He nodded to himself, then stood and walked to the gun rack, selected one, and headed out of the cave.

Pop Duval squatted before the heavy track and traced it with one finger. The two boys stood on either side of him, staring at the embedded hoof print with a mixture of awe and wonder.

" 'Bout an hour or so old," Pop said, raising a hand and pointing up a small rise. "Went that way. Movin' nice, an' slow, an' easy."

"How can you tell?" Tim asked, staring in the direction Pop had pointed toward, almost as though he expected the deer to be standing there watching them.

"Moisture in the track tells ya how old it is," Pop said. "Ain't hardened much yet. Ain't dried out much. Know the direction by the shape of the hoof. Gots that little separation, wheres it's cloven-like. Tells ya which is the front part real easy."

"Could we catch up to him?" Robbie asked.

"Could. If we moved real quiet like, an' stayed downwind. Course we don't know it's a him. Big enough to be a buck. But could be a fat old doe, jus' as easy."

"Let's see if we can catch him," Tim pleaded, excited now about the prospect.

When they had entered the woods with Pop, both boys had been apprehensive. The old man had looked as if he belonged there. The well-used red and black checkered jacket he wore seemed to blend into the surroundings; the rifle, slung over one shoulder, a force as powerful as the forest itself. The boys felt naked and vulnerable next to him. But they also felt safe, and the old man's gentle way of explaining things soon put them at ease as well.

They started up the rise, following Pop closely, each boy trying to place his feet in the same spot the old man had chosen. He had explained the need for quiet when they started out; had told them about the ability of animals to hear even the faintest sounds, and to recognize if they were natural to the woods or a warning of possible danger.

"Can smell real good too," he had explained. " 'Specially iffin the wind's not too strong like. Heavy wind makes it hard on 'em to pick up scents. Kinda blows it up an' away from 'em. You get yerself a strong wind you kin move a right might smarter. Kin even smoke a little iffin you like." He had nodded at them with that, choosing not to say they were too young, and both boys were quietly grateful he had not.

Pop stopped at the top of the rise, then held out one hand, directing the boys to hold up. He waited, watching, then motioned them up beside him.

"Over there, near that thick brush, lost all its leaves already," he whispered, nodding with his head.

The boys followed his gesture and at first saw nothing. Then the buck lowered its head toward the ground to graze and they each saw it.

"Jeez," Robbie whispered. "It's got horns and everything."

"Good size," Pop said. "Go maybe hundred forty, hundred fifty pounds field dressed. Feed ya all winter, iffin ya decided to take 'em."

Robbie and Tim continued to watch the buck. It seemed impervious to their presence, even though it was no more than 200 yards away.

"Could you shoot it this far away?" Tim asked.

The old man nodded. "Pretty clear shot," he said. He glanced down at the boy. "Course ya gotta be sure ya hit 'em right.

Wanna drop 'em with the one shot. Don't wanna make 'em suffer none. Ain't no sport ta make no animal suffer."

"Where would you try to shoot him?" Robbie asked.

"Neck's the best place," Pop said. "Top part, that is. Breaks the spine and kills 'em right quick. Don't even take a step. Heart's next best. Just behind the elbow joint of that front leg. 'Bout the same result. Though I seen 'em run with the heart blown right outta them. Don't feel nothin' though. They's in shock, an jus' runnin' on pure instinct. Mighty strong animals, deer. Lot stronger'en you'd guess, jus' seein' 'em."

Robbie took a step forward, and the deer suddenly raised its head and stared in their direction. Before Robbie could speak, it turned and bolted into the brush.

"It saw me," Robbie said, embarrassed.

"Saw ya move," Pop said. "Deer don't see things too good. Can't see no color. Everythin's jus' kinda gray to 'em. But they pick up real good on movement. An' that spooks 'em real fast. Jus' like you seen."

"Sorry," Robbie said.

"Ain't nothin' to be sorry about. We wasn't gonna shoot 'im anyways. Good for ya to learn this way, then find out when ya wanna take one."

"I guess," Robbie said, still not sure.

Jubal squatted in a stand of birch, situated on a ridge 100 yards north of where the old man and the boys stood. He had watched them for the past half hour. Watched them track the deer. Watched as the old man instructed the boys, as he had once instructed Jubal many years before. He could almost hear the words he was speaking, despite the distance. The old man was his father, the only one who had as much right to the mountain as he himself. Now he was sharing it with these children. Did that mean they belonged here too? No, that couldn't be. He would have to watch and study them to be sure. He nodded to himself. Yes, he'd watch them; then he'd know.

Pop had taken the boys down to where the buck had stood grazing, had shown them the fresh excrement it had left, had explained that the buck, though startled enough to run, had probably moved only a few hundred yards, where it could stand and watch them unseen.

Both boys stared hard into the distance, their eyes roaming

the terrain, trying to locate the deer they had frightened off.

The old man fought off a smile, not wanting to patronize the boys. "Look real careful," he said. "He'll be standin' still as a stone. An' he'll be in fronta somethin', or behind somethin', or next ta somethin', that'll give him real good cover. Somethin' that his own color'll blend in with."

"How's he know what his own color is?" Robbie asked.

"Jus' knows," Pop said. "Taught by his mamma 'bout that, when he was jus' a skipper, suckin' on her milk."

Robbie nodded, his face serious, all knowing. His eyes continued to roam the distant brush and outcroppings. Suddenly his body stiffened, and his hand shot up involuntarily, pointing. He caught himself, again embarrassed by his foolish movement.

"I thought I saw something," he said, his voice shy and uncertain.

Pop's eyes moved to the ridge in time to see Jubal drop to a prone shooting position, his rifle cradled in his arms, a flash of sunlight reflecting off the lens of the scope. He stepped in front of the boys, his own rifle slipping from his shoulder into his hands.

"You be movin' off, Jubal," he shouted.

Light reflected off the lens again, as Jubal's rifle moved slightly. The old man's own weapon snapped to his shoulder, and both boys heard a click as he disengaged the safety.

"Damn your eyes, Jubal. Don't make me ta stop ya."

The boys watched as a figure clad in camouflage rose slowly and stood staring down at them.

Robbie looked up at the old man, shaken and uncertain about what he had become a part of. When he turned back toward the ridge the camouflaged man was gone.

"Who was that?" he asked.

Pop was silent, his eyes still fixed on the ridge.

"Was he going to shoot at us?" Tim asked.

Pop looked down at the boy, his eyes showing pain. "Can't never tell what Jubal might do," he said. His eyes hardened and he turned to Robbie. "Jubal's my boy," he said. "But he ain't well, like. You see him—'specially in these here woods—you steer clear."

"Were you gonna shoot him?" Robbie asked.

The old man looked away, the muscles dancing along his

jaw. "Let's get on back now," he said. "It'll be near dark 'fore you boys get home."

The stores along the main street of East Blake blazed with exterior light, although most were now closed, and the German restaurant, Wolfgang's—which had moved to the Vermont town from New York City—was festooned in the small white Christmas lights that it wore year round. Paul Devlin sat at a small corner table with his daughter, enjoying a quiet meal with her, and making up, in part, for the unanticipated absences he had been forced to impose on her.

Phillipa loved the restaurant, partly because it was located in an old church that had gone bankrupt—an idea that fascinated her—and partly because it, and its owner, Gunter Kline, had come to Vermont for the same reasons as she and her father. None had wanted to deal with the endless pressures of New York any longer.

Devlin had polished off his sauerbraten with relish, and Phillipa her schwein schnitzel, and now each were faced with enormous portions of *käsekuchen* and *schokoladenauflauf*, respectively.

"I'm gonna explode," Devlin said, as he stuffed another forkful of cheesecake into his mouth. He stared pointedly at Phillipa's chocolate souffle, which was already half gone. "But I suppose you'll be able to eat the rest of *my* dessert too."

"Definitely," Phillipa said. "That's why I like you to bring me here. You can never finish your dessert, and, that way, I get two."

"You keep eating like that, and growing the way you are, and you'll drive me into bankruptcy," Devlin said.

"Just like this church." Phillipa wrinkled up her nose, thinking. "You said this used to be a Congregational church. Do Catholic churches ever go broke?"

"No. The pope's got too much money," Devlin said.

Phillipa giggled. "Then how come you have to put money in the basket *whenever*"—she rolled her eyes—"you go to church?"

"I'm trying to buy my way into heaven."

"Then you should go more. Besides, you'll never get in as long as you keep making me go to bed at nine o'clock every night."

"That's a sin?" Devlin asked.

"Sure. The priest at Sunday school told us that God loves little kids. So, if he does, a father who abuses his daughter that way doesn't have much of a chance."

"I'll mend my ways," Devlin said. "Tonight you can go to bed at nine fifteen."

"Not exactly what I had in mind," Phillipa said.

"Best I can do."

"Well, I suppose you'll have to settle for twenty years in purgatory."

"Hard time?" Devlin asked.

"Very hard. Shoveling coal, stoking fires. All that hot, sweaty stuff."

"Whew." Devlin made a weary face. "What about nine thirty?"

"Ten years," Phillipa said. "But no stoking, just shoveling."

"I suppose ten o'clock might let me cut a little better deal, huh?"

"Eleven o'clock and you could go straight to heaven."

Devlin fought back a laugh. "I'll settle for ten years, and you'll settle for nine thirty. The way the parole boards work today, I think I'll take my chances."

Phillipa's nose screwed into a tiny button. "I was afraid I might be pushing too hard. Can we start again, and work our way to ten?"

"Not a chance. Court's closed."

"Pooh."

"You're not going *pooh* for your *schokoladenauflauf,* I hope."

Phillipa looked up into Gunter Kline's smiling face. She returned the smile. She liked the man, liked his round, red face, and stocky body, all of which made him seem like a young, fit Santa Claus in a suit. But most of all she liked the story about how he inherited the New York restaurant from his father, then just said, okay, but not here, and promptly moved it all to Vermont.

"No," she said. "The dessert's great. We were just negotiating bedtime hours, and I lost."

"You won an extra half hour," Devlin said.

Phillipa shrugged. "Not exactly a breakthrough," she said.

Gunter began to laugh, his chunky body shaking with delight. "Where does she get this?" he asked, not expecting an answer. He looked down at Phillipa. "Sometimes I think you're a forty-year-old midget."

"I wish I was," Phillipa said. "Then I could stay up as long as I wanted."

"Life's tough in the big city, kid," Devlin said.

Phillipa gave him a wide-eyed stare. "The big city? Somebody better tell the cows." She began to giggle again. "Or maybe tell the farmers you're going to start enforcing the pooper scooper law."

"Never mind," Devlin said, unable to hold back his laughter. "I've got enough problems without getting the farmers mad at me."

"Still working on—" Gunter let the question hang in deference to the child.

Devlin nodded. Eva Hyde had worked for Gunter as a waitress, and he had liked the young woman; had found a decency in her that transcended her reputation.

"Tough one," he said. "But we'll break it." He decided not to add that he hoped it would happen before another victim turned up.

Gunter shifted uncomfortably. There were other questions he wanted to ask, but knew they'd be inappropriate in front of Phillipa. Perhaps in front of anyone. He simply nodded. "I've been thinking about it," he said at length. "Maybe I could come in and talk with you tomorrow."

"I'll be in at nine," Devlin said. "Anytime after that."

Gunter nodded again, then turned his attention back to Phillipa, his features changing from somber to smiling. "Now, mein kind," he said. "How would you like another schokoladenauflauf?"

Phillipa's eyes widened with delight. "Great," she said, not even bothering to glance at her father for approval.

It was 7:30 when they left the restaurant, and as they walked to their jeep, Devlin spotted Jubal's battered pickup parked across the street.

He took Phillipa's arm and bent to her. "You wait in the car a minute," he said. "I have to see somebody, but it won't take long."

When he reached the pickup it was empty. Devlin hesitated, wondering if he should wait. He turned to go, deciding he would catch him another time, then saw Jubal walking toward him, face like a stone mask.

"Good evening, Jubal," he said, as the man reached him. Jubal just stared at him, offering not so much as a grunt. "Missed you the other day," Devlin continued. "Guess you were in a hurry."

"Ain't hard ta find," Jubal said, standing his ground. He didn't ask what Devlin wanted; acted as though he didn't care.

"I understand you were at the roadhouse the night Eva Hyde was killed."

No word; no gesture. Silence.

"That true?" Devlin asked.

"Go there sometimes."

"Were you there that night?"

A shrug.

Devlin bristled at the man's reticence but held himself in check. "You see anybody leave with her?"

Another shrug.

"What does that mean?" A slight edge had crept into Devlin's voice, and Jubal's eyes narrowed at the sound of it.

"Didn't pay no attention."

"You spend any time with her that night? Talking, or whatever?"

Jubal snorted derision. "Don't pay no mind to no Saigon whores," he said.

"That what you thought she was?"

Jubal stared at him for a moment, then started past, headed for the door of his truck.

"You know anything about a fox carcass left in somebody's backyard?"

"Heard about it," Jubal said, opening the door of the truck.

"You put it there?"

Jubal turned and stared at Devlin, eye to eye. "What I do is my business. I don't bother you 'bout your business."

Devlin felt his body tense. He didn't want the man to come at him; wasn't really sure he could handle that. But he'd be damned if he'd let the sonofabitch cow him. "It *is* my business," he said, staring back into Jubal's flat, vacant eyes. "So answer the damned question."

A small smile began to form on Jubal's lips, almost as though he was admiring his antagonist's bravado, someone he knew he could crush like a bug. The smile disappeared. "Don't know nothin' 'bout no fox."

"What about Eva Hyde?"

"Don't know nothin' 'bout that neither."

Devlin nodded. "Hope I don't find out you're kiddin' me, Jubal." He waited, watching the small smile begin to form again, then fail as quickly as before. "Probably be a good idea to stay out of people's backyards. Somebody saw you there, they might get the wrong idea, given what's been going on."

Jubal didn't respond. He stared at Devlin for several seconds, then turned and climbed into his pickup.

Devlin stood there and watched him drive off.

When he climbed into the jeep Phillipa leaned across, put her arms around his neck, and hugged him. He knew what she had witnessed had frightened her.

"Hey, pretty good. And I was only gone a few minutes." He hugged her back.

"It was really scary watching you talk to crazy Jubal," Phillipa said.

"He's all right," Devlin said, releasing her. "And don't call him that. It's not his fault what happened to him."

"I know," she said. "But he is scary, just the same."

He sure as hell is, Devlin thought. He reached across and stroked her hair, then smiled. "I think maybe we'll experiment with ten o'clock tonight," he said. "Just to see if you're over-tired in the morning."

"Great," Phillipa said. "And I won't be overtired. You'll see."


Billy Perot sat in his truck farther down Main Street, his girlfriend, Linnie French, beside him. He had watched the confrontation between Jubal and Devlin, and, although he had been too far away to tell how much talking Jubal had done, the brevity of the session had satisfied him that little had been said. Good ol', stupid ol' Jubal, he thought. Like tryin' to get conversation out of a clam. He grinned at the idea.

"What are you so happy about?" Linnie asked. She was a slender young woman, pretty in a pouty sort of way, with vapid blue eyes and blond hair that had been red the week before. She smiled at Billy, aware that her perfect, even teeth were her most attractive feature.

"You honey," Billy said, turning his own smile on her. "Just hopin' you're gonna do somethin' to make me happy."

Linnie gave him a coy look. "Maybe I will," she said, looking off down the street. "If you're good to me."

Billy stroked her cheek. The woman thought she knew all the moves, he told himself. Thought she knew how to play it out, so you'd be ready to come in your pants waitin' for her to put out. Then she'd drop her drawers, jus' like she wanted to all along. It was all bullshit. But he enjoyed beating her at her own game; enjoyed the sense of power it gave him.

Billy's eyes returned to the sidewalk, and what he found there added to his enjoyment. Tommy Robatoy was walking toward the truck, a package in his arms, just as Billy had known he would be.

"Here comes ol' Tommy, just like I said. Bringin' his ol' man's nightly bottle."

"I can't believe they'd give a bottle to a kid his age," Linnie said. "He could be drinkin' it himself."

"So what," Billy said. "And it ain't really no State Store anyway. It's just part of Elson's store, that's supposed to be a State Store. And El knows Tommy ain't gonna drink it, 'cause if he did his old man would beat his ass to death for cuttin' into his supply."

Billy rolled down his window. He had parked on the wrong side of the street so he could talk with Tommy without getting out of his truck. He thought it would make the conversation seem more natural, less planned, as though Tommy had seen him and stopped to say hello.

Billy motioned with his head, and Tommy came to the truck's window, a slightly nervous look in his eyes. He didn't really like Billy; didn't trust him. But he very much wanted Billy to like him. It was safer that way.

"Understand you got a new city boy in your school," Billy said.

"Yeah," Tommy said. "How'd you know?"

Billy grinned at him, as if saying he knew everything there was to know. "I was out at his place the other day—helpin' his sister out." He grinned again as if there was more he could say, but couldn't now because Linnie was there. "Heard him makin' fun of the local kids. Sayin' they were all a bunch of farmboy assholes. Just thought you'd like to know."

"He really say that?" Tommy asked.

Billy's eyes hardened on the boy. "What are you sayin', Tommy? You sayin' I'm lyin', or somthin'?"

Tommy blanched and began to stutter. "N-n-no. I j-j-just didn't think he'd have the g-g-guts to say nothin' like that."

"Must think you local boys a bunch a pussies." Billy's grin returned. "Maybe you oughtta smack him real good. Let him know we don't shit our pants over no city kids."

Tommy nodded, but there was a look of doubt in his eyes. Billy picked up on it.

"But maybe you do shit your pants." He cocked his head and gave Tommy a questioning look.

Tommy snorted. "I'll show him." He paused. "Just haveta do it away from school, that's all. I get any more detentions, my old man's gonna beat my ass for sure."

Billy thought of telling him to tell his old man that he, Billy, just might kick *his* ass, if he didn't keep his hands off the boy. But he decided against it. Probably did Tommy a lot of good to get his ass beat every so often, anyway. Billy thought about that. For sure, he told himself.

"You let me know what happens," he said instead. "I wanna hear all about it." His grin widened. "And, who knows. I jus' might have some even better ideas for you."

He watched Tommy nod his head, then rolled up his window, dismissing him, and turned to Linnie, the grin still spread across his face.

"So what were you doin' out there with his sister?" she asked, an edge to her voice.

"Just helpin' her out. Somethin' my daddy asked me to do," Billy lied. He leaned over and kissed her ear. "You don't haveta worry. You're all the woman I can handle."

Linnie's head snapped away and she stared up the street, her face flushed with anger. "You better make sure I am. I don't wanna catch somethin'," she said at length. "All the women you're *helpin' out* all the time."

Billy put his truck in gear and pulled out, spinning the tires. "Oh, baby, I wish you'd trust me," he said. He wasn't angry, more amused than anything else. "Let's take us a ride. Maybe stop someplace nice and quiet."

Linnie turned back to him, then slid over on the seat and put her head on his shoulder. "Let's go out by the bend," she said. "That spot near the river. I like it there." She dropped her hand to his thigh, then ran it up to his crotch and began rubbing softly. "You promise me you won't be with nobody else?" she said, her voice soft, yet demanding.

"You know I won't," Billy said. He grinned. "But you keep doin' *that*, I do promise you somethin' real hard to play with."

Linnie rubbed harder. "I'll keep doin' it, Billy," she said. "You jus' keep it hard 'til we get there."

He reached over and stroked one breast, allowing his finger to linger on the nipple. Linnie nuzzled her head against his shoulder.

Jubal, who had circled around, and had parked well behind Billy's truck, sat and watched them leave. From the front window of the restaurant, Gunter Kline also watched them drive past. Like Jubal, his eyes were filled with hate.

# CHAPTER
## 5

The ground fog is so concealing, so comforting. It rises up, swallowing the trees around you, hiding everything that needs to be hidden. From here, among the trees, you can barely make out the boy as he reaches the end of the driveway and rises into the school bus, which sits there hovering, like some great yellow monster. But you can see her. Standing there waving. Acting as though she really cares. Dressed in her tight jeans. Flaunting her beauty.

She stops waving and stands now with her hands on her hips. There is a box beside her, and she bends, picks it up, turns and starts toward the open door of the barn.

The figure stands rigid, staring, body covered by a hooded camouflage poncho that hangs like a shroud, eyes boring out from two holes cut into a gauzelike camouflage mask. A hand slips beneath the poncho and withdraws holding a long, slender knife, the glistening blade already moistened by the dew carried on the fog. The figure takes one step forward, then another, then stops abruptly, as a pickup truck rumbles into the driveway and slides to a halt at the entrace to the barn.

The woman exits the barn just as the old man climbs down from the truck.

"Gettin' started on makin' yer studio?" the old man asks.

"A start's about it," the woman says. "But at least I'll have a place to work. I'll just keep improving it as I go along. As I can afford it."

"Best way," the old man says. "Tell me what I kin do to help." He pauses. "Watcha gonna do with that old freezer in there? We could get it out if ya want."

The woman turns, eyes wide with surprise. "No. No, it's too heavy. I'll just keep it there. Just, just in case I need it."

The old man nods and follows her into the barn, as the hand returns the knife beneath the poncho. The eyes are glaring now, and as the hand withdraws it is holding a red rose, dry and withered with age. A second hand covers the flower, closing into a fist, grinding and crushing the petals into a fine powder. Then the figure turns and disappears into the fog.

Devlin was at his desk. He had been trying to review the Eva Hyde file but his mind had been drifting. He had been up late the previous night reading the new book he had received, plying his two-year-long avocation. The words kept returning to him even now: "For years we have believed that men who killed again and again—so-called serial killers—were driven by insane furies, mad possessions, or wild longings. But what if they simply enjoyed killing; enjoyed it so much they wanted, perhaps even needed, to relive the experience, recapture the pleasure they derived from it?" Devlin's hand, laying atop Eva Hyde's file, began to tremble slightly, and he closed it into a fist, fighting off the tremor. When he looked up, Gunter Kline was standing in his office door.

It was 10 a.m. and Gunter was dressed casually in a blue Burberry sportshirt, gray Harris Tweed jacket, and pale gray slacks, near formal attire for East Blake, but a far cry from the severe double-breasted suits he wore when greeting customers at his restaurant. He was about Devlin's age, but far more regal looking in a European sense. Even his longish blond hair was trimmed to perfection. He placed a plastic bag, containing two dressed and cleaned partridge, on Devlin's desk. "I got lucky hunting the other day," he said. "I thought you and Phillipa might enjoy them."

Devlin thanked him, then watched as Gunter sat heavily on

one end of the imitation leather sofa, stared at the floor for a moment, then looked up, drawing a weary breath.

"I think Eva was killed. Murdered," he said. "And I wanted to tell you why."

Devlin nodded, declining to say he agreed with this man, who had become his friend over the past two years. "What makes you think so?" he asked.

Gunter rubbed his palms together and drew another deep breath. "First let me tell you that I liked her very much." He raised a hand as though fending off an anticipated objection, even though none had been raised. "She was a good person, very kind, very sweet. I know what her reputation was, but that's not the side of her I saw every day. She worked hard, and she had a generous heart."

"Why would that make her a possible murder victim?" Devlin asked. He suspected that Gunter had felt more for Eva than he was saying, but he wanted to keep him away from maudlin memories; keep him as near to facts as possible.

"She was so meticulous about her appearance." He raised his hand again. "Oh, I know she was a bit gaudy with her makeup, and the way she dressed when she wasn't working. But that was because she didn't know *how* to dress. And she was insecure about herself, and the excessive makeup was a way to cover it up. If someone had only shown her how, she would have been a ravishing woman."

There was a deep regret in Gunter's voice, and Devlin noticed he had begun to twist his fingers nervously.

"So, what I'm saying is that she never would have been out in some field at night, unless she was running from someone." His face hardened. "And then there was that damned Perot kid. He used to show up, sit at the bar, and harass her. Wait for her to get off work." His jaw tightened. "Several times I offered to see her home, but—" He shrugged helplessly.

"Did Billy ever threaten her?"

Gunter's eyes narrowed. "Billy's too slick for that. He's a threat without even opening his mouth. People know what a vindictive bastard he is when he doesn't get his way; that if he can't smooth-talk his way into something, he'll get it any way he can. Or get his sonofabitch of a father to get it for him."

Devlin wondered what pressure Ray Perot had brought to

bear on Gunter. Wondered if he had tried to keep Billy out of his restaurant and had suddenly found his note at the bank Ray Perot controlled being called into question.

"You think Billy killed her?"

"Somebody did. I know that here." He thumped one fist against his chest. "And I know he was always after her."

"Maybe he got what he wanted." Devlin said the words softly, without condemnation. He didn't want to hurt the man.

"I'm sure he did," Gunter said, looking away. "But that was never enough for him. He has to feel he controls people, has to be able to humiliate them. I know Eva would have fought that. She was trying so hard to be a different person. To stop letting people walk all over her. I know. We talked about it."

Devlin thought about what he knew of Eva's past, about the abuse and abandonment she had known most of her life. He liked Gunter for attempting to help the woman, even if it wasn't totally unselfish.

"There's nothing in Billy's record to indicate he's ever been violent with a woman."

Gunter snorted. "That's because his father buys them off. What about this new woman in town, this Adams woman, and what happened to her?"

Devlin leaned forward, his eyes as tense now as Gunter's. "What are you talking about?"

Devlin listened, his eyes growing cold as Gunter explained. "Where'd you hear about this?" he asked.

"Jim McCloud. You know he has a problem with his drinking. Well, he was in the bar last night, and apparently Electa Litchfield—she lives next door to the Adams woman—saw the whole thing from her window." Gunter smiled. "Electa likes to keep watch on things from her window, I'm told. Anyway, McCloud was in his cups, and was really enjoying the story of Billy getting thrashed by a woman, and then being run off by an old man." He shook his head. "But it's not funny. And it shows what he's capable of. You see that, don't you, Paul?"

Devlin sat back in his chair, his fingers steepled before his face. There was a slight tic in his right eye that caused the small scar on his cheek to do a nervous dance. "Yeah, I see. I see I should have done something about that arrogant bastard a long time ago."

Gunter watched him, realizing he had touched a nerve;

pleased that he had. "I know he was with Eva that night. I can't prove it, but I know it's true." He began twisting his fingers again. "When she finished work that night—the night she disappeared—she told me she was going to the roadhouse. And Billy's always there. Always."

Devlin didn't explain he already had that information, or that it proved little one way or the other. He was thinking of Billy now, and what he wanted to do to him. But first he'd play it straight. Speak to Leslie; see if he could get her to sign a complaint, with Pop Duval as a witness. Then lock the bastard up and pray he'd resist arrest.

He looked up at Gunter and forced a smile. "I promise you I'll look into it. And if he had anything to do with Eva's death, I'll find out, and I'll nail his ass to a wall."

Gunter nodded and returned the smile, his own equally as full of venom as Devlin's. The smile faded. "Just watch out for his father," he warned. "You go after Billy, and he'll come after you. He has a great deal of hidden power here. And he enjoys using it."

"Yeah," Devlin said. "I know how that game's played. I lived with it in New York for nine years."

"This is a very small pond, here," Gunter said. "And it's a lot harder to avoid the big fish. There are fewer places to hide."

"Yeah, I know that too," Devlin said. His smile widened, growing even harder. "But it's not easy for a big fish to hide either. And I've got sharp teeth."

Louis Ferris stood behind his desk, holding a sheaf of papers in his hand. He was smiling as he looked out at the class. It was an odd smile, both sly and happy at the same time, and it struck a note of nervousness in his students that he appeared to enjoy.

"Well, it would seem that everyone managed to get his paper in yesterday . . . something of a minor miracle." He paused, thumbing through the papers, stopping at the one he was seeking. "It would appear we also have one student courageous enough even to attempt a poem." His eyes scanned the class, then settled on Robbie. "Mr. Adams, would you do us the honor of reading your poem?"

Robbie felt a surge of panic; remained glued to his seat, then finally rose on shaky legs and went to the front of the class.

He accepted the paper from Loopy Louie and turned to face the class only to find himself met by a mixture of curious stares and smirks. Even Tim had lowered his eyes, as if too embarrassed to look at his friend.

Robbie's voice caught in his throat, and he had to wait for it to fight itself free. He had titled the poem "Nod," and he read it in a voice that was weak and barely audible.

> Our loveliness died,
> In a place called Nod.
> And the people came out,
> And they stood all agog.
> Then they lifted her up,
> And carried her away,
> To an old, gray graveyard,
> By the edge of a bay.
> Then they buried her deep,
> And covered her with clay,
> And some said a prayer,
> While others went away.
> Then they set up a marker,
> That said she was there,
> Buried deep down below,
> With flowers round her hair.
> And the children of Nod,
> Went on with their play,
> And the boy kissed the girl,
> In the field full of hay.
> And the preacher said a prayer.
> And the harlot made a date.
> And the clerk in the store,
> Sold at a bargain rate.
> And some people laughed,
> While other people cried.
> And they all soon forgot,
> That our loveliness had died.

There was quiet, then a smattering of giggles, then quiet again when Robbie finished. He handed the paper back to Loopy Louie, pleased by the *A* he saw written next to his name, yet still mortified at having read it to the class. He started to turn away, but Ferris held him with his eyes.

"Where did you ever hear the word *harlot?*" he asked. A

picture of Robbie's sister, whom he had met when the boy registered for school, flashed into his mind.

Robbie swallowed, sure more giggling would come. None did, the other children apparently not knowing the word. "Sunday school," he said, his voice barely a whisper.

Ferris raised his eyebrows momentarily, then seemed satisfied with the answer. He looked out at the class. "A harlot is a loose woman," he intoned, "an evil woman." His eyes took on a wild look, then quickly returned to normal. He achieved the giggles that had not come before, albeit uncertain ones. "In any event, an excellent job. An *A*," he added. "And," he paused for emphasis, "an example for you all."

Robbie was still mortified when he and Tim made their way into the schoolyard for recess. Being singled out and praised in front of a bunch of kids he hardly knew was one of the worst things he could think of. Maybe being singled out and yelled at would be worse, but right now he wasn't sure.

"Jeez," Tim said. "Why'd you ever write a poem? You *want* all these farmers to get on your case?"

Robbie shrugged. He had written the poem for a class in his school in Philadelphia and had gotten a good grade. It had seemed like a good idea just to turn it in again with the corrections and changes his teacher, then, had made. Almost like getting away with something. Now, having had it backfire the way it had, he didn't even want to admit what he had done. "I guess it wasn't such a great idea," he said, wanting to let the whole thing drop.

"Not one of your more brilliant ones," Tim said. "Especially in Loopy Louie's class. There's nothing he likes better than to get everything all stirred up."

"You wanna go out in the woods today?" Robbie asked, hoping to change the subject. "I mean alone this time?"

"Yeah, sure," Tim said, his voice less than certain.

"Me too. I don't want to miss it this time."

It was Phillipa. She had come up behind them. A dental appointment had kept her from going with Pop and the boys the day before.

"You may not want to when you hear what happened to us," Tim said. He quickly began to relate their encounter with Jubal, and Pop's warning to steer clear of him in the woods. Then he added the part about the deer, and the things Pop had taught them, slightly uncertain he was getting it all right.

"I'm not afraid of Jubal," Phillipa said. "My father says he's not dangerous, just very mixed up."

"Yeah, well my father thinks he's a psycho," Tim said. "He said he saw guys just like him when he was a war correspondent in Vietnam."

"I know. You told us all that before," Phillipa said, a note of dismissive boredom in her tone.

"Well, just so you know," Tim said defensively. "I don't want you claiming later that we never told you."

"Oh, stop trying to scare everybody," Phillipa said. She turned to Robbie. "I hear you wrote a poem," she said.

"Jeez," Robbie said. "Does everybody know?"

"Even the cows, by now," Tim said. He looked away and groaned at what he saw.

Robbie and Phillipa followed his gaze and saw Tommy Robatoy headed toward them with three of his gang tagging along.

"Hello, assholes," Tommy said as he pulled up before them. "Or maybe I should call you faggots, since that's what you are." He glared at Robbie. "You like to write poems, faggot?"

When Robbie didn't respond, Tommy turned to his friends. "Sure he likes it," he said. "Probably jerks off every time he writes one. Or maybe he lets this faggot"—he gestured at Tim—"play with his dick while he's writin' them."

"If you don't stop it, I'm going to tell the yard monitor," Phillipa interjected.

Tommy stepped toward her, jabbing his finger in her face. "You do and I'll punch you right in the mouth. Girl or no girl."

Tommy cocked his arm and began throwing a mock punch at Phillipa. Robbie stepped quickly between them. "Leave her alone," he said. There was a slight quaver in his voice, but he hoped Tommy wouldn't notice.

Tommy didn't wait to notice. He recocked his hand and drove his fist into Robbie's face, knocking him back into Tim, and finally to the ground.

"How'd you like that one, faggot," he said, standing over him. "I got lots more if you want."

The sneer on Tommy's face turned to a grimace, and he cried out in pain. Phillipa had kicked him in one ankle, and was now attacking the other. "Stop it," he shouted, swinging a backhand at her, but missing badly.

"Fight! Fight!" Phillipa began to shout.

Tommy stepped back quickly and glanced over his shoulder, looking for the schoolyard monitor. "I'll get you," he snarled at Phillipa. "And I'll have more for you too," he snapped at Robbie, who was getting up now, wiping a blood trail from beneath his nose. Then he turned and hurried off, the other boys following close at his heels.

"Jeez, he really socked you one," Tim said, staring at Robbie's swelling nose.

"Yeah, it's been a great day so far," Robbie said. He felt his nose gingerly. "It feels bigger," he said.

"It is," Tim said. "Lots."

"Jeez," Robbie said.

"I think you were terrific," Phillipa said.

"Oh, God," Robbie said, wishing he could crawl into a hole and hide.

Ray Perot stared at his son, his lips curled in disgust. "So the woman kicked you in the balls, and then the old man drove you off like some useless piece a shit."

"It wasn't like that," Billy said. His voice had a wheedling sound to it, and Ray stepped quickly forward and slapped him across the face.

"What'd you do that for?" Billy demanded, one palm pressed to his cheek.

"Don't whine at me, boy," Ray snapped. "Or you'll get worse than that."

Ray Perot was much smaller than his son, a thin stick of a man, who was fast approaching 60. He had a narrow face, and mean, self-centered eyes, set wide apart, thinning hair, and a flat, homely face accented only by badly yellowed teeth. He had no fear Billy might hit him back. He knew it was something Billy would never do. Billy was terrified of him. Just the way Ray wanted him to be.

He continued to glare at his son. "You're a disgrace to me; always have been and, I expect, always will be."

"It wasn't nothin' like you heard," Billy insisted. "She come on to me. Then she got scared when she saw the old man comin' outta the woods."

Ray's sneer returned. "Yeah. So she kicked your nuts for ya, just to cover up." He raised his hand again, but held back when Billy flinched. "And you were just out there cleanin' up her trash to be neighborly, huh?" He could see Billy's mind working, trying to figure out another tact. The boy was pitiful. "And I suppose the chief was all over your ass the other day just because he doesn't like the way you look."

"It didn't have nothin' to do with that," Billy said, his voice insistent, stronger this time.

"Then what was it?" Ray demanded.

Billy felt suddenly vindicated and hurried on without thinking. "He was all over me about Eva Hyde."

Ray's eyes grew cold, narrow. "What you know about that bitch gettin' herself killed?"

"Nothing," Billy said, the whine back. "He was just pushin' me, 'cause I was with her a couple a times."

Ray studied him closely, appeared satisfied. "Shit, everybody fucked that girl." He seemed about to say more, then decided not to. "I'll take care of that," he added at length. "But you." He jabbed a finger at Billy. "You clean up your act. And you let these people know they ain't pushin' no Perot around. Not in this fuckin' county. Anybody pushes you, I wanna hear they got problems like they never wanted."

Billy nodded. He too was about to say something but thought better of it.

Robbie searched the ground, trying to find a deer track. It had seemed so simple the other day with Pop, but now it was as if all the signs that had been everywhere had simply disappeared. He stared at a young tree, only a few inches in diameter, its bark scarred only a few feet above the ground.

"This could be a rub," he said, doubt heavy in his voice.

"What's a rub?" Phillipa asked.

"Pop says it's when a deer rubs its horns against a tree to sharpen them and get the felt off that covers them when they grow every year." Tim interrupted, taking charge of the explanation.

"It's a buck, not a deer. And it's antlers, not horns," Robbie said, reasserting himself under the guise of accuracy.

Tim made a face, while Phillipa glanced between the two, trying to decide what the competition was all about.

"And there's scrapes too," Robbie continued. "That's when a buck scrapes out an area of ground, maybe this wide." He held his hands about two feet apart. "Maybe bigger, if it's a big buck. It's to let the does know it's his territory, in case they want to join up with him."

"And if the doe does, she pees in the scrape," Tim said, giggling.

"Oh, gross," Phillipa said.

"It's just the way they do things," Robbie said, posturing an unfelt authority in both voice and stance.

"It's still gross," Phillipa said, earning a "girls" look in reply.

"Let's see if we can find a scrape," Tim said. "Pop said bucks put them all over their territory, then visit each one a couple of times a day to see if any does have been there."

Phillipa seemed uncertain, but shrugged agreement, as if there was nothing better to do, and tagged behind the boys as they headed toward a large deadfall.

A heavy breeze pushed through the woods, sending sporadic showers of leaves filtering through the trees, the colors flashing in the bright sun as the leaves twisted lazily as they floated to the ground. The boys ran ahead, jumping to catch a particular leaf, often missing as another gust carried it out of reach, regrouping and racing after it again.

"Look at this one," Phillipa said, stooping to retrieve a bright red leaf, laced with yellow.

"It's a maple," Tim said. It was the only leaf he could identify, but his voice sounded positive, knowledgeable.

"What's this one?" Phillipa said, stooping and picking up a bright yellow birch leaf.

Tim turned away, as though he had not heard, searched the ground, and came up with a broken branch, shaped naturally like a cane. He drew it to his shoulder, turning it into an instant gun, and began sighting along its shaft.

Robbie forged ahead toward the deadfall. It was a large tree, three feet in diameter at its base, with a web of twisted boughs, one forming a couchlike seat only a foot off the ground. The base was pitted with rot, and it looked as though it had simply fallen over, the strength to hold itself erect eaten away from within. Robbie thought about that, wished he had been there when it had come crashing to the earth, then realized he could just as easily have been under it when it fell. He looked nervously at the surrounding trees, wondering if the disease had spread to them as well.

He hesitated, decided it was too much to worry about, and continued toward the deadfall, wondering if he could convince the others it could be used as a fort, maybe covered with branches and leaves, with a crawlspace they could use as a secret entrance.

Jubal rose from behind the base of the fallen tree, his face, smeared with camouflage grease, a grotesque mask. Robbie took three quick steps back, stumbled on a hidden root, and landed on the seat of his pants. He struggled to his feet and glanced back at the others, who had seen Jubal now, and stood staring, frozen in place.

"Run!" Robbie yelled, then turned and raced past the others, grabbing at Phillipa's arm and spinning her around.

The three children ran with abandon, weaving between trees and around boulders that seemed suddenly placed in their path. They were no more than a thousand yards from Robbie's backyard, but the density of the wood made it impossible to see the safety they sought. They rounded a small hillock and started down a steep slope. Thirty yards ahead Jubal stepped from behind a cluster of boulders.

The children stopped, staring in disbelief. They were panting, more from fear than exertion, and their faces glistened with sweat. Jubal's eyes moved from one to the other.

"Leave us alone!" Phillipa screamed, her voice choked, close to tears.

Jubal's eyes riveted on her, looking surprised, almost hurt. He stood still, silent. Slowly, carefully, the children began moving in a wide circle, their eyes never leaving him. Jubal turned with their movement, his own imperceptible to the eye, and it made the children feel they had not moved at all; were still fixed to the same spot, and only their bodies told them it wasn't true, that they were going around him, away from the danger.

When they were behind him, behind the rock formation that had hidden him, they again began to run, racing even more wildly this time, miraculously staying erect, avoiding the roots and branches and rocks hidden beneath the carpet of leaves.

When he could see the outline of his barn between the trees, Robbie chanced a look back. Jubal was nowhere to be seen. At the edge of the wood, only a dozen or so steps from his backyard, Robbie stopped, raising his arms to halt the others. The three children stared at each other, panting, sweating, uncertain what to say. From the barn they could hear Pop Duval hammering, still replacing the rotted planks he had been working on when they had left.

"You think we should tell Pop?" Tim asked.

"What could we tell him?" Robbie said. "He didn't *do* anything to us. He just scared us."

"He sure did," Phillipa said.

"But he chased us," Tim insisted.

"How did he get ahead of us like that?" Robbie asked, as much of himself as the others, ignoring Tim's complaint.

"But he chased us," Tim repeated.

"He didn't do anything," Robbie said.

"I don't want to go back there," Tim said.

"He's not keeping me out of the woods," Robbie said, his voice shaky but firm. "Not if I want to go back." He looked at the others, not certain if, indeed, he did want to go back.

The children looked at each other, then started toward the yard. As they did, Jubal stepped from behind a tree only 10 feet from where they had stood. He stepped toward them, smiling. The children bolted and ran.

It was seven o'clock when Devlin pulled into Leslie's yard. The children were all at McCloud's house for the night, and he had thought it would be a good opportunity to speak with her about Billy Perot. He had called, and she had invited him for dinner, and he had accepted, deciding to speak with her after they had eaten. She was a strong-willed woman, and he saw no sense in being tossed out before eating. He had smiled at the thought, knowing he simply wanted to prolong his time with her before falling into a potential conflict.

Leslie was wearing a silk skirt and blouse when she opened the door, and it clung to her, moved with her, made Devlin notice everything about her. He was dressed in jeans and loafers, a tweed jacket over a plaid shirt and blue V-neck sweater, and he had shaved at the office before leaving. But, looking at her, he felt underdressed, even a bit grubby, and he wished he had taken the time to go home and at least put on a dressier shirt and tie.

Leslie seated him at the harvest table and poured them each a glass of white wine.

"It's the only liquor I ever keep in the house," she said with a slight shrug. "And I hope you don't mind sitting in here. Dinner's not quite under control, and, to be honest, neither is the rest of the house. At least not for receiving guests."

"We live in the kitchen too," Devlin said. "It seems to be a Vermont thing—at least in the country—and it kinda creeps up on you."

"A lot of things creep up on you here," Leslie said, a bit sardonically, Devlin thought.

"Like people roaming around backyards and leaving dead animals behind?"

"Among other things," Leslie said.

She turned and smiled, her dark hair swinging with the movement, giving off hints of blond and red under the overhead light. She didn't want the conversation to hinge on the morbid. It had been a long time since she had entertained a man in her home; a long time since she had spent a pleasant evening with a man, and she wanted this evening to break the mold.

"I hope you like coq au vin," she said. "It was one of the things I always did well, and I wanted to see if I'd lost my touch. Robbie and I have been terrors of the takeout set for the past few months."

"Not much of that here in the woods," Devlin said.

"Robbie's major complaint," she said. "But at least it's driving me back to the kitchen. Believe it or not, I used to take a lot of pride in that sort of thing."

There was a touch of wistfulness in her voice, Devlin thought, and he wanted to understand it. He knew it wasn't just his cop instincts kicking in, but rather the woman herself that made him want to know. "What made you decide to move up here?" he asked.

Leslie fussed at the stove absently, then came back to the table and sat across from him. "Just looking for a good place to hide," she said, picking up her wine glass and staring into it.

"Hide?"

Leslie sipped the wine and smiled. "Nothing sinister. At least not criminal." She paused for a moment, smiling, wondering what she should tell him. If she should tell him anything at all. She decided telling everything was a good place to start. He *was* a cop, and if Jack ever showed up, she just might need him. She drew a long breath.

"Hide from my husband," she said. "At least until I get up the guts to file for divorce."

"Are you afraid you'll change your mind if he finds you?" The words out before Devlin could stop them.

A weak, self-amused smile crossed Leslie's lips, then faded as she looked past him, out the window. She shook her head. "No. I'm afraid of what he'll do to me if he finds me." Her eyes became hard as they returned to him. "Jack's one of those men who thinks a marriage license comes equipped with an owner's manual; and that he has a right to control what he owns. And, when the car doesn't work the way he wants it to, the right to get annoyed and kick the door in."

"There are laws to stop that," Devlin said, knowing the words were nonsense—that the law seldom stopped domestic violence—seeing in Leslie's eyes that she knew it too. He wanted to tell her she was safer here, that the size of the town would make it harder for him to get to her unnoticed; harder to force her to leave if she didn't want to. He knew that was a lie as well. The F.B.I.'s statistics showed that half of all women, and two thirds of all married women, were battered at least once in their lives. "Help's here if you need it," he said at length.

Leslie smiled, nodded again. "I hope I never do." Her eyes, then her entire face, softened. "What sent *you* scurrying to the woods?"

It was Devlin's turn now, and his face clouded momentarily. "I was forced to retire from the New York Police Department," he began, smiled at himself, then started again. "I was hurt on the job, and they didn't exactly have to twist my arm to get rid of me."

"Shot?" she asked.

"Knife," he said. "Lost a lot of the use of one arm. At least in high performance situations." He smiled again. "That was the term they used. It meant I might not be able to protect myself, or my partner, to full capacity in a bad situation." He shrugged. "So it was retire, or ride a desk. I walked; then decided to come here. Get Phillipa away from the city, and live in a place where the pension would go farther." He pulled on his nose. "Raise chickens, maybe." His smile turned to a grin. "Then this job came up, and I was already bored stiff, so here I am, riding a desk after all."

"And you don't have to carry a gun." Leslie was puzzled by that earlier revealed fact. That a cop, who might not be able to defend himself fully, who had already been viciously attacked, would now decide not to carry a weapon. Her face apparently asked the unspoken question.

"The man who cut me was shot; killed," Devlin said. His mind kicked in. Killed by you. No, executed by you. Even if he forced it; wanted it. Or was it you who wanted it? He pushed it all away. "It was something I never wanted any part of again," he said simply. He hesitated, drawing the words from his guts. "The man was my partner; my friend."

"He was a police officer?" Leslie's expression was blank with shock, surprise, all of that, mixed with confusion and a growing compassion. "That must have been terrible."

Devlin forced a weak smile. "I don't know why I told you that. I haven't talked about it to anyone in two years."

Leslie understood. Self-forgiveness was something she had struggled with; still did. But guilt seemed capable of launching new assaults, even when unwarranted. Logic, she knew, was impotent in that battle. She remained silent.

Devlin acknowledged her reticence; was grateful for it. "Dinner smells wonderful," he said, ending the subject. "Mattie Shover, the woman who keeps house for me, is a great cook. But it's strictly meat and potatoes. Usually in quantities an elephant would have trouble with." He paused momentarily. "My late wife cooked that way. But she always added a note of tragedy by burning a lot of stuff."

He had smiled warmly at the memory. A loving recollection. Leslie found that appealing in the man, despite the inexplicable tinge of senseless jealousy it produced. She rejected it. "How long ago did she . . . die?" she asked.

"A long time. Phillipa was only a baby." He looked out the window, then back at her. "Phillipa tells me your parents are dead," he said, closing the book on another subject.

He was good at shutting down subjects he didn't want to deal with, couldn't deal with, Leslie decided. She knew the malady. "My father died earlier this year," she said. "My mother died years ago, when I was quite young."

Leslie stood, returned to the stove, and inspected the

chicken. "It's ready," she said. "Now we'll see if my one talent atrophied at the hands of Colonel Sanders."

The meal was everything Leslie had hoped it would be, the food as good as she had ever managed, the conversation witty and casual and relaxed. Devlin charmed her with stories about local people, their foibles, their humor, their apparent ability to overcome the accidents of fate by simply ignoring them.

"You make most of the people here sound so charming, I find myself wondering if I'm living in a different place," Leslie said.

"They're hard, at first," Devlin said. "Very reserved, and even suspicious until they get to know you; know that you accept them for what they are."

"Then it gets easier?"

He smiled at the thought, thinking of the men who worked for him. "Some of them never stop being an enormous pain in the ass. Because sometimes you just can't do things the way they're used to, or think they have to be done. But, for the most part, they're fine. You just have to take them as they are." He toyed with the little food that remained on his plate, rearranging it with his fork. "They're very insular, and I think they feel vulnerable because they are, because they're so far removed from what goes on in the world." He thought of his men again, and wondered if he was being too kind. Probably, he decided. At least in certain cases.

Leslie sipped her wine, her eyes on Devlin's face. There seemed to be an underlying core of gentleness there, not necessarily in how he looked, or in his words, but a certain softness that came to his eyes, at times, when he spoke. Yet he had told her about the violence that had been part of his life, and she had found it hard to reconcile such a man with the one she perceived before her. She hadn't pursued it then. Now she felt she must.

She shifted nervously. "You told me the man who hurt you . . . that he was a police officer. Why?" She hesitated, uncertain how to phrase her words. "I mean why would another cop try to . . ." She failed again.

Devlin smiled weakly and looked down into his own glass. "It's a long story."

"You don't have to—"

"No. It's okay." He looked up at Leslie, his eyes suddenly

very tired. "He was a lieutenant, who ran a special homicide task force. And he was also my partner." Devlin hesitated, catching his breath, which suddenly seemed labored. "Years before he had killed his wife and child, and had gotten away with it. I think it must have driven him crazy." He shook his head, trying to drive reality back, or away, he wasn't sure. "Maybe he was crazy already by then. I don't know. But no one ever noticed, suspected. Then this brutal series of killings started. Women being . . ." He let the words die. "It was all tied to an obscure religious ritual that he had learned about. I stumbled into one of those killings while he was still there. But I didn't know it was him—he was wearing this cape and mask—and he attacked me. Later, the evidence just caught up with him. It was an accident the way it did. Although, who knows, maybe he wanted to be caught." He fought his breathing again. "But when he was confronted, he wouldn't give it up. And he was killed." Devlin's mind kicked in. Or did you decide that yourself? Was it just to save him the trial, the humiliation? Or worse?

"God, I read about that," Leslie said. "Those women. The way they were mutilated." She hesitated, the present pushing itself in on her. "And now you have this killing. How awful for you." She offered him a wan smile. "I'm sorry. That sounds stupid, doesn't it? Saying how awful it is for you."

"Don't apologize. The thought's crossed my mind too. You see one mutilated body, you've seen enough for a lifetime. I've never known a cop who needed a second look." He shook his head. "It's like autopsies. When you're a rookie, you want to go; see what it's about; prove you can handle it. But after that, every time you have to go, it's the last thing in the world you want. Then you steel yourself against it, so it won't bother you anymore, unless it's something really bad, like a kid, or something. And, one day, it doesn't. And that bothers you even more, the fact that you've become immune to it." He forced a small smile. "Does that make any sense to you?"

Leslie nodded.

"Anyway, I guess the idea of a serial killer just scares hell out of me. As a cop, I mean."

"Why?"

"The guilt it pushes on you." He gestured with his hands,

as if using them to find the right words. "In any murder, the faster you solve it the better. Statistically the odds of finding a murderer drop like crazy after forty-eight hours. But that's partly because the caseloads are so heavy in a big city. You just don't have enough time to devote to each one. But in reality, you have all the time in the world. Especially in a small place like this." He folded his hands on the table. "But in serial killings you don't have that time. And each new body means you've failed to beat the clock, and that somebody's dead because you didn't."

Leslie nodded at the suggestion. "I guess I never thought about that. That the police might take it as a personal failure. It gives the killer a great deal of power, doesn't it? He must enjoy that, knowing he's won again."

Devlin stared off, his eyes distant.

"What is it?" Leslie asked.

"It just reminded me of something Rolk—my dead partner—used to say. 'Let's clear the case, and beat the bastard.' I used to think he treated it all like some kind of contest."

"Maybe it is in a way."

Devlin gave her a peculiar look. "I hope not," he said. "Anyway, this won't be that kind of thing." He wondered if he was saying that to reassure the woman, or himself.

"*Anyway*," Leslie said, exaggerating the word. "I have some dessert. It's only sorbet, but I thought anything else would have been too heavy after the coq au vin."

"Sounds great to me," Devlin said. "Then there's something I want to talk to you about."

Leslie raised her eyebrows but didn't pursue it.

"How did you find out about it?" she asked, her eyes showing her annoyance.

"It's a small town," Devlin said. "If it happens outdoors everybody knows about it. Sometimes even the doors don't help."

"Well, it had to be Pop, or Electa. Or Billy."

"Pop wouldn't, and even Billy's not that dumb. He'd tell a different story." Devlin watched Leslie's face darken at what that "different story" would be. Then she seemed to dismiss it.

"That nosey old witch," she said. "She was probably on the phone thirty seconds later, and probably stayed on until she got everyone in town."

Devlin decided to let it drop. Not to bring up McCloud. It might cost Leslie a job she obviously needed. "I'd like you to make a complaint," he said, taking her in the direction he had initially intended. "I'd like to bust him for it, with Pop as a witness."

Leslie shook her head. "I just want to forget about it. I've had enough of courts—getting relief from abuse orders against Jack, my husband. It never seemed to work. It only got worse. The courts never seemed to want to do anything. They just wanted the problem to go away." She looked at him sharply. "Finally it was me who had to go away." She shook her head with finality. "If he comes back, okay. But if he doesn't, I just want to be left alone."

Devlin couldn't argue with her. He knew she was wrong in doing nothing. But he knew she was right too. The system couldn't stop a threat, it could only react to it when it was carried out. "I'll talk to him," he said. "Hard."

"That, I'd appreciate," Leslie said.

Devlin sat back and looked at her. "How about showing me the rest of the house?"

"It's a pigsty," Leslie complained.

"I know pigsties," Devlin said. "I'm a bachelor with a small child. This is only unpacked boxes."

"A bachelor with a housekeeper," Leslie corrected. She shrugged. "But you might as well know the whole truth about me." She stared at him as she started to rise from her chair. "Everybody else in this damn town seems to, whether I want them to or not."

The tour of her new digs, as she termed it, became far more elaborate than intended, and Leslie found herself explaining not only changes she had already begun but some that were little more than vague ideas for the future. She wondered about that: whether she was trying to impress Devlin with her competency, her ability to take care of herself, or if it was something more. Perhaps gain his approval. The latter thought grated, and she studied the idea and him as he gazed about the living room. She couldn't deny she was attracted to the man; liked him. Liked the way he listened to her plans without offering advice. There also hadn't been the typical male-female first encounter, in which the male seems impelled to establish how important and interesting he is within the first two hours of conversation. If anything, Devlin was reticent about himself; had to be drawn out, and spoke more freely about others. And he listened to her. God, he actually listened.

Almost without realizing it, she found herself looking at his mouth, the shape of his lips; wondering what it would be like to kiss him; whether he would be aggressive or gentle, and she suddenly felt the nipples of her breasts hardening and a moist, almost wet, warmth begin to spread through her vagina. She began to resist it, then stopped herself. There was nothing wrong with the feeling. She hadn't been with a man in a long time. Not since that one, brief fling she had had after leaving Jack, and that had been more of an animal coupling, an expression of recaptured freedom, than an act of lovemaking.

She pulled herself up. Is that what she wanted to do? Make love to this man? God, the women in the store were right. She was like a spider luring flies into her web.

"Well, that's about it," she said. "Upstairs there are only three average-sized bedrooms, which will stay pretty much as they are." God, did she sound as defensive as she felt. "And the barn, which will be my studio. If it wasn't for the money my father left me, I wouldn't even have this." Leslie glanced around the room as if searching for some escape. Stop being an idiot, she told herself.

"If you don't mind the boxes, we could put on some music," she suggested lightly. "The first thing I did was put the stereo together." There, proving yourself again, she thought. Annoyed.

"I'd love it," Devlin said. "Phillipa's already into rock, and she claims the stuff I listen to is like everybody playing a different song at the same time."

"What do you listen to?" Leslie asked.

"Jazz, mostly. But anything's okay. Really."

Leslie smiled at his quick attempt to cover a possible faux pas, then moved to the stereo and inserted a compact disc. The strains of Wynton Marsalis' trumpet soothed into the room. "How's that?" Leslie asked.

"Couldn't be better," Devlin said. "I saw him one night at Fat Tuesday's in New York. Dizzy Gillespie was playing, and

Marsalis just came and sat in. It was something, the two of them together on the same stage."

"No more of that up here in the woods."

"You'd be surprised. Both Marsalis and Gillespie gave concerts in Burlington last year. I forced Phillipa to go to both of them, but it didn't do anything for her taste in music."

"That's right," Leslie said. "I always forget there's a university up here." She said it like they were at the ends of the earth, and it made Devlin smile. "But it's a long drive to Burlington, isn't it?"

"An hour and a half. But, in this case, well worth it."

"Move some boxes and sit down," Leslie said. "I'll get us some more wine."

In the kitchen she refilled both glasses, then paused to study her reflection in the large multipaned window. She ran her fingers through her hair, shook it for good measure, then looked again, and unfastened one more button on her blouse. Interesting without being blatant, she told herself. Inviting? She shrugged and returned to the living room with the wine.

Electa Litchfield sat before her bedroom window, her bentwood rocker moving almost imperceptibly beneath her, one hand absently stroking the large, gray Angora cat perched in her lap. She had seen the boy leave earlier in the day, a small bag packed for an overnight stay; had seen Devlin arrive and remain. She had watched the glow of light from the kitchen, then a fainter light from the living room, and, finally, a light from an upstairs bedroom, briefly lighted, then extinguished.

City slut, she told herself again, as she had earlier. Thinks she can get what she wants just by opening her legs. Doesn't have to *have* anything else about her worthwhile. She ran her hand along the length of the cat's back and watched the darkened bedroom window and wondered why it had remained dark for so long. She had only had one man in her life. She had been 19, and he had laughed at her inexperience, had used her and then laughed at her, and she had never been with another man after that. She glanced at the clock on her bedside table. More than an hour had passed since the light had gone off in the bedroom. She had never read about sex—had avoided doing so—nor had she viewed it on film. She knew it was quick and brutal and unnecessary, except for women who wanted to use it to get their way with men.

A half hour later she watched the kitchen door open and Devlin emerge, stop, then turn and reach out one hand. Leslie moved into the doorway, dressed only in a flimsy robe, and Electa watched as Devlin's hand caressed her cheek. A strange, unbidden sensation coursed through Electa's stomach as she stared at the scene beyond the vast expanse of darkened lawn. "Slut," she whispered aloud. "See the whoremaster and his slut, kitty. See them standin' out there brazen as can be."

Only when Devlin's jeep had backed down the driveway, and the kitchen door had closed behind Leslie, did Electa rise from her rocker. She continued to stare at the closed kitchen door, her eyes glaring anger. Then she placed the cat on top of a dresser and stroked its head a final time. "Another slut who needs God's punishment," she said to the animal. The mounted cat stared back at her, its glass eyes reflecting the faint glow of the nightlight in Electa's bedroom, offering neither approval nor disapproval of its former mistress's words.

# CHAPTER
## 6

The hand reaches out, placing the rose atop the closed coffin. It's cold; the wind cuts knifelike through clothing, then flesh. The hand is encased in a glove, just like Mother encased in her coffin. Now the hand leaves the coffin and encircles your thin, child's shoulders. Father's hand. So comforting to feel it there.

The man in gray mourning clothes gives you a rose, a different rose, and father's hand guides you forward. You place it next to his, and you're glad she's locked inside. Gone now. Gone for good.

Other people are given roses. Dozens of them, and soon the coffin is covered in a sea of red flowers. Mother had so many friends it seems. So many friends. So many who came to see her when Father was away. You stare at the roses, so much like the one that fell into the pool of blood on her bed. The one that you hid away so Father would never know. The one you still have. Just as you have all the roses. All of them.

A small smile forms, then fades. Eyes grow wary and begin to dart around the bright, white-walled room. The mind speaks to itself, answering its own interrogatories with impatience, annoyance.

They know now.

Of course they do. It's about time.

So now they're after you. Now they'll hound you. You think that doesn't make you prey?

I'm still the hunter. Nothing has changed.

Except that they're hunting you.

Only Devlin. A mental and physical cripple.

Maybe he's smarter than you. More experienced.

No one is smarter. And I make the rules in this game.

Then why are you frightened?

Don't confuse caution with fear.

He'll find the hearts and take them away.

Never.

He'll find the roses.

Never!

The final word shouted in the mind, bringing pain to the temples. The hands begin to tremble, causing the polished fingernails to shimmer in the bright light of the room.

I'll kill him if I have to. Angry, snarling. But it won't be necessary. His own fear will stop him.

You hope so.

I know.

Shouted again. The pain piercing. A finger, the nail glinting, points at the table where the hearts lay frozen in their plastic bags.

He's coming now. Coming. Coming. Coming.

If he comes too close he'll die.

Perhaps.

Leslie sat in an Adirondack chair on the rear lawn, the unseasonably warm morning sun matching the inner warmth she had felt since rising. Robbie had telephoned to say he was off to school and now she was enjoying the quiet solitude of her thoughts, the memory of the previous night, the remembered pleasure mixed with the slightest doubt that too much had happened too quickly. She pushed the latter away.

He had been such a gentle lover, so tender and attentive and patient at first, then so urgent and hungry for her when his own passion overwhelmed him. It had begun so oddly, so unexpectedly, even though it was what she had wanted so unquestionably.

She had returned from the kitchen with their glasses of wine and found that he had cleared the couch of boxes—and only the couch—placing them on other chairs that might have been used; leaving her only the place there next to him. It had been so blatant that she had had to force herself not to smile. Yet the look of boyish uncertainty in his eyes had made it all seem acceptable, not the move of some presumptuous Lothario whom she would have been tempted to dispatch quickly and wickedly.

She smiled at the idea. The man was lucky she hadn't torn his clothes from his body. God, she had wanted it; wanted it badly. But at least she had wanted it on her own terms. At least she hadn't degenerated into some horny slut, who was willing to take on any acceptable man to satisfy her need. Over the past six months, except for that one, brief—and now embarrassing—affair, she had pushed sex far back in her mind, afraid of her need of it, perhaps; afraid of what it might lead her into, and with whom.

And what had it led her into? she wondered now. Something warm and comforting, she told herself. Something that might, or might not, become more. She smiled, thinking back on it. They had sat talking quietly, inconsequentially, enjoying each other's company, each other's closeness. Then their eyes had become more intense, more urging, and he had reached out for her gently, and she had gone into his arms so easily, so quickly, she had surprised herself. And his lips had felt so soft, so exciting, just as she had imagined they would, and the wetness she had felt earlier became a flood, and her nipples so hard she longed for his hands to brush them, caress them. And he did, almost as though he had read her thoughts.

He had taken her hand without a word, and had led her upstairs, and they had undressed each other slowly, stroking and fondling each other as if they had known each other, each other's bodies, for weeks or months. He had seemed to savor each part of her, allowing his mouth to roam her neck, her breasts, moving to her stomach, her inner thigh, her. . . . She felt herself growing wet again, thinking of his mouth, his tongue, on her vagina. She had come so quickly, so fully, her body arched with the sheer pleasure of it, and then he had moved slowly up her body and had entered her, filling her, and she had cried out for the pure joy of it and had come again, even more intensely than before. And she had felt his own urgency then and realized that he too had pushed sex away for months now, and it comforted her to know that she was not giving herself to a man who was merely adding one more name to his list of conquests.

They had made love again, even more slowly and tenderly. He had used his fingers that time, stroking her clitoris almost imperceptibly; whispering to her, telling her how soft and wet she felt, and the sound of his voice, combined with the gentleness of his touch, drove her into an unabashed frenzy that left her squirming in his arms, her voice asking for more and more and more. . . .

The heat of the sun disappeared from her face and Leslie opened her eyes, startled to find Electa Litchfield hovering over her, and the warm wetness of her vagina washed her with an irrational sense of guilt and her voice stammered badly.

"E . . . E . . . Electa. God. I didn't even hear you."

"Father used to say I walked like an Indian." The woman's dark, close-set eyes bored into her, prying, almost menacing. More like a bloody snoop, Leslie thought. "Would you like some coffee?" she asked.

"Another time, maybe." Electa's stare narrowed. "Had the chief by last night, I see. Have more trouble?"

Oh, Christ, Leslie thought. "No. I invited him for dinner. Just to thank him for the other night."

A small smile rose and fell from Electa's lips, saying far more than any words. "Phillipa didn't come, eh?"

"No." A hint of annoyance now. "She and Robbie camped out with Tim."

The smile. There and gone again. "So Jim said." Leslie was about to snap a response but was stopped by Electa's words. "Called to ask me to come in early. Seems there's been another killing."

"Oh, no. Who? Where?"

"Down the road. 'Bout half a mile."

"This road? Our road?"

Electa nodded. "Jim wanted me to meet him there. Thought you might like to come. Do an artist's sketch, or something."

"Did Jim ask that I come? Do a sketch?" Leslie's voice was incredulous.

"No. Just my idea. Thought you might like to show some enterprise."

There had been no maliciousness in Electa's voice, but the suggestion itself was enough. "No. I don't think so. Even if he asked, I don't think I'd want to."

Electa shrugged, indicating it was of little consequence to her.

"You still haven't told me who," Leslie said, as the woman turned to leave.

Electa glanced back over her shoulder. She was dressed all in green again and looked as though she had sprouted straight from the lawn, rigid and immovable. "Don't know," she said. "Some high school girl, Jim said."

"A *child?*"

Electa's eyes hardened, then began to glitter with some inner fury. "No," she snapped. "Not a child. 'Bout seventeen, Jim said. Not a child by any means. Full grown and frisky, no doubt."

Leslie stared at the woman in disbelief. *Full grown and frisky.* What she hadn't said, but what her eyes seemed to say for her, were the words *and got just what she deserved.* Leslie opened her mouth, trying to find words for her outrage, but before she could speak Electa had started off across the wide green lawn, almost as if she were part of it, blown by some strong, unnoticed wind.

Devlin stood over the body, his stomach churning, his mouth dry and pasty. She must have been a pretty child, he thought. At least until whoever did this got at her.

"Funny how that last look of terror stays on their faces, ain't it?"

It was the young state cop who had been called in to guard the scene for the BCI's mobile crime lab. Devlin turned to face him. He was dressed in full regalia, pressed and polished, right up to the leather band on his Smokey hat. And Devlin was glad to have him. It was a helluva lot better than having Buzzy, or Luther, or Gaylord in charge. He just didn't need the kid's mouth, or his attempts to show how "experienced" he was when it came to blood and gore. But maybe the kid was just compensating for the way his own gut was twisting in on itself.

"It would be nice if it was different, wouldn't it?"

"How do ya mean?" the trooper asked. He wore a name tag that said Wilson.

Devlin turned back to the body. "I mean if death was like you see it in museums, in those old Renaissance paintings. All restful and quiet, with the angels and the family gathered around the bed. Not shit and piss in your pants and those God awful empty, staring eyes." He looked back at the trooper. "And sure as hell not some young girl gutted from pubis to sternum."

Wilson's face paled, and Devlin noticed he was keeping his eyes off the victim. "How long you been a cop, Wilson?" he asked.

"Graduated from the academy six months ago," Wilson said.

Devlin nodded, more to himself than the trooper. "You're doin' fine. First bad homicide I caught, I almost puked on the victim. Would have too, if my partner hadn't grabbed me by the seat of the pants and dragged me away. Lab boys would have loved that: barf all over their evidence scene."

Wilson smiled weakly at the story; seemed to appreciate its intent. "Does anybody ever get used to it?" he asked.

"Some do. But if it ever happens to you, remember that it means you're getting as sick as the bastard who did it."

And what about the things you don't get used to? Devlin asked himself. What do you do with those things? His mind brought him back to that day two years ago. Rolk was standing before him, the long, wicked knife in his hand, his eyes filled with the insane realization that it was over; that the killings had come to an end. And with it the slow understanding of what lay ahead, the court appearances, the press, the years and years in a mental institution. Endless humiliation that would be dredged up again and again until he was dead.

He had stepped forward then, the knife rising above his head. "Clear the case, Paul," he had whispered. "Just clear the case."

And Devlin could see himself, raising the pistol again, sighting along the barrel, through tear-filled eyes, on the center of Rolk's forehead. He could hear the woman screaming—the woman whose life he had just saved—begging him not to do it. And he could see Rolk smiling at him as the pistol exploded in his hand, the blood and brains and bone, splattering a wide swath of wall behind him.

He closed his eyes tightly. But even then it hadn't been over.

Then there was the departmental investigation, and the battle among the political factions there over what would be done about the cop who had executed another cop to spare him the humiliation of a trial. But the ones who had wanted to butcher him publicly had lost out. The department had been spared Rolk's trial and the further damage that would bring. He would escape; be allowed to retire because of his injury, and what he had done would be ruled "justifiable." And he would not receive the punishment that might cleanse his heart and mind.

So now he lived with it; fought to hide it away except when it returned at night, waking him in a cold sweat. And he hid his weapons away, knowing he could never use them again; afraid of what he might feel if he had to. Except that now perhaps he would have to. Now that a hunter had found Amy Little's mutilated body in this God-forsaken field. Now that it had all begun again.

And he was sure that it had. In his inside coat pocket, sealed in a plastic bag, was the dried and pressed red rose that had been left next to Amy Little's body. It was a piece of evidence he was going to withhold—identifying it only in a written report that would remain locked in his desk—something only he and the killer would know about. Something that might produce the one slip he desperately needed. He wouldn't even tell Eric Mooers and his BCI cronies. It was lousy police procedure but he knew it was necessary if that one bit of information was to be kept quiet.

Devlin's thoughts were cut short by the voice of Orlando Quint, the town's only doctor, and the local coroner. Good, Devlin told himself. Saved from your own mind, from memories you thought you put away and buried. But you don't bury life. Not until you end it.

Quint was in his early 60s, short and scruffy, with an unruly thatch of silver hair, and the most delicate hands Devlin had ever seen on a man. He stared at the body, his soft, heavily lined face seeming to darken with each passing moment. He pulled on his flat, fleshy nose, and Devlin noticed his eyes had grown moist.

"Know her, Doc?" he asked. Devlin had already seen the ID in her purse.

Quint nodded. "Delivered her," he said. "And her brother and sister. Her name's Amy Little. Always called her Little

Amy, as a joke." He shook his head in disgust, or anger, or both. "Guess you were right about Eva Hyde," he said. "I should have listened. I guess I just didn't want to believe it."

Devlin ignored the apology. "What else do you know about the victim?" he asked, using the word instead of the child's name, trying to distance himself.

"Senior in high school. Nice family. Worked part time for Ray Perot."

"Ever have any trouble? Boyfriends? Anything like that?"

Quint hesitated, as if deciding what to say, if anything. He looked at the child again, then surrendered to the reality that nothing he said could hurt her now. "It was years ago. I was giving her an exam, and she told me one of her teachers had been kind of fondling her. Nothing serious," he added quickly. "But it scared her. Scared me too. Thought it could *get* serious if it wasn't stopped."

"Who was the teacher?"

"Louis Ferris."

Devlin's face darkened. "What happened? He's still teaching."

"Child's parents didn't want to expose her to all the fuss and fury," Quint said, obviously displeased, even after so many years. "We all agreed I'd talk to the head of the school board without identifying Amy. Ferris must've gotten the message, 'cause I never heard any more complaints."

"You're sure she was telling the truth?" Devlin anticipated an angry reaction, but none came.

"She wasn't that type of kid. And her fear was either real or she was the best twelve-year-old actress I ever saw." He shrugged, as if conceding a point. "She could have misunderstood some friendly hugs, or whatever—Ferris *is* a little strange—" He let the thought die.

"But you don't think so," Devlin said.

Quint shook his head. "No, dammit, I don't."

Devlin filed the information away. It was one more thing to speak to Ferris about. He hadn't yet spoken to him about being at the roadhouse the last night Eva Hyde had been there, and he knew if the man turned out to be the killer, it would be a long time before he would be able to forgive the delay.

He looked down at the body, then back at Quint. "I guess we better get to it," he said.

Quint nodded, knelt beside the body, and opened his old, battered Gladstone bag. "I'll do as thorough a preliminary as I can," he said. "I suspect the state medical examiner is going to want to do the post. This is going to draw a lot of press coverage, and they won't want some aging quack from the backwoods handling it." He still hadn't taken his eyes off the child's face. "But I want to give you everything I can, so you can move ahead and catch this bastard before he butchers another one."

"You think it's a serial killer?" the young state trooper asked, his voice a little too eager, a little too excited for Devlin.

"I think it's a fucking maniac," Devlin said. "And I think he's found something he really enjoys doing." Devlin turned to the sound of a car stopping on the road 100 yards from the patch of scrub oak where the girl's body had been found. He watched Jim McCloud climb from the car, a camera slung around his neck.

He turned to Wilson. "Get down there and tell him he has to stay on the road," Devlin ordered. "I don't want anyone tramping around this crime scene. He's already fucked up any tire tracks we might have found."

Quint looked up from the body, his eyes weary and brimming tears. "The heart's missing," he said. "Dear God, this poor little thing." His face looked as though it had collapsed in upon itself.

"I don't want anybody to know about that," Devlin said. "Nobody outside the investigation. Or we'll have a panic on our hands."

Ray Perot's office was in the rear of a massive apple warehouse, located on Perot Road, a deadend street that was little more than a wide driveway, and holding nothing but the man's sizable home, and the more than 500 acres of orchards that were the core of his financial holdings. At first the locals were amused by Ray's "conceit" at having his driveway turned into a road and named after him. That amusement turned sour the following winter, when they found the town plowing snow from the driveway, and even more so when the next town budget was struck, and Perot Road was listed as a capital expense for repaving. Yet no complaints were made to town officials. Those locals who did not work for Ray Perot had mortgages or loans at the bank he controlled. And Ray had a longstanding reputation of repaying those who offended him. With interest.

When Devlin arrived at Perot's office, he was greeted by a middle-aged woman seated at an institutional metal desk outside a set of double mahogany doors that led to the man's inner sanctum. Not knowing the woman, Devlin identified himself and told her he had to see Perot. She looked at him skeptically, picked up her telephone, and pressed an intercom button. Devlin noticed that her bare metal furnishings and file cabinets were made complete by a kerosene space heater behind her desk.

The woman put down the telephone and gave him a cool look. "Mr. Perot says perhaps tomorrow," she said.

Devlin offered her a broad grin. "Chief Devlin says definitely today." With that he moved past her desk and headed for the double doors.

"You can't go in there," the woman shouted, her voice so strident Devlin wondered if it was meant to stop him or simply as a warning to Perot.

He didn't really care; he turned and winked at her, then knocked perfunctorily on one door and opened it.

A young woman was quickly backing away from Perot's desk as he entered. Devlin had seen her before; tried to place her now. She was pretty and blond and dressed to show off her body; now she was blushing very badly. Linnie French, Devlin told himself. Billy's sometime girlfriend. Perot sat behind the massive mahogany desk, his face incredulous.

"It's okay, Linnie. We'll finish up later," he said, his eyes never leaving Devlin. "It must be important for the chief to lose his manners this way."

Linnie moved quickly toward the office doors, her face still red, her eyes avoiding Devlin. Perot followed her progress, his yellow teeth showing themselves as he admired her well-shaped bottom.

The smile disappeared as the doors closed, and Perot turned his mean, wide-set eyes back to Devlin. "So, what's so important you'd come barging in here uninvited?" he asked.

"Nice kid," Devlin said. "How old is she, seventeen, eighteen?"

Perot's yellow teeth poked through his lips again, without

warmth. "She's twenty. Worked for me ever since she got out of high school. Just like her father works for me. Some of her uncles too." He stared hard at Devlin. "Most everybody around here does. One way or the other."

"I imagine most folks feel real lucky about that, Ray," Devlin said.

Perot leaned back in his high-backed leather chair and cupped his hands behind his head. "You didn't barge in here to tell me how lucky my employees are, Devlin. What is it? Some trouble Billy's got himself into?"

"Just investigating a couple of murders, Ray."

"A couple of murders? Didn't know we've *had* a couple of murders."

"Eva Hyde—"

"Thought that was an accident," Perot said. A bit too quickly, Devlin thought.

"And Amy Little," Devlin finished.

Perot sat forward, his face a mask. "When that happen?" he finally asked.

"Yesterday. Early evening, probably. I understand she worked for you. When did you see her last?"

"What are you tryin' to get at, Devlin?" Perot's eyes had narrowed, his face becoming even more pinched.

"I'm trying to trace her movements. What time she left here; who saw her; who she might have been with." He offered Perot a false smile. "Stuff like that, Ray."

Perot ran one hand through his thinning hair. "Can't tell you when I last saw her. I know I had to speak to her a while back—couple of days, maybe. She wasn't workin' out too well."

"Not like Linnie, huh?" Devlin tossed the remark off without emphasis.

Perot glared at him. "You tryin' to say somethin', just spit it out."

"You were at Pearlie's roadhouse the night Eva Hyde disappeared, weren't you?" Devlin asked, ignoring him.

"What the hell's that got to do with anything?" Perot demanded.

"Need information about her too. You spend any time with her that night?"

Perot leaned back in his chair again, appearing relaxed.

Feigning it, Devlin thought. "I might of spoke to her. Speak to most people." He looked at Devlin as though, in future, he might not be one of those so honored.

"Ever date her, Ray?"

Perot's jaw tightened, then relaxed. He offered Devlin a yellow grin. "Wouldn't exactly call it a date. Eva was kinda free with her favors, you know what I mean. And I've been a widower a long time."

"I understand Billy dated her too," Devlin said. "You two kind of competing for her?"

"Eva wasn't the kind you competed for," he snapped. The flash of anger disappeared. "Fact is, I told Billy to stay away from her. He's young, and even though he's quite a stud, that boy of mine, he's not too experienced. I didn't want her gettin' her hooks into him."

"Was she trying?"

Perot shrugged. "Be a fool not to. But Billy was wise to it. He does what I tell him."

Like most people, Devlin thought. "When was the last time *you* had a date with her, Ray? For lack of a better word."

"Maybe a week ago. Maybe a little more. Can't be sure. Wasn't somethin' I kept track of."

"Where'd you go?"

"Didn't go anyplace, Devlin. She came here. Usually did." He nodded toward a large leather sofa.

Devlin studied the sofa, plush and expensive. He wondered if Linnie had been invited on to it. Wondered if anyone Billy pursued also got a rush from Ray too. And he wondered what happened if they ever said no.

"Billy ever date Amy Little?"

Ray glared at him. "She was just a kid." He jabbed a finger across the desk. "But she was legal. She was seventeen."

What are we talking about here, fish? Devlin asked himself.

"Does that mean yes or no, Ray?"

Perot shot forward in his chair again. "It means I don't know," he snapped.

"What about you, Ray? You date her?"

"That's insulting," he snapped. "The kid worked for me. That's all." His eyes narrowed, radiating all the meanness and threat he could muster. "I'm gettin' a little tired of this."

"Almost finished," Devlin said, ignoring the implication.

"Did Amy have any boyfriend problems? Anybody she seemed afraid of?"

"Look, Devlin. People work for me. I don't get involved in their personal lives. They got problems in their love lives, that's their business." Perot's eyes still radiated an implied threat.

"You see her when she left yesterday?"

"I already told you. I saw her a couple of days ago. That was the last time."

"Where'd you go after work last night, Ray?"

"Now wait a God damned minute!"

Devlin placed both hands on Perot's desk and leaned forward. "Just answer the question, Ray. Here, or down at my office."

The two men glared at each other.

"You must not like your job very much," Perot said, almost a hiss.

"Answer the question."

"I worked late. Here!"

"Anybody see you?"

"No. I was alone!"

Devlin straightened up and smiled down at the livid face that looked back at him. "Thanks, Ray," he said. "I'll be talking to you."

Louis Ferris was at the desk in his classroom when Devlin arrived. He was looking through papers turned in by his students, and his face changed constantly, showing annoyance, exasperation, disgust; never pleasure. He looked up as Devlin approached his desk and seemed suddenly nervous. He caught himself and smiled.

"Hello, chief. Are you looking for someone? Has one of my miscreants run afoul of the law?"

"I'm looking for you, Louis."

The nervousness returned; was masked again. Ferris forced a smile. It in itself was disconcerting. Juxtaposed with his eyes, each seeming to look in a different direction, the smile appeared blank, unnatural; almost like one fixed to the head of a doll.

"I'd offer you a chair, but all I have are these school desks, which appear a bit small for you." A slight tic appeared in

Ferris's cheek. He waited for Devlin to explain the visit, and when he didn't, was forced to ask, just as Devlin knew he would.

"It's about Eva Hyde, Louis," Devlin said. "I understand you were at Pearlie's the night she was killed. I wondered if you spoke to her; saw her speaking to anyone else; heard her make plans to meet anyone when she left, or whatever." Devlin watched the teacher's eyes, aware that what he found there might prove more valuable than anything he was told.

Ferris hesitated, as if deciding what to say; what Devlin might already have been told by others. "I tried to speak to her, but I was quickly pushed aside by that philistine, Billy Perot. He dominated her time, at least until his father showed up. Then *he* was pushed aside." Ferris let out a small, snide laugh. "It was like watching cave-dwelling males asserting dominance. It always is when those two are around a woman."

"Did she leave with either of them?"

"No. Eva left alone." He paused, taking on a self-satisfied look. "Billy whispered something to her when his father went to the men's room. Then Eva left. Before Ray came out. He seemed annoyed by that. Asked where she went." Again the self-satisfied look, as though Ray's displeasure gratified him. "Billy left a short time after that. And Ray followed almost immediately." He shrugged and smirked. "Maybe he followed his son to see if he was meeting her."

"Anybody else leave around that time?"

"That neanderthal, Jubal Duval. Right after Billy and Ray."

"When did you leave?"

"A short time after that. The place had pretty much cleared out."

Ferris had twisted a bit in his seat as he answered. "You ever date Eva?" Devlin asked.

"No. She wasn't my type."

Too emphatic. "Ever try to?"

Ferris twisted again. "I was friendly with her. But I try to be with everyone."

Devlin smiled at the idea of Ferris's self-professed friendliness. "I heard you asked her out and she turned you down; made fun of the idea."

Ferris reddened. "That's a lie. In fact I drove her home one night, when her car wouldn't start. But that was from Wolfgang's, not Pearlie's." He seemed to catch himself, realizing he had said too much. "Look, it was a dreadful accident, but she was the type of woman—"

"Is that why you went to her funeral, Louis? Because she was that type of woman?"

Ferris drew an annoyed breath, and the color in his face deepened. "I knew the woman. It was a simple gesture of respect." He hesitated, as if suddenly understanding the contradictory nature of his two statements. "Look, as I said, it was a dreadful accident and I—"

"It was no accident, Louis. A second body was found. Amy Little. You knew her too, didn't you?"

Ferris's eyes became cold and flat and empty. Devlin could read nothing there, almost as though all feeling had left the man. "I knew her," he said, his voice small and distant. "She was a student of mine five years ago." He looked straight at Devlin, and his eyes seemed to glitter with something, perhaps hate. "You say she's dead, too?"

There was no surprise in Ferris's voice. There was nothing there at all. "She was killed the same way Eva was," Devlin said. No reaction. "You had a problem with her, I hear."

"The child misunderstood warmth for . . . for something else." Ferris composed himself willfully; only his hands, which were worrying a pencil on his desk, betrayed any emotion. "I'd forgotten all about that."

But you remember exactly how many years ago she was your student, Devlin thought. Not four or five years ago, or five or six years ago. But exactly five years ago. "If someone accused me of something like that, I don't think I'd ever forget."

"Those things happen in teaching. It was looked into and nothing came of it."

Not exactly accurate, Devlin thought. But it was Ferris's version. "When's the last time you saw Amy?" he asked.

Ferris's jaw tightened. "I haven't had any contact with her at all. Not in five years. I was . . . advised not to. If I saw her approaching me on a street, I crossed to the other side." The same indefinable look crossed his eyes, mixed this time with what seemed a sense of satisfaction.

"You don't seem very upset by what I've told you," Devlin observed.

"Anything adverse that affects a child disturbs me, chief.

But there's little I can do, except warn my present students to be careful."

"I'd like to believe that, Louis." Devlin stared down at the man, his eyes as flat and cold as the teacher's. "I hope I don't find anything that changes my mind."

Alone at his desk, Ferris's eyes remained riveted on the door that had closed behind Devlin. The tic in his cheek was more pronounced now, and the fingers of both hands were wrapped tightly around the pencil he had been worrying earlier. "It's just like Mother said," he told himself. "What goes around, comes around." The pencil snapped in his hands.

Leslie opened the door of her truck and stopped, staring at the seat. A dried, pressed red rose lay there. A small smile came to her lips and she thought immediately of Paul Devlin. How surprisingly romantic and old fashioned, she told herself. Her mother had always pressed flowers in books, and, for a time, when she was very young, so had she.

The smile faded. Why did she even think of that. She had hated her mother, hated her so deeply it had taken years of therapy to remove the guilt, to make her understand that it was right to hate her. No, the flower must have come from Paul. Then the memory of another flower—a rose too, she thought—came to mind. It had been near that hideous fox behind her barn, and she had forgotten it completely after seeing the figure in the woods. A chill ran along her spine. No, she told herself. There couldn't be any connection. It had to have been Paul. Perhaps he had come early this morning and left it for her. It had to have been. She would ask him first chance she had. And, in the meantime, she would stop being silly.

Leslie pulled out of her driveway and turned left onto the dirt road, enroute to the newspaper office to pick up the assignments she would complete later at home. As she passed Electa's house, she slowed and stared up at the small blue cape that sat alone on a slight hill. It was neat and well cared for, with sheer curtains drawn across every window. Yet something about it sent a chill down Leslie's spine. It was almost as though the house sat there, staring out at the world through those sheer curtains, feigning its own quiet perfection, denying the certitude that something was going on inside, something that would never be known or seen. She shook the thought away. It was just the woman, she told herself. She was enough to give anyone chills.

When she entered the newspaper office, Jim McCloud was pacing up and down in front of Electa's desk, red faced and angry.

"Did I come at a bad time?" Leslie asked, not certain if it was Electa he was fuming over or something else.

McCloud stopped and turned, eyes blinking, as though his mind was struggling to register her presence. "No, I'm just raving. Raving at Paul Devlin," he said. "You do the man a favor one day, because he's supposed to be a friend, and the next day he stabs you in the back without even batting an eye."

"What did he do?" Leslie asked.

"It's not always what he does. Sometimes it's what he doesn't do."

The voice had come from behind Leslie, and when she glanced over her shoulder, she found a thin, balding man staring intently at her bottom.

He raised his eyes slowly, not at all concerned at being caught, and offered a yellow toothed smile. "I'm Ray Perot. And you must be the new lady in town. Understand you already met my boy."

Leslie glared at him. "Yes. Regretfully."

Perot's smile hardened, then he looked past her, almost as though he had dismissed her from the earth. "Need to talk to you, Jim," he said. "In private."

Leslie watched McCloud lead Perot into the press room, then glanced down at Electa. She too was watching them, her stare as intense as the stuffed black bird perched on her desk.

"Does he always order people around like that?" Leslie asked.

Electa kept her eyes on the press room door. "Thinks he has a right to when his bank holds the mortgage on somebody's business or house."

"And he—?"

Electa nodded, as she swiveled her head to take in the younger woman. "Probably holds it on your house too. If you used the local bank, that is."

"No. I used a bank in Saint Johnsbury, thank God." A stream of obscenities ran through Leslie's mind.

"Then all he could do is try'n get Jim to fire you," Electa said.

"And Jim would do that?" Incredulous.

A small smile played on Electa's lips. "Never know what Jim's gonna do under pressure. 'Cept have a drink, maybe."

Leslie stared at her. She thought she had detected a tremendous sense of loyalty for McCloud every time his name had come up. Now she seemed to be getting just the opposite. Or was it just blatant, unadulterated candor.

Before she could question it the press room door opened and McCloud walked Perot through the office to the front door. As he passed, Perot again allowed his eyes to roam Leslie's body, as if he were inspecting something he might want to buy. Leslie's jaw tightened, and her mind shouted every obscenity she had thought of earlier. When the door closed behind the two men, she turned back and found Electa's eyes dancing with vindictive amusement.

"Like the wise man said: A silk purse and a sow's ear," the older woman said.

Leslie gave her a false smile. "I like an adulteration of Gertrude Stein's line better. A pig is a pig is a pig."

McCloud pushed back through the door, ending the conversation, marched to his desk and picked up his coat.

As he headed back for the door, he stopped before Electa's desk. "I'm going over to Devlin's office," he said. "Would you see that Leslie gets the advertising copy on my desk." He turned to Leslie. "I think it's self-explanatory, but if you have any questions, call me here, or at home later." He hesitated, as if trying to regroup. "By the way, the kids were no problem last night. They were great."

"What are you seein' Paul Devlin about?" Electa demanded.

"I want to let him know what's going to happen if he ever tries to run me off at a murder scene again."

"What else?"

McCloud drew a deep breath as if girding himself. "And I want to find out if he's investigating Jubal Duval in all this," he said.

"That what Ray Perot wants?" Electa snapped.

"Look, Electa, I know Jubal's one of your favorites, and has been for years. But the man's dangerous."

Electa snorted derision. "He might a killed that poor animal, an' put it behind her house." She nodded toward Leslie, then motioned toward the stuffed black bird with her chin. "But he's 'bout as dangerous as that thing."

McCloud held up both hands and backed toward the door. "I'll see you later," he said. Then he was gone.

"Maybe he really thinks the man's dangerous," Leslie offered, uncertain why she even bothered.

Electa pursed her lips; her eyes narrowed. "Man doesn't always know what he's talkin' about. Like what he said about the children." She paused, allowing Leslie's curiosity to build. "Saw all three of them walkin' on our road last night, 'bout dinner time."

"But that's at least a mile from Jim's house," Leslie said.

Electa nodded. "And right close to where they found Amy Little," Electa said.

"Dear God. Are you sure? It must have been dark by then."

"Can still see what I see," Electa snapped. She gave Leslie a hard look. "Sometimes I even see more'n some people'd like me to."

Ray Perot drove directly back to his warehouse office, his foot jammed down on the accelerator, his mind racing along with the engine of the large, black Lincoln Town Car. McCloud had resisted him, but only at first. McCloud was angry with Devlin, yes. He disagreed with the way he was handling the case, yes. But he had confidence in Devlin. Considered him more than competent. Considered him a friend.

Bullshit.

A little pressure was all it took. A little more than usual, but still not that much. The man knew where the purse strings originated. That was the bottom line, just like it was for everyone.

Perot pushed his way through the office door, ignoring his secretary, who he knew wouldn't dare bother him with messages until told he was ready for them, entered his own office, and went directly to his private bathroom. His stomach was churning; felt as though it was devouring itself. He stared into the mirror, displeased at what stared back. He looked so fucking old, so used up. He was 58, but his fucking face seemed 10 years older. Damn. He needed a woman. A young woman whose body would excite him, rejuvenate him. And one who wouldn't be out fucking everything else in sight like his wife had. Like they all had.

He thought of his late wife, wishing she had died 20 years ago instead of 10. Then he would have still been young enough to find someone else, find someone who didn't want to use him just for his money; just for the power it would give her just being with him. He had waited too long. Too fucking long. Living with that cheating whore.

But every one he had found since then had been like that. He had offered Eva everything except marriage, something she had said she had no interest in anyway. All she had to do was keep her legs closed to everyone else, and he would have given her a car, clothes, even a small house somewhere close by. But she even had to fuck his own son, and every other sonofabitch with a stiff prick.

He splashed water into his hands and doused his face, noticing that he was trembling slightly. Even Amy Little, who hadn't had a pot to piss in, and never would have, had turned down what he'd offered her, and then let herself get knocked up by some pimply faced kid. And then the little bitch had come to him for money, so she could go away and have an abortion someplace where nobody would ever know.

But he had fixed her. He had gotten the word around, made sure people knew about her. But even that hadn't been enough to ease the pain the little slut had caused. But maybe Linnie would be different. She seemed willing to tell Billy to take a walk. Save it only for him when he wanted it. He'd see if she would. Yeah, he'd see.

His mind flashed on Leslie Adams. What an ass that woman had. Tits too. Nice and firm and round. You could tell that even under the loose shirt she was wearing. And she had told Billy to fuck off; had kicked him in the balls for even trying. But a snotty little bitch. Oh, you could tell that all right. But she'd learn you didn't get snotty with Ray Perot. Oh, yes, she'd learn that. And he'd have her. He'd have her even if she wouldn't stay with him. It was what he needed. Some good, young flesh to keep it up.

He wiped his hands on a thick, soft hand towel and stared at his image in the mirror again. He needed some now. Right now. He'd call Linnie in. Let her hunker down on him a bit. Yeah. Let her do what she did so well for him.

He smiled at the mirror, the uneven, yellow teeth grinning back. It would be all right. Everything would be all right now. Just like it always was. Like it always would be.

When Devlin returned to his office, he found Eric Mooers seated behind his desk, reading through the Eva Hyde file. He stood in the doorway, staring down at the BCI detective sergeant, the scar on his cheek a vivid white line.

Mooers looked up and offered a cold smile. "Pretty complete file," he said. "Anything more to add to it?"

"You mind if I sit in my chair?" Devlin's voice was soft, low.

Mooers' smile widened, but not with warmth, and he stood slowly and gestured Devlin toward the chair. "It's our case. Just thought you'd like me to see everything you got."

"Half of what we *got* would be missing if I'd listened to you, Mooers." He stared at the man as he slid into his chair. "Some asshole game warden would have buried it, and right now you'd be trying to keep the state's attorney from finding out how badly you fucked everything up. So as far as it being *your case* goes, you can kiss my ass."

Mooers glared at him, the soft tone of Devlin's voice juxtaposed with the harsh words confused him. He was short and stocky, powerfully built, and like most short men, especially cops, he had a need for physical intimidation. When it became obvious it wouldn't work with Devlin he turned to words, far from his forte.

"You know we supersede you on major crimes. And there ain't no state's attorney gonna change that. Especially not for some flatlander from *New York City*."

Devlin studied him. His flat, dull eyes. His bushy eyebrows, ginger colored like his close-cropped hair. His badly fitted blue checked sports jacket that left his gun bulging on his hip and defied any coordination with his green Vermont State Seal necktie. Ready for a fucking circus, he told himself.

A slow smile came to Devlin's lips. "Supersede's a big word for you. But you're probably right. After we both talk to him, the state's attorney will undoubtedly tell me BCI is in charge." The smile disappeared. "But I promise you one thing, clown. You won't be the one I'm dealing with when we're through." Devlin paused a beat taking in Mooers' darkening face. "And

I promise you one other thing. You ever come into this office again when I'm not here, I'll put my foot so far up your ass, you'll be spit shining my shoe."

Mooers' face looked as though it might implode with rage. "One tough, fucking asshole, aren't you?"

Devlin smiled at him.

"You think you can push me around?"

The smile widened, nothing more, not even a raised eyebrow.

Mooers caught himself with obvious difficulty, the hint of hatred still flickering behind his eyes. "Look, Devlin." He paused to light a cigarette. "We gotta get along. I was just out at the scene of this latest hog butchering. Ain't nobody gonna put up with us fightin' with each other with this goin' on. Not your bosses, or mine."

Devlin stared at his desk, fighting off renewed disgust at Mooers' description of Amy Little's murder. "So let's get along," he said at length, looking up. His voice was calm, the only hint of anger, the thin white line on his cheek. "You stay off my ass, and I'll give you what I have, when I have it. If you need something from me, you tell me, and I'll get it."

Mooers gritted his teeth, forcing the words through. "Sounds fine." He paused a beat. "You talk to anybody not in the reports I read?"

"Two. Today."

"Wanna tell me about 'em?"

"Louis Ferris, a local school teacher, who was suspected— but never formally accused—of sexually harassing Amy Little when she was twelve."

"Shiiit," Mooers said, interrupting, drawing the word out. "We do got our pre-verts livin' back here in the woods. But they usually ain't school teachers." Mooers grinned. "Hell, a game warden told me once"—he paused, offering Devlin an apologetic shrug—"told me how he caught this old woodchuck makin' his boy fuck this deer he'd shot. Told the warden it was the boy's first deer and it was a tradition like." Mooers watched Devlin squeeze his eyes shut and grinned again. "Anybody else?"

"Local businessman. Has a reputation as a pretty heavy womanizer. Name's Ray Perot, and the girl worked—"

"Perot! Shit, Devlin. You go after him, you won't have to

worry about me. You'll have half the state legislature on your ass." Mooers was grinning again, this time with true pleasure.

Devlin started to respond, then caught himself as Jim McCloud appeared in his doorway. He stared at the newspaperman, who under other circumstances he considered a friend, and drew a long breath. "What can I do for you, Jim?" he asked.

"Well, you can start by not ordering me away from any more crime scenes," McCloud began.

"When you drive your car over potential evidence, I don't have much choice, Jim. What else?"

"I want to know what you're doing about Jubal Duval? Why you haven't brought him in for questioning on these murders?"

"I've questioned Jubal," Devlin said.

"And?"

"And, I've questioned him. Period."

"Who's Jubal Duval?" Mooers interrupted.

McCloud turned to the BCI sergeant, whom he knew. "Local psychopath, Eric. Former Green Beret, who got a section eight discharge because he was even too crazy for them. Saw Eva Hyde a few hours before she was killed."

"Your facts are fucked up as usual, Jim," Devlin snapped. "At least as far as his discharge is concerned. I know. I've seen the paperwork."

"Then why was he discharged?" McCloud demanded.

"That's none of your damned business."

"This guy sounds pretty good to me," Mooers interjected. "Sure worth a pretty heavy look."

Devlin ignored him, his eyes intent on McCloud. "Somebody we both know put this bug up your ass?" he asked. "Like, maybe, Ray Perot?"

McCloud's jaw tightened, giving Devlin all the answer he needed.

"This Jubal's gettin' to sound even better," Mooers said, a grin spreading across his broad face.

"Then you pull him in," Devlin snapped. "Like you keep telling me, you're in charge of this show."

Mooers stared down at Devlin, his eyes hard now. "I just might do that," he said.

"Good luck," Devlin said.

# CHAPTER
# 7

The room is dark and cool, the curtains drawn across the small windows, blocking out the light of day. The figure sits alone in the center of the room, draped in the hooded poncho, eyes fixed on the blank, bare, blackened wall. Amy Little had been even better than Eva Hyde. She had squealed and begged; promised that she would never again do the things that she had done. It had been hard not to touch her before she died. Hard not to make her repeat things she had done that made it necessary for her to be punished. But she knew. It had been there in her eyes, wide and staring and terrified. It had been so exciting, seeing the realization there, seeing her last, fleeting look into her life; the knowledge that she had brought this final act on herself.

She had been walking along the road, on her way home from work, and, when offered a ride, she had accepted it, reluctantly, foolishly. But why shouldn't she? Everything had seemed so safe. Hands seize the poncho, twisting it. Hitting her with the pipe had been so easy. Then driving up the old hunter's trail, until the car was hidden from the road, and tying and gagging her. The hands tighten into white-knuckled fists, the palms inside them wet with sweat. She had seemed so heavy at first, dragging her unconscious body across the field. But then, as they neared the chosen place, her body had seemed to lighten, to weigh almost nothing at all. Maybe it was because she had awakened, and the terror had come to her eyes. And, when the gag was removed, the pleading, the begging, had begun, the words running together with such sweet desperation.

The gag had been replaced before she saw the knife. It had been smart to do it that way. It had kept her from screaming in terror. A shiver courses through the body, shaking the poncho. Oh, how her body had jumped when the tip of the knife punctured the skin. It had bounced on the ground in uncontrollable spasms as the blade moved up from the soft, smooth point just above her pubic hair, inching upward to the spot just below the sternum, and then, finally, cutting through the firm cartilage, the warm, rich blood flowing along her body, the body now shaking more violently as she went into shock. And, at last, reaching in, the body now soft and quiet, and feeling the still-beating heart in your hand. Then, after cutting it free, holding it out before you, how it had lain there, still beating in your hand, pulsing and pulsing and pulsing, until it had gradually slowed and stopped with a slight, oh so slight, shudder.

It had been so much better, driving the stake into her later. So much better than Eva, who hadn't seen and felt the cutting, hadn't surrendered a still-beating heart in payment for her wrongs.

The eyes leave the blackened wall and drop to the table in the center of the room. There, freshly removed from the plastic bag, the frozen heart sits, duller and lifeless now, but still there, as it always will be.

The hands tighten into fists again. And now there's the boy, who's seen what he shouldn't have seen. If he hadn't intruded he could have been spared. He didn't belong there. Now you know that. Now there's no choice. He and his sister will both be marked for punishment. But you wanted someone to see you. You needed it to make those fools understand. No, it makes no difference. Now the boy and his sister will both get what they deserve. And so will the others who have abused you. Then maybe it will be over. Maybe it will be time to rest again. Rest and wait. Yes. As long as others don't interfere. If they do, then they'll also get what they deserve. A smile forms. They'll get roses. Roses dropped on their bodies. Just like Mother. No! Placed *in* their bodies. And on their coffins.

Hands come away from the poncho, then slowly lower again and smooth the dark olive-green fabric. The hands tremble with anticipation.

Robbie sat at the cafeteria table, staring at the sandwich Jim McCloud had made for him that morning, uncertain what to do about what he had seen. He glanced across the table where Tim and Phillipa munched greedily on their sandwiches. It wasn't their problem, he told himself. They hadn't seen it. Only he had.

But it was their fault. They were the ones who had wanted to sneak away when Jim had gone into his study to read and "have a few pops," as Tim had put it. They had been supposed to stay in the yard, but Tim had suggested they explore the old logging road that cut across the ridge from his road to the one Phillipa and Robbie lived on. There was nothing to worry about, it wasn't Jubal's territory, Tim had argued, when Robbie had objected, and Phillipa had looked at him like he was being some kind of wimp. So he had gone along. And now he was in it up to his neck.

He could probably have just kept his mouth shut if that old witch, Electa, hadn't seen them when they came out on his road. And she was sure to blab to his sister. Christ, the woman had been a teacher. What else could he expect.

He recalled how Electa had stared at them from the window of her car, her eyes like a hawk, watching a group of mice. But they had continued on the road, even though he knew they should have turned back right then. Then about five minutes later stupid Phillipa had decided to pick some flowers, and dumb Tim had agreed to help her. And you, you had to keep walking and go around that curve.

He had seen the hooded figure then, dragging something into the thick brush about 200 yards off the road. It was almost dark, and all he could make out was the chalk-white face against the dark fabric of the hood. He hadn't even been able to tell how big or small the figure was, the way the poncho the hood was attached to billowed out in the wind. But he knew the figure was the same one his sister had described the night they found the gutted fox behind their barn. And he knew one other thing. That what it was dragging looked like somebody's legs.

He had tried to tell Phillipa and Tim, but they had just looked at him like he was nuts and insisted he was still spooked by the run-in with Jubal. And now he didn't know what to do, whether to tell anybody or not. If he told, he was in trouble, and maybe he was just imagining about the legs. But what if he wasn't? And what if the person he had seen didn't want to be seen? Jesus, he thought. And all because you went for a stupid walk.

"So now we know that the car was parked on that long, narrow path that's been beaten down by hunters pulling their trucks in over the years, and that the body was dragged from there, across that small field and into the brush about a hundred yards from the main road." Devlin stared across his desk at Quint. "But why? Why not kill her right there? Why take the chance of dragging her through an open area? Is the M.E. sure she was alive then?"

Quint, who had attended the autopsy at the state medical examiner's office then hurried back to give Devlin the results, nodded slowly. He seemed torn by the need to be scientifically objective and by the fact that the victim was a child he had known; had treated all her life.

"She sustained a mild concussion prior to death, which indicates the killer hit her in the head then transported her unconscious to the scene. She was killed there; the amount of blood makes that indisputable."

"And the only physical evidence were those green, water-proof cotton fibers under her nails." Devlin offered the question as fact. "No sign of sexual assault. Nothing else."

The aging coroner shook his head. "I know it would help if she had been," he said. "But thank Christ she didn't have to endure that horror. Jesus, she was alive when the bastard gutted her."

"Dammit," Devlin snapped. "What we need is somebody who saw him. Or, at least, saw the car." Devlin leaned forward, his eyes boring into Quint as though he might find something there. "Why that place? There are dozens—shit, hundreds—of more isolated places to dump a body."

"It's only a mile from the place we found Eva Hyde. The same road. Maybe it's his territory, someplace he feels safe," Quint offered. "Or, maybe, he just wants to make sure they're found." Quint tightened his arms against his sides, as if controlling a shiver. "Just find the bastard before it happens again," he said.

"I will," Devlin said. "As soon as I find the connection between the two victims."

Quint hesitated. "They were both young and sexually active."

"Amy Little?"

Quint nodded. "I performed an abortion on her two months ago."

"Why the hell didn't you tell me that before?" Devlin snapped.

Quint stared at his hands and shook his head. "Being protective, I guess. I'm sorry. It was wrong to do that."

"Who was the father?" Devlin asked, his voice eager now.

"She wouldn't say, and I didn't press it. I gave her a prescription for birth control pills, and let it go at that."

"Did anybody else know?"

Quint snorted. "In this town? Christ, find me somebody who didn't."

Devlin lowered his head, massaging his forehead with his fingertips.

"There's one other thing," Quint said.

Devlin's head snapped up.

"It's so crazy, I'm not sure what it means."

"What?"

"The roses. The ones found next to Eva and Amy; even that damned fox. They're old. Very old."

"How old?"

"The M.E.'s office can't be sure. They don't have the equipment necessary to determine exact age, so they've sent them off to a university laboratory." Quint stared at Devlin, his eyes revealing disbelief in his own words. "Christ, Paul. They're at least twenty years old."

Devlin closed his eyes as a shudder coursed through his body.

The clear, oily texture of the martini bespoke a coolness far beyond the faint mist that clouded the top of the long-stemmed glass. Jack Chambers studied it with pleasure. It was the first drink of the day, and always the best, the one he most looked forward to, the initial step to controlled oblivion.

He took a long sip, draining half the glass, then nodded approval to the young bartender who awaited his signal. He had been staying at the Logger's Inn on Blake Mountain Road for five days now and had succeeded in training the bartender well during that time. The young man—a tall, reedy kid, with straw blond hair—was a senior at nearby Lyndonville State College, who had aspirations toward law school and later a job with a big city firm. In short, Jack had concluded early on, he wants to grow up to be just like me.

Jack finished the drink and watched with satisfaction as the young bartender removed the glass and started on an immediate refill.

"Heading out to hit some of the local nightspots tonight, Mr. Chambers?" the kid bartender asked.

"I think I've seen all there is to see," Jack said. "Besides, I'm expecting a call from one of my partners, so I have to hang about."

"Big case, huh?"

"They're all big cases as far as the clients are concerned," Jack said. There was no call expected, and no case, but it sounded right.

Jack sipped the second drink, nursing now. The two heavy hits of the first had gone straight to his brain, giving the soft, foggy glow that put everything into a nice, easy perspective. He hunched over the glass, his broad shoulders and large hands dwarfing the glass, his normally handsome, slightly Ivy League features, hard now, matching the cold, blue sheen of his eyes. He had watched the bitch for five days; knew what she was doing, and where she was doing it. She had thought herself so smart. Thought she could hide from him. He smiled inwardly at the idea. All it had taken to access the U-Haul computer was a quick hundred slipped to a clerk. And he had been right on the first guess; hadn't even had to check the other truck rental companies. She was such a predictable little cunt.

He gulped down the second martini without realizing it and watched as his faithful bartender quickly grabbed up the glass and started on another. Today was the day he'd telephone her, let her know that her little plan to run away had blown up in her face. He checked his watch. It was 4:30, plenty of time yet.

He picked up the new drink and sipped. She had caused him enough trouble, and now she'd pay for it. She'd forced him to take time off from work he could ill afford. Christ, she'd ravaged his whole career. Everything had started going downhill as soon as he'd married her. He'd never had trouble getting clients before. Men had always been drawn to him, had liked his fraternity-boy/grown-up demeanor. But now they had stopped staying with him, claiming the work wasn't done on time, or was fucked up somehow. And it was all because of her, because she wouldn't be the wife she was supposed to be. Wouldn't give him what he needed at home so he could concentrate on work during the day. But she had plenty of time to dote on that little shit of a brother. Even brought him into his home. And now his partners were getting nervous about his clients leaving him. And if he wasn't careful he'd be on his own soon, scratching out an income to pay off the bank loans he'd need to live on. But she'd pay for it all. He'd see to that.

He gulped half the drink and sat fingering the glass. She'd come crawling back now. Once she knew she couldn't get the best of him, she'd have no choice. She'd humiliated him by leaving, made him out a fool to his friends and his peers. But that would all resolve itself when she came back, tail between her legs. Then they'd know she couldn't stay away from him. He grinned at the idea. Maybe he'd give her a good fuck when he saw her. She always liked that big sausage of his. Squirmed on it like a fucking eel; begged for more of it. She'd only stopped putting out for him to punish him; to get what she wanted from him. Probably laid in the guest bedroom playing with herself, dreaming of it, wishing she could have it. Well, he'd give it to her. And then he'd tell everybody how he had. How she couldn't resist it. He'd told them that anyway, after she'd left—that he was still seeing her, still banging her. But he could tell from their eyes they thought it was so much bullshit, because she still hadn't come home. But now it would be different.

He finished off the drink and thought about the local bitch he'd had a few nights ago. He'd had to force her head down to get her to take it in her mouth. Had to hurt her a little to get her to do what was right. Had to—. He pushed the thought away and looked up, startled. His new drink was already in front of him. He winked at the bartender. "Keep that cool for me," he said. "Have to make a phone call. Seems like my partner is sitting on his ass."

Jack got up from his stool, slightly unsteady. But no one else would notice. He could drink all night and never let it show. It was time for the bitch to get a little message. Maybe he'd even be generous. Let her know everything could be forgiven if she did the right thing. He smiled at the idea.

"We came as soon as he told me. He didn't know about the girl, about what happened to her." Leslie glanced at Robbie, then back at Devlin. "If he had, I know he would have told me sooner."

Devlin watched her, ready to defend the boy against any attack that might come. He could only imagine what she would be like with her own child; he decided it would be awesome. He had thought about her a great deal during the day, about their night together, the sensuality he had found in her, the abandon that had ignited all the urges and feelings he had repressed for so long. And he had found himself wanting her again, just as he wanted her now.

He glanced at Robbie and smiled. "I'm glad you came in," he said. "It's important in a lot of ways." He leaned forward, closing the distance between himself and the boy. They were sitting in his office, in chairs facing each other, Leslie and the boy on one side, he on the other. He had not wanted his desk between them as a barrier.

"Was anything about this person you saw familiar?"

Robbie shook his head. "He was just too far away."

"But you think it was a man?"

The boy shrugged. "I guess."

"What about size, weight, anything like that?"

"It was hard to tell. The coat, or poncho, or whatever it was, was kinda blowing out with the wind."

"But he was dragging something, and it looked like somebody's legs?"

Robbie nodded.

Devlin paused, pulling on his nose, gathering his thoughts. "How long was it from the time Electa went by to the time you saw this person?"

Robbie twisted in his chair. "Five minutes, I guess," he said at length.

Too long, Devlin thought. She had probably gone by before he started into the field. But he'd have to ask her anyway. "What about a parked car or truck? Did you see one?"

Again Robbie shook his head.

"Tell me about the poncho this person was wearing."

Robbie seemed to struggle with the question. "It was green." He shrugged. "You know, like the kind they wear in the army."

"Camouflage," Devlin said.

"I guess."

"Maybe it was that Jubal person," Leslie interjected, a hint of excitement, an eagerness to have the question resolved, present in her voice.

Devlin's jaw tightened. "Just about every damned hunter in the state owns a camouflage poncho or jacket," he snapped. He looked quickly at Leslie. "Sorry," he said. "I'm just getting pushed a little too much about Jubal these days.

"Okay," Devlin said, turning back to Robbie and forcing another smile. "I want you to keep thinking about it, and let me know if anything comes to you. Anything you might have forgotten."

"I'd like him to try to put it out of his mind," Leslie said.

Devlin stared at her. She didn't want him to think about it, because she didn't want him to recognize the danger he might be in just by having seen the killer. But that was wrong. He had to recognize it, no matter how much it scared him.

Devlin leaned forward again, forcing a closeness, a greater intimacy. "Robbie, I also want you to keep an eye out for anyone—*anyone*—who reminds you of the person you saw. And if you see someone like that, I want you to get to me, or your sister, or any other adult you trust right away. Okay?"

When Robbie nodded, Devlin turned quickly to Leslie to blunt any objection. "And I'll be checking your house several times a day, and I'll have my patrols doing the same thing." He watched Leslie's face, the mixture of anger and relief. For a moment she seemed about to tell him something, then thought better of it. He smiled at her. "It's better that way. Believe me, it is."

Leslie could hear the telephone ringing as she climbed out of her truck, and she hurried to the kitchen door, fought the key into the lock, and made it to the phone on what had to be the ninth or tenth ring.

"Hello," she said, her voice slightly breathless from the effort.

"Where were you? Out playing in your little red barn? Or just picking apples off your tree?"

Leslie froze, the sound of Jack's voice chilling every part of her. He'd been there. Seen where she lived. Watched her. She thought about the rose in her truck; her decision not to tell Devlin about it in front of Robbie. Oh, God. Jack.

"I don't want to talk to you, Jack," she said, fighting for control in her voice, not sure if she had managed it. She heard a sound behind her, turned and found Robbie staring at her, his face concerned, a little frightened.

"Oh, you'll talk to me," Jack said. "You'll—"

Leslie put the phone back in its cradle, cutting him off, then removed it again, leaving it off the hook.

"He found us," Robbie said.

"Yeah," Leslie said. "Looks like he has."

# CHAPTER
## 8

Devlin knocked on the rear door of Electa Litchfield's house, waited, then knocked again. Her car was in the driveway, and he was about to try the door when it flew open and he found himself facing the woman, dressed in rubber gloves and apron, a long, slender knife in one hand, her eyes glaring with a barely controlled rage. He jumped back quickly.

"E . . . E . . . Easy, Electa," he said, stammering. "I just came by to ask you some questions."

The woman's face seemed to soften, and Devlin let out a long breath. He could feel the sweat in his palms, and he realized she had scared the hell out of him. He forced a smile. "You keep opening the door like that, you're gonna give your visitors heart attacks," he said.

Irritation flooded her eyes, then she turned abruptly. "You want to talk, then come inside," she snapped, leaving Devlin to follow her or not.

She moved down a narrow hall, Devlin close behind, then entered a large ground-floor room that seemed to have once been a cold storage area. There was only one small window, but the long strips of fluorescent light that had been added to the ceiling filled the room with an almost blinding brilliance that caused Devlin to stop short in the doorway. His jaw dropped as he looked about him.

The room was immaculate, almost clinically so; dominated by a large stainless steel table and deep sink at its center. Arrayed on the table, glistening under the lights, were several surgeon's scalpels, kitchen paring and grapefruit knives, a butcher's skinning knife, heavy surgeon's bone cutters, an assortment of forceps and surgical scissors, all juxtaposed with a set of artist's oils and brushes and an assortment of hammers, saws, files, shears, pliers, wood rasps, and tools he couldn't begin to identify. On each wall glass-fronted cabinets held boxes of cotton and wood wool, blocks of balsa wood and Styrofoam, plaster of paris, glue, modeling clay, an enormous box of salt, and myriad bottles, the labels of which he could not read.

"Jesus Christ," he whispered. "What the hell is all this?" His eyes were fixed on yet another cabinet containing large glass jars, filled with fluid, and holding the entrails of dozens and dozens of small animals.

Electa sneered and stepped to one side, revealing a smaller wooden table, on which the hide of a raccoon lay pinned, its exposed flesh covered with salt. "It's called taxidermy. Probably don't see much of it in New York City," she emphasized the words, almost as though pronouncing some exotic plague. "But up here in the backwater, some folks have a regard for it. I learned it from my father, as he did from his."

Devlin gave his head a slight shake, more to clear it from the shock than any display of judgment. He moved to the cabinet holding the entrails. "What are these for?" He stared at the collection of viscera floating in liquid that had turned slightly yellow, perhaps with age, he thought.

"I used to use them when I taught," Electa said, her voice stiff. "It helped the children understand the workings of the body."

Devlin recalled that Electa had taught high school and he envisioned his own reaction at that age if forced to view this collection of twisted remains. His back was to Electa, and he grimaced at the thought, then turned, his eyes roaming the stainless steel table and the collection of scalpels and skinning knives. "That's a pretty awesome display of weaponry and whatever," he said.

Electa grunted, dismissing his opinion. "You said you had some questions," she snapped.

Devlin nodded and began by telling her what Robbie had seen, and the subsequent discovery of Amy Little's mutilated body.

"Killed the same as Eva?" Electa asked. When Devlin nodded, she shook her head. "Knew her as a small child. She was a sweet, innocent thing then. Too bad she couldn't stay that way."

Devlin stared at the woman, openly surprised at her ability to fix some responsibility for the murder on the child herself.

"Did the boy see who did it?" she asked, almost as if it were of lesser consequence than the victim's own guilt.

"We think so. But no one he could see clearly enough to identify." He stepped closer to Electa, a faint hint of formaldehyde assaulting his nostrils. It reminded him of autopsies he had witnessed; the pervading smell of death he had always hated. "He said you had driven by a few minutes earlier. I was hoping you might have seen something."

Electa snorted again. "You remind me of children I had in school. Always looking for someone else to do their work for them." She stared at him disapprovingly, as though he was still such a child. "No, I didn't see anything except the children."

"What about a parked car?" Devlin asked.

"Nothing," Electa snapped. "I'm afraid you'll just have to do your own work."

The rented Toyota turned into the driveway, skidded slightly on the gravel, then rolled to a halt at the kitchen door. Leslie watched from the door's glass panel as Jack climbed out from behind the wheel, staggered almost imperceptibly, then started for the door. She pulled down the shade that covered the panel and moved quickly to the telephone.

A heavy fist rapped against the wood. "Jack's back, Leslie. Time to open up and welcome your lord and master."

Robbie had come into the kitchen and looked from the door to his sister, and back again. Leslie held up a hand requesting quiet. "Yes. This is Leslie Adams," she said into the telephone. "I have someone trying to force their way into my house. Can you send somebody?" She waited, listening, her foot tapping a tattoo on the floor. "Look, I don't have time to explain things. Can you *please* send somebody. *Please* just tell Chief Devlin." She slammed the phone down and stared at her brother. "Go upstairs," she ordered.

Robbie shook his head, defiantly.

"Please, Robbie!"

Another shake, more determined this time.

"Open . . . the . . . fucking . . . door . . . , Leslie." Each word a commanding shout.

Leslie shrank back against the wall. Her arms and legs were trembling; her jaw was clenched. "Leave me alone, damn you," she whispered. "Just leave me alone."

Jack rattled the knob of the locked door, then stared at the glass panel, debating whether to smash his hand through the glass to open it. Instead he pounded on the door again. "I told you to *open* it!"

"I think you better hold up there, clown." Paul Devlin had heard the pounding as he had left Electa's house, and had hurried across the wide lawn. Now he stood directly behind Jack Chambers wondering if he would need the service revolver locked in his glove compartment.

Jack spun around and glared at him. "And who the fuck are you?" he demanded.

"Chief of police will do for a start. Now get the fuck away from that door and show me some identification."

"Big fucking deal," Jack snapped and, turning, began to pound on the door again.

Devlin was on him in two steps, driving Jack's arm up behind his back, and slamming his face against the side of the house. "You just bought yourself a trip to the station, asshole." His voice was soft and low, and far more threatening because it was.

"You can't do that. I'm a lawyer, and I have—"

Devlin jammed his arm up higher, cutting his words off with pain. "Then you oughta know better, shouldn't you?" He grabbed Chambers by the hair, pulled him away from the house and released his arm. "Spread 'em," he snapped. "And do it right," he added, almost whispering. "Or you go out of here in a fucking ambulance."

Jack did as he was told, then drew a deep breath and spoke through clenched teeth. "What's the charge?"

"Well, we could start with being an asshole," Devlin said. "But Vermont doesn't have a statute against that, counselor. So we'll start with failing to obey the lawful command of a police officer; disturbing the peace; trespassing; and, from the smell of you, drunk and disorderly, and since you drove up here, suspicion of drunken driving. How's that for starters? You give me a little more time, and a little more mouth, and I can really start to get creative."

"I'm the woman's husband, jerk," Jack snarled. "So I technically own half of anything she owns. And I can't trespass on my own property, or be stopped from pounding on my own door. So you had no right to approach me in the first place."

"Well, we'll just start with the drunken driving I observed and go from there." Devlin patted him down for weapons, then took one wrist, brought it behind Chambers' back, withdrew handcuffs from the rear of his belt, and snapped them in place.

"Don't you dare cuff me," Jack ordered.

Devlin shouldered him into the wall and brought the other hand behind his back. "Shut up," he said, as he snapped the second cuff into place.

The kitchen door opened and Leslie stood there, eyes wide, mouth slightly agape. "How did you get here so fast?" she asked. "I just called."

"You called the fucking cops?" Jack snarled.

"Shut up," Devlin said, pushing him against the wall again. "I was at Electa's when I heard this clown doing a *big, bad wolf* on your door."

Leslie stared at Jack's hands cuffed behind his back. "Are you arresting him?" she asked.

"That's right. And I'm doing it whether you press charges or not. He drove up here drunk." Devlin noticed her voice was shaky, uncertain. He had handled enough domestic violence incidents as a young cop to know that women often panicked when faced with locking up their abusers, either from fear of economic loss, if the man lived with them, or from the near certain knowledge that reprisals would follow once the police released him. "Look," Devlin said. "There are several other charges I can file—that *should* be filed—but I need you for that. In any event, I want you to ask for a relief from abuse order, so the court can order him to stay away from you under threat of arrest."

Leslie seemed overwhelmed by the information flying at her. "Will it work here?" she asked.

Jack twisted his head around and glared at her. "No, it won't. You won't even get one," he snarled.

Devlin slammed him back into the wall, harder than necessary. "He must have missed that class in law school," he said, his eyes on Leslie. "You request it, the judge will grant it. Automatically, no question. Then, later, there'll be a hearing, at which I'll testify. And then his ass gets locked up every time he comes within a hundred yards of you. *I'll* see to that."

Leslie began to stammer, still uncertain, and Jack seized on it, twisting his head around again, staring at her. "This hick cop is forgetting that we're *married*. We're not even legally separated. And that I had every right to be here, that legally I own half this property, and that he had no right to even approach me."

"Wrong again, counselor," Devlin said, pressing Jack to the wall again. "We've had two murders in the area, and we have reason to believe the people in this house are in danger. It's been under protective surveillance since this afternoon."

He could see Chambers' mind begin to work furiously, seeking out some advantage. He twisted his head toward Leslie again. "Danger?" His face took on a look of shocked concern. "Baby, why didn't you tell me? Look, if you need protection—"

"Oh, shit," Devlin said, spinning him around, cutting off the words. "We're on our way now, counselor," he said. He grabbed Chambers by the seat of the pants and the collar of his shirt and began frog marching him across the lawn toward his car. He glanced back at Leslie. "You let me know what you want to do," he said. The last thing Leslie heard was Devlin reciting Miranda rights to her husband.

Twenty-five yards back in the woods, Jubal Duval watched the chief march the stranger toward his car in Electa's driveway. He had been on his way to watch the woman's house when he had heard the pounding, and he had seen everything that had taken place.

Jubal nodded to himself, then began to fade back into the wood, making himself more a part of it, unseen, unnoticed by anyone at all.

# CHAPTER
## 9

Jack Chambers sat in Devlin's office with a smirk on his face that was purely for Devlin's benefit. He had tried to befriend the man, using a *look, we're both guys, and she's only a woman* approach that had always worked with other men. But the asshole had ignored him, had continued to play hardass. So he had played it right back.

He had refused the breath test Devlin had directed him to take, aware the refusal would produce a charge of its own. But he could live with that. He could delay any trial until his business with the bitch was finished. Then what did he care if his driving privileges in Vermont were suspended for six months. As far as he knew there was no reciprocity with Pennsylvania, so a conviction wouldn't follow him there. And even if it did, he'd live with it. It was the threat of the other charges that worried him. Those could end up with the bar association and prove embarrassing, if not worse. And none of it would help with his already wavering partners. His features darkened. It was the bitch's fault. She had set him up; was the one behind everything that had happened. He twisted in his chair, then caught himself. He couldn't afford to show any nervousness. He needed to scotch this thing now. Devlin had already called the inn to confirm his residence there, and in a hick place like this that would be enough to start some tongues wagging. It might even bring that woman he had met out of the woodwork to file a complaint against him. He should have stayed away from her. Or he should have shut her up the way he always shut them up. No, she'd keep her mouth shut. She wouldn't want every asshole in this hick town to know she'd sucked his cock.

He had telephoned a local attorney, and now both he and Devlin were waiting for him to show. But there had to be something he could do, something to break through the barrier this clown of a cop had set up.

"Tell me about these murders you've had," Jack said out of the blue.

"Why?" Devlin asked.

"Well, you said they somehow threaten my wife. So naturally I'm interested."

Devlin looked at him with an amused disgust.

Jack turned both palms up in a gesture of helplessness. "Look. Just because we're having some domestic problems doesn't mean I'm not concerned."

Devlin came around his desk and stood so he was towering over Jack. "You get around much in the five days you've been in town?" he asked. He could see Chambers' mind begin to work, weighing the probability that whatever he said would be checked.

"Sure. I hit a few places. Just to relieve the boredom."

"Been to a place called Pearlie's?" A nervous twitch hit Jack's eye, then disappeared just as quickly.

"I think so. Yeah."

"And you didn't hear anything about a woman being killed."

"Look, I haven't found the locals too friendly. And that includes today." He offered the comment with a boyish grin. The liquor had begun to wear off and he was playing his charm for all it was worth.

"Why'd it take you five days to get in touch with Ms. Adams?"

"Mrs. Chambers," Jack said, more like someone asserting property rights than out of belligerence.

Devlin ignored him and waited for an answer.

"Look, I just wanted to see what she was up to. If there was another guy. Whatever. I'm a lawyer. I believe in checking things out before I take any action." He smiled boyishly again. "She pulled out without any warning. I wanted to see what was behind it."

"Never dawned on you that beating the hell out of her might have been the reason." There was no question in Devlin's words, merely a simple, statement of fact.

"Look, I never laid a hand on her," Chambers said, wounded. "You're dealing with a lady who's had some severe emotional problems. You don't believe me, you call Lawrence Withers, her shrink in Philly. He even hospitalized her for a couple of weeks about a year ago."

Before Devlin could respond his doorway was filled with the large, overweight figure of Milton Atwater, one of the town's three lawyers.

"Hello, Milton," Devlin said, taking in the man's balding head, filmed with perspiration despite the cool temperature. "This is Mr. Chambers, your client."

Milton nodded, then turned a thick-lipped smile on Jack, his round, red face exuding pleasure. At an anticipated fee, Devlin thought.

"Can we have a few minutes?" Milton asked.

"Use the office," Devlin said.

When he closed the door behind them, Devlin found Free staring at him expectantly from his desk. He had asked him earlier to telephone Leslie and find out when she was coming to the station, and now Free was waiting to learn the connection between this new woman and Devlin's prisoner, a surefire font of gossip for the bars that night.

"Did you reach Ms. Adams?" Devlin asked.

"Yup. Said she'd be down when she could."

The man continued to stare at him, eyes eager. When she could, Devlin repeated to himself, wondering if that meant when she found the courage, or what. He looked Free up and down. "I thought you were going to get that uniform pressed," he said.

"Did," Free said. "Ironed it myself."

"Well, it didn't work," Devlin snapped. "Try a cleaner."

Free grunted then turned quickly away and began busying himself with the papers strewn across his desk. Don't take it out on the poor slob, Devlin cautioned himself. It's the man inside your office who's got you bugged, not him.

Devlin took a seat at an empty desk in the outer office, thought about calling Leslie himself, then quickly dismissed the idea. He wanted to nail that smug bastard sitting in his office, wanted to hit him with every chargeable offense he could conjure up. And he wanted that relief from abuse order so he could nail him again if he ever came near her. The thought of Chambers ever having been with her in the past, ever being with her again, ate at him, made him want to slam his fist into the man's face, let him feel the physical cost of trying to hurt her again. Or was it more than that?

Devlin picked up a pencil and began turning it in his hands. Christ, the woman had run from the man; hidden from him. His experience as a cop told him that few women did that unless they had finally had enough, wanted to get away no matter the cost. He shook his head. There was something in women, he believed, that made them hang on in a bad situation far longer than could reasonably be expected. Maybe it had something to do with the nurturing instinct. Something that made them believe they could change a selfish, abusive prick into something decent. He ground his teeth, tightened his grip on the pencil. But how much did she want to escape him, if she wouldn't take the steps needed to thwart him from coming back at her again and again? He tried to push the thought away; found it returning. As a young cop he had dealt with other women in the same, or worse, situations; had suggested they take similar action. But when they refused, he had let it go, hadn't let it eat away at him. But now it was different, and even though he didn't want to admit it, he understood, in his gut, why it was so.

When the front door of the station opened he looked up quickly, expectantly, but found only Gunter Kline moving toward him, his face agitated and etched with worry.

"Can I speak to you privately?" Gunter asked. He was dressed impeccably, as always, in blue blazer and tan slacks, his Gucci loafers polished to a sheen, his custom-tailored yellow shirt set off by a regimental blue and red tie.

"If you don't mind the interrogation room," Devlin said. "My office is being used."

Gunter winced at the idea of the closed, barren room that Devlin had converted from a windowless storeroom. "Could we just talk outside?" Gunter asked.

Devlin nodded, came around the desk, and started for the door, Gunter at his heels. "If there are any calls, I'll be right outside," he told Free needlessly. The man's ears were perked and pink with anticipation.

Devlin led Gunter to a small bench outside the building, smiled at the stocky restauranteur, and slouched onto one end. "You look like something's eating at you, Gunter. What's up?"

"Amy Little."

"Me too. You know something about it I should know?"

"She worked for me summers. You knew that?" Gunter said.

"No, I didn't. I mean, I may have seen her there, but it never registered," Devlin said.

Gunter's hands attacked each other. "It's just that both of them worked there. And now both of them have been killed, murdered so horribly. Amy, she was like a niece to me. So sweet, so lovely. And Eva—" He let the sentence die.

"It's just coincidence, Gunter. Nothing more." Devlin listened to the falseness of his own words. Each had worked there. And each could have been seen there; watched there. But there was no sense in laying that on the man. Especially not the way he had felt about Eva.

"Paul, you know I hunt. Birds, deer, rabbit. It's something in my German heritage, perhaps." He shrugged away his own small joke. "But, Paul, I know this area. I've learned it in the years I've been here. There are so many places, Paul. So many places where a body would not be found for years. Places where it might not ever be found. This person, this monster who killed them. He wants the bodies found, Paul. But why? And why women who have worked for me?"

"It's got nothing to do with you, or the restaurant, Gunter. It's a small town. Not that many places to work." He listened to the falseness again; was irritated by it. "And I agree with you. Whoever's doing this wants the bodies found. Wants us to know he's done it again. It's part of his damned madness."

"He's got to be stopped, Paul. Killed. Stopped for good."

Devlin raised both hands. The wild look, which had come so suddenly to Gunter's eyes, momentarily unnerved him. The man just didn't understand what killing someone meant, the explosion of flesh, the spray of blood and bone and skin. "I'll settle for catching him, putting him away."

"No!" Gunter's eyes glittered with hatred. "That's not good enough, Paul. He deserves worse than that."

Devlin hesitated, was about to answer, then spotted Leslie coming toward them. Saved, he told himself. Or am I? Maybe it's just another bit of madness to cap off the day.

Devlin, then Gunter, stood as Leslie reached them. "You okay?" Devlin asked.

"Fine." Leslie's hands twisted together. "I'm here to do what you suggested." She glanced at her hands, then balled them into fists. Within seconds they were opening and closing as nerves reasserted themselves.

"That's great," Devlin said. He was about to go on when he realized he had left Gunter standing there like a fool. "Excuse me," he said. "Leslie Adams, this is Gunter—"

"I know Gunter," Leslie said, cutting off the formality.

"You've met?"

"One of my first nights in town," Leslie said. "Robbie and I were so exhausted from running around, we decided to treat ourselves to a night out." She smiled warmly at Gunter. "I had the best dinner I've had anywhere. Plus the personal attention of the owner. I wish we could go there every week."

"You come anytime," Gunter said, obviously delighted. "As my guest. And if you want something at home, you come see me, and I take you down to my meat room in the cellar. You pick what you want."

Devlin glanced from one to the other: Leslie, who had arrived with nerves frayed; Gunter, who had come to demand the execution of a killer, each now brimming smiles. He reached for Leslie's elbow, felt her stiffen under the paternal gesture, and immediately released it.

"Gunter? Can I get back to you later? There's some business we have to take care of."

"Certainly," Gunter said, still smiling at Leslie. "And, please, you shouldn't forget my offer of dinner," he added. His eyes seemed to brighten suddenly. "In fact I have a wonderful idea," he said. "The two of you come to my home for dinner tonight, and I shall cook it for you myself."

"Oh, I'd love to," Leslie said. "I'd love to have a normal, pleasant evening. But Robbie, I just couldn't leave him. Not after today."

"I could ask my housekeeper, Mattie, to watch both kids at my place," Devlin said.

Leslie hesitated; bit her lower lip, then smiled. "Then let's do it," she said.

"Excellent," Gunter said. "Seven o'clock, then."

"Done," Leslie said.

"On one condition," Devlin added. "No talk about police business. From anyone."

"Agreed," Gunter said. "Seven o'clock."

As Devlin and Leslie turned to go, Gunter reached out and took Devlin's arm, halting him. He allowed Leslie to move a few steps further toward the door, then leaned toward Devlin and whispered. "You make sure you watch her closely," he said, indicating Leslie with his eyes. "She's beautiful like the others. She needs to be protected."

Devlin stared at the dapper restauranteur, wondering if he might inadvertently have stumbled onto something. That being beautiful might be a criterion for dying. Or was it more than that? Something more personal. He felt a twinge of jealousy. "I'll protect her," he said. "That much I promise you."

Gunter watched as Devlin caught up with Leslie and led her inside, then he turned and started up the street, his nattily dressed figure appearing almost alien among the well-worn jeans and hunting shirts favored by the other men he passed. But being the odd man out was something he understood, something he had lived with since boyhood, when his then stubby, overweight body had made him little more than a pet for other children, someone to be derided or befriended dependent upon whim. But not so at home. There, demands for perfection were made that could never be met, whether working in his father's restaurant or existing in his mother's parlor. In that life everything had to be meticulous, be it mixing a sauce or matching the colors of his clothing. It was something he had hated desperately, yet something he had carried with him, almost religiously, throughout his life. He was a perfectionist, and he took a self-deprecating pride in the fact, whether it was serving up a souffle or shooting a rifle. And no matter the occasion, Gunter Kline was dressed for the part.

Now he would dress for another part: finding the monster who had destroyed his Eva and young Amy. And if Paul wouldn't listen, and allow him to help, then he would do it alone, just as he had done most things in his life. The monster would be put to rest. If he did nothing else in his life, he would see to that.

When he reached the restaurant, Gunter found it bereft of customers, save one: Jim McCloud, seated alone at the bar, doing what he did each day—soaking his brain with numbing fluid—only, today, a bit later that usual.

Gunter slid onto the stool next to him. "Bad day?" he asked.

"I'm still waiting for a good one," McCloud said, speaking to Gunter's reflection in the mirror behind the bar.

"You won't find one here," Gunter said. "Not unless you eat my food."

"No lectures about alcohol abuse, Gunter. I'm not up to that today."

"From a German, never." He waved to the bartender, who promptly brought him a bottle of German beer, then gestured with his head toward the empty dining room. "Has it been this slow all evening?" he asked the bartender.

"There was a big rush earlier, but since then, nothing," the bartender said.

Gunter shrugged in resignation. It was something that happened from time to time, although it was still disconcerting. He turned back to McCloud. "Looks like we're both having a bad day," he said.

McCloud eyed him in the mirror. "At least you didn't have to deal with Ray Perot. That's enough to throw a black cloud over anybody."

Gunter's mouth hardened into a thin line. "And what did the great benefactor want?"

"What he usually wants. His own way." McCloud toyed with his near-empty glass, then raised it to his lips, drained it, and nodded to the bartender for a refill. "He's all hot and bothered about the murders. Probably because both victims had a connection to him and his asshole son. So now he's convinced himself Jubal Duval is involved somehow, and he wants me to use the newspaper to put pressure on Paul to haul his ass in."

Gunter's face had turned scarlet, and he seemed about to

speak, but McCloud ignored him. "What really pisses me off, is that I think he may be right. I just don't like anybody telling me how to run my God damned newspaper." He glared at the new drink. "Even if it is a one-horse operation in a one-horse town, it's my fucking horse."

Gunter's hand tightened around his beer glass and he caught himself just before it smashed under the power of his grip. He drew a deep breath, calming himself. "Why Jubal?" he asked.

McCloud seemed uncertain about what he could, or should, say. He glanced toward the bartender to make sure he was out of earshot, then lowered his voice. "You've heard about the mutilations?"

Gunter nodded; his eyes glistened.

"And you heard about the fox left behind Leslie Adams' house?"

Again Gunter nodded. There was a tic near his left eye.

"Its heart was taken. Just like Eva and Amy."

The beer glass smashed in Gunter's hand. He didn't look at it; seemed oblivious to it. "Their hearts?" His voice came out in a growl, low, bestial.

McCloud started, then stared at the bar. Blood dripped into the spilled beer and broken glass, a shard of which protruded from Gunter's palm. "Gunter. Your hand."

Gunter's eyes glared at McCloud. "Whoever he is, I'll find him and I'll destroy him." He raised his hands. "I'll destroy him with these."

McCloud watched as blood dripped down onto Gunter's sharply creased trousers, then raised his eyes to Gunter's. They brimmed hatred. It sent a sudden chill through him, but he wasn't certain why. He had a vision of the man confronting Jubal Duval and the terrible result that would produce. Was that it? He wasn't sure. "Gunter. You're talking madness. You've got to let Paul handle this. Paul and the state cops."

Gunter's eyes glittered. "But they don't do anything. None of you do anything at all."

Jim McCloud pulled his car off the road about 200 yards from Paul Devlin's house. His hands gripped the steering wheel and he stared blindly through the windshield. The booze was already clouding his brain. But he knew he had to

get it over with; run his little errand for Ray Perot. He had put
it off all day, and he knew it was only a question of time before
Perot called to find out what had happened. God, how he hated
that sleazy sonofabitch. The bastard controlled a bank, and
now, by controlling it, he controlled his newspaper.

And the God damned booze wasn't helping. He was hitting
it every day now; hitting it so hard he was having blackouts
that scared the living hell out of him. He was awakening mornings unable to remember what had happened the night before.
Unable to remember what he had done, what he had said.
There were times that Tim and his wife, Mary, stared at him
in the mornings, or, even worse, seemed unable to look at him
at all, that made him feel that something had happened, or
had been said, that had hurt them. But he had never had the
courage to ask about it. And now the blackouts were coming
during the day, and, at times, he found himself unable to remember what he had done a half hour earlier. It was like a
God damned black hole he couldn't account for at all.

Yeah, he told himself. And you know the solution to that
problem too. You've known it for years. You just don't have
the guts to do it.

He took his hands from the wheel and stared at the trembling
fingers. He wondered if it was from the booze or the fear of
what he was thinking. He gritted his teeth and squeezed his
eyes shut.

Go run your errand, he told himself. Be a good little puppy
and do what you're told.

Paul Devlin sat on the wide rear deck of his house and stared
out into the woods. His heart was racing and perspiration
filmed his forehead and ran rivulets beneath his shirt. He had
dozed off in the chair and the dream had come again, until
the intensity of it finally jarred him awake. He looked down
at the revolver that lay on the low table in front of him, its
empty cylinder open. The cleaning kit lay next to it. He had
brought the weapon out to clean and oil it but had not done
so. He looked away from it now.

It was a different revolver from the one in the dream, a
backup weapon he had never carried on the job. The other one
was still in the police property room in New York. He had

never retrieved it after the routine ballistics tests were completed . . . after they had exonerated him . . . after . . . He shook his head, driving the thought away.

The dream had been bad, that was all. Rolk's face so clear, so real. Staring at him, as it always did, over the barrel of the revolver. The same pleading eyes, changing then to relief, and finally to pleasure. That final, knowing smile. He closed his eyes, fighting off the final image, the one that always ended the dream, the one when he pulled the trigger and sent the bullet smashing into Rolk's forehead.

The sound of the car coming up the gravel driveway made him jump. His hands gripped the arms of the chair, and he realized, for the first time, his heart was racing. He drew three quick breaths, then turned and saw Jim McCloud starting up the steps of the rear deck. Devlin studied him quickly, the redder than usual face, the slight hesitation to his step. You could probably lock him up for drunk driving, he thought. Oh, shit, he told himself. There's been enough of that today.

"Hi, Jim. Want some coffee?"

McCloud shook his head. "Need to talk to you a minute."

He took a chair opposite Devlin, then stared briefly at the revolver and cleaning kit on the table between them. "Thought you didn't use one of those things," he said.

"Looks like I may have to start carrying it again," he said.

McCloud nodded. "Yeah. Somebody who likes to carve people's hearts out, it wouldn't be too bright to confront him with empty hands."

Devlin's eyes hardened. "How'd you find out about the hearts? We haven't released that. Not to anyone."

"In this town? You kidding?"

Devlin glanced down at the revolver, then back at McCloud. "That what you wanted to talk about?" he asked, angry, but glad to be off the subject of the revolver.

"In a way."

McCloud twisted in his chair, as though trying to settle himself. He clasped his hands together in front of him. "I want to know when you're going to bring Jubal in and lean on him?"

"We already talked about that. You know something new I don't?"

"Just that he's the most logical suspect you've got."

"Not to me."

"Come on. For Christsake, Paul, the man's mentally unbalanced. He was even too homicidal for Special Forces."

"That's only a rumor. I told you I've seen his records."

"That they threw him *out* on a section eight." McCloud's voice was incredulous.

"But not for *that* reason." He leaned forward. "What else makes you think I should bring him in?"

"The way these people were killed, Paul. The mutilation. That fucking fox." He too leaned forward to meet Devlin across the table, across the revolver. "I was in Vietnam, Paul. As a correspondent. I saw the kind of terror campaigns Special Forces ran behind enemy lines to demoralize Charlie. This is the kind of stuff they were taught. They called it the Phoenix Program."

Devlin leaned back in his chair. His face was tired. "We had a series of murders in New York, about ten years ago. Somebody was picking up hookers, taking them to cheap hotels that offered kitchenettes, then screwing them; killing them; cutting out their hearts, and cooking and eating them. *The Daily News* nicknamed him 'the hearteater.' "

"So what's the point?" McCloud demanded.

"The point is that when the detectives working the case caught him, he turned out to be this nice, quiet kid. The point is, he was never in Vietnam, never in Special Forces. He was never anywhere. He was just fucking crazy."

Devlin's voice had remained calm, quiet, and the fact that it had seemed to irritate McCloud. "Nice story. But what does it mean?" he snapped.

"It means I'm not gonna drag Jubal's ass in until I have more to go on than the fact he was in Special Forces. It means I'm not gonna label him a monster in everybody's mind until *I* know he is. And it means I'm not gonna spin my wheels going in one direction, and only one direction, until I'm sure it's the right one."

"And if you're wrong?"

"I've been wrong before."

"The odds are heavier if you're wrong now."

"You think I don't know that, Jim." An edge had come into Devlin's voice and his eyes had narrowed. He fought the anger. "I'm gonna do this the way it has to be done, Jim. Just like you run your newspaper the way it has to be done."

McCloud's color deepened; his lips moved soundlessly for a moment, and Devlin wondered what he wanted to say but could not.

"I'm afraid I just can't support you on this, Paul."

"I'm sorry about that, Jim. I wish you could."

"So do I," McCloud said.

Gunter Kline lived in a converted carriage house at the rear of his restaurant. The first floor remained what it had always been—a garage now housing Gunter's station wagon and restored twenty-year-old Porsche, rather than the horses and carriages it had once held—but the upper floor had become pure elegance, one enormous room that had obviously felt the hand of a decorator, with an open kitchen, dining area, and a massive living room dotted with an eclectic selection of antiques that gave it the feel of a small museum.

Leslie felt her breath catch as she and Devlin stepped into the room—were swallowed by it.

"Gunter, this is wonderful. Tell me you found all this beautiful furniture at estate sales here in Vermont."

"I wish I could," Gunter said. "But I'm afraid most of it belonged to my parents—part of their legacy to me."

"You can take the rich boy out of New York," Devlin quipped, allowing the rest of the altered saying to remain unspoken.

Gunter smiled with pleasure. He was dressed in a black silk jacket and white slacks that were obviously tailored for him, a pale blue shirt and—something Leslie had never seen outside of films—a red patterned ascot at his neck.

"And you look as elegant as the room," she said.

"And you make the room seem truly lovely for the first time," Gunter responded, kissing her cheek.

"What about me?" Devlin said, gesturing to his brown tweed jacket and tan turtleneck.

Gunter shrugged. "You, Paul, look as you always do, I'm afraid."

"And how's that?" Devlin asked, fighting back a smile.

"Like a cop on his way to Sunday mass."

Devlin tried to look hurt, then joined the laughter. "Well, you can take the poor boy out of New York too," he said.

Gunter seated them on an elegant red Victorian sofa that, to

Devlin, looked like it had come from a turn-of-the-century bordello, served wine from a chilled bucket beside his own chair, and gestured to a tray of canapes on the small table before them.

"This is my first night out for a social evening in Vermont," Leslie said. "I doubt any future ones will quite match it." She gave a small smile. "Of course I haven't been inundated with invitations," she added. "I don't think scarlet women are in this year."

"You've apparently found your reception less than friendly," Gunter said. He waved a dismissive hand. "It will pass. Not quickly, but it will."

"Will I still be young enough to enjoy it?" Leslie asked.

Gunter grinned at her. "Just barely." He leaned forward, cupping his wine glass in both hands. "The people here are very insular. And, in many ways, very unsure of themselves with outsiders. But once they know that you accept them as they are, they can be very warm, very giving."

"Even the women?" Leslie asked, allowing her skepticism to hang heavy in her voice. "They all act like I'm here to lure their bovine boyfriends and husbands along the path of perdition."

"You probably terrify them," Gunter said. "A beautiful woman who could obviously have any man she wanted, but who, just as obviously, doesn't need one. That's so far out of their realm of experience, it's truly alien." He offered her another smile. "But even that too will pass."

"When?" Leslie demanded.

"Sometime before you die," Devlin offered. "As long as you live to be ninety."

"That's what I thought," Leslie said. "I'll have to outlive them."

"Paul exaggerates," Gunter said, taking Leslie's glass and pouring more wine. "It will take no more than two or three years."

Leslie accepted her wine and rolled her eyes.

"But think of how you lived in the city," Gunter said. "People who lived down the hall from you for years, who didn't even know your name, or care to."

"And who probably wouldn't have taken the time to call the cops if they'd heard you screaming," Devlin added.

Leslie raised one hand in self-defense. "Okay, I'll give it time." She giggled. "But not more than one or two years. After that I'm going to get annoyed." She raised her glass in a mock salute. "Thank God there are enough fellow aliens here."

Gunter deftly changed the subject and began regaling them with stories of his father's restaurant before he moved it from New York. The stories were witty and outrageous, and Gunter told them with a natural panache that seemed to enthrall Leslie, invoking alternating bits of laughter, disbelief, and wonder. Devlin sat and watched, wishing he could add his own repertoire of cop stories; knowing without question how inappropriate they would be to the tone of the evening.

You're feeling a bit of jealousy, he told himself. Seeing your "date" stolen away from you like this.

He watched Leslie pick up a silver framed photograph on the table beside her. It was a formal portrait of a man and woman. The woman appeared to be sitting in the same high-backed Victorian chair in which Gunter was now seated. The man, at least 20 years the woman's senior, stood behind her.

"This is a lovely picture," Leslie said.

"My parents," Gunter offered. "Both dead, I'm afraid."

"Your mother was very, very beautiful."

"Yes, she was. I think I worshiped her as a boy. I was so proud of her. So proud to be seen with her. She had the kind of external beauty that made everyone look at her."

"External?" Leslie asked.

"Well, that's all they could see, of course. Her internal beauty was even greater." He smiled, almost sheepishly, Leslie thought. "Of course little boys all think their mothers are so very perfect," he added. "It sort of goes with the territory, I think. It certainly did with me."

Leslie smiled at the idea, replaced the photograph, and allowed her eyes to roam the room, noticing for the first time that other photos of Gunter's mother were strategically placed on other tables and shelves, along with a portrait hanging on one wall. She silently hoped that one day a child of her own would think of her with such love.

"And now, if you are ready," Gunter said, "you will taste sauerbraten as you have never tasted it before. Not even in my own restaurant." He raised his hands, holding them like a surgeon prepared to enter the operating theater, the long, strong fingers spread apart. "Sauerbraten made with these own hands, from my mother's favorite recipe."

"I can't wait," Devlin said. "When she finds out you cooked for us yourself, Phillipa will never forgive me for leaving her at home."

"You tell her that next time I will invite only her and cook an even better dinner."

"If I tell her, she'll hound you until you do it," Devlin said.

"Tell her," Gunter said. "And now to the dining table."

# CHAPTER
## 10

Watching her. Just as you watched her standing outside police headquarters. She is beautiful; knows how to make herself beautiful to men. Knows how to smile, how to use her eyes on them. Letting them know there's so much more available if she decides to offer it as well.

She is coarse. Nothing but a cheap bolt of cloth made to seem fine by dyes and display. But you won't be fooled.

But she *is* beautiful. Watch how she uses her body. The way she leans toward a man; the supple movement. Her body cries out, telling him how much he'd enjoy lying with her, how much pleasure it would give him to reach out and touch the parts of her she only hints about. She is a whore. Coarse and whorish. Inside her there is nothing but evil and rot.

Oh, God, how beautiful she is, though. The line of her cheek and jaw. The shape of her lips, full and rich and offering that slight hint of a pout. Her long, thin neck, which makes her seem so much taller than she is. And her blouse, the way it plunges down; it makes it seem as if her neck reaches all the way to . . . Hands begin to open and close and breath becomes ragged. . . . All the way to those filthy things that cover her lying, beating heart. Filthy, lying, rotten, cheating slut. Using those filthy things to cover a heart so black and cruel. Saying: Look how beautiful these are. How could they hide anything evil, anything vile and punishing.

But even now you can hear it beating. Steady and hard and cold. Oh, so cold and cruel. And she knows it too. Knows in time it will be discovered. Knows that those soft, round breasts can only hide it for so long. Knows that the blackness beneath that soft, white innocence will come out. You can feel it now just from the sound. That steady, pulsing beat. Hard and dark and threatening. And only the knife can stop it, can cut out the evil, can stop that constant beating that keeps growing louder and louder and louder until you want to take your hands and cover your ears to stop it.

But even then it won't stop. You know that. And if you covered your ears they'd all look at you, and they'd know you were hearing it; know you were the one who could hear the evil inside her. No, you can't let that happen. Not ever. Because you know they'd stop you then, and the evil would go on.

It's good how you can move among them, and they can't tell that you know; that you hear it. No, they must not know. Not until you're finished. Maybe not even then. But how you wish you could tell someone. But *they* know. Just before you stop the evil. *They* know. And tonight you'll stop it again. And she'll be the one. And *she* will know. Just before you take her heart in your hands and watch the beating stop. She will know. And deep inside—inside her immortal soul—she will be grateful.

Paul Devlin watched his daughter's small chest rise and fall in the gentleness of sleep. She had already been asleep when he returned home from Gunter's, and she seemed so lovely to him, so innocent, so perfect. He adjusted her covers and slipped quietly out of the room, then moved down the uncarpeted stairs as softly as possible to avoid disturbing her.

He went to the desk, set in a living room alcove that he used as an in-home office, sat, and began to review the list of names he had made after Jim McCloud had left. McCloud. The damned fool thought it was all so simple. Just pick the likeliest suspect and haul his ass in and everything would resolve itself. Likeliest suspect, shit. He had learned about likeliest suspects. Learned it in the worst possible way. And he had learned something about this killer too. He wanted his work known; wanted his slaughter understood. And if you go in the wrong direction, he's going to point it out to you. And he's going to point it out with his knife.

A quiet terror seeped into his mind. He knew this killer so well, deep inside, knew him, understood him. And, yet, didn't. It was the veil drawn across his mind that he had felt before; that was keeping him from finding the one thing he needed to clear the case.

*Clear the case.* The phrase Rolk had used. *Clear the case, Paul.* His last words. Rolk, who had never carried a gun, just like you refuse to carry one now. So maybe you're becoming Rolk? Maybe you've done that already. Maybe your mind, ridden with guilt, turned you into the man, the mentor, you executed. A shiver went through him and he fought it. He stared at the book on his desk, his book on the pleasure of killing. That's why you understand this killer, he told himself. Because you know what he feels; because you've felt it yourself.

Devlin stared at the legal pad holding the list of names. It included everyone who had been at Eva Hyde's funeral; everyone who had been anywhere near her the night she died. Anyone who had been part of Amy Little's past, regardless of whether the names made any sense or not. Anyone with any connection to anything even remotely close to the murders. He stared at the last two names. Jack Chambers. Leslie Adams.

So why do you keep calling the killer *him.* Electa Litchfield's on the list too. You know better than that. You know the killer could be anyone. *Anyone.* Don't do the same idiotic thing McCloud is telling you to do with Jubal.

Devlin picked up the telephone and dialed. His hand was shaking. The number was still burned in his memory; always would be, he suspected. A familiar voice answered on the third ring—the man there, working late, as they always had.

"Moriarty, you hump. Don't you ever get your fat ass out of a chair?"

There was an irritated pause on the other end of the line. "Paul? Is that you? You useless piece of shit?" The voice was suddenly pure pleasure. "How you been, hotshot?"

"Up to my ass in cow shit and maple syrup. How about you?"

"Ugh. It's the same down here. The same fucking zoo. The

assholes are icing each other so fast, we don't need a homicide task force. All we need is more overtime for the Sanitation Department so they can pick up the fucking stiffs faster."

"How's the new boss working out?" Devlin asked.

"Shit, we got another new one last month. A tough little dago. Pain in the fucking ass. But at least he knows what he's doing. Not like the scumbag he replaced. But it's still not like the old days."

There was a heavy note of sadness in Moriarty's voice, one Devlin understood and shared. The man was his friend, had been for many years, and he understood what had happened. Understood and sympathized. He doubted he would ever fully forgive him for it, but, then, Devlin knew he would never forgive himself.

"Sounds like I'm not missing much," Devlin said.

"Not unless you miss lots of overtime, lousy coffee, and bags under your fucking eyes. So tell me what's happening up there. You still sodomizing cows in your spare time?"

"Only on Fridays." Devlin hesitated, then pushed ahead. "But I do have a problem I could use some help on."

"Tell me, and if I can do it, it's yours. You covered my ass enough times all the years we worked together."

Devlin felt relief course through his gut. Not because the help would be given, but because Moriarty still wanted to give it.

"Thanks," he said, then moved on quickly to avoid embarrassing either of them. "What I got is a couple of murders up here. Same perp, no motive. Uses a knife. Cuts their hearts out."

"Jesus. Nice guy. When you catch him, tell him he coulda worked steady in the Port Authority Bus Terminal, he wasn't so fonda cow shit."

"Yeah, I hear you," Devlin said. "Anyway, what I've got is a list of names, d.o.b.'s and descriptions. A couple from Philly, one from the city, one from Boston, the rest all from up here. I need NCIC* checks on all of them, and local checks on the ones from Philly, Boston, and New York. I thought I'd get it all a lot faster if an NYPD dick asked for it than if it came from some police chief in Boonieville."

---

* National Crime Information Computer.

"State cops no good for you up there, huh?" It was more a statement than a question.

"I'm not sure they'd even be interested. And if they were, I'm not sure I'd ever get all the info back."

"Fucking assholes," Moriarty said. "Give me until tomorrow night. I should have most of it, if not all by then."

"Thanks, babe. I knew I could count on you," Devlin said, then began reading off the information.

"Can we keep it? Can we?"

Leslie stared down at the cat that was rubbing itself, back and forth, against her legs. Robbie had found the animal sitting on the back porch when they had gotten home from Paul's house and had immediately called her back out to see it. Now the plea to keep the animal was urgent, almost desperate.

"I guess so," she said. "As long as it doesn't belong to anybody."

"It doesn't," Robbie assured her. "Just look at it. It's too raggedy to belong to anyone."

Leslie stared at the cat. It certainly was raggedy. But it was easy to see it could be a lovely-looking animal too. If it was cared for.

The cat, about nine months old, she guessed, continued to rub against her legs. It was long and sleek, a pale gray, without a spot of any other color, and striking blue eyes. It must have some Siamese back in it somewhere, she told herself.

She stooped down and began stroking its back. "What shall we call it?" she asked, grinning.

"Oh, great!" Robbie exclaimed. He became suddenly serious. "Uh, is it a guy or a girl?" he asked.

Leslie picked up the animal, turned it over and examined it. "A girl, I think." She shrugged. "I was never much good at telling about cats."

"So you think, maybe, it's a girl." He spoke the question as fact.

Leslie nodded again. "Best I can do, tiger."

"So, let's call her 'Maybe,' " Robbie said.

Leslie's smile widened with the idea. "I love it," she said. She was still holding the cat and now extended it out before her. "I dub you Maybe," she intoned. "Which means, maybe you'll get fed; maybe, if you're good, you'll be allowed in the house—"

"And, maybe, she'll catch the mice in the barn," Robbie added.

"As long as she doesn't bring them around to show us," Leslie said. She glanced back toward the barn, thinking of what had been found behind it. No, she thought. I've definitely had enough of dead and mutilated animals. "Time to go to bed," she said to Robbie. "School tomorrow."

"I know," he said. He hesitated, thinking, then looked at her with worried eyes. "You think we're safe from Jack now?" he asked.

"I don't know," she said, deciding not to minimize the situation with Robbie and thereby minimize him as well. "I got a temporary order from the court that says he has to stay away from us, or he goes to jail. Paul says he'll enforce it, personally. Whether Jack will listen or not, who knows?"

"You like Paul, don't you?" Robbie asked.

Leslie smiled and nodded. "How about you?"

Robbie shrugged. "He seems okay. I don't know."

Leslie reached out and stroked his cheek, touched by the bit of proprietorship she sensed. "You're still my main man," she said. "But only if you get your butt up to bed."

"I'm goin', boss lady." He glanced at her a little sheepishly. "Can I take Maybe?"

"Maybe you can. Maybe not." She grinned at him, then ruffled his hair. "Sure. I just hope it doesn't have fleas. I'd hate to have a brother who scratches himself with his hind leg all the time."

Business had picked up at Gunter's restaurant by the time Jim McCloud returned. He had been frustrated and angry with himself after his talk with Paul Devlin and had decided he needed a drink and companionship to soothe the feelings of self-reproach that boiled inside him.

He had driven home, checked on Tim, and told his wife he was going back to work for a couple of hours. The look on her face had not helped.

Now he wondered if it was worth it. The bar had livened up in his absence, but not the way he had hoped. Billy Perot and Linnie French dominated the center stools—something that seemed to have ruined Gunter's mood as well—and supercilious Louis Ferris anchored one corner, gazing at Linnie like a starving dog in front of a butcher shop. Even Electa was there, seated at a small table in the dining room, surveying the bar scene—and him, he decided—with abject disgust.

McCloud took a stool at the other end of the bar, away from everyone, waved to Electa, then turned away from her disapproval. Gunter came over and took the stool next to him.

"You decided to come back, I see."

"Like the proverbial bad penny," McCloud said. "Glad to see business has picked up for you." He made no attempt to hide the sarcasm in his voice.

Gunter grunted. Over his shoulder McCloud could see Linnie French talking to Billy with all the body English she could muster—ample chest pushed forward, coy pout on her lips, hips wiggling on her stool to emphasize her words. Louis Ferris, watching intently, seemed one step short of drool.

McCloud was about to say something to Gunter when the front door opened and Ray Perot marched in. McCloud let out an audible sigh, causing Gunter to look over his shoulder. His glower deepened.

Perot walked up to his son and Linnie, stroked Linnie's cheek, then stared at Billy. "Wait here," he said, then continued toward McCloud and Gunter.

"You take care of that matter we talked about?" he asked McCloud without preamble, ignoring Gunter.

McCloud nodded. "It wasn't well received." McCloud prayed the man would not discuss his "errand" openly in front of Gunter. He glanced at Gunter, then back to Perot, hoping he'd pick up on the message.

"Well, I guess you know what to do, then." Perot kept his eyes steady on McCloud, emphasizing his own message, then turned to Gunter. "'Lo Gunter," he said, pivoting abruptly and heading back to his son and Linnie.

"You seem to have discovered the knack of being ignored by the great man," McCloud said.

Gunter stared at him, then looked away. "I work at it," he said. The expression on his face was not dissimilar to Electa's, McCloud thought. He glanced into the dining room. Electa was staring at Perot, Billy, and Linnie. She seemed engulfed by a near-maniacal rage.

Perot stared down at Linnie. Her blouse plunged deeply; one button was open to make it even more revealing. She leaned slightly forward and hunched her shoulders, improving his view. She had an image in her mind of his old cock stiffening. It amused and pleased her, especially since she knew he wasn't going to get what he coveted.

She smiled at him. She had been teasing him, leading him on for months now, giving in only when she had to. To her he was just like that little creep Loopy Louie, whose eyes she could feel boring into her back. The only one she had given anything to regularly was Billy, and she wasn't sure why she had done even that, except that he was the only semi-decent thing around who had shown any interest. But it would only be a few more months now before she had enough money together to leave this God-forsaken hole and move to Burlington, or Rutland, or some other place where she'd have a chance to meet somebody, *anybody*, who wanted something more from her than her mouth wrapped around his fat prick.

Linnie giggled. "Oh, Ray, you say the funniest things." She had only a vague idea what Perot had said—she'd been only half listening—but the leering grin on his face told her *he* thought it was funny, or dirty, or both.

"Just want you to be up to par at work, honey," Perot said. "Can't do that if you're out to all hours with Billy boy, here."

Billy sat stonefaced and silent, the only hint at his feelings showing in the red that had come to his neck and ears. Ray hadn't turned on him yet, hadn't humiliated him in front of the woman and the others, but that could be coming at any moment. It was something that was never far away.

Almost as if given a cue by Billy's thoughts, Ray turned and stared at him. The look was hard and level, and Billy knew that whatever words Ray offered would be an order, no matter how they were phrased.

"It wouldn't do you no harm to have an early night either," Ray said. He turned back to Linnie. "*Boy* likes to burn it at both ends. Can't wait until he becomes *man* enough to learn how to pace himself."

Linnie giggled and picked up the line Ray had offered her,

wanted her to use. "Oh, he'll be man enough one of these days." She giggled again. "Don't you worry about that, Ray."

Billy glared at her, and Linnie knew she'd be in for a rough ride if she were alone with him now. But she wasn't going to be alone with him tonight. Ray had already made that clear. And by tomorrow Billy would have forgotten it, like he always did, his mind filled with whatever new need had seized it, or whatever new insult had fixed itself in his head.

"But I think you're right, Ray. I think it's going to be early to bed for me tonight." She looked at Ray coyly, knowing he wanted her to, knowing that he wanted to think about her in bed, but not alone. Too bad, Ray, she told herself. But like you said, I need my rest, not some horny old billygoat.

Ray turned back to Billy and fished some change out of his pocket. "Get me some cigarettes, will ya son?" he asked.

When Billy had started for the cigarette machine Ray turned back to Linnie. "You go on home," he said. "And I'll stop by a little later. Got somethin' I'd like to talk to you about."

"Oh, Ray, I really am tired," she said. "Can't we talk about it now?" She saw the irritation begin to form in his eyes, and she turned coy again to ease him out of it. "I mean, I'd love to have you stop by if I thought I was up to a visit from you. And, besides, my sister's visiting me from Rutland. It wouldn't be private at all."

Ray's eyes narrowed. "Didn't know you had a sister in Rutland."

"She's really a half-sister. But she's got a whole mouth," Linnie added quickly, knowing Ray's penchant for discretion. "And she sure likes to flap it."

"Well, she'll be asleep later," Ray said. "You just try to keep yourself awake."

Shit, Linnie thought. "I'll try," she said, the coy look returning, knowing she wouldn't any more than she'd produce her imaginary sister. But it was enough for Ray. She could tell that by the way he was smiling.

Billy returned and placed a pack of Pall Malls on the bar. Ray scooped it up, without looking at him, or acknowledging they had been offered to him, opened the pack, and lit one.

" 'Bout time, ain't it, Billy?" he asked. "I got a truckload full a work for you tomorrow."

"Yeah, I was just thinkin' the same thing myself," Billy said.

His neck and ears were almost scarlet now. "I'll talk to you tomorrow, Linnie." His eyes laid hard on her face, letting her know she wasn't going to like that "talk" one little bit.

Linnie smiled at him with all the warmth she could muster; all the disappointment she could force into her eyes. "I hope so," she said.

Billy moved quickly to the front door, pushed through it, and almost collided with Jubal Duval, who was standing on the wide deck that led to the entrance, staring through the front window.

"What the hell you doin' here?" Billy snapped, realizing quickly it was the wrong question, the wrong tone of voice, by the sudden narrowing of Jubal's eyes.

"You tellin' me where I can be now, Billy?" Jubal asked. His voice was low and soft, but still carried a very real threat in it.

Billy faltered, then caught hold of himself. "Just wondered what you were doin' snoopin' around out here."

Jubal's hand shot out like a snake and had Billy's windpipe squeezed between his fingers before he could move. His ability to breathe disappeared and his eyes bulged. "Don't never snoop, Billy," Jubal hissed. "Just watch what I wanna watch." His eyes narrowed and his head tilted questioningly to one side. "You wanna be with them Saigon whores, that's your business, your soul you gotta worry 'bout. I wanna watch, that's my business."

Jubal released his throat, and Billy took two involuntary steps back, his own hand moving to his throat to massage the pain. "What the hell you talkin' about, Saigon whores?" he croaked.

Jubal stared at him, then turned and walked away. Billy watched him as he walked across the street to his truck, climbed in, and sat there, unmoving.

"Crazy motherfucker," Billy hissed under his breath. Saigon fucking whores. He was talkin' about Linnie. And she was nothin' but a fuckin' Vermont whore. And he was sure gonna fix her fuckin' ass. Fix it good.

From his seat at the near corner of the bar, Louis Ferris had had a clear view of the window and of Billy's confrontation with Jubal. He grinned openly, then the grin hardened into an ugly mask. His eyes moved back to Linnie French and he wondered if that old fool Perot would ever leave so he could speak to her. He glanced into the dining room and caught Electa Litchfield's eye. They had seen each other often before she retired, and had been reasonably cordial—at least before that bitch Amy Little had placed that cloud around him. But now Electa was staring at him like he was some kind of filth. The same way his mother had always looked at him, the way so many women had looked at him.

Movement at the bar brought his attention back. Linnie was up and preparing to leave. And it seemed she was leaving alone. Good, he thought. Good, good, good.

Jim McCloud also watched Linnie leave and decided it was time for him as well. His mind was already clouded, and he couldn't remember if he had been home yet or not. Didn't matter. Didn't matter. He eased himself from his stool, making sure his feet were firmly beneath him.

"Time to go, Gunter. Good night," he mumbled.

Gunter stared straight ahead, eyes fixed on the mirror behind the bar. He grunted, and McCloud couldn't tell if it was intended as a response or not. He didn't really care.

You can hear it. Just behind the door. Beating, beating. Such a small, ugly little house, holding all that evil. All that cruelty. But it's there, waiting for you. Waiting for you to cut it out. You just have to be careful. Have to circle the house quietly. So quietly. Have to make sure she's alone. Alone and waiting for you. Waiting for your knife.

The hands tremble slightly. Not in fear, but rather in anticipation. Perspiration beads the forehead, even though the outside temperature is only 45 degrees. There is no breeze, and no moon. The night is still and dark and quiet.

The windows are small and square and each is lighted from within. They are high enough off the ground so your chin rests easily on the sill as you look inside. The living room: nothing. Slowly. Quietly. The bedroom: clothes scattered on chairs and floor. But no person. No one. The bathroom window. Too high; the glass frosted. Noise coming from inside. Water running; someone moving. Quickly. Quickly now. Can't hear you with all the noise in the bathroom. Second bedroom: empty, even the bed's stripped down to the mattress. Back porch. Quickly. But quietly, just in case. Kitchen: empty, empty. Can see through to the small dining area and living room. No one. No one at all.

A small laugh comes out as a hiss. The pulsing, beating, throbbing. Stronger now. Surging in the temples until it's almost painful. A hand opens and closes rhythmically on a foot-long piece of lead pipe held loosely, almost tenderly. The head snaps up, registering an end to the water sounds. The empty hand closes into a fist, rises, and beats a loud tattoo on the glass panel of the door.

Movement. It stops. Hesitation. Now movement again. She's in the kitchen, standing, looking toward the door. A look of confusion, concern on her face. There's a towel wrapped around her head, and she's wearing a flimsy, whorish bathrobe. She comes forward, her breasts jiggling, stops and stares through the glass panel, eyes suspicious. Recognition. A smile fills her lips. As false as her filthy, beating heart. The door swings back; the smile remains.

"Hi. I was in the shower. Have you—"

The hand snakes out from behind the back. The lead pipe crashes into her temple, and she falls back, her body sprawled on the floor, legs twitching, eyes rolled back. Closing now. Closing.

Quickly, quickly. Tape across the mouth. Now drag her by the hair, through the kitchen, into the small hall. Now into the bedroom. Heavy. Heavy. Lift her on to the bed. Heavy, awkward. Dead weight. But not dead yet. Breathing. Breathing. The heart beating. Beating so loud it almost hurts your ears.

Tape on the ankle. Now to the bedpost. Now the other. Quickly, before she wakes. Now the wrist. Yes, yes. Now the other. Oh, yes.

Hands reach for the robe, ripping it away, exposing her filthy nakedness. Yes, yes. Now only need to wait. Wait for her to wake up. Wake up and see. See.

The knife rises before the eyes, glinting, gleaming in the light. Beautiful, so beautiful.

Minutes pass. Waiting. Hours. Days. So long. So long.

The eyelids flutter. Open, then close again. Snap open. Wide. Filled with fear. The head turning, staring at her hands, her feet. Humming, moaning. Words beneath the tape. Slip on top of her, straddling her thighs. Just above that filthy, black thatch of hair. Eyes terrified. And the beating—louder, harder, stronger.

Hands reach out to the mouth; fingers grip the tape and rip it to one side. A cry. Now a whimper. Tears fill the eyes.

"Oh, God . . . Oh, God . . . Please . . . Please let me go . . . Don't hurt me . . . I didn't do anything." The words punctuated by sobs, gasping, pleading. "I'll do anything you want . . . Please . . . Just don't hurt me."

"Filthy slut!" A hissing growl.

"Noooo . . ." Begging. Chest rising and falling, faster and faster and faster. "Are . . . you . . . crazy? . . . Pleeease!"

"Bitch! Filthy, cruel bitch!" Shouted. Hands trembling uncontrollably. Chin quivering with rage. Must control yourself. Control, control, control, control. Hands reach for the tape.

"Noooo." Head shaking back and forth, fighting the tape. "Pleeease . . . Pleee—"

Mumbling now. Mumbling and moaning behind the tape. Almost drowned out by the heart beating stronger and stronger and stronger.

The knife rises again, gleaming, glinting. The body freezes, eyes fixed wide and terrified on the blade.

"It's time." Panting, sweating. Hands trembling in anticipation. The beating louder now. Louder and louder and louder.

The knife lowers to a point just above the pubis. The body stiffens, tries to press itself into the bed. The point touches the skin, and the body jumps involuntarily, driving the point into the flesh. Doing the blade's work for it, surrendering to the need for punishment.

A scream behind the tape, muffled, useless. The point slides in and begins to move upward, slicing the flesh as the bright red blood pours over the stomach. The body arches and begins to shake. Spasm after spasm after spasm. Then it falls back, shaking violently, and the eyes roll back in the head, and suddenly it is still. The knife slices up into the sternum, sawing now, as steam rises from the open wound into the colder air of the room.

A hand slides under the chest, seizing the heart, beating and beating and beating. Then the other, with the knife, probing for the veins and arteries and cutting them away.

The hands retreat in a spray of blood; the knife falls away. The heart lays cupped in both blood-smeared hands, still beating and pulsing.

"Oh, God!" the voice shouts.

Beneath the figure the body lays still and silent and dead.

# CHAPTER
# 11

The heart slips into the plastic bag, is placed on the bed, rolls and quivers slightly with the movement, then is still. The beating has stopped now. There is quiet, profound quiet. Hands slide into the poncho and remove a pressed, withered rose, then a short, sharpened stake. Different from the ones used before. Shorter, easier to carry. A refinement.

A shrill laugh fills the small bedroom. Hands rise above the head, holding the stake, steadying it; then plunge down, driving it, until the body's own resistance stops all movement. A hand moves to the rose.

"Oh, yes." Deep breaths, almost panting, as the rose is used. "Yes . . . yes . . . yes . . ." With each breath expelled, the words come like the ticking of a clock.

Dangerous. It's dangerous here. Another voice, another person, from deep within. Escape, escape, escape, escape.

Eyelids begin to flutter; the eyes roll back; the body sways. "Mother . . . Mother . . . Mother." The words issued in a hiss. "See what filth begets." A soft moan, almost like the lowing of a wounded animal.

*Leave this place!* The other voice shouting into the brain, demanding, ordering.

Eyes snap open and stare wildly at the bed. "Oh, my God!" Run . . . run . . . run . . . run . . .

Ray Perot sagged against the doorjamb, his body doubled over. He retched violently, hands rushing unsuccessfully to his mouth to stem the flow, vomit pushing past his fingers and splattering the bare wood floor.

He turned and rushed into the small hall, his body careening against the walls, eyes blurred, staggering to the rear door, and out into the cold crisp air. At the front of the house he stopped, leaned against a tree and vomited again, spewing sickly bile from an empty stomach. He gasped, the back of one hand wiping away the remnants from mouth and chin, his stomach and chest aching from the sudden, violent expulsion. Face bathed in sweat, he stumbled toward the large, shiny Lincoln parked in the driveway, hands trembling as he leaned against it, steadying himself.

"Dear God. Jesus," he moaned. A shiver moved from his hands to his shoulders, then along the length of his body. His fingers gripped the top of the car fighting off the tremors that wracked his body. His hand sought purchase on the door handle, which seemed to move, evading him. Got to get out of here. Now. Fast. Fast as you can. His mind screaming in his ears, the tremors again wracking his body, almost buckling his knees.

From the cab of the truck, backed into a narrow dirt logging road; obscured by leaf-heavy, overhanging branches, across and slightly down from the house, Billy Perot watched his father. There was a twisted, sneering smile spread across his lips, and his eyes, narrowed to pinpoints, seemed to rivet the man to the spot. His hands tightened on the steering wheel, and he felt a hatred, mixed with satisfaction surge inside him.

Puke your guts out; shake in your boots, his mind cheered on, and he wished he could scream the words out, drive them into the old man's white, fear-filled face. If only he could have been inside the house and witnessed what had caused the reaction. But this was good. As good as he could have right now.

He watched his father climb weakly behind the wheel of the car, fumble there momentarily, then start the engine. He had no fear of being seen. The car would turn in the other direction. He had known that before he had chosen his place. There was nothing in the other direction but a long strip of dirt road, leading to a distant town.

He watched the bright red taillights of the car diminish, and he thought, for a moment, of going inside. No, he told himself. Keep what you have. Keep it, and hold it, and use it. Yeah. Use it. Use it like a sharp knife.

It was 10 o'clock, Sunday morning, and in the distance Devlin could hear the peal of the Congregational church bell, echoing across the valley from the center of East Blake.

From the kitchen he could also hear the sobs of the young woman who had found Linnie French's body, wracking and fearful, filled more with fear and horror than pain or loss. Her name was Ellen Moody, and she had tried to reach Linnie all day Saturday, both at work and at home, and had finally become concerned, and had come to the small house on her way to church that morning.

Devlin stared at what the woman had found, as Quint moved perfunctorily about the body, seeking quick conclusions that could later be confirmed by the post. The body lay on its back, arms and legs spread, marks on the wrists and ankles, indicating each had been tied down. The face, once pretty and young and fresh, was now a bloodless gray, the lips drawn back in a rictus, the eyes filmed and blank and lifeless. The wound, running from pubis through the sternum, had curled back, and the tissue along its edges was dry and crusted, puckering up and away from the sagging musculature. From the right breast, a short wooden stake protruded, the absence of blood around the puncture showing it was inflicted after death. There was a sweet, cloying odor to the body, the start of putrefaction. In all, it was a scene from a butcher shop, no longer human, having no place, no reality in a room where someone had lived and laughed and rested and loved. And yet it had.

And then there was the rose, protruding from Linnie French's vagina, so only the withered flower and an inch or two of stem could be seen. Devlin shuddered.

"Talk to me," Devlin said, eyes fixed on Quint.

"More than a day ago. Late Friday, early Saturday. That's my best guess," Quint said. He removed his glasses, cleaned them, then placed them carefully back. His face looked beaten with weariness. He looked terrified. He shook his head. "Same as Amy Little, best as I can see," he added. "Except for the rose; the way he used it this time."

"And the stake's different," Devlin said.

"Yeah, it is."

"I wonder why?"

Quint gritted his teeth, forced a shrug. "Maybe he ran out of the other kind. Or maybe he couldn't carry a large one with him this time, coming to her house the way he did." He looked down at the rose. "Oh, God, he's a sick bastard. And he's getting sicker. I wish we could find him and kill him."

The force, the ferocity of Quint's words jolted Devlin. It was as if the man had read his own thoughts, thoughts that terrified him. He forced it away.

Devlin nodded. "He didn't take her away either. Didn't take her to a place in the woods like the others."

Quint's head snapped up. "You think he's getting anxious? Impatient, maybe?"

"I hope not," Devlin said. "If he is, he'll start killing faster. Faster even than now."

Devlin turned and stared at the dried vomit just inside the bedroom doorway, dried pieces of food and once-foamy liquid. Quint followed his gaze. "You think it made him sick this time?"

"Either that or somebody else came in here and never called us." Devlin's head snapped up. "If it was the killer, why would it make him sick this time and not the others?"

Quint shrugged. "The closed room. The smell of an open body cavity wouldn't hit as strongly out in the open air." He stared hard at Devlin, as though considering something for the first time. "Or, maybe, he's been killing in a psychotic haze, and this time he came back to himself while he was still with the body. I've read about that in journals. It's something that can happen."

Devlin snorted, acknowledging that speculation was all it gave him. "At least we'll know what he had for dinner."

"That could help. If it was something exotic. We'll know when we analyze it."

"Yeah," Devlin said. "If he ate in a restaurant. And if he paid with a credit card. And if the order slip and the credit slip are still attached to each other. Or, if not, if he'll simply tell us what he ate on Friday and Saturday. Too many fucking ifs."

"Calm down, Paul. It might narrow the suspects. It's more than we've had up to now."

Devlin placed his hands on his hips, causing the windbreaker he was wearing to spread open, revealing a .38 snub-nosed revolver tucked into his waistband in an inside-the-belt holster.

Quint stared at the weapon. "I haven't seen you wearing one of those before," Quint said.

Devlin looked down at the revolver, then away. "Yeah. Well, I don't seem to have much choice anymore. Maybe one of your journals can do an article on how much my hand shakes if I ever have to take it out."

"I hope you do have to take it out, Paul," Quint said. "And I don't think your hand will shake if you do."

"Don't make book on it, Doc. It shook when I put it on this morning." Devlin turned, walked in a circle, then looked at his watch. "I wish those assholes from BCI would get here with their God damned crime lab. The way things are going, they might as well park it here."

Quint looked down at Linnie French. He understood what Devlin was feeling. He too felt the repulsion and frustration of dealing with still another mutilated body. But he also knew it was worse this time, and that made it worse for Devlin. It was Devlin's job to stop it, and he had failed to do that again. Quint found himself wondering what the man would do when he finally caught this monster. Or, even worse, what would happen to him if he didn't. Killers, especially those who were psychopaths, had a tendency to stop, or disappear, or kill themselves before they were caught. And he wondered, given Devlin's history, if the man could deal with such an injustice.

Jack Chambers stared down at his plate of Belgian waffles, wondering why he had ordered them. He picked up his bloody mary—his second—and sipped it, hesitated, then took a longer, more meaningful swallow. Food seemed to have lost its charm, he decided, as he picked up a fork and absently cut into the rich brunch.

It was time to do something. That was the problem. Ever since his arrest he had holed up at the inn, plotting and brooding, but doing nothing. It was time to act; time to show her who was in control. Show her that her relief from abuse order was nothing more than a useless piece of paper; that a smart lawyer could beat it whenever he wanted.

He bit into the waffle and chewed, not tasting it. Of course that wasn't true. The judge would slam him, and slam him hard, if he went anywhere near her without her consent. A small smile played across his lips. And that was the key. To manufacture some proof that she had asked to see him—to vindictively try and set him up, or for whatever reason. Or to show her to be a mentally unstable liar. That might even be easier. There was the history—however brief—of psychiatric treatment. And Larry Withers, her shrink, would attest to that if necessary. All he needed, then, were two other pieces of the puzzle. An absence of witnesses when he went to her and an alibi proving he was somewhere else when she claimed he had violated the order. He took another long pull on the bloody mary. Not easy. But not impossible either. All it would take was a little time and work. He stopped, the glass halfway to his mouth again. And caution. This time he damned well had to be careful.

"Excuse me. Are you Mr. Chambers?"

Jack lowered his glass and looked up into the smiling face of Louis Ferris. He sat back, assuming a practiced look of disinterested importance, tilted his head slightly to one side, and nodded. "Can I help you?" he asked, making it clear he doubted that he could.

Ferris fought to hold his smile, a bit nervously, Jack thought, then leaned slightly forward, as though ready to impart some secret. "Actually, I thought I might be able to help you." He glanced at a vacant chair. "May I join you for a moment?"

Jack nodded toward the chair, then sat forward and steepled his fingers before his eyes, so he could look at Ferris through them. "How did you know who I was?" Jack asked at length.

"Small town, big talk," Ferris said, offering a conciliatory shrug.

Jack stiffened, wondering who the man was; whether he had been sent by that prick Devlin or, perhaps, even Leslie herself. "So what do you want from me?" he said, unable to keep a trace of hostility from his voice.

Ferris's smile flickered, faded, then fought to reassert itself. "As I said, I thought I might be able to help you."

"Why?" Jack's voice was cold and flat.

Ferris toyed with a spoon before him; kept his eyes on it as he spoke. "Let's just say I too was once the victim of accusations made by a female." He looked up. "But that's something that's past, and not germane. In any event, I've met your wife." He smiled again. "Her brother's in my class. Oh, I'm a teacher, by the way. I guess I forgot to tell you that."

"So you met her. And you know her brat brother. So what does that have to do with me?" Jack made no attempt to hide his impatience.

"Well, nothing really," Ferris said. "But, as I said, it's a small town. And there was an instance where she made an accusation against another man. Not a formal one, but enough to get the word around."

Jack sat back, sipping his bloody mary. "Tell me about it."

"Man's name is Billy Perot. Not a very nice young man. Rather unpleasant, really. The son of a very important man around here. The most important, probably." He smiled again. "I think that's why no formal allegations were made, myself." Ferris twisted in his chair, seeking comfort. "But, then, she did invite him to her house, even if it was under the guise of doing some work for her." Ferris's smile came close to a leer. "In my experience, young men who live with their rich daddies don't hire out as handymen."

Jack leaned forward again. "Tell me all about it," he said, his own features switching to a fraternity-boy warmth.

When Ferris had finished his recitation, Jack studied him in silence. He couldn't quite fathom what the man was up to. Whether he was out to cause problems for Billy, or Leslie, or was simply one of those individuals who liked to stir the pot. But one thing he did know was that he just might have found himself the ally he needed.

"So she supposedly fought this Billy Perot off," he offered at length.

"So the story goes. But only after somebody walked in on them." Ferris grinned again. "One can only suspect that also may have contributed to the lack of a formal complaint."

"And, obviously, this Billy was not happy."

Ferris's knowing grin widened. "Would you be?" he asked.

"Where can I find this Billy?" Jack asked.

Ferris leaned forward, his voice low, conspiratorial. He loved it when people who thought they were so smart, so important, showed they weren't very smart at all. "You know Pearlie's roadhouse?"

"Yeah. I know it."

"He's always there on Sunday nights." Ferris sat back. "So am I. If you stop by, I'll be happy to point him out." He stared at Jack, the foolish grin gone now. "Just one thing. Our conversation is private. To Billy or anyone else."

"I don't have a problem with that," Jack said. "You haven't even told me your name." Ferris remained silent. "What time do you suggest?" Jack finally asked.

"Nine o'clock is usually best."

"Nine o'clock then," Jack said.

It was four o'clock when Devlin finally got back to his office and found Billy Perot waiting for him. It had been a frustrating day. Dealing with state police arrogance toward a supposedly small-town cop was infuriating. Especially so since they made it so obvious they were all nothing but a bunch of traffic cops who had taken some courses on how to investigate a homicide.

Devlin slid behind his desk and stared at Billy. And now another flaming asshole to deal with, he told himself.

"What can I do for you, Billy?" he asked, his tone indicating there were a number of things he'd like to do for him, none of which Billy would enjoy.

Billy glanced over his shoulder. "Can we close the door?" he asked.

"Close it," Devlin said. He waited until Billy had done so and returned to his chair. "So tell me why you're here."

Billy's hands attacked each other. Then he seemed to notice and held them still. "I heard about Linnie," he said.

"You come in to confess?"

"Come on, Devlin. Gimme a break."

The hands were at war with each other again.

"Go on," Devlin said.

"My old man was there last night. At Linnie's."

Devlin sat forward, forearms on the desk, eyes intense. "How do you know?"

"I just know, all right?"

"No, it's not all right. The state crime lab is there now, dusting for prints. If your old man's are there, we'll know it. And if yours are, we'll know that too."

"Jesus, Devlin, I dated her. I was there lots of times. You know?"

Devlin jabbed a finger at him. "Just tell me how you know your father was there last night."

Billy's hands twisted together. "I went there and waited outside to see if he'd show up."

"Why?"

Devlin listened as Billy related the Friday night scene at Gunter's restaurant; how his father had ordered him home; ordered Linnie home as well, and how he had been sure some plan had been made between her and Ray to meet up later.

"So you went there to spy on them," Devlin offered.

"I just wanted to see how they were fuckin' with me," Billy snapped. "I had a right to know that, didn't I?"

Devlin raised both hands. "So your father went there. Then what?"

"Well, he's in there, ya know. And then he comes out, all shook up, like. And he leans against a tree and pukes his guts out. And I'm thinkin', holy shit, what the fuck did she do to him, kick him in the nuts, or somethin'." Billy hesitated, distressed by his choice of words, knowing it would remind Devlin of his own confrontation with Leslie Adams.

"Go on," Devlin said.

"Well, then he drives off. That's all. And then, today, I hear about Linnie, and I figure I gotta let somebody know."

Yeah, Devlin thought. Just like Nazi Germany, you gotta inform on your own father. Christ, you must really hate that sonofabitch.

"And you didn't go inside to see what it was all about? After you saw him come out?"

"No. I was supposed to be home, and I figured he'd check to see if I was. And I figured I could tell him I stopped for one last beer at Pearlie's, or somethin'. But I couldn't take the time to get hung up with Linnie."

Devlin leaned back in his chair. Billy Perot. Big, bad Billy. Scared absolutely shitless of old Ray. And hating him for it. Really hating him. And this is your big chance, isn't it? he thought. You not only get rid of a father you hate, but you end up with everything he's got. Yeah, that's the best-case scenario for you, isn't it, Billy? And the worst is, you get me to make his life a living hell, just like he's made yours.

"Okay, Billy. You did the right thing telling me. I'll check it out."

A nervous smile formed on Billy's lips, then disappeared. "Listen. You gotta understand somethin'. I ain't gonna testify against him, or nothin'. I mean, this is between you and me. You can't tell him I told you. You do, and I deny it. I ain't puttin' my ass in the middle. You gotta understand that."

"Don't worry, Billy. I understand. I'll protect your confidentiality, as long as you're straight with me." Devlin emphasized the final words. "But you fuck with me, and I won't care who knows what. Understood?"

Devlin could see Billy's mind working, playing out the probable results of his treachery should his father learn of it. Gotcha, Billy boy, he told himself. From now on your ass belongs to me.

"Yeah, no problem," Billy assured him, his eyes very nervous now. "I just wanna do what's right."

"That's all I want too, Billy. I just want you to do the right thing."

Billy hadn't been gone five minutes when Gunter Kline marched into Devlin's office, his face torn, haggard, every bit the man who was about to do something he detested.

"I saw your car outside," Gunter began. "I was going to wait and talk to you on Monday, but then I saw your car as I was going by."

Devlin smiled. "Yeah, it's okay, Gunter. I'm here. It's not a problem."

"It's just—" Gunter stopped, then took the chair Billy had just vacated. "It's just that I like McCloud. I consider him a friend. It's just what he's doing. What I think he's doing. I just can't stomach it."

Jesus, Devlin thought. What is this? Rat on your friend or relative day. The God damned moon must be full. "Ease up, Gunter. If it's something I should know, then that's the bottom line."

Gunter nodded and seemed to draw himself up, but the haggard look remained. He was dressed for the out of doors, unusual in itself, and he lacked any trace of his normal, dapper self.

"Last Friday night, at the restaurant, I overheard Jim and Ray Perot talking." He shook his head. "No, that's wrong. Ray was talking, giving orders really. To Jim. And the gist of it, as far as I could tell, involved you. It seemed like Perot wanted him to use the paper against you. To stop you from doing something, or get you to do something. I'm not sure."

"And Jim?" Devlin asked.

"He didn't say much. He didn't have to. The look on his face, when Perot left, said it for him."

Gunter's face was red and angry, mixed with shame, Devlin thought, over what he was doing. "I appreciate you telling me." He paused. "Who else was there that night, Gunter?"

Gunter seemed momentarily confused. "Why . . . Billy was there . . ." He paused to think. "And that girl of his. Linnie something. And Louis Ferris, I think. Yes. Louis, definitely. And Electa Litchfield. Although she was in the dining room."

Full house, Devlin thought.

"Why do you ask?" There was a look of confusion in Gunter's eyes.

Devlin drew a long breath, telling himself Gunter would learn of it eventually. He just didn't like being the one to tell him. Not given his reaction to Eva Hyde's and Amy Little's deaths, and their connections to his restaurant.

"Linnie French was found murdered this morning. Same as the others."

The color drained from Gunter's face. "And she was at my restaurant, she was at Wolfgang's that night."

Devlin said nothing, he simply watched Gunter as the man stared at his desktop. Then his head snapped up and he glared at Devlin. "And Jubal was there." His eyes blazed. "I forgot all about that. Louis Ferris saw him and told the bartender, who told me. Jubal was outside, looking in the window. And when Billy left, Jubal apparently grabbed him. But he was there, damn it. He was there watching her.''

"Wait a minute, Gunter. We don't know who he was watching, or if he was watching anybody. Maybe he was just trying to decide if he wanted to come in.''

Gunter stood abruptly, almost knocking the chair over. "Why do you protect him?" He was almost shouting. "Why do you protect him? Why can't you see what a menace the man is?''

Devlin stood, his own face red now. "I'm not protecting anyone, dammit. Every fucking suspect I have—or almost every damned one—was in your restaurant that night. But I'll be God damned if I'm going to forget about the rest of them just because Jubal Duval was standing outside.''

Gunter turned and began pacing the floor, and Devlin wished he could tell him that Ray Perot's big plot—the thing he was so damned concerned about—was nothing more than an attempt to force him to go after Jubal, just what Gunter himself was demanding.

"I just don't understand why you can't see it.''

"I see it, Gunter. I see it damned well. And one of the things I see is that there's not a damned thing—not one damned thing—that makes Jubal Duval any more of a suspect than half a dozen other people.''

"But he's always there. *Always.*" Gunter's face was scarlet now; a blood vessel throbbed in his forehead.

"And so are some other people," Devlin snapped.

"Who!" Gunter demanded.

"That's none of your business, Gunter. Nobody's made you the official vigilante in this thing. And no matter how much you may have loved Eva, you're not getting carte blanche to go after anybody. And certainly not Jubal Duval. Christ, man, he'll chew you up and spit you out before you know what's happening.''

Gunter glared at Devlin. "Don't underestimate me, Paul." His hands had begun to tremble. "People have underestimated me all my life. And, in most cases, they have been very sorry that they have.''

Devlin sank back in his chair, shaking his head. "I'm not underestimating anyone, Gunter. I'm just telling you something. Very plain. Very simple. Stay the hell away from Jubal Duval. Run your restaurant, and let me run this investigation." Devlin paused, letting his eyes lay heavily on Gunter's flushed, angry face. "Or else, Gunter. *Or else.*"

Devlin sat watching as Gunter turned and stalked from the room.

# CHAPTER
## 12

The leaves are wet under foot and it makes everything so soft, so silent. Like the beating of a sleeping heart. Each step so steady, so rhythmical, you can set the sound, the actual beat, to anything you want, from slow, gentle relaxation, to the thumping speed of anger, fear, anxiety, pain. Oh, yes, you can control it, manipulate it. The ability to do that is yours, yours.

*But it's dangerous, very, very dangerous.*

No it's not! Not dangerous at all.

*It is. She's so protected. You cannot reach her. Not unless you want to die.*

No! Not true! Soon they'll be looking for someone else. Are already looking for someone else. I know it, feel it. Hands rush to the temples, pulling at hair along the sides of the head. Fall away now, calmer, brushing the folds of the green camouflage poncho.

"You'll see." The voice a whisper. Soon they'll all be sure they have the person they want. The words internal again, accented by a thin smile, played across full lips. Then she'll be mine, mine, mine, mine.

The steps resume, moving in a steady, even rhythm, the soft ground offering up a constant pulse, growing louder now, as feet slam down harder with each step. Yes, yes, yes, yes, yes, yes . . .

Silence. Standing stone still now. Eyes staring ahead. The animal lies in the snare, still, quiet, unmoving. The wire about its neck drawn tight. The eyes bulging, almost bursting from the sockets. The tongue protruding, long and gray and cold. Kneeling, a gloved hand reaches out and strokes soft fur, matted here and there with traces of blood thrown up by the once-spurting wound in the neck.

Dead. Soft and still and dead. Tears course down cheeks and begin the drop steadily on the patterned camouflage. The hand strokes the animal again. The heart is not beating. It is still and dead and quiet. You cannot hold it in your hand and feel the rhythm. The hand closes into a fist, rises, and crashes down into the dead beast, again and again.

No! No! No! No! No!

Ray Perot's lips trembled slightly as he came into the spacious study where Devlin awaited him. Devlin's back was turned as he perused the books that lined one wall behind the leaded glass doors that enclosed the bookcase.

Turning, Devlin offered the man a false smile. "Sorry to disturb you on a Sunday, Ray. But it's important."

Perot scowled and waved Devlin to a leather chair. "Every time I see you, you tell me it's important." He took a chair opposite, his face finally composed behind a mask.

"Wouldn't be much reason for me to come if it wasn't important, eh, Ray?"

Perot's jaw tightened. "What is it."

"Linnie French."

Fear flickered across Perot's eyes; was quickly hidden, but not before Devlin had seen it. "What about her? She didn't come to work yesterday. Supposed to. It's picking time. Our busiest time of year."

Devlin crossed one leg atop the other. "I know she didn't, Ray. But you knew she wouldn't be in either. The dead aren't supposed to rise until the last day."

Perot looked as though he had been punched. Punched by someone small, and weak, and previously unthreatening. "What the hell are you talking about?" he demanded.

Devlin couldn't help a small smile. Bravado to cover fear.

What bullshit. "I'm talking about Linnie French. And the fact that she's dead. But you already knew that. You've known it since Friday, when you puked your guts out in her bedroom."

Perot gripped the arms of the leather chair, fighting to stop the trembling in his hands. But the trembling moved to his arms; then his shoulders. "I don't know what you're talking about." The words were forced and clipped and lifeless.

Devlin stared at Perot's feet. He was wearing hunting boots that still held fresh traces of mud and rotting leaves. "Been out in the woods, Ray? Must be nice this time of year."

Perot seemed bewildered, thrown off balance by the sudden change, and he too stared at his boots for a moment. "Out in the orchards," he snapped, almost as though defending himself. "Just checking on things."

"Somebody saw you come out of Linnie French's house late Friday night," Devlin said, his voice crisp and sharp, like the jab of a good boxer. "Saw you lean against a tree in the front yard and puke your guts out there too. Said it looked like what happened inside upset you a lot, Ray. You want to tell me about it? *Now!*" The final word was almost a growl and it made Perot jump slightly in his chair.

The muscles in his jaw danced wildly, as Perot's mind struggled for a response. "Who? Who says they saw me?"

Devlin's eyes were cold and flat now. "That's not the way we play this game, Ray. We play by me asking the questions and you giving the answers. You don't want to play here, that's okay. Then we go down to my office and we try again. You still don't want to play, then you get a chance to call in your lawyer. And, when he gets there, he finds he's got a criminal charge to deal with, not just some client who wants to keep his lips together."

"What charge!" Perot's face was scarlet, and the trembling had moved to his jaw, part anger, part fear, Devlin thought.

"Failing to report a crime, for starters. Obstruction of justice; concealing evidence, and any other thing I can think of." Devlin paused and offered Perot a cold smile. "How does suspicion of murder sound to you, Ray. It has a nice, fucking ring to me."

"That's bullshit. You can't prove any of it." Perot's voice was loud, firm, but his eyes looked as though they were about to melt

"You left enough physical evidence in there to fill a good-sized file cabinet," Devlin snapped, tiring of the man now. "We've even got the contents of your fucking stomach, and enough saliva to match your blood type fifty times over. And we've got fingerprints all over that doorjamb that I'd bet a year's pay are gonna match yours to a tee. Now, you wanna play, Ray, that's fine with me. But, by the time I'm through, every dirty little secret you've got is gonna be spread out like a bad movie. And I'll be running the God damned projector."

Perot twisted in his chair, his hands opening and closing as though he wanted to reach out and wrap them around Devlin's throat. Devlin smiled at the hands, wishing he would try.

The hands fell to Perot's lap, and his face fell as well. "I didn't kill anybody." His voice was little more than a croak. "You know that. You know I'm not that stupid." He studied Devlin's face, but found nothing there. "I went there. To her house. She'd asked me to come. Later, after I got rid of Billy." He sat forward, his face strained, almost pleading. "But, when I got there . . ." He struggled with the memory, almost as though it might make him ill again. "Christ. Somebody had gutted her. Cut her open like some God damned animal." He began to tremble openly now, either unable or unwilling to control it. He stared at Devlin. "I never touched her. I was there, and I ran like hell when I saw her. I was scared shitless, Devlin. I'm still scared shitless. But I never hurt that woman. I never put one hand on her." Perot leaned even further forward, looking as though he might fall out of his chair and onto his knees. "You know who did this, Devlin. There's only one person in this town crazy enough to cut somebody up like that. Jesus Christ, Devlin, you gotta realize that."

Devlin sat and stared at the man, took in his fear, could almost feel it across the room. If he had killed Linnie French he was the best actor Devlin had ever met. But then, psychopaths were supposed to be great actors, weren't they. Like two different people. Like day and night. Like his former partner. Like Rolk had been.

"I want a formal statement from you, Ray. And I want it now." He watched the man nod his head. The movement seemed almost doll-like. "And you better not plan any trips. None at all. And, if I were you, I'd talk to my lawyer real soon."

———

Robbie held the long cookie tin under one arm, the kitten, Maybe, crooked in the other. He knocked gently on Electa Litchfield's back door and waited, then knocked a second time, a bit harder.

When the door pulled back Electa stared down at the boy, at the cookie tin, at the kitten. She was wearing a rubber apron and rubber gloves, and her normally rigid hair hung in wisps over her forehead. Robbie thought she looked like a witch who had been interrupted while mixing up some scary brew.

"My sister wanted me to bring back your cookie tin," he said, almost apologetically.

"Bring it in," Electa said. "My gloves are covered with fur." She turned abruptly and walked back down the small hall and into a large back room. Robbie followed, stopping short as he entered the taxidermy room, his eyes wide as he took in the instrument-covered table, the stacks of supplies, the wall of jars that held the floating entrails of long-dead animals. On one table the hide of a large hare lay stretched out, the holes where its eyes had been stuffed with cotton. "Jeez," he whispered, not certain if he had spoken aloud or to himself.

"Put the tin on that table over there," Electa said, pointing with her chin. She removed the gloves, the apron, and smoothed out the dark green sweater she wore beneath. "Never seen a taxidermy room before, eh?"

Robbie shook his head. He felt a shiver building along his back and hunched his shoulders to fight it off.

Electa turned and stared down at the pelt of the hare. "Just getting ready to poison the hide on this one," she said matter-of-factly.

"Poison?" Robbie said, uncertain he had heard correctly.

"That's what it's called," Electa said. "Means it has to be brushed with a formula of water, powdered borax, and formaldehyde. Gets it ready for mounting." She looked back at the boy, then his kitten. "Could mount that'un for you some day, if you wanted."

"Huh? . . . I . . . I . . ."

"I mean after it's dead," Electa snapped. "You can mount just about anything. Could mount a person if ya wanted to. Though, some folks, there'd be no point in preservin'." She continued to stare at the boy, watching him try to sort out what she was saying. It scared him, she could tell, and she didn't really want that. He was just a boy; innocent enough for now. Some day, not too many years away, he'd be a man, and he'd be just like all the others she had known. Mean and selfish and abusive. Just out to satisfy his needs, and to use anybody willing to let him.

Her mind paused, the thought attacking her. Willing just like you were willing that one time. A little whore, no better than the little whores who've been gettin' their hearts cut out. Broken, battered hearts. She shook the thought away; shook her head to force it to happen. When she looked down again the boy was staring at her, confused.

"What's your kitten's name?" she asked.

"Maybe."

"Eh?"

"His name's Maybe," Robbie said.

"Like maybe I'll go to the store?" Electa asked.

Robbie nodded and watched a brief smile come and go from her mouth.

"Strange name for a cat. Strange name for anything."

"It's kinda a joke between my sister and me," Robbie explained.

Electa snorted. "Guess ya had to be there." She watched Robbie's eyes survey the room again. He looked back and saw her studying him.

"I didn't know you did this stuff," he said. "I mean stuff animals."

"Mount 'em, don't stuff 'em," Electa said. "There's a difference. When ya mount 'em, ya gotta carve the body outta wood ta fit the skin on. Gotta be the same size as when they were alive. Else it won't fit; won't look natural."

The sound of the back door opening and closing stopped her dissertation, and Electa turned, along with Robbie, listening to the sound of heavy steps in the hall. When the door to the taxidermy room swung open, Jubal Duval filled the door frame, one hand holding the body of a fisher by its neck, its two-foot length leaving the tip of its tail only inches from the floor.

Jubal's eyes snapped to the boy and watched as he took a frightened step back.

"Got one, I see, 'eh Jubal?" Electa said. She turned to Robbie, saw the frightened look on his face, and chose to ignore it. Jubal had that effect on people.

"That's a fisher," she said to Robbie. "Some folks call it a marten. Rare to see one, let alone catch one. But Jubal here, he's real good. Been bringin' me animals ever since I had him in school. Isn't that right, Jubal?"

Electa looked at Jubal, saw he was still staring at the boy; saw the tic in the corner of one eye. "Jubal!" she snapped. "Stop actin' the fool!"

Jubal's head swung around to face her. "Yes'm," he said, darting another quick look at the boy, then turning his eyes obediently back to Electa.

Robbie watched him, stunned by the sudden subservience he had shown to Electa, the flicker of fear that had seemed to come to his eyes when he had given him a final, fast look. Almost as if Jubal was afraid of him, afraid to take his eyes off him.

"You know Jubal?" Electa asked, turning to look at the boy.

Robbie nodded, still staring at the hulking man. "I'm . . . I'm sorry we bothered you in your woods," he said.

Jubal looked down at him, eyes blinking. He appeared confused, uncertain. Then he nodded his head and grunted before looking back at Electa. His eyes seemed filled with unspoken questions only the woman could answer.

But Electa didn't seem to notice. Carefully she picked up the skin of the hare and placed it aside. "Put that fisher up here, Jubal," she ordered, patting the now-empty table.

As Jubal did, she quickly slipped on her apron and gloves and picked up a narrow, short-bladed knife. She turned the animal on its back, stroking its fur gently, almost as if soothing it to sleep. Then the knife flashed forward, piercing the belly, sliding up in a smooth, fast motion. As she allowed the animal to fall back on its side, the entrails oozed out through the gaping wound, and with one gloved hand, Electa seized them up, and the other hand, holding the knife, slipped quickly into the incision and began several quick slashing motions.

Robbie stood and stared, mouth open, both repulsed and fascinated by what he was witnessing. Electa's hand seemed to move wildly, angrily—cutting and slashing—and her breathing seemed to increase with the effort until her breath came in short, panting gasps.

Then all motion stopped, and Electa stood hunched over the animal, staring down at the wound. "It was a male," she said, although Robbie couldn't be sure if she was speaking to him, to Jubal, or to anyone at all. Slowly Electa raised the hand holding the now-severed entrails and stared at them, almost as if she were reading some divine message inscribed there. Then her hand dropped away, allowing remains of the evisceration to fall away into a trash can next to the table.

Robbie continued to watch as Electa hunched forward, her breathing slower, more even now. Slowly he started to move away, but Jubal took one quick step forward, stopping him. The man and the boy stared at each other for a moment, then Jubal raised one finger to his lips, indicating quiet. He turned and looked at Electa's back, watching for several moments. Then he turned back to Robbie and motioned toward the door with his head.

Robbie didn't hesitate. Clutching Maybe to his chest, he moved quickly through the door of the taxidermy room, down the hall, and out the rear door. He was still moving quickly when he saw his sister come out their kitchen door, stop, and wave to him. Only then did the beating of his young heart begin to slow.

Jim McCloud sat at his desk, his head cupped in one hand, his other hand trembling slightly as he reached for the glass of straight bourbon that sat next to a half-empty bottle that had been full only two hours earlier. He was thinking about that bottle. That last bottle, which was just one more in a long line of last bottles he had bought in recent years. That was why he didn't hear Ray Perot enter, didn't hear the newspaper's front door open and close; didn't hear the footsteps move across the hardwood floor. The first thing he heard was Perot's voice. And that alone made his stomach twist. That and thinking about the booze.

"I have to talk to you, McCloud," Perot began, without benefit of any preamble. "Christ, I've already been to your house. Thought you'd be there on a God damned Sunday. Your boy told me you were down here." Perot's mouth was rambling, seemingly out of control. Suddenly his eyes spotted the bottle on the desk, and he stared down at McCloud more closely. "You all right?" he asked.

McCloud looked up wearily. "I'm fine, Ray. What can I do for you?"

Perot leaned over the desk, both fists supporting his weight, crowding McCloud until he was forced to push his chair back. "It's that God damned Devlin. Same as before. Now Linnie French has been killed, and that sonofabitch is trying to tie me to it. Me! God damn it."

McCloud raised both hands, fending Perot off. "Wait a minute, Ray. Go a little slower. You say Linnie French has been murdered? That's the woman who was at Gunter's place last Friday, right?"

"Yeah, that's right. She worked for me. Just like Amy Little did. And now that sonofabitch Devlin is trying to make some kind of blind-ass connection."

Perot continued to ramble, but McCloud had turned him off. He was trying to remember what he could of the previous Friday night, trying to recall what had happened at Gunter's. He remembered talking to Perot, and he vaguely recalled starting to leave. But the rest, actually leaving the restaurant, the drive home, getting himself to bed, were all a blank.

"So what are you going to do, dammit?"

McCloud looked back at Perot, refocused on him, then drew a long breath. "The paper's due out on Wednesday. I'll have an editorial ready for it. I don't know what the hell else I can do."

"Just make sure it's a damned strong one," Perot snapped. "And make sure it's on the God damned front page. I want this sonofabitch stopped. I already talked to that Mooers guy at the state cops. I want this investigation taken away from that smartassed bastard. I want somebody handling it who's gonna go after the right God damned person. And we all know who that is. Christ, everybody knows who that is."

McCloud closed his eyes, fighting off the pain that surged through his head. "I'll take care of it, Ray. I'll do everything I can."

"You just make damn sure you do," Perot snapped. "This thing has gotten outta hand. Way outta hand."

McCloud stared at him, bristling under the commands being showered on him. The man was losing it, he told himself. He's right on the edge, frantic. And he suddenly wished he could make it worse for him, add to it all by telling him to take his theories about Jubal Duval and shove them. But he couldn't do that. Not if he wanted to survive economically. And besides, he honestly thought the man was right. He just had to keep telling himself that. Then maybe he could stand looking at himself in the mirror each morning. No. That wouldn't be enough. He'd have to stop drinking to be able to do that.

Perot had been gone for the better part of a half hour before Electa Litchfield arrived at the paper to copyedit the articles Jim had put together that afternoon, and the bottle on McCloud's desk had dipped well below the halfway mark.

Electa stared fiercely at the bottle as she moved past, and McCloud offered her a wan smile, then quietly slipped the bottle into a desk drawer when her back was turned. Carefully he gathered up the copy she had come to work on, drew himself up, and made his way to her desk.

"It's all pretty straightforward," he said, placing the collection of articles before her. "The long piece on last week's Board of Selectmen meeting will have to be cut about ten inches. There's been another murder. Young woman named Linnie French. And I'm putting together what I have on it now. But it's not much."

"Same as the others?" Electa asked. Her eyes were bright now, almost glistening.

"Yeah, afraid so. And we're getting about the same amount of information out of Devlin." He paused, drawing a breath. "There'll be an editorial too, which we'll run on the front page."

" 'Bout the killings?" Electa asked.

"Yeah. About the killings."

Before Electa could respond the front door opened again, producing the smiling face of Leslie Adams, a portfolio under one arm, bearing the advertising copy she had been assigned that week.

McCloud smiled, nodded, then decided to beat a hasty retreat to the men's room. He didn't need further conversation. He didn't need anything, really, except maybe another drink.

Leslie watched his retreating back as she approached Electa's desk. She placed the portfolio on one corner, then glanced again toward the door McCloud had disappeared behind.

"What's wrong with Jim?" she asked. "He looks a little battered."

Electa snorted. "Looks rode hard and put up wet to me," she snapped.

"Drinking?" Leslie asked.

Electa smirked up at her. "That. And there's been another murder too."

"Oh, God, no. Who this time?"

"Young tramp named Linnie French. Know her?"

Leslie winced openly. "No, I didn't." There was an edge to Leslie's voice. "God, Electa. Can't you show some compassion for the poor thing."

"Save my compassion for where it's deserved," Electa snapped back.

"Like who?" Leslie demanded. "Jim, maybe?"

"Never met a man who deserved compassion. Not ever. Not once."

Leslie stared down at the woman, not knowing how to respond; realizing any attempt would be useless.

It was nine o'clock precisely when Louis Ferris saw Jack Chambers push through the door of Pearlie's roadhouse. Chambers stopped just inside the door, took in the worn, seedy decor—the old, molting deer heads that had gathered dust for years on strategic portions of wall, the illuminated beer signs, the plastic plaques of would-be quaint and humorous sayings—all pervaded by the ever-present odor of stale beer. He seemed to smile to himself, then quickly scanned the long, battered bar, spotted Ferris, nodded, and moved to the empty stool beside him.

Ferris was unable to keep the smirk from his face. "When you're given a time to be someplace, you get there, don't you?"

Jack bristled inwardly. Being perceived as overanxious was something he had been trained to avoid. Now he had done just that, and he had done it with this little worm. He offered up his most charming smile, covering himself as best he could. "Not much going on in this town to make you late. And a nice cold one was just what I needed."

The smirk remained. Ferris was not convinced. Chambers tried to ignore it, looked away, and signaled the bartender for a beer, along with another for Ferris. "Is the man you told me about here?" Chambers asked, unable to keep his eyes off the teacher's face.

Ferris nodded, but did nothing else.

Anger flickered through Chambers' eyes, but he pushed it away with another smile. "Would you like to point him out to me?"

Ferris looked down the bar. "Husky young man in the blue shirt, sitting alone at the center of the bar," he said. The smirk returned. "Used to be in here with one of his girlfriends all the time. But he seems to be running out of them lately."

Ferris giggled at his own small joke, but Chambers ignored him, concentrating on the man he had indicated, studying him, sizing him up. He was a good-looking kid, and obviously cocky about it. Jack could tell by the way he used the mirror behind the bar to constantly adjust his hair; moved his head to check different poses, different expressions. He'd be a wise ass too. That was easy to see. But he'd dealt with all kinds of wise asses as a lawyer. He knew how to handle them. You just blow some smoke up their ass, puff up their ego a bit, and then you could play them like a flute.

He turned back to Ferris, thinking how much he'd like to tell the little squirt to go fuck himself. But he might need him later. And there was no sense in burning bridges. He'd done enough of that already.

"I'm going to talk to him," Jack said.

"Just remember our deal." Ferris said. "I never told you anything. If anyone should ask, you just happened to sit next to me, and struck up a conversation." The smirk was gone now, the eyes flat and intense. The man suddenly looked potentially dangerous, and it surprised Jack.

His smile flashed assurance. "It's not a problem. Remember, I don't even know your name." He offered Ferris a conspiratorial wink. "I'll let you know what happens."

"No you won't," Ferris said. "I won't be interested."

Jack shrugged. "Any way you like it." He picked up his beer, nodded, and moved down the bar.

Ferris watched him go. Idiot, he told himself. The two of you will make a perfect team. But only because I want you to. His thought was interrupted by a young woman, no more than 16 or 17, entering the bar. She took a stool three seats away from him and ordered a Coke.

Ferris stared at her. There was something vaguely familiar about her profile, something he couldn't quite place. She could have been a student of his a few years back, but he doubted it. He never forgot what they looked like—especially the girls—for he watched them too closely for that. Of course, she could have been very heavy then and simply grown out of it. Well, she certainly wasn't too heavy now. He studied the line of her breasts, her waist; the slender legs showing through the tight jeans she wore. He picked up his beer and moved to the stool next to her.

"Hello," he said. "I haven't seen you in here before."

The young woman turned, blushing. "Oh, hi, Mr. Ferris." She saw the confusion on his face. "I'm Jenny Bower," she said. "I usta be in your class a long time ago." She seemed momentarily flustered and leaned closer to him, whispering: "You won't tell anybody you saw me here, will ya? My father'd have a fit."

Ferris's smile filled his face. "Of course not, Jenny. Let me buy you a drink, and then tell me what you've been doing."

Billy stared at Jack and grinned. "So you're married to the bitch." The grin became disparaging. "That must be a living, fucking nightmare."

Jack offered a hard, street-tough smile. "Only until I fix her tight little ass," he said.

"That I'd like to see," Billy said.

"And I'd very much like you to see it." Jack tilted his head to one side. "If you're interested."

Billy puffed himself up, thinking of his own eventual plans for Leslie; of his plans for her little shit of a brother through Tommy Robatoy. He was flushed with his own success against his father; had seen him that evening, pacing and twitching like a cat locked in a room with a large dog. Maybe it was time to settle all the scores. Do it now, while his luck was running fast and steady.

"I might be interested," Billy said. "Depends what you have in mind. I just gotta be careful about our local asshole police chief. He's got a thing about protecting her." He grinned again. "You gotta forgive me for sayin' so, but I think he's probably dickin' her."

Jack felt a surge of proprietorial anger, but covered it with another fraternity-boy smile. "I guess I forgot to tell you I'm a lawyer," Jack said. "And even your local Wyatt Earp can't do anything to you when you've got a solid alibi." The smile broadened. "And who could be a better alibi than the husband of the woman making a complaint?"

Billy began to laugh. "You got a point there, counselor. You got one fine, fuckin' point."

# CHAPTER
# 13

The three of them just playing there in front of Elson's store. Taking turns posing with the cigar store Indian, giggling and jumping around, not behaving well at all, acting like the rotten little fools they are.

The hands close into fists, open, then close again. Mother would never allow that, would never stand for it. But these three can do whatever they please. Especially the boy, a little brat whose sister lets him roam the streets at will, causing whatever trouble he likes. But you'll use him soon. Use him to get to her. And then she'll pay, just like they all pay in the end. Filthy little whores who play with people's hearts.

And they don't even know you're watching them. No one knows. You walk the streets and people say hello, and you say hello back, and none of them—none of them at all—know what you know. And they never will, not one of them.

But you have to be careful, just like you were years ago when you did what had to be done and no one dared even say it, say aloud what you knew they were thinking. Not even that fool psychiatrist who talked to you and talked to you. And you just sat there looking sad until he finally decided you were so upset about Mother, you needed care and comfort and treatment. But you weren't depressed, were you? You were so happy to have things the way they were. Just as you're having them now. Just as you'll always have them. Because no one loves you; no one will ever give their heart to you. They'll hurt you and hurt you and hurt you. And you'll stop them, just like you finally stopped Mother.

But it's dangerous, still so dangerous. They're getting closer and closer, and you have to make them look somewhere else. They're too close to you now, making it hard for you to move. They have to be misdirected, sent off chasing their own tails.

Oh, no. Here comes some stupid fool. Go away. Go away.

"Oh, Hello. Yes, it is. A really nice day."

Fools, fools, fools, fools. Hands open and close, open and close. They'll never know. Never, never, never, never.

*But be careful.* A voice whispered in the ear.

"I will!" The answer hissed aloud.

Devlin stared at the notes he had taken during his phone call with Moriarty. His former colleague on the homicide task force had done a more than thorough job, putting together more information, he was sure, than the Vermont state cops would come up with in the next year. The only thing that was missing was one juvenile report that the courts were sitting on. But that would come within the next few days, Moriarty had assured him. *Just a question of a little sleight of hand,* he had said.

But the J.V. record wasn't what was bothering him. A lot of kids got their tails in a jam; he had done so himself. What bothered him was that nothing he now had gave him anything on anybody that pointed him in a new direction. The only incriminating information sat in the U.S. Army's records on Jubal Duval. And that was something he had largely known already.

He tapped a pencil absently on his desk. Maybe Perot and McCloud were right. Maybe he was just being stubborn. Maybe he *should* drag Jubal's tail in and work on him. Maybe he was just being thick. Just the way he had been about Rolk.

He sat back in his chair. He had dreamed about Rolk again last night, and this time he had had the new gun in his hand.

The one he carried now, the one that made his hand shake every time he slipped it inside his belt.

He stood and paced the office, trying to drive the memory away; trying to get a handle on something, anything, out of the information he had put together. He walked back to his desk and stared down at his notes, then at his watch. It was 10 a.m. There was one thing he hadn't done that he might as well do now. He sat down, dialed the number he had gotten days ago, and waited. Just doing it made him feel like shit.

When Dr. Lawrence Withers finally got on the phone, Devlin found himself dealing with a deep, soft, melodious voice, one he was sure provided the Philadelphia shrink with a fat income whether his talents deserved it or not.

After listening to Devlin's preamble—the problems with Jack Chambers, Leslie's escape to Vermont, Jack's sudden appearance there, and his claim that she was a disturbed person, whom Withers had treated and hospitalized—the psychologist agreed to speak with Devlin, but only after he called him back, thereby verifying with whom he was indeed speaking.

When Devlin again picked up the phone, Withers apologized for his caution, then went on to caution Devlin again that he would be strictly limited in what he could discuss by the ethical question of patient confidentiality.

"I just need a handle on the woman," Devlin assured him. "She's involved in a case I'm investigating, so I'm trying to find out as much as I can."

Withers, assuming the "case" involved the physical abuse Devlin had mentioned earlier, began by explaining that he too had heard those same allegations from Leslie.

"I treated her for some rather severe bouts of depression," Withers began. Devlin could almost see him stroking an imaginary beard as he spoke. "Her father had just been killed in a car accident. Something about brakes failing, something of that type, even some concern about faulty work by a mechanic, or some deliberate vandalism that caused it. This was compounded by the fact that her mother had also died tragically when she was very young.

"Anyway, Leslie had had long and serious problems with her mother that were never reconciled. At the same time, she and her father were very close. He was a gentle and kind man, but not much of a disciplinarian, which apparently her mother was."

There was a pause, and Devlin could hear what sounded like the sucking sounds of a pipe being lit.

"In any event," Withers resumed, "Leslie felt a subconscious guilt for feeling great pain over her father's death, and less so over her mother's.

"It was at this point that the matter of Jack's alleged physical abuse arose." He paused again. "Now you must understand that Leslie, because of her father's laxity in that area, grew up to have great difficulty with male authority. And, as such, any forcefulness on her husband's part might well be viewed as abuse.

"Now I know Jack Chambers—have known him personally for years—and I highly doubt he is the type of man who would physically abuse his wife."

"Is that a professional opinion?" Devlin asked.

Withers coughed, then began sucking on his pipe again. "Yes, I'd categorize it as such, based upon what I know. You see, chief, I always felt Leslie had a subconscious but very intense desire to hurt herself, and I believe she fantasized about Jack hurting her to sublimate that wish and thereby make it more acceptable."

"That, of course, assumes that he wasn't beating the hell out of her," Devlin said.

Withers coughed again. "Well, yes, of course. If he was, the diagnosis wouldn't be of much value." He concluded the comment with a deep, rolling laugh.

"You said she was hospitalized. What was that all about?" Devlin asked.

"The depression over the death of her father, and especially her unresolved conflicts with her mother. It was only for a week, just as a precaution. And later, her younger brother came to live with her, and I believe that helped resolve some of those problems for her."

"Is there anything else you can tell me?" Devlin asked, thinking about Withers' earlier caution about patient confidentiality, and how little that had proven to mean to the babbling idiot.

"No, I don't believe so. I'd just again emphasize my own skepticism about Leslie's abuse fantasies."

"Yeah, I got that, Doc," Devlin said. "And thank you for your help."

Devlin replaced the receiver and squeezed his eyes shut, wondering what Withers would have thought if he had seen Jack Chambers pounding the shit out of his wife's back door.

He opened his eyes and stared at the telephone. *And what would you think if what he said turned out to be true? What would that mean to your investigation? And what would it mean to you?*

Leslie's smile seemed to shoot out the doorway; her eyes glittered with pleasure, and Devlin immediately wanted to reach out and draw her into his arms. It had been a long time since he had shown up at a woman's door and had her look at him that way. A very, very long time.

Leslie closed the door and quickly pressed herself against him. "I've been so happy since you called to say you were coming by," she said, her head resting against his chest.

Devlin slid his arms around her and ran them slowly along her back. She felt so good to him, so incredibly good. He drew a deep breath and took in the scent of her hair. There was a near-physical discomfort in the pit of his stomach, just knowing he would soon be trying to draw information out of her. And doing it in a way she would hopefully not suspect. It made him feel sleazy, and he didn't like it. He didn't want it to be part of the emotion he felt for her.

"You feel tense," she said, still resting against him.

"It's been a long day. And not a very good one."

Leslie eased herself back and looked up at him. "Are you feeling guilty about this new murder?" she asked.

"I don't know. Maybe I am."

"You shouldn't do that to yourself. You can't stop people from doing terrible things."

"It's my job to stop them."

"No. It's your job to catch them. There's a difference."

He stepped back, holding her hips at arm's length, and forced a small smile. "No matter how you describe it, I'm not doing it very well." He glanced about the kitchen. "Where's Robbie?"

"In bed. He was in town with your daughter and Tim today— they all went shopping with me after school—and he wore himself out." She hesitated, studying his face, acknowledging how much she liked the way he looked, even found the small scar on his cheek attractive. "I saw your friend, Gunter, in town today," she said, trying to lighten the conversation. "I was going to ask him for some of that sauerbraten he offered me. But he seemed in a really black mood."

"He is," Devlin said. "But it has nothing to do with you. He's furious with me, with the way I'm handling this investigation." Paul's jaw tightened momentarily. "He was in love with Eva Hyde, and her death hit him pretty hard. He also knew the other two women. From the restaurant."

Leslie shook her head. "I didn't know. How awful for him. But why is he unhappy with you? He must know you're doing everything you can."

The muscles along Paul's jaw danced. "He's fixated on Jubal Duval; he's convinced himself he's behind all of it. And he thinks I should drop everything else and just go after him. I think he might even do something rash, himself, if I don't."

Leslie continued to stare up at him, her own doubts flickering in her eyes. "And you don't feel that's the right thing to do," she said at length.

Paul dropped his hands from her hips and took a small step back. "You seem to have your own doubts about that," he said.

"No. Not at all," Leslie said, shaking her head. "I'm just trying to understand."

The lie didn't carry very well, but Devlin knew there was nothing he could do about that. Nothing he could do about anyone's doubts, not even his own. He just had to play it out the way he had been taught. Slow, steady, and methodical—waiting for the break to appear. It was the way it worked. The only way it worked.

"Let's not talk about it anymore," he said.

"No, let's not," Leslie said. She smiled. "You look like you could use a glass of wine."

"I could use a bottle of wine," he said.

"Then go in the living room, put on some music, and I'll bring us one."

The lighting was low and soft, and it shaded Leslie's features making her seem sultry and available, and, combined with the Roberta Flack album he had chosen, it made Paul want her with an urgency he hadn't felt in days. Not since the last time he was with her, he realized.

"Have you had any problems with Chambers?" he asked, pushing his own needs away.

She shook her head. "No. Nothing. Why? Are you afraid I will?"

"It's just some comments he made when I had him at head-quarters," Paul said. "It made me feel he was trying to build a future defense."

"What were they?" A hardness had come to Leslie's eyes, an anger that seemed to rise up from deep within her.

"Well, he insists he never hit you; that it's all a fantasy you dreamed up." The kitten, Maybe, attacked Paul's foot, then quickly climbed his trouser leg. He picked the cat up and placed it back on the floor.

"He mentioned the name of some shrink he says you saw in Philly. Claims he treated you, and put you in a hospital for a short time. I'm afraid he might think that's some kind of hook he can use to defend any further complaints. And, if he's think-ing that way, it could mean he hasn't given up."

Leslie sipped her wine through tight, angry lips. "I never should have gone to that chauvinist idiot," she finally said. She placed the wine glass on the low cocktail table, then looked up at Paul, her face softening. "It was after my father was killed," she began. "I needed to talk to someone, and Jack suggested Larry Withers. They were fraternity brothers in col-lege and had remained friends. I didn't realize it at the time, but what Jack was doing was finding someone safe for me to go to, just in case any other issues came up." Leslie shook her head; her hands had closed into fists. "I was really worn down; hadn't been eating, and he put me in a hospital for four days to have some tests run." She stared at Paul, her eyes hard. "Medical tests," she added. "And to build myself back up. There was no psychiatry involved, other than the visits I made to his office."

Devlin reached out and stroked her cheek. "You don't have to explain that to me," he said, knowing it was a lie, that she had already explained what he had needed to know.

Leslie sat staring at him, silent, looking for something in his eyes that would tell her what he really thought. She had known him for such a short time, and already he knew more about her than anyone. More than Jack ever had. More than she had ever allowed anyone to know. She felt suddenly unsafe with the fact, vulnerable; not sure she could afford to be.

The cat climbed Paul's trouser leg again, and he plucked it off, holding it this time, stroking its head.

Was she in love with him? She wasn't sure. Thought perhaps she wanted to be. But was it just a present emptiness she wanted him to fill? She stared at him; watched the way he looked at her. Softly. Gently.

The hands open and close. The eyes stare at the face filled with lust. He wants her, wants to devour her. And she will let him. Oh, yes. She'll let him do whatever he wants. The sound of her heart. You can hear it. Beating faster and faster and faster. He'll use her, and she'll let him. And she'll use him as well. Wrenching, tearing, taking. Her heart beating faster, grunting and sweating. Filthy, dirty words. Mother's voice, harsh, belittling, ugly. Groaning, crying out. Filthy slut.

Leslie's head snapped up, turned toward the window.

"What is it?" Paul asked.

"I thought I heard something. Felt something."

"Where?"

Her eyes fixed on the window. "Out there."

Paul stood, placing the cat in her lap. "I'll check," he said, moving toward the front door.

"Be careful, Paul."

Devlin reached for the handle of the front door, his right hand instinctively moving to the revolver tucked into his belt beneath his jacket. His hand began to tremble as he touched it, and he pulled it back.

Stepping outside, the cold chill of the autumn night hit him, cutting through his clothes, sending a shiver through his arms and shoulders. He moved in a small circle toward the window Leslie had indicated. There, the lawn abutted the house, broken only by several wide, ground-hugging shrubs, offering no chance of footprints, or any other indication someone had been there. He circled the house slowly, stopping and listening for any sound of movement, watching for any change in the texture of shadows that patterned the grounds. Nothing.

He reentered the house through the kitchen door, locked it behind him, then went to the living room and locked the front door. In his absence Leslie had closed the curtains at the front windows and drawn the shades. She was back on the sofa now, the kitten cradled in her arms.

"Nothing out there," Paul said, approaching her.

"It's probably just nerves," she said. "Talking about Jack has a tendency to put me on edge." She continued to look up at him, her eyes warm, hopeful. She held out the cat. "Please put him in the kitchen and close the door," she said. "Then come back and make love to me."

Paul took the cat. "What about Robbie?" he asked.

"He never wakes up once he's asleep."

He looked down at her and nodded. Her eyes seemed to swallow him up, and he could see a faint trace of moistness on her lips. He turned and walked toward the kitchen, forcing himself to move more slowly than he wanted.

# CHAPTER
## 14

The sounds come through the bedroom wall, faint at first, then rising, rising, rising. Whispers, soft laughter, changing to sighs and gasps for breath, then moans, long and pleasurable, short and desperate. Voices, filthy words; cries, almost on the verge of pain.

Father will come home. He'll come home and he'll find her. Giving her heart so freely. So many nights when he's at work, thinking I'm asleep. Thinking I'll never hear her; never know. I'll just lie here and wait. Wait for Father to come home. Wait for him to catch her and punish her.

She slaps my face. "Don't you ever say that to me!" she screams. "Look at you. Dumpy and stupid and dirty. Ten years old and you can't keep yourself clean. Sneaking around, spying, listening. Imagining things that never happen. Can't tell the difference between what's real and what's a stupid, filthy dream."

She stalks into my room and stares at me, disgust on her face. "Can't you dress yourself properly. Look at you. Who's ever going to care about you when you walk around looking like a fool. Like a fat, stupid clown in the circus. What will people think when they see you? What kind of mother will they think I am?''

If they knew about you, I know what they'd think. If they could hear you grunting like a pig; hear you saying your filthy words; hear the man telling you what to do, telling how good it feels, telling you to do it harder, faster, harder, faster, harder, faster . . .

The figure sits bolt upright in the bed, body shaking, sweat coursing down the face. A low, deep moan fills the room. A memory comes racing back. The knife plunging and plunging and plunging.

The body falls back on the bed, the breath fast, ragged. Sleep. Have to go back to sleep.

Minutes pass and the breathing evens out, deep, steady.

The children race through the woods, trying to hide. They are there, almost within your grasp, but then they slip away. Slip away and run. Faster and faster and faster. Gaining distance. You chase them, forcing yourself to move as fast as you can.

"But you're too slow and stupid and lazy." Mother's voice, screaming at you. But it can't be her. She's dead. In her grave rotting in her own filth. The voice gets louder and louder and louder, and you cover your ears but you can still hear her. And the children. Where are they? Where have they gone? You have to find them. It's the only way you can get to her. The only way you can stop her voice. The only way you can stop her filthy, filthy voice.

The words force themselves through your hands.

Nooooooo . . . Stop it! Stop it! Stop it! Stop it! Stop it!

Oh God, no. The face has changed. The body too. It's Jack, and he's with you in the room. And you're trapped. There are no doors, no windows, no way to escape.

"Jack's back, bitch." The words scream out at you; the face twisted and cruel, already anticipating the pleasure he will find in his fists, in the points of his shoes.

"Jack's back. Jack's back. Jack's back." His head, grinning wildly, is tilted obscenely to one side, then slowly begins to pivot, turning impossibly on its axis until it rotates in a full circle. The head comes to a stop. The eyes are staring straight ahead; the grin is wide and fixed. There is something odd about the head, but Leslie can't quite decide what it is. Perhaps it's not a real head. Perhaps it's really made of wax, something being used by someone only pretending to be Jack. The head begins to turn again, the eyebrows arch, almost as if surprised by the sudden movement. The speed increases, and suddenly the head is spinning wildly, spinning like a top.

The head stops, and suddenly Jack has her by the throat, his face all too real now, glaring down at her, his lips twisted in a snarl. His free hand draws back in a fist, and Leslie throws up her hands to fend off the blow. But he's too strong, and his fist comes crashing through her hands and slams into her forehead just above the eye. The impact of the blow rocks her head back, and she feels the skin split and the blood begin to flow down her face.

He always stops when he makes you bleed, she tells herself. He always does. So he'll stop now. He'll stop, he'll stop, he'll stop.

The fist draws back again and she ducks her head, flinching as it comes forward. Her nose flattens against her face in a sickening crunch, and two teeth shatter, filling her mouth with jagged shards and the sweet, coppery taste of her own blood. The punch drives her back, staggering, staggering, staggering, until her back slams into the kitchen counter that has suddenly materialized behind her.

There is a knife in her hand now as Jack advances. He doesn't seem to see it, or doesn't care. He keeps coming, fists clenched, body hunched slightly forward, machinelike, bent on destruction. He stops; hovers over her, both arms raised above his head, the hands curved into claws. His eyes gleam with a murderous rage, like a wild animal about to tear her to shreds.

Leslie closes her eyes and thrusts out with the knife, feels it plunge into Jack with almost no resistance. She opens her eyes and stares up at him. His face is a blend of shock and horror. Suddenly she wants to pull the knife away, make him well, heal the harm she has done him.

But as she starts to withdraw the knife, his face changes; the murderous rage returns to his eyes, the snarling smile contorts the lower half of his face into a hideous mask.

Leslie grabs the handle of the knife with both hands, and instead of withdrawing it, she pulls it upward, slicing Jack open, cleaving him. Now his face is filled with agony, and he falls back and crashes to the floor. But Leslie no longer wants to end his pain. She stares down at him, his shirt and the skin beneath it slit open and gaping up at her. She raises the knife above her head. Below, she can see his heart beating inside the open wound in his chest. She brings the knife down, plunging toward the now swelling and receding heart. Die. Die. Die. Die. Die. Nooooooo . . .

Just as the knife plunges into Jack's heart, the eyes staring wildly up at her, change. Now the face changes too, and Leslie finds herself staring down at a young woman she has never seen before, eyes wide with terror, mouth twisted into an unbearable scream of agony.

A harsh, brittle sound assaults her back, and her head snaps around. Jack stands there, behind her, legs spread apart, towering above her. His head is thrown back, and he is laughing at her.

A faint, almost foglike haze of early morning light filled the room. Leslie sat bolt upright in her bed, eyes wide, hands trembling. "Jesus," she whispered. Her hands moved to opposite arms, hugging herself.

She shook her head, driving out still-clinging remnants of the dream, then swung her legs over the side of the bed. It was chilly, and she quickly slipped into a heavy terry cloth robe and thick, fuzzy slippers. She hugged herself again. God, that final image in her dream. It seemed fixed in her mind, unshakable. It was as though someone had erected a photograph behind her eyes, and now flooded it with light, at will, forcing her to look at it again and again and again.

Leslie shuffled out of her room and down the stairs, her arms still wrapped about her. It was just the cumulative effect of all the horrors of recent days, she told herself. Those women being killed so terribly one after the other. The incident with Billy Perot. The mutilated fox, left behind her barn like some hideous warning. Jack's sudden appearance, and the terror that had rekindled in her. Even what she was now feeling for Paul Devlin. That too had put her nerves on edge. At best it was confusing; at worst it scared the hell out of her.

Leslie moved about the kitchen, awake yet not awake. She

put the coffee on, checked the wall clock, then listened to see if she could hear Robbie stirring overhead. She could let him sleep a bit longer, she decided. And if he missed the bus, she would simply drive him to school.

She stared at the coffee pot, willing it to brew more quickly, then decided to walk down the driveway and get the morning newspaper, a task she normally left for Robbie. She poured some coffee from the still-brewing pot, then moved to the back door, sipping it gratefully.

As the door opened into the kitchen, Leslie froze in mid-step. The coffee cup fell from her hand, smashing on the kitchen floor in a shower of hot liquid and pottery fragments. Her eyes stared at the door, unable to look away. Even as her head turned instinctively, fighting to escape the vision, her eyes refused to move; they remained fixed on the spot, until, her head turned fully away, found herself still staring at it out of the corners of her eyes.

Leslie staggered back; her arms and legs trembled uncontrollably. Her mouth, frozen in mid-scream, began to move, as though fighting to speak. But the only sound to emerge were the retching, gagging noises of someone about to be sick.

The sound of a car engine and tires crunching gravel in her driveway snapped her back, and her eyes were able to break away and stare out at Pop Duval's truck moving past the kitchen door toward the barn.

Yes, she told herself. Oh, yes. He was supposed to be there this morning to pick up a load of trash for the dump. She started forward, then stopped, her eyes riveted to the door again. The kitten hung there, its fur spattered with blood. A nail had been driven through its throat, pinning it to the door, and its belly and chest had been slit, the entrails left dangling from the gaping wound, which now held only a single, withered rose. Tears rolled down Leslie's cheeks. The kitten's eyes were wide and blank, giving it a look of terrified surprise that seemed somehow wrong for something so young, and its mouth was open, the lips drawn back in a final screech that seemed ready to burst forth at any moment.

Leslie pulled her arms into her sides, as though trying to make herself smaller, and pushed herself out the doorway.

Pop was just getting out of his truck when he saw her, standing there waving frantically, her robe flapping loosely about her slender body. But it was her eyes that stopped him cold. The wide, terrified, almost mad look in her eyes.

Devlin squatted next to Pop. The kitten had been wrapped in a cloth and placed inside the barn. Now it lay open before the two men. The nail, removed from its throat, lay beside it, next to the rose.

"Why'd you take it down?" Devlin asked. "It would have been good if the forensic people saw it the way it was found."

"Lady wanted it down," Pop said. "Didn't want the boy ta see the critter thattaway."

Devlin shook his head. "That's a hard one to argue against," he said. "You notice anything when you took it down?"

Pop stared at the kitten. "Jus' that its heart was missin'."

"How'd you happen to notice that?"

Pop glanced at him, then back at the cat. "Whoever done it fixed it up so's its guts was hangin' out. Could see its heart wasn't there." Pop hesitated. "But even if I couldn't, I woulda looked."

"Why?"

Pop kept his eyes averted, almost as though he couldn't look at Devlin. "Been findin' animals in the woods the past six months or so. Killed. Cut open like this'un. But only their hearts missin'. Always with a stake driven in 'em."

"Why the hell haven't you told anybody?" Devlin snapped.

Pop stared at him, then looked away.

Devlin understood. The old man was afraid of getting people stirred up about his son, afraid of what that might lead to.

"You think Jubal did this?" he asked.

Pop drew a long breath, pulling strength from it. "Jubal was always partial to small critters. Even when he trapped as a boy, always tried ta make sure his traps wasn't near no dens the younguns 'ud be stayin' close to." He pressed his lips together and slowly began to rewrap the mutilated body of the kitten, his large, callused hands moving gently, tenderly.

When he was finished he looked back at Devlin. "But that's when he was a boy," he said softly. "It's been twenty years since I know'd what Jubal might do, or might not do. Mostly he stays by hisself, which is the bes' thing."

Devlin picked up a stick and began scratching in the dust-covered floor. "I've read army reports about what happened to Jubal, Pop. I've gotten reports on a lot of people because of these murders." Devlin wasn't sure why he had added the last. Whether he was trying to comfort the old man or just assure him he hadn't condemned his son out of hand.

"You'll be needin' to talk to him, I suppose," Pop said.

"It would help," Devlin said. "It would also help if I didn't have to go looking for him." He smiled, more at himself than anything else. "I'm not sure I could find him on that damned mountain anyway."

"Plenty of folks would be willin' to help ya," Pop said.

"Yeah. I'm afraid you might be right. You intend to find him?"

"Was thinkin' I might," Pop said.

"Tell him I need to see him," Devlin said.

Pop nodded. "I'll tell him. Can't promise ya nothin' after that."

When Devlin returned to the kitchen, Leslie was still badly shaken. He had considered asking Electa to come and stay with her while he examined the cat, but had thought better of it. Electa's presence wasn't exactly a comfort.

Now, seated at the harvest table, he could see Leslie's hands were still trembling as she tried to control the cup of coffee he had poured for her.

"This is getting to be a horror show for you," he said.

"It's even worse than that." She stared at him. "That rose that was left . . ." She grimaced. "Inside that poor cat. It was meant for me."

Devlin hesitated, not knowing what to say. Finally he settled for a question. "Why do you say that?"

"Because whoever did this . . ." She tried to steady her voice. "He left me one before. I found it in my truck. The morning after you came for dinner."

"Why didn't you tell me?"

Leslie shook her head. "I meant to. At first I thought it was from you. After what happened that night . . ." She shook her head again. "Then, later, I thought maybe Jack had done it. But, after that, with what happened with Jack and all, I just forgot. I kept meaning to tell you, but it kept slipping my mind." She stared at him, frightened; wanting to know why it was all happening. "What does it mean?"

Devlin knew he couldn't tell her. Not only because it would

only intensify her fear, but because it would violate the confidentiality at the very core of his investigation.

"I want you to do something for me," he said at length. "I want you and Robbie to come stay at my house until this is over."

Leslie stared at him, surprised. Then she shook her head slowly. "I can't do that, Paul," she said. "Not in this town." She forced a smile, albeit a weak one. "They'd fire you, and they'd probably burn me at the stake."

"I don't care what they think," Devlin said.

She shook her head again. "It's not just us, Paul. Think what they'd do to Robbie. And Phillipa."

Devlin let out a long, frustrated breath. "Well, they can't stop me from increasing protective surveillance. You better get used to having a cop around a lot of the time. Mainly me."

Leslie's weak smile returned. "That I'd like," she said.

Pop took his rifle from the truck and entered the woods behind the Adams' house. It was as good a place as any, he had decided, and close to the last spot he had seen Jubal.

He didn't bother to check for tracks as he entered. With the children's use of the woods near the house, there were tracks upon tracks. That, together with the heavy fall of leaves, would make spotting and identifying recent movement a random and difficult thing at best. What he would do, Pop had decided, was move in the direction from which Jubal had previously come. Move and make no effort to mask his presence. Let Jubal find him. He had little doubt the boy would do just that. And just as quickly as it pleased him.

Pop made his way halfway up a steep ridge, then began to work east, allowing his eyes to sweep above and below him. He smiled inwardly at what he was doing. Workin' this hill jus' like an ol' ridge runnin' buck would. Never usin' the top, 'cept to cross over t'other side. Always runnin' the edges, so's he can see ahead what's over 'n' under 'em.

He stopped, squatting over a deer track that had escaped the leaf cover, one that moved down and away. He followed the line. Headin' toward McCreedy's overgrowed apple orchard, he told himself, thinking how the unpicked drops would be brown and soft now, after several weeks on the ground. Jus' the way them deer likes 'em.

He stood, stretched his stiff legs, then continued along the ridge. He heard a sound far back behind him, stopped, turned, and scanned the terrain. Coulda been anythin', he told himself. But itta only be Jubal iffin he wants ya ta know he's behind ya.

The ridge ended at a deep hollow, and Pop made his way down, crossed it, then moved up the gently rising slope on the other side. There were rock ledges ahead. Places where he had once hunted bear. In those days he had worked the area in a wide circle, from the berry bushes deep in the hollow to the acorn-bearing hardwoods and on up to the line of dense pines, always ending back at the rock ledges that were dotted with the small caves the bears would den up in.

He started a wide circle now, moving to his left away from the main concentration of caves. This was also the area he had always thought Jubal would use as a base camp. He had hunted here as a boy; had come and played here outside of hunting season. The cliffs and ledges and caves had provided a perfect setting for whatever games had then occupied his mind.

And now it provided a perfect setting for a war, if Jubal decided to fight one. Iffin they make him fight one, Pop corrected himself.

The old man knew he had been terrified about that possibility for a long time now. Not so much that Jubal would come to harm. He had unhappily accepted that probability years ago. What truly frightened him was how many others Jubal would harm along the way. How much destruction Jubal would bring to any confrontation, any attempt to capture or control him.

And it was only a question of time; he knew that with equal certainty. Sooner or later Jubal would no longer content himself with frightening hunters and children off "his" portion of the mountain. His fantasy world would become his real world, his only world. And then the killing would start—if it hadn't started already—and Pop knew when that happened, he would have to come for Jubal himself. And when he did, he would probably have to kill him.

Pop stopped to rest before a rockface that jutted from the hillside, a small stand of cedar almost obscuring it from view. He knelt to retie his boot, then lit a cigarette. When he looked up again, Jubal was standing 10 yards away, staring down at him.

" 'Lo, Jubal," he said. "How ya been?"

" 'Lo, Pop. Ya got another of them cigarettes?"

Pop fished one from a pack in his shirt pocket, along with a book of matches, and tossed them to his son.

He watched Jubal light the cigarette. "Been watchin' me long?" he asked.

"Nope. Jus' heard ya a bit ago."

"Wasn't tryin' ta walk quiet."

"Guess ya jus' do it natural like."

Pop sat, his back against a tree, and drew heavily on his cigarette. "Want ya ta come back ta town with me," he said at length.

Jubal's eyes narrowed. "What for?"

"Chief of police wants ta talk ta ya."

"Already talked to him." Jubal's hand brought his own cigarette to his lips. A bit too quickly; with a touch of nervousness, Pop thought.

"Needs ta talk ta ya again," Pop said.

" 'Bout what?"

"These killin's that been happenin'."

"Ain't got nothin' ta say 'bout that. Jus' a bunch a Saigon whores."

Pop glared at his son, his face flushed with anger, a lone vein throbbing in his forehead. "Damn your eyes, Jubal. There ain't no God damned Saigon whores anywheres aroun' here."

Jubal stared back at him and snorted. "Might 'spect ya ta say that, since you're workin' for one."

"Ya takin' 'bout that Adams woman?" Pop snapped.

Jubal shuffled his feet and looked away. His face seemed suddenly confused and nervous. "See what I see," he said, his voice soft, distant.

"Then you're a damn fool," Pop said, keeping all animosity out of his voice. "Prob'ly been listenin' to that other damn fool, Electa Litchfield."

Jubal began to speak, but Pop silenced him with a single look. "That woman you think's one a them Saigon whores a yours, is jus' tryin' ta get herself by. Herself, an' her brother, too. An' she's got Billy Perot an' some crazy husband makin' her life harder'n it has ta be." He stared hard at Jubal. "An' maybe somebody else too."

Pop stood and faced his son. "An' them young women that's

been killed, they's only been local gals, children practic'ly, that some crazy sumbitch's been guttin' like they was hogs set out ta butcher." He took a step forward. "An some folks beginnin' ta think maybe it's you been doin' it."

Pop felt the bullet whistle between his head and Jubal's a full heartbeat before he heard the crack of the high-powered rifle. He threw himself to the ground and crawled behind a tree, then glanced around and saw that Jubal had also taken cover behind a cluster of large rocks.

From a ledge on the other side of the hollow, some 300 yards away, Gunter cursed himself for chancing a shot at that distance. He had been in the woods, hunting Jubal, when he had first seen Pop; had realized the old man was undoubtedly looking for Jubal as well, and had decided to follow him and take advantage of the old man's superior skills.

Now he had blown it. He waited, watching as Jubal moved out from behind the small rock pile he had used as cover, and disappeared behind the row of cedars that fronted the nearby rockface. Seconds later he watched Jubal emerge with a rifle in his hands. A cold smile spread across Gunter's lips. Maybe it's not blown after all, he told himself. Slowly, staying low to the ground, he eased himself back along the ridge until he could not be seen by the two men across the hollow. Then he stood and began to backtrack his way out of the woods. But only for now, he told himself. Then, when you're ready, you'll know where to come.

Pop stared out across the hollow. "Whoever it was, he's gone," he said.

Jubal nodded. "Ain't seen no movement, nothin'."

"It's what I was afeared of," Pop said. "I want ya ta come back ta town with me."

Jubal shook his head. "Got things I gotta do here. Gotta secure my perimeter."

"Damn it ta hell, Jubal! You ain't got no perimeter." Pop stared angrily at the large, glowering man who was his son. "You have anything to do with hurtin' them women?" He waited, getting nothing but silence in return. "You know who did?" he demanded.

"Gotta secure my perimeter," Jubal said, turning and heading back toward the row of cedars that covered the entrance to his cave.

Pop followed him with his eyes, then shook his head and turned away. "Damn your eyes, Jubal," he whispered under his breath. He knew he'd have to return soon. And, when he did, he'd have to do something he'd dreaded for more than a dozen years now. He closed his eyes and drew a deep breath, then slipped his rifle over his shoulder and started down the hill, toward the hollow and home.

Leslie had been fighting for composure all day, and all day had felt the battle slipping from her. Even Paul's assurances hadn't helped. She had told Robbie what had happened that morning; had seen his face crumble in hurt disbelief, and she had tried to soothe the unsoothable. At least the kitten had been gone by the time he had come downstairs, and she had managed—with more than a little difficulty—to get the blood washed from the rear door before he could see even that much of their morning horror. Paul hadn't been pleased with that destruction of evidence when he had arrived, but right then Robbie had been her first concern.

But that didn't erase the fact that there was someone out there doing these things to her. Someone cold and cruel and brutal enough to nail an innocent kitten to a door and disembowel it. Someone crazy enough, sick enough, to imitate what had been done to three young women. Or maybe worse than that. Maybe the very same madman, telling her she was also on his insane list.

And so what are you doing? Leslie asked herself, as she pulled a gallon of milk from the cooler in Elson's store. You're out shopping as though nothing at all is going on, when you should be home barricading the doors and windows.

She glanced around the store, taking in its very serene, quiet, country flavor. So much for escaping to the safety of rural Vermont, she told herself. I should take out an ad in The Times, warning people to ignore those photographs on postcards and bank calendars. This place offers about the same level of serenity as Beruit.

Leslie turned to head for the counter and was forced to pull up abruptly to avoid crashing head on into Louis Ferris.

"Oh, I'm sorry," she said. "I'm walking around in a daze today."

Ferris bathed her in a wide, unpleasant smile. "My fault,"

he said. "I was just coming over to speak with you." He paused, his smile fading then reasserting itself. "You remember me, don't you? I'm Louis Ferris, one of Robbie's teachers."

"Of course I do," Leslie said. Concern flashed into her eyes, and she looked quickly at her watch. "Is my watch wrong?" she asked. "Is school out already?" She had a sudden dread of Robbie coming home alone to an empty house.

"Oh, no. Don't concern yourself." Ferris's grin widened. "The last period is a free one for me—my lunch hour, so to speak—so I'm able to leave early some days."

Leslie let out a relieved breath. "I just had this vision of Robbie coming home to an empty house," she said.

"Surely he's old enough for that," Ferris offered, his smile becoming slightly patronizing, in that way so often used by teachers.

Leslie bristled under the official rebuke. "I guess it's a hold-over from living in a city," she said defensively, annoyed that she was even bothering to explain. "You said you wanted to speak to me," she said, abruptly throwing the onus back on him.

Ferris stuttered briefly. "Y-y-yes, I d-did." He drew himself up, fighting off a last-minute nervousness.

"Actually, it involves something I inadvertently overheard." The smile flashed and faded from Ferris's lips. "It was a conversation between Billy Perot and someone I gathered was your husband."

Leslie stared at him, silent, waiting. There was something in the man's eyes, something she found repellent. Something that told her he was anticipating her discomfort, waiting to enjoy it, perhaps even exploit it somehow. Her silence seemed to make him nervous, and she held to it.

"I couldn't hear everything that was said," Ferris continued, his smile appearing and fading again. "But it seemed to me they were planning to cause you some difficulty."

Still nothing from Leslie.

Ferris shifted his feet. It was not going as he had anticipated. The woman seemed repulsed by him rather than grateful for his concern. He had to let her know he was there to help her; was someone she could turn to if difficulties arose.

"I just thought you should know," he said, his voice brittle and nervous. "And I want you to know that I'm here to help, if you need help."

Leslie stared at him, openly incredulous. "Did you hear anything specific?" she asked. "Anything they said they were going to do?" The image of the cat flashed in her mind, was dismissed, then slowly reasserted itself.

"No, I'm afraid not." Ferris's smile became wan, flickering. "Just things like 'fixing you,' and 'see how she likes that,' nothing much more specific than that."

"Well, I want to thank you for telling me, Mr. Ferris," Leslie said, fighting off a shudder the man seemed to loose in her.

"If I can help, please call me," Ferris said, much too eagerly, Leslie decided.

"I shall. Thank you again." Leslie moved past him, headed for the counter. A chill crept up her back, and she couldn't help but wonder if it came from what Ferris had told her or from the man himself. She thought it was probably the latter.

As she placed her groceries on the counter she could feel his eyes boring into her back. Yes, it was the man, she told herself. Definitely the man.

# CHAPTER
## 15

"Cats and rats and elephants,
As sure as you're born,
But you're never gonna find,
A unicorn."

Hysterical laughter fills the room, drowning out the echoing refrain of the song's lyric, which still reverberates off the walls. The laughter stops as suddenly as it began and the eyes glare at the long, battered, butcher-block table where three frozen hearts, wrapped in plastic, sit in a semicircle around the tiny, grayish-red lump that once throbbed in the chest of a kitten called Maybe.

"Mother had a kitten. She did, she did, she did." The voice singsong, childish.

*Yes she did. And you killed it. She beat you, and the next day you killed her cat.*

"Yes, I killed it. I killed it. I killed it."

*And you're not sorry!* The shouted voice banging around inside the head.

Eyes close, wincing in pain from the sound. Then a sickly smile returns. "No, I'm not. No, I'm not. No, I'm not."

Wild, hysterical laughter again, as eyes glare down at the stark wooden table.

"Room for one more. Room for one more. Room for one more."

"I can't believe anybody could be that gross." Phillipa looked up at Robbie and immediately wanted to hug him. But he would hate that, she told herself. Probably hate it even more than what happened to his cat. So you better not.

She offered him a sympathetic smile. He looks so sad, she thought. Sad and confused and angry. She wished boys weren't so weird about affection. She knew she'd never understand how they could reject something that felt so good both to give and to get.

"You think it was Jubal who did it?" Tim asked. There was an ominous tone in his voice. "Or just some kids?"

They were seated under a large oak in the center of the schoolyard, using up the last half of their lunch break.

"I dunno who did it," Robbie said. "I know crazy old Electa offered to stuff the kitten for me."

"When!" Phillipa demanded.

"When I was over at her house the other day." Robbie hesitated. "And Jubal was there too. He was bringin' her some other animal she wanted to stuff."

"Whaddya mean, stuff?" Tim asked.

"She does that taxidermy junk. You know, she stuffs animals and things." Robbie knew stuffed was the wrong word, recalled Electa emphatically telling him so. But he just didn't care right now.

"Ugh, that's disgusting," Tim said. "And you said Jubal was there helping her?"

Robbie nodded. "You can't believe how disgusting it is. You'd have to see the room she does it in. There are bottles filled with animal guts, and everything."

"Oh, double gross," Phillipa said.

"What kind of animal did Jubal bring her?" Tim asked, unable to let go of Jubal's part in it all.

"I forget what it was. Some big, ugly weasel kind of thing," Robbie said. He paused, recalling something. "But it was really strange. Jubal wasn't scary at all, when he was there. It was like he was all nervous and scared himself."

"Scared of what?" Phillipa asked.

"I dunno. Scared of Electa, maybe."

"I know what you oughtta be scared of, asshole."

They all looked up and found Tommy Robatoy and one of his eighth-grade goons grinning down at them.

Robbie gritted his teeth. If there was one thing he didn't need today, it was having idiot, shitkicker Tommy on his case.

"Why don't you go fuck off, Tommy."

Robbie's words were met with stunned silence. Not only from Phillipa and Tim but from Tommy and his goon as well. Tommy's jaw was left hanging open, his mouth fixed in a circle of stupefied surprise, his eyes wide, blank, and disbelieving. His sidekick looked utterly confused; almost ready to scratch his head in bewilderment.

"You little shit," Tommy began, recovering at last.

"You're the shit, Tommy," Robbie snapped back.

The words seemed to hit Tommy like a punch, and he appeared to hesitate physically, not quite knowing what to do next.

Suddenly, Tommy seemed to sense the isolation his inaction had produced, the impotence Robbie's words had forced on him. Anger twisted his mouth and his hands balled into fists as he took a quick step toward his still-seated tormentor.

"Now you're gonna bleed," Tommy snarled as he reached down, trying to grab Robbie by the shirt front.

But before his hand got there, Phillipa surged up from the ground. Both of her arms were held straight out in front of her, and her upturned palms slammed into Tommy's chest, and sent him staggering back.

"Leave us alone!" she screamed at him, causing nearby children to turn and stare at them.

It was more than Tommy could bear. Rage flushed his face scarlet. "Bitch!" he screamed, his mind unconsciously imitating a scene he had seen his own father play out many times. His arm swung out, even before he realized it, and the back of his hand caught Phillipa flush in the face, bloodying her nose and knocking her back on the seat of her pants.

But the violence produced another reaction Tommy had not anticipated. Fully out of concert, Robbie and Tim heaved themselves off the ground and independently threw themselves on the older boy, knocking him on his back, where they proceeded to pummel his face and head without mercy.

Tommy's eighth-grade goon stood in shocked disbelief, until a yelp from Tommy snapped him back to reality. He jumped forward, reaching for Tim, ready to pull him from the fight, when a sharp pain engulfed his arm, and he looked down to see Phillipa's teeth firmly attached to his own flesh.

Yelping now with his own pain, the boy pulled back, twisting, pushing at her head with his free hand, fighting to break a hold that would not be denied, all the while forgetting Tommy, who was struggling to block the four fists that rained down on him.

"Stop it! Stop it! Stop it!" Louis Ferris marched across the schoolyard, face white, lips trembling.

When he reached the children he grabbed Robbie and Tim by the backs of the neck and pulled them off Tommy Robatoy, then turned wild-eyed on Phillipa, his voice rising to a scream: "Stop biting that boy!"

Phillipa obeyed, but not before biting down hard one last time and bringing a wail of new pain from her victim.

Ferris was beside himself, shaking with outrage and indignation. He seized Phillipa by the shoulders and glared into her face.

"How dare you bite that boy! How dare you!"

Phillipa glared right back at him. "He deserved it," she snapped. Her head whipped around to her victim, who was still rubbing his forearm. "And, if I get the chance, I'm gonna bite him again," she added through tightened lips.

"No you will not!" Ferris shouted. "Girls don't bite boys. They're not allowed to."

"The two of you jumped me. Two of you!" Tommy Robatoy's shouted complaint almost drowned Ferris out.

"That's right," Robbie shot back. "And every time you bother us, we're both gonna jump you again. And if you have kids there to help you, we'll wait 'til we get you alone, and we'll jump you then."

Ferris wheeled on Robbie. "Stop this! Stop this! Stop this!" he screeched. "You will not jump *anyone!*"

"That's what you think, Loopy," Robbie snapped. "We've had enough of this shitkicker."

"You bet we have," Phillipa said, stamping her foot for emphasis.

Ferris's eyes darted back and forth between the raging children. This was madness, and it could not be allowed. And this one—he stared down at Robbie—this one had actually called him *Loopy*. Denigrated him, just like that bitch of a sister of his had yesterday. His face tightened with anger. Oh, but he'd be punished, and punished hard now. And not just here at school. No, not just here. Not if he could help it.

Ferris raised one hand, the index finger pointing toward the school like some symbol of doom. "All of you. Get to the office. Now!"

Leslie put down the phone, not knowing whether to be upset or to laugh out loud. Louis Ferris had sounded on the verge of some uncontrolled frenzy. He had described the *horrific* fight, which had sounded, to Leslie, like little more than some younger kids standing up to a couple of older bullies. He had also described their attitudes as *arrogant* and *abusive*, which obviously meant they hadn't agreed with him that what they had done was wrong. But at the center of it all was the name Robbie had called Ferris. Leslie put her hand to her mouth. *Loopy*. God, she thought. If the man only understood what a gentle name that was to describe the sleazy way he came across to others.

She bit her lower lip. She had played the responsible parent and had promised Ferris she would deal firmly with Robbie's transgressions. Fighting she could handle, even if deep down she felt it had been the right thing for him to do. His supposed arrogance to school authority: ditto. The name-calling incident with Ferris? She began to laugh softly. Better stay clear of that one, she warned herself. You'll never do it without breaking up. The hard part will be not calling him Loopy yourself in the future.

Devlin stood far back from the mourners surrounding Amy Little's grave. He didn't want to intrude, didn't want his presence to make it harder for the family who was burying their child. If anything *could* make it harder.

The graveside, on the sloping hillside cemetery, was

crowded. It was as though the people of the town realized that something young and precious had been taken from them, something that was part of them, a part of their future. It spoke well of the people he lived among, the same people he often found very hard to understand.

Devlin hated funerals; had hated them ever since he had buried his wife six years ago. They were events that changed people's lives forever, often lessened them without hope of recompense. He stared at Amy Little's parents, a middle-aged couple who looked bewildered and beaten, and whose eyes held the promise of forever carrying some vestige of that imposed punishment.

Devlin understood. He had mourned at a similar graveside six years ago, after a young woman who had spent the evening partying at a bar had ended his wife's life in a fiery auto crash. And he too still bore the pain of those days, still felt the confusion and the anger of that needless loss.

He glanced about, hating the fact he was even there, hating that he would be back again. First for Eva Hyde; now Amy Little. And, in a few days, Linnie French, and the people driven to pain by her death.

He turned away from the grave as the minister began his final prayers and started across the cemetery, moving through the rows of tombstones, each of different age and shape and color, yet each markedly the same in purpose.

And now there'll be two more because you haven't found a killer. *A killer whose mind you understand as well as your own.* That acknowledgment terrified him, made him feel a fear that seemed to invade his mind, seize it, wring it dry. He had spent most of his life denying fear, and now it was controlling him, possessing him more completely than he had ever imagined possible. He no longer even knew if he was well or as mad as the killer he pursued, whether uncontrollable fear was a form of madness in itself, one that denied you the ability to act rationally, competently. Made you act because of the fear, not in spite of it. He felt the pressure of the pistol in his waistband. The pistol he had forced himself to wear, and he knew it was there because of his fear of it, his fear of using it again, using it and enjoying the power it gave him.

Ahead, slightly to his left, a mound of freshly turned earth caught his attention. He veered instinctively toward it and suddenly realized he had stood in this same spot not very long ago. It was Eva Hyde's grave.

Devlin felt sweat filling his palms, and he wondered about it. It was the one death for which he bore no responsibility; could not have stopped, unless he had happened by. Perhaps it just reminded him of his failure, and what it had produced.

He was standing at the head of the grave, and he began to move slowly around it. When he reached the foot, he abruptly stopped, his breath catching momentarily as he stared at the ground. There, at the edge of the fresh mound, lay a pressed and withered long-stemmed red rose.

"Paul?"

Devlin spun around at the sound of his name, his right hand instinctively moving toward the revolver under his coat. He stopped it inches from the butt, pulling it back before he was completely turned.

Gunter Kline stood staring at him, his face a mix of surprise and immediate concern. Devlin wondered what his own face looked like to cause such a reaction. He was sure it had not been caused by the movement of his hand. His back had still been turned when he caught himself.

"What is it, Paul? You look terrified."

Gunter was at the head of the grave, and he too moved slowly to its foot. He stared down at the rose, then squatted and reached out a hand.

"Don't touch it!" Devlin snapped.

Gunter looked up, confused. "Why, Paul?"

Devlin let out a long breath. He was regaining control now, overcoming his initial shock. "It could have been left by the killer. I want to have it examined."

Gunter's hand had remained outstretched toward the rose. Now it snapped back, the hand balling into a fist. "You think Jubal left this?" His face filled with a simmering rage, as though the grave had been desecrated; Eva's body as well.

"I said the killer," Devlin said, his voice softer, more controlled. "I don't know who that is, and neither do you."

Gunter ignored him. His eyes still glittered with hatred as he looked back at the rose. "I thought . . . I thought it was from someone else who cared about her. So many people did."

No, just you, Devlin thought. The others just used her. He

glanced back toward Amy Little's grave. The graveside was empty now, as the few remaining people entered their cars. He knelt next to Gunter, spread a handkerchief on the ground, and carefully levered the rose onto it with a pen.

"I'm going to find this killer, Gunter," Devlin said, as he stood, holding the rose in the handkerchief. "I'll find him, and I'll stop him."

Gunter glared at him. "Will you, Paul? When?" The anger in his voice seemed to break with the final word, and his head dropped, his shoulders suddenly heaving with heavy sobs. "Why can't he leave her alone?" he asked, his voice hoarse with emotion. "Why can't he leave her alone, even now?"

Billy Perot sat fidgeting in the passenger seat of Jack Chambers' car. At first Chambers thought it was simple nervousness. Now he recognized it for what it was. Anticipation. You really want to get at her, don't you, kid?

Chambers felt mixed emotions about that. He hated the idea of someone messing with his property. And yet, at the same time, he wanted her to hurt for what she had done. He would simply prefer to inflict the pain himself and not be forced to give up something that was rightfully his just to get the job done. But that just wasn't practical.

"There she is now," Billy said, bringing Jack back.

They were parked down the road from Leslie's house, far enough away not to arouse suspicion, but with a clear view of her kitchen door and side yard. Jack sat quietly as he watched her move toward the barn, a large carton held against one shapely hip. Billy twisted in his seat, no doubt watching the sway of her tight little ass, Jack thought.

"The barn's a good place," Billy said. "You just drop me at the driveway, and make sure you wait."

Good place for what? Jack thought. "Just make it fast. We don't need a patrolcar showing up and blowing me as your alibi." There was little chance of that, Jack knew. Only 10 minutes ago he had telephoned in the report of a school bus accident in the farthest reaches of the town. It would have sent every working patrolcar in that direction, along with every other yahoo on the rescue squad and volunteer fire department. They were safe and he knew it.

"Be as quick as I can," Billy said, grinning.

The grin was gone two minutes later as he loped up the driveway, staying on the soft grass along its edge to avoid giving any warning of his approach. Leslie stood only 30 feet away as he slipped through the barn door, her back to him, her attention fixed on an old freezer that sat in one corner.

He moved up behind her, his steps unheard on the well-worn floorboards, until he was almost close enough to touch her.

"Maybe I'll stuff what's left of you in that freezer when I'm through," he said.

Leslie jumped forward at the sound of his voice and spun around, eyes wide with surprise, shock. He was grinning at her, but didn't move forward. His body blocked any chance of escape, and he seemed to know it. His eyes roamed her body, and the grin took on a cruel twist. She began to shake, and was immediately enraged by her own reaction.

"Get out of here!" she screamed. "Get out! Get out! Get out!"

Billy took one quick step forward, his hand lashing out across his body in the same motion and crashing into the side of her head.

He growled the word *bitch* just as the blow struck, but Leslie barely heard it, as the force of the impact deadened her senses and sent her flying back. Her shoulders hit the floor first, momentarily driving the breath from her, and she lay there, rage mixing with the fear now that this was all happening to her again.

She needed a weapon, something she could hurt him with, stop him. Her eyes darted about her. The old butcher-block table next to the freezer had a knife rack at its side, but it was empty now. The pieces of wood that had once littered the floor had all been carried away by Pop.

Billy stepped over her, staring down; leering. Leslie lashed out with her foot, but he was ready for it and stepped away quickly.

"Not this time, bitch," he snarled. "You got away with that once, but not this time." He reared back with his foot and sent his boot smashing into her thigh.

Leslie grunted in pain and tears filled her eyes. Her mind screamed at her. No tears, dammit. Don't let him make you cry. She spun quickly, fighting through the pain, rose to her hands and knees, and started to crawl away. Even the act of crawling enraged her. *Crawling* in front of this filth. But she needed a weapon. She needed to hurt him. Kill him. It didn't matter anymore how much he hurt her. If only she could *get* him. Get *him*.

Billy grabbed her by the hair, twisting it hard in his fist, forcing her head to turn, then her body, until she fell back. He quickly straddled her, pinning her legs beneath him. Leslie's hands formed into claws and she raked at his face, going for his eyes.

"Bitch," he growled again, and sent his fist smashing into her temple, stunning her.

His hands ripped at her shirt, buttons flying in all directions, exposing her breasts. He grabbed one, squeezing it with all his strength, until she cried out in pain.

"Nice tits," he hissed. "Maybe I'll bite it off; cut it off."

Leslie slashed at his face again, raking one cheek, but missing his eyes. "I'll kill you! Kill you!" she screamed.

His fist came down again, aiming for her jaw, but missing, driving into her neck with such force it numbed one entire side of her body.

Leslie grunted, the pain robbing her lungs of air; tears filled her eyes, blinding her.

"Kill you. Kill you," she panted.

Billy ignored her and began to force open her jeans; to pull them down.

"I'm gonna fuck you so hard, you won't be able to walk," he hissed. Sweat had begun to form on his face, and his breathing had become shallow. "You're gonna love it. You're gonna beg for more."

Leslie began to fight beneath him, bucking wildly, trying to throw him off, her hand raking at him again, the tears blinding her, her nails only getting his shoulder, protected by a thick denim shirt.

"You move like that when I get it in you," Billy said, his voice almost laughing now. "Oh, now that's gonna feel so good."

Leslie screamed in rage, her arms flailing, teeth bared like a trapped animal. Through the haze of tears she saw Billy's arm draw back, then a large shadow appeared behind him and Billy was suddenly lifted up and away, freeing her.

Quickly, instinctively, she pulled her jeans up and began

pushing herself back along the floor. She heard a deep grunt, and as her eyes began to clear, she saw Billy's body tumble across the floor. Standing above him was the hulking figure of Jubal Duval.

Billy struggled to his knees, one arm pressed against his side, where Jubal's boot had caught him.

"You fuck," he hissed, forcing himself to his feet.

Jubal's face was cold and impassive, like a man taking on a task that bored him. He didn't speak; simply stepped forward, his right hand held flat and rigidly straight. Then it struck out—so quickly Leslie barely saw it—driving the rigid fingers into the base of Billy's throat.

Billy gagged, eyes wide, and both hands went defensively to his throat. Jubal's arms swung wide now, the palms slightly cupped, then flashed rapidly together, each striking one of Billy's ears simultaneously.

Billy let out a howl of pain, as one eardrum burst and the other came close to rupture. Leslie watched, fascinated, as Jubal continued without hesitation. Both hands shot out, grabbing Billy's shirtfront, and pulled him violently forward, as Jubal tucked his chin to his chest and drove the top of his head into Billy's face, breaking his nose and smashing teeth in a spray of blood. Billy sagged, but Jubal, still holding his shirtfront, lifted him and drove his knee into his crotch, then released him, watching with open indifference as he crumbled to the ground.

Then, as Billy retched uncontrollably, Jubal reached down, took his wrist, and, extending his arm, drove his knee into the back of Billy's elbow.

The resounding crack filled the barn like a gunshot, followed by Billy's agonized scream. But still Jubal wasn't finished, and as Billy's body curled into a fetal position, Jubal cocked his arm and drove his fist into Billy's kidney. A final scream was cut short as Billy fainted from the pain.

Jubal stared down at the wasted, battered figure of Billy Perot. He felt nothing, but was quietly reassessing his earlier evaluation that Billy might have made it in Special Forces. Slowly he turned to look at Leslie.

She was still sitting on the floor stunned, her shirt still ripped open, so transfixed she was unaware her breasts were exposed. It had all happened so fast. Only seconds, she realized. And the terror that had been Billy had been turned into a broken bloody pulp.

Leslie struggled to her feet, still unconscious of her swaying breasts. She stared at the hunting knife hanging from Jubal's belt and stepped quickly forward and reached for it.

"I'm going to kill him," she said, her voice not even recognizable.

Jubal's hand snapped onto her wrist with a pressure so intense she released the knife. The pressure eased and he stared into her face.

"You all right?" he asked, the voice flat, dispassionate.

She nodded, slightly frightened by him now.

"Cover yourself," he said, without looking at her nakedness.

Leslie looked down and quickly drew her shirt together.

"Now go call the chief," he said.

"How did you get here?" Leslie asked.

Jubal just stared at her. "Call him," he repeated.

Leslie looked down at Billy. "What about him? He'll wake up and get away."

"Ain't goin' noplace," Jubal said. He hesitated, eyeing her. "But I'll stay 'til I see the chief's come. Now go."

He walked to the barn door with Leslie, and as they stepped outside, the engine of a car parked across the driveway roared, throwing back a plume of gravel as it sped away. But not before Leslie saw the shocked face of the driver. Rage returned to her eyes.

"Other fella was waitin'," Jubal said needlessly. "Now go. I'll wait here."

Jubal watched as Leslie staggered quickly toward the kitchen door. I'll wait, he told himself, so's you don't come back and send Billy where he really belongs. There was no doubt in his mind that she would. He knew it. For sure, he told himself.

Jubal Duval entered the woods as Devlin's car pulled into the driveway, followed the edge for a hundred yards, then reemerged and slipped quietly into Electa Litchfield's back door. Devlin never saw him.

Leslie came out the kitchen door as he climbed from his jeep, and she could see the shock, then the anger in his eyes as he stared at her already swollen face.

"Where is he?" he asked, his voice low and threatening.

"The barn," Leslie said. "Jubal's watching him."

She had explained everything to Devlin on the phone. He had just walked into his office, returning from the cemetery, and he had raced back out to his car, after telling Free to send the rescue squad for Billy. Now, after seeing Leslie's face, he wished he had forgotten the last part.

Leslie led him to the barn, wondering why he hadn't reached out to her, tried to comfort her. It was as though all he could think of was getting to Billy. They entered the barn and found Billy alone, still unconscious.

"Where's Jubal?" Devlin asked.

Leslie glanced around and shrugged. "He said he was going to leave when he saw you'd come. I'm sorry, I didn't even think to tell him to stay."

"He wouldn't have listened."

He was still staring at Billy; his fists were clenched and the scar on his cheek was a bright white line. If he had been here when it happened, he would have let me kill him, Leslie thought. She found the idea confusing.

"Jubal didn't leave a helluva lot of him," Devlin said.

"It was . . ." She couldn't find an adequate word. "He was like a machine." She stared down at Billy's body. His arm was twisted at an obscene angle, and his face was pulp, covered with drying blood. "It only took him a few seconds to do this. And . . . and there was no emotion. He could have been combing his hair, or eating a sandwich for all the feeling he showed." She turned to look at Devlin. "Paul, he wasn't even angry."

"It's the training he's had," Devlin said. "He's been trained to react, not to feel."

"That's frightening," Leslie said.

Devlin looked at her, then back at Billy. He still hadn't moved. "You're lucky he was here," he said. "I should have been here." He wondered what he would have done if he had been. But he knew that answer all too well. Right now the thought didn't upset him at all. "Or at least one of my men should have been here. Somebody called in a phoney report of a school bus accident." He turned back to her. "I suspect it was Chambers. I think Billy's too cocky even to think of covering his ass that way. Anyway, they were prepared to have plenty of uninterrupted time with you."

A shiver went through Leslie's body and she hunched her

shoulders to stop it. In the distance, she could hear the sound of a siren. The ambulance, she told herself. She stared at Billy. His eyelids were fluttering now, and he let out a low moan. She hoped he died before anyone could help him. She hunched her shoulders again, fighting off another shiver. What's happening to you? she asked herself.

The sound of the arriving ambulance grew louder and Leslie suddenly squared herself on Devlin. "Hold me, will you?" Her voice held an imploring tone. "You haven't even touched me since you got here."

Devlin reached out and moved her gently into his arms. "I'm just so angry," he said. "I'm afraid to touch anyone."

Leslie laid her head against his chest. The bruises on her face hurt as she did so, and she winced in pain. But she kept her head against him.

"What will you do now?" she asked.

"I'll question Billy, as soon as the doctors let me, and then I'll find your husband."

The men from the rescue squad entered the barn, but neither Devlin nor Leslie moved.

"Get him," Leslie whispered. "Get him for me." There was a look of utter hatred in her eyes that she didn't want Devlin to see. She felt his body stiffen, but he said nothing.

A similar look of hatred filled Electa Litchfield's eyes as she stared out her upstairs bedroom window, her mounted cat pressed tightly against her breast. Jubal had left minutes earlier, after telling Electa what had occurred in the Adams' barn, and the woman had gone immediately to her room to watch the aftermath.

Her hands tightened into fists, squeezing the cat's fur between her fingers, then releasing it. She should have been there, she told herself. She should have, should have. Her fingers tightened on the fur again, and tears of anger filled her eyes.

# CHAPTER
# 16

The figure paces the darkened room. An animal trapped in a cage. The eyes are fearful, angry. Perspiration beads the brow and upper lip; strong fingers open and close, open and close. The voice comes in a harsh whisper, intended for no other ears.

"Someone else almost got her. Someone else."

The eyes seem close to panic now, and the figure quickly moves to the large box set on a table. Inside are dozens of crushed red roses. All the flowers from Mother's grave. All the flowers, so carefully preserved and protected all these years.

Fingers, slightly trembling, the nails painted a bright red, fly to the sides of the head and begin forcing their way through long, silky hair.

"No one else must harm her. No one."

Panic fills the eyes. "No one."

A hand enters the box, withdrawing three flowers. The figure turns and moves stiffly across the room to a small mirror attached to the wall.

Time to change, an inner voice commands. Time to become your other self. Time to do what must be done.

———

Devlin stood at the window of Billy's hospital room, while the doctors worked on him behind a drawn curtain. It was raining, and the window was sheeted with water, giving the lights and buildings outside the strange, wavering quality of a surrealist painting.

The hospital was in the small city of St. Johnsbury, 15 miles south of East Blake, and Devlin had followed the ambulance there, then waited for the doctors to finish tending Billy's injuries so he could question him. Three hours had passed and he was still waiting.

But it was better this way. It had given him some time to gain control of himself; allowed some degree of professionalism to creep back in. If Billy had been awake and vertical—no, just capable of being made vertical—he would have come close to killing him. No, closer than close. And he would have enjoyed it.

Devlin thought about the rage he had felt. He wondered if his feelings about Leslie were already that strong. He had known her for such a short time; really knew so little about her. Yet the rage had been there, and it had been so overwhelming. It could not have been stronger if Billy had attacked Phillipa. And that, somehow, didn't make sense to him.

The need to kill? To feel the power that gave? The text he had been reading talked about that. Talked about the monsters who felt that urge, that need. Devlin's jaw clenched even tighter, and he realized it had been held that way so long, the muscles there were beginning to hurt.

A doctor came through the closed curtain and approached Devlin. He was young and quite thin, and his name tag identified him as Dr. McCoy. There was a sunken quality to his eyes, something that seemed to be emphasized by a long, sharp nose and receding hairline. But it was simply exhaustion, Devlin thought. The man looks dead on his feet.

"Our friend's not in very good shape," McCoy said. "He'll need surgery on the arm, one eardrum has been ruptured, and we're concerned about the damage he may have sustained to one kidney." He paused, looking at Devlin sharply. "What the hell happened to him?" he asked.

"Somebody beat the shit out of him," Devlin said.

"One of your people?" the doctor accused.

I wish, Devlin thought. He shook his head. "Our little victim in there was in the process of beating and raping a woman, when somebody caught him and stopped him."

The doctor shook his head. "Well, they stopped him. For a good, long time. His balls are about the size of grapefruits." McCoy drew a breath. "Look, I know you want to question—"

"Doc, this whole thing may be tied in to some pretty grim murders we've had—"

McCoy raised a hand, returning the interruption. "Yeah, I heard about them. Okay, but only ten minutes. And keep your voice as low as possible or all you'll get out of him will be screams of pain." He tapped his own ear for emphasis.

A nurse was just pulling back the curtain as Devlin approached Billy's bed. The bruises and bandages made him look worse than he had on the floor of the barn. There was a tube coming from his nose and an I.V. attached to the back of his wrist. A catheter bag hung from the side of the bed, so Devlin knew there was another tube as well.

"Did you arrest him?" Billy croaked, as Devlin reached his side. His voice was barely audible, barely understandable through the pain.

"Who?"

"Jubal. Did you lock his ass up?"

"We're giving him a fucking medal," Devlin said.

"Look what he did to me!"

Devlin leaned close, keeping his voice soft. "You offer up a little prayer, Billy. Just to say thank you that Jubal got to you before I did."

Fear flickered across Billy's eyes. It was as though he had just realized he was alone with someone who wanted to harm him, hurt him badly, and that he was in no position to defend himself. His eyes looked past Devlin, searching for someone who could do that for him.

Devlin recognized the look; knew he had seen it before, although he couldn't recall where. He knew Billy had seen it before as well. He had seen it in Leslie's eyes only hours before, Devlin told himself. How do you like it, Billy boy? How do you really like it?

"What are you gonna do?" Billy asked. His eyes were wide and frightened, and there was perspiration on his forehead.

"First, I'm arresting you for assault, and attempted rape,"

Devlin said. He took a card from his pocket and slowly read Billy his Miranda rights. When he had finished, he simply stared at Billy for several minutes.

"Now," he said at length, "you're going to tell me everything you know about this. Who else was involved. What the deal was. Everything you did to this woman over the past couple of weeks." He took a small tape recorder from his pocket as he finished, but did not activate it.

"You just said I had the right to remain silent," Billy said. "And a lawyer."

Devlin nodded. "Billy, a few days ago you came to me with a story. A story about your daddy. You remember?"

Billy just stared at him, his eyes wary now behind the swollen tissue and bandages.

Devlin offered Billy a smile that did not carry to his eyes. "Well, Billy. If you don't talk to *me*, I guess, I'm going to have to talk to *him*. And I guess I'm going to have to tell him what you said. Hell, I may even embellish on it a bit." Devlin paused to smile again. "So then you'll get to talk to the lawyer *he* hires. A lawyer, I'd bet, who's going to do what *he* says. But, hell, Billy, he might not even hire a lawyer. Shit, he might not even make your bail. He might just say: Fuck the little shit, and have your clothes sent over to your cell. Then you'll be able to hire your own lawyer. Hell, it might even be better than that. When you get out of prison, you might never have to pick another fucking apple for as long as you live."

Billy's voice came in a frightened whine. "You said what I told you was confidential. You said you'd never tell him. I told you I wouldn't even testify, and you said that was okay, as long as I was straight with you."

"I lied to you, Billy," Devlin said.

Billy's mouth began to work, but no words came.

Devlin held up the tape recorder. "It's up to you, Billy. But this is the only chance you get."

Tears began to form in Billy's eyes. Christ, he's gonna start to cry, Devlin thought.

"You're a fuck, Devlin. You're a rotten fuck."

"Yes, Billy, I am." Devlin pushed the tape recorder forward, then depressed the record button and gave the time, date, location of the interview, and the names of those present.

"What kind of deal do I get, if I do this?" Billy snapped.

"For what you did *today*, Billy? You don't get any deal at all," Devlin said.

Billy's swollen lips began to tremble. "You ready?" Devlin asked.

"Yeah."

Billy told it all. The earlier incident with Leslie, when Pop had driven him off. The subsequent approach by Chambers; the plan they formulated, and the failed execution of that plan. It was enough to guarantee he'd do time, Devlin told himself. Even old Ray wouldn't be able to buy him out of that.

"What else did you do to this woman?" Devlin asked.

Billy hesitated, then told him about his own deal with Tommy Robatoy. He hesitated again. "And then there was that deal I made with Jubal about that fox," he said. A small smile came briefly to Billy's battered lips. At least he was getting back at that big prick, he told himself.

Devlin fought for control. He didn't want Billy to see how eager he was for information about the fox. He didn't want to give him any edge that would make him withhold information in the hope of finessing a deal for himself.

"So you paid Jubal to put the fox there? Just to scare her before you went there the next day?"

Billy nodded.

"What about the rose? You tell him to put that there, too?"

"What rose?"

Devlin stared at him. He really didn't know about it. He could tell that. Billy wasn't acting. And that meant that either Jubal left it, or someone else came along and did it before he, Devlin, had found it. Shit.

"What about Leslie's cat?" Devlin asked.

"I don't know about any cat."

Devlin turned to the sound of footsteps behind him, and immediately snapped off the tape recorder. Jim McCloud moved toward the bed, his eyes wary, anxious.

"I heard what happened," McCloud said without preamble. "So I came down to get the story." He stared at Billy, then turned to Devlin. "You still think Jubal's not dangerous?"

"I never said that. I said I didn't have any evidence that he was a killer. I still don't." He inclined his head toward Billy.

"He left this asshole alive, and in a lot better shape than I would have."

"He couldn't kill him. There was a witness present," McCloud snapped back.

Devlin looked at him, startled. "How much do you know about this?" he asked.

"I know that Jubal attacked him, while he was at Leslie's house. Electa saw Jubal running away, and she saw you, and then the ambulance come and get Billy."

Devlin nodded. "What Electa didn't see—because it happened inside the barn—was Billy beating Leslie, and then trying to rape her. And Jubal coming along and stopping him." He held up the tape recorder. "It's all here, in Billy boy's own words." He paused, enjoying the shock, then the anger on McCloud's face. "Now, you want me to go out and lock Jubal up for what he did?"

McCloud stared down at Billy. His face was scarlet with a sudden rage that surprised Devlin, and for a moment he thought he might have to grab McCloud to keep him away from Billy's throat.

"You little shit," McCloud said. "You fucking, little shit."

Billy hissed at him. "You just keep this out of your newspaper. You do anything to fuck up my trial, my father'll have your ass."

McCloud took a step forward, and Devlin moved quickly to place himself between the man and Billy. What the hell was this all about? he wondered. McCloud's anger seemed far in excess of what he would have expected.

McCloud stood there for a moment, his hands trembling with rage. Then he turned and walked quickly from the room.

Out in the hall McCloud moved toward the elevator. He didn't even notice Gaylord French coming toward him, his gunbelt swaying on his hip, his police badge gleaming. Gaylord grabbed his arm as McCloud began to pass him.

"Heah, I got a message for you," the town cop said.

"What?" McCloud snapped.

"I was just over Ray Perot's place. Telling him about Billy. He said I was to find you, and tell you to get down here to the hospital." Gaylord paused, confused. "But I guess you're already here." He grinned at his own small joke.

McCloud glared at him. "You tell Ray you found me. And you tell him I said he should go fuck himself."

The cop's jaw dropped. "You don't want me to tell him that," he said.

"Tell him," McCloud snapped, as he moved past the dumbfounded man and headed for the elevator.

It was already evening when Devlin pulled up in front of police headquarters and saw Jack Chambers entering El's store across the street. He had already been to Chambers' hotel, learned that he was not there, and had not checked out, and had resigned himself to the idea that the man had fled without even getting his luggage. This was more luck than he had hoped for.

When he entered the store, Jack was hunched over the counter, filling out a traveler's check. Another one, already completed, lay beside it. Just getting the local shopkeep to provide a little traveling money, Devlin told himself.

"You won't need to cash those, El," Devlin said. "Mr. Chambers isn't going anywhere except across the street."

Chambers, recognizing Devlin's voice, slowly straightened and turned. "What's this all about, chief?" he asked. He was forcing one of his best fraternity-boy smiles, but it wasn't quite working.

Devlin stepped up to him. "You're under arrest, Chambers."

"Like hell I am," Chambers snapped. He started to take a step back.

Devlin's right fist came from his hip, catching Chambers squarely on the chin. His knees buckled and he hit the floor flat on his back.

"Have to add resisting arrest to the charges," Devlin said, as he again withdrew the Miranda card from his pocket.

Chambers' face was white with shock, perhaps fear, Devlin thought. "What are the charges?" he demanded, his voice guarded now.

"Conspiracy to commit assault. Conspiracy to commit rape. Aiding and abetting assault. Aiding and abetting rape. Contempt of court, for violating a relief from abuse order." Devlin stopped to offer a cold smile. "And, like I said. Resisting arrest."

Devlin started to read the Miranda card.

"You're crazy," Chambers shouted, shaken now. "I know why you're doing this. You think I don't know you've been seeing my wife." He glanced at El, trying to make sure his message was getting across. "You're just setting me up, and I'm not going to take it." He was close to whining now. "I'm charging you with assault." He turned back to El, looking far from forceful as he lay on the floor. "I'll need you as a witness," he said. "You'll have to tell them what you saw."

El stared down at him with contempt. "You mean how you resisted arrest?" he said.

Devlin kept reading.

It had been late evening before the paperwork on Chambers' arrest had been completed, too late for Devlin to stop back at Leslie's house. He had called earlier to tell her of Jack's arrest and Billy's confession, and he had heard the relief in her voice. All she needed, she had told him, was sleep.

As he pulled into her driveway the following morning, he found others had reached her first. Pop Duval's pickup was parked next to the barn, and Gunter's stationwagon and Jim McCloud's Ford sat in tandem behind it.

Devlin climbed from his Jeep and suddenly jerked into a crouch as a shot echoed from behind the barn. Then a second and a third. His hand instinctively went toward his pistol, stopping again, almost with a will of its own, before he reached it. Perspiration burst into his palms, and his body seemed frozen in place. Oh, God, his mind shouted at him. Move. Move.

He pushed himself forward and ran along the edge of the barn, until he reached the corner, then took a quick, defensive look around it, his heart hammering, his breath coming in gasps. There, 50 yards back near the edge of the wood, Leslie stood in a combat shooting stance, leveling an automatic pistol at a silhouette target 30 feet in front of her. Pop, Gunter, and McCloud stood in a tight semicircle behind her.

Two more shots came in rapid succession, the final one leaving the pistol's slide mechanism open, indicating the weapon was now empty.

Devlin approached the group, still fighting to get himself under control as Leslie and the others moved toward the target. When she finally turned, Leslie found Devlin facing her, the look on his face a mask of feelings she couldn't even begin to identify.

"How'd you do?" he asked, his voice strange, distant.

Leslie stammered momentarily. "Not too well." She paused. "I hope what we're doing isn't against some town law," she said.

"Not in Vermont it isn't."

He glanced at the target. None of the bullets had hit the silhouette figure of a man. "What made you decide to do this?" he asked.

Leslie stared at him, irritated by his annoyed tone of voice. "Don't you think I've had enough reasons in the past few days?"

"For this? No." He waited a beat, watching her face redden. With anger, he told himself. "Where'd you get the pistol?"

"I gave it to her," Gunter interjected.

Devlin ignored him, extending his hand to Leslie. "May I see it?"

She handed him the pistol and he turned it in his hand, examining it. It was a Walther PPK/S, .380 caliber; several years old but well cared for.

He handed it back. "It'll cut anyone you don't like in half," he said, then glanced back at the target. "But from the looks of that, you'd be better off throwing it at him."

Leslie's face was crimson now. "I'll practice," she snapped. "I'm just learning. Gunter's teaching me."

Devlin turned to Gunter. "What made you decide to do that?" he asked.

Gunter seemed equally annoyed. "I heard what happened, and I offered this as a way to help. The woman needs to be able to defend herself."

"Why not a shotgun?" Devlin asked. "At least she'd be able to hit something."

Leslie interrupted before Gunter could reply. "Is it just the type of weapon you object to?"

"No. I think any weapon will cause you more trouble than it will ever help you. Unless you're *really* trained to use it. And that doesn't mean plunking a few shots in the backyard." She started to object, but he cut her off. "But if you're determined to slaughter somebody, at least you'd have a decent chance with a shotgun." He turned to Pop. "What do you think?" His voice seemed to demand a negative answer.

Pop looked down and toed the ground, then he looked up at Leslie. "Never cared for pistols much," he said.

"I can't carry a shotgun around with me. I can carry this." Leslie directed her words at Devlin, choosing to ignore Pop. Her eyes were defiant.

"Look, Paul, the lady does have some need to be able to defend herself. Just because you're uncomfortable about guns—"

It was McCloud, and Devlin's look stopped him in mid-sentence. He turned back to Leslie. "I hope you never have to use it," he said. "I just stopped by to see if you were all right." He paused again. "Your ex-husband will be arraigned later this morning, but there's no need for you to be there."

"Thanks for telling me," Leslie said, her voice still cold, but her eyes confused now.

"Call if you need me," Devlin said, turning and starting back to his car.

Leslie stared after him, wishing she could go to him, stop him from leaving.

Gunter stepped to her side, sliding one arm around her shoulder. "Don't let it bother you," he said. "Cops never like to see anybody else carrying a gun. It's something that's bred into them, I think."

"With Devlin it's worse than that," McCloud said. "I think he'd even take the guns away from the cops. Must come from having had to kill his partner when he was working in New York."

"What?" Leslie's head snapped toward McCloud. "What did you say about Paul killing his partner?"

McCloud was momentarily taken aback by the force of Leslie's question. "Yeah. Well, he killed him." He hesitated, finding the right words. "I mean he didn't have much choice. The guy had committed some pretty brutal murders. Oh, there was some stink about Paul doing it to keep him from going to trial. Sort of a mercy thing. But in the long run they ruled it to be a justified shooting."

McCloud had been rambling, and Leslie had just stared at him, hanging on every word.

"What's wrong?" Gunter asked.

"He told me about his partner. Told me he was killed," Leslie said. "He even told me the man had wounded him." She stared at Gunter, her eyes cold now. "But he never told me he was the one who killed him. In fact he made it sound like other cops did it. He deliberately made it sound that way."

"Well, I'm sure he meant—" The cold, angry look in Leslie's eyes shut off the rest of McCloud's words. He wondered why she was so angry about an obvious misunderstanding.

Devlin sat at his desk, feelings of self-disgust assaulting him. He had been like a child out there, shaking like a leaf, and then had put those feelings into words when he objected to Leslie's having a gun. It had been more of a tantrum than a rational, reasoned argument. Still, he knew he was right. A pistol would do her about as much good as a bloody bow and arrow, unless she had the proficiency gained through long-term training. And even then. . . . He shook his head.

And how much of it involved her ability to do something he could no longer even force upon himself? No, it was more than that. The scene this morning was insane. Gunter and McCloud, standing there with Pop Duval, while Leslie learned to handle a powerful handgun—both of them convinced that Pop's son was responsible for all the killings. What the hell were they doing? Teaching her to use a weapon in front of Pop, a weapon they hoped she'd use to blow Jubal's brains out? Jesus.

And the hell of it was they were both responsible men. Men who shouldn't want any kind of weapon in the hands of an amateur.

It was the killings. It was driving everyone slightly off balance. Scaring the shit out of them, even if they wouldn't admit it to themselves. Christ, it was surprising everyone in town wasn't walking around with a gun. He let his own thoughts sink in. Even you are. Again.

But all this didn't solve a damned thing. He had to go back and talk to Leslie. Talk her out of this nonsense. Make her see that toting around an automatic wasn't going to solve her problem. It would only create a new one.

*And what if she asks why it scares you so much? What do you tell her then?*

Leslie had the drawings spread out on a long table in her barn/studio. She had repositioned the table so she could see the open door, so she could not be crept up on again. But that was not the reason for the frightened, disturbed look in her eyes. The drawings were first drafts of work she had done for the newspaper, but in the corners and edges of each were the figures of murdered and mutilated women—pictures she had obviously penned when her concentration had flagged, when her mind had drifted from the work at hand. What terrified her was that she did not remember drawing them. Yet they were in her own style; there was no question of that.

Why these horrible pictures? she asked herself now. Why things you don't even *want* to think about. She looked down and saw that her hands were trembling.

She had started drawing after her mother's death, at the urging of the psychologist she had seen then, and the pictures had often been violent and terrible, an expression of the horror and fear she had felt. She had been terrified her father would die as well, and that she would be abandoned. So she had painted the scenes of death because it had filled so much of her child's mind. Later, she had worried that her father would find someone else to love, and that she would lose him in that way, and she had drawn him with other women, who were always ugly and cruel and unsuitable for him.

But why now? Why all the violence and ugliness now?

Because you're surrounded by it, she told herself. It's there, everywhere you turn, and you're drowning in it.

Her eyes darted around the barn. It had happened here, right here, only yesterday. Her eyes fell on the abandoned old freezer in one corner. She had been staring at it when Billy had crept up on her. She had been staring, frightened by its presence, concentrating so hard she hadn't even heard him until it was too late. And looking at it now unnerved her as well. She had wanted to be rid of it as soon as she had first seen it in the barn. She hadn't even wanted to look inside it; didn't want to even now. The idea chilled her. But she had known it was far too heavy for Pop to move alone, and she had decided to fight the fear, or at least to wait until she could afford to hire enough people to do it.

But if it frightens you so, why don't you just cover it with something. At least then you won't have to look at it.

A shadow filled the doorway, and Leslie reached for the carryall bag next to the table. It held the loaded automatic.

"Don't shoot. It's me." Devlin stepped through the door and walked slowly toward her.

Anger flared in Leslie as she watched him approach, a small, contrite smile on his face. She covered the drawings she had been studying and stepped around the table.

"You can help me do something," she said. Her voice was cold and distant.

"What?"

"I want to cover that freezer. There's an old tarp in the corner behind you."

"Don't like the way it looks?" Devlin asked as he dragged the tarp forward.

"It makes me nervous," Leslie said. "A neighbor's child suffocated in one when I was growing up. I've never felt comfortable about them since."

Devlin lifted the tarp and began fitting it over the freezer. The lid, he saw, was fitted with a bicycle lock. It looked new. "This is locked," he said.

Leslie stared at the lock. "I never noticed it before. But I don't think it was there when I first saw it."

"Maybe Pop put it on because of Robbie," Devlin said.

When the tarp was in place, Leslie started for the door, Devlin a step behind.

"I want to talk to you about this morning," he said.

"I don't want to discuss it," Leslie said, her voice still cold, angry.

"I just want to explain my reasons. Please hear me out?"

They were outside now, and Leslie spun on him, her eyes brimming anger. "I heard you out once, and you lied to me," she snapped.

"What the hell are you talking about?"

"You told me about your partner in New York. You told me how he was killed. But you left out one small part. That it was you who killed him."

Devlin froze, unable to speak for several moments. "Does it matter?" he finally asked.

Leslie seemed confused by the question; by what answer she could give. "You couldn't be honest with me. That matters. I've dealt with people who couldn't be honest with me all my life. So, yes, it matters."

Devlin stared at her, trying to understand, finding he could not. "I shot him," he said at length. "He was standing not much farther away from me than you are. He had a knife, and I told him to put it down. Told him it was over. He started toward me. He wanted me to kill him, didn't want to face what he knew he'd have to go through." His eyes continued to stare at her, cold and flat. "And I didn't want him to go through it either, because I knew what they'd do to him, the newspapers, television, the lawyers, all of them. Maybe some kind of unspoken agreement passed between us. I don't know. I still keep asking myself that. But in the end it didn't matter. In the end I raised the gun and I pointed it right at his forehead. And I pulled the trigger. And his brains and blood and pieces of his skull splattered all over the wall." Leslie's eyes were wide now, but he didn't stop. "It's an easy thing to do. You'd be surprised how easy. Just a little pressure from your finger and someone who was standing and breathing and talking to you isn't standing and breathing and talking anymore." He stopped to draw a breath, and his voice softened. "It can give you a tremendous sense of power. And, if you're unlucky enough, you can find you like that power. That maybe you wouldn't even mind doing it again."

He reached out and held each of her arms. "It's why I don't want you involved with it. If you're lucky, if it doesn't give you a thrill, the best it will do is give you nightmares for the rest of your life."

Leslie tried to speak, stammered, then tried again. "I have to be able to protect myself," she said. The anger was gone from her face now; from her voice. "I understand why it's hard for you—"

"Hard? Hard?" Devlin took her wrist, turned, and pulled her after him. He walked her to the silhouette target and the rear of the barn, released her arm, pulled the revolver from his holster, and turned toward the target. He fired five rapid rounds, each striking the target in the chest in a pattern no larger than his fist.

He turned back to her. "It's not hard, Leslie. It's easy. You just have to practice. Then you can kill someone too." His voice was trembling, and he tried to say more, but couldn't. Then he turned and walked away.

•

Devlin entered Gunter's restaurant and took a seat at the bar next to his friend.

"Drinking on duty?" Gunter asked.

"Just coffee," Devlin said to the bartender. He looked at Gunter in the mirror behind the bar. "Ever have one of those days when everybody seems to be telling you that you don't know what you're doing?" he asked.

"Many," Gunter said. "I had a mother who specialized in that, every day of her life."

"Black sheep of the family, huh?"

"Right up to the day she died." He shook his head with a touch of old regret. "Now everyone tells me the same thing. I didn't know how good I had it then. With just one person telling me."

Devlin sipped his coffee.

"How's the case going? Anything new?"

Devlin shook his head, still watching Gunter in the mirror.

"It's not going to stop, you know," Gunter said. "Not until someone stops it."

He knew what Gunter meant—knew that he too thought his chief of police didn't know what he was doing—but at least he wasn't saying it outright.

"I know," Devlin said.

Gunter toyed with the glass in front of him. "I got back about an hour ago," he said. "We stopped practicing right after you left."

"I know. I saw your car go through town."

"Are you still mad about the gun?" he asked at length.

"I'm not happy about it," Devlin said.

"Is that all?" Gunter asked.

Devlin looked at him in the mirror, but didn't say anything.

"I am attracted to her, Paul. I can't deny that."

"It would be hard not to be," Devlin said.

"And I am worried about her."

"Can't argue with that either."

"But you want me to stay away from her."

"I just don't want you telling her that a God damned gun is going to make her any safer." Devlin turned to look at him directly now. "It just might make her overconfident. And she can't go pulling it on everyone she meets. And this madman just might be somebody we all know."

"I just want to make sure she's protected," Gunter said.

"That's my job," Devlin said.

"I'm afraid that's not good enough, Paul."

Devlin stood, took a dollar from his pocket, and laid it on the bar. "Thanks for the coffee," he said.

# CHAPTER
# 17

The rose is laid at the foot of Amy Little's grave; the eyes stare at it, at the freshly turned earth, which seems so much like Mother's grave the day Father went to gather the roses from the funeral.

"We can keep them, and remember her by them," Father had said. And we did. We kept them all those years, until Father died too. And then you kept them. But only until you could find someone like Mother to give them to.

The figure turns and moves across the graveyard to the place where the hole has been dug for Linnie French, and a second rose is laid there. Now only one rose is left in the hand. Only one more to give. But that will be given with other final gifts. Gifts that only Leslie Adams can have.

A smile begins to form, then breaks into a huge grin. Final gifts. Only for her.

Jack Chambers had been arraigned and then released in his own recognizance, not because the charges against him weren't serious, but because the judge had believed that, as a lawyer, Chambers would not fail to appear in court when required.

But it was more than that, and Chambers knew it. Judges

viewed complaints by one spouse against another with skepticism. And, even more, they understood how easily a legal career could be smashed. It was something they were loath to participate in until the evidence was overwhelming.

And it would be, Chambers knew, as soon as Billy started singing his guts out, or the man he had seen standing in the barn doorway with Leslie was brought into court to corroborate her identification. Worse still, he didn't dare try to reach Billy, and he didn't even know who the other man was.

So his career was smashed, just as she had always wanted it to be. The word was out in this pissy-assed little town, and it would soon spread all the way back home. That had been confirmed to him as soon as he had walked into the bar of the Logger's Inn. The bartender, who had treated him like Christ returned to earth only a few days ago, now couldn't stay far enough away. He might as well have a leper's bell around his neck. And it would only get worse.

Seated at the bar now, Jack wondered how long it would be before his partners took the necessary steps to strike his name from the firm's door. Not long. Not unless Leslie withdrew the charges against him and Billy. Or unless she wasn't able . . .

He let the thought die, afraid even to think it. Not that he wouldn't like to. He could almost feel the pleasure of putting his hands around. . . . He stopped himself again. The consequences were too grave. But there was still a chance. Perhaps she'd listen to reason. Although she never had, never once during their entire relationship. He'd have to offer her something. Something she wanted. He swallowed the rest of his drink. Bitch, he told himself. Fucking miserable bitch.

He waved the bartender over, ordering another martini. His third, he thought. Or maybe his fourth.

"Do it again," he said, offering the would-be lawyer/bartender one of his better smiles.

You've always been a great negotiator, he told himself. Always been able to wear people down; work them into seeing your side of things. Perhaps you can even use repentance as a tool this time. Or perhaps you can make her see that the alimony you might agree to just wouldn't be there if you were disbarred and ended up working in some fucking supermarket. His hand tightened around his empty glass. Maybe you should just grab her by her fucking throat . . .

The bartender placed the new drink in front of him, and Jack offered up another smile. "You know, you're going to discover something when you finally start practicing law," he said, his voice slightly slurred. "You'll find negotiation is the real key to everything. For example, I'm about to start a negotiation now that—"

"With your wife?" the bartender interrupted.

The smile faded from Jack's face, replaced by the bartender's smirk as he turned and walked away.

"Beats the shit out of strangling her, doesn't it?" Jack snarled at the young man's back. "Just barely," he added to himself as he drained half the new drink.

"Two of them," Gaylord French said, as he laid a pair of pressed red roses on Devlin's desk. "One at Amy Little's grave and one at the hole they just dug out for Linnie. What's goin' on?"

Gaylord had been a distant cousin of Linnie French, and Devlin noted a hint of proprietorial anger in his tone.

"Nothing," Devlin said. He had sent Gaylord out to check the graves; had decided not to have it staked out the previous night due to manpower limitations. At least that's what he had told himself when he had made that decision.

Devlin nodded to Gaylord, dismissing him, then looked across his desk at Quint, who had come in to review the autopsy findings.

"I should have had the place watched round the clock," he said.

"You can only do so much with a five-man department," Quint observed.

"Yeah," Devlin said. "That's what I told myself yesterday." He stared at the flowers. "I should have asked the staties to do it."

Quint said nothing, knew there was nothing he could say. He knew Devlin had checked every florist in a 50-mile radius, had even checked wholesalers for individuals, who bought flowers in quantity on a regular basis. It had all proven fruitless.

"We don't even know if it's the killer doing this," Devlin said.

"It's the killer," Quint said.

"Yeah. It's him." Devlin stared at the wall for a moment, then turned back to Quint. "Why this new twist?" he asked. "And why put the rose inside Linnie's vagina, and not the others?"

"Maybe he did it with the others too," Quint said. "Linnie was the only one found inside. The others were all where animals could have fouled up the scene. We know that was true with Eva. Amy?" he shrugged. "She was found pretty quick. Before any animals started feeding on her." Quint shook his head at his own words. "But that doesn't mean they weren't sniffin' around."

Quint paused a minute, thinking. "There's also the possibility that the killer knew he'd been seen—by the boy—and was just in too much of a hurry to do that."

"Then you think it could be part of his . . . his . . ." Devlin couldn't find the right word.

"Yes, I do," Quint said. "I think, when he does it, he may even be playing out the real reasons for the killings. Either that or he's just getting crazier and crazier."

"And we keep saying *him*," Devlin said. "I wonder if we're just as crazy for doing that."

Quint stared at him, openly surprised. "You know something you're not telling me?" he asked.

Before Devlin could answer, Eric Mooers rapped on the doorframe of Devlin's office and stepped inside. "Even knocked this time," he said, grinning.

"I'm shocked," Devlin said. "What can I do for you?"

"I need one of your men," Mooers said. "One who knows the woods hereabouts."

"May I ask why?"

"Goin' after your boy Jubal," Mooers said. "Can't seem to find him in town, so I thought I'd go pluck him off his mountain."

"For these murders?" Devlin asked.

"That's what I'll talk to him about. By thumpin' on Billy Perot the way he did, he gave me a good reason to pull him in an' hold him a bit."

"He saved a woman from being raped," Devlin said.

"Well, that ain't been proven yet," Mooers said, grinning again. "So, technically, what we got is a pretty serious aggravated assault, Billy bein' in the hospital an' all." He stared at the angry expression on Devlin's face. "Shit, Devlin. He's the best suspect we got. Even the army said he was a fuckin' lunatic."

"You ever read the circumstances of his discharge?" Devlin asked.

"Nope. But I know it was a section eight, and that's good enough for me."

"If I were you, I'd read it first."

Mooers shook his head. "Plenty of time for that. Do I get one of your men, or not."

Devlin nodded. "Take Gaylord French. And good luck on that mountain, Mooers. You're gonna need it."

When Mooers had left, Devlin sat staring at the roses. "If he's right, if it turns out to be Jubal, I'm going to look like one horse's ass," Devlin said.

"Maybe," Quint said. "But at least you'll have done it the right way."

"I wonder if Eva Hyde, Amy Little, and Linnie French will understand that," Devlin said.

Robbie was out of breath when he reached the top of the incline. It was the farthest he had gone into the woods, even when he had been with the other children. But he had wanted to go, and the thought of meeting Jubal no longer frightened him.

He wasn't sure exactly why. Maybe it was what he had done for Leslie. Or maybe it had been the way Jubal had looked at him when they met at Electa's animal stuffing room. He hadn't seemed scary at all then. In fact he had seemed a little scared himself. Besides, there was a question he had to ask him.

Ahead of the boy a row of conifers stood against a rock wall and slightly to the left of the row a large patch of leaves and sticks lay scattered on the ground. Robbie thought he'd pick out a stout walking stick to make his trek back down the mountainside a little easier.

He walked to the fallen sticks, still trying to catch his breath.

"Don't go no closer!"

The harsh voice stopped him, and he spun around to see Jubal stepping out from behind the line of trees.

"Why?" Robbie asked, surprised the sudden appearance of the man hadn't unnerved him.

"Dangerous," Jubal said. "It's a trap."

Robbie wrinkled his nose. "Whaddya mean, a trap?"

Jubal came over and took his arm and led him to the edge of the fallen leaves and sticks. Using one foot, he pushed some of them aside. Beneath was a pit about four feet deep, and embedded in its floor were more than a dozen stakes, the sharpened points rising up like knives.

"It's a punji trap," Jubal said. "V.C. used 'em in Nam. Keeps an enemy from sneakin' up on ya."

"Who you think's gonna sneak up on you?" Robbie asked.

"Same fella tried to shoot me," Jubal said.

"Somebody tried to shoot you?"

Jubal nodded. "Don't want 'em to get close enough so's he don't miss. What you doin' here?"

"Lookin' for you," Robbie said.

"How come?"

"Somebody killed my cat. I wanted to know if it was you."

Jubal's eyes hardened and for a moment Robbie felt a resurgence of his old fear. "Don't kill no animals I ain't gonna eat," Jubal said. "An' I don't eat no cats."

"What about the animals you bring to Electa?" Robbie asked.

"Them's for her. For her taxidry. She usually saves me the meat when she's through. Been bringin' her stuff since I was in school." He stared hard at Robbie again. "I didn't do nothin' to yer cat. But I'm sorry to hear it's dead." Jubal shuffled his feet. "How's that lady you live with?"

"She's okay. She says you helped her. That you beat Billy Perot up bad."

"Don't like Billy much," Jubal said. "Not sure 'bout the lady you live with."

"Why?" Robbie asked.

"Could be one of them Saigon . . ." Jubal hesitated, not wanting to use the word *whore* with the boy. "Could be one of them bad ladies," he finally said.

"She is not," Robbie snapped. "And anybody who says so's a first-class asshole."

Jubal took a step back, surprised by Robbie's sudden vehemence; his angry choice of words.

"Didn't mean no harm," Jubal said.

"Well, you should watch out what you say about people. She's a really good person. She's my sister."

Jubal nodded slowly. "You better get on home," he said. "An' don't come up here no more. It ain't safe now."

Ray Perot stormed away from Jim McCloud's front door, leaving his wife standing there with a dumbfounded look on her face. He had been to the newspaper office, and now to McCloud's home, along with the various bars he knew Mc-Cloud frequented, and still had been unable to locate him.

He had gotten McCloud's message from Gaylord French the previous evening and had spent most of today trying to find him. The sonofabitch needed to be squared away. And he needed to be squared away fast.

At least the state cops were now looking for Jubal. He'd seen to that. But he needed McCloud to put the pressure on. And the sonofabitch was going to do it one way or the other.

Perot stood in front of his Lincoln thinking of where to go next. Electa Litchfield, he told himself. If anyone knew where to find that stupid bastard, she'd be the one.

Perot climbed behind the wheel of his Lincoln and gunned the engine.

"Come on, I'll buy you some lunch," Devlin said, grabbing his coat and following Quint out his office door.

"Chief, we just got a call maybe you should know about." Free's voice stopped them before they reached the front door.

"What is it?" Devlin asked.

"Bartender up at the Logger's Inn just called. Said your boy Chambers just got himself all liquored up and kinda hinted he was headed out to see his wife."

"How long ago did he leave?" Devlin asked. He could feel the sweat forming on his palms.

"Didn't say. Said he called as soon as he could."

"Shit," Devlin said. "Doc, you better come with me." The images of Chambers pounding on Leslie's door and of her firing at the silhouette target flashed through his mind. "I'm afraid I might need you."

# CHAPTER
# 18

The gifts are hers. The gifts are hers. The gifts are hers.

A harsh, uncontrolled laugh filled the room, forcing the figure to bend at the waist, sending a cascade of long, silky hair in front of the eyes.

The laughter stopped abruptly, leaving only a faint echo in the room. The figure straightened. The eyes hard now.

"It's time," the voice hissed. "Now it's time."

Leslie entered the barn, the carryall, which was always with her now, hanging from one hand. When she reached her drawing table, she stopped short. The drawings she had covered yesterday when Devlin arrived were now exposed and spread about the tabletop. She stared at them, wondering if she had inadvertently done it herself; knowing she had not.

She looked closely at the corner of one. It showed a woman, horribly cut, a bloody knife beside her body. But something new had been added. Now a crudely drawn flower lay beside the knife. Her hands began to tremble. She didn't think the flower was by her own hand, and she was almost certain it had not been there yesterday.

Leslie began to pull the drawings together, looking quickly

at each one to see if something new had been added. As she pulled the final one atop the newly formed pile, she jumped back and let out a small cry. There, on the table, hidden by the final drawing, lay a pressed red rose.

Leslie's hands flew to her head, her fingers raking through her long, dark hair.

"Oh, God," she whispered. "Dear God, please, no, no."

Leslie backed away from the table. Her hands and arms and legs were trembling badly now, and her breathing had become ragged, almost as though she had just run a long way. She turned her eyes from the table, and they were immediately drawn to the old freezer she and Devlin had covered yesterday. Now there was an awkward bulge beneath the tarp they had placed there, a large mound, as though something, some things, had been placed beneath it.

She stepped toward it, her hands shaking even more badly now. She didn't want to look beneath the tarp, but she knew she had to; had to learn what had been left there for her.

The tarp hung down, covering the face of the freezer, and she bent over, lifting it up and back until her hands were well over her head, the extended tarp obscuring her view of the freezer's top. The cascade of falling objects, disturbed by the movement of the cloth, brushed her thighs, then fell along her legs, landing in a pile at her feet.

Leslie jumped back, her heart racing now. There, lying in front of her, were dozens of pressed red roses, a tangled mass of stems and leaves and dead, withered flowers.

The trembling was out of control now, and Leslie began to move back, one slow, short step at a time, her legs fragile and unsteady beneath her.

"Leslie."

The voice sent a shock wave through her, and she spun around, staggering, almost falling. Jack filled the doorway, blocking out much of the light. His face radiated a nervous, uncertain aggression, and he stepped forward, holding up his hands, palms out, as if to ward off an anticipated objection.

"I need to talk to you. That's all, just talk."

Leslie glanced toward her work table, to the carryall that held the automatic. It was too far away, she told herself. Too far.

"Get out of here, Jack. Just get out. Right now. Right this minute."

She was glaring at him, and Jack's anger rose with the look. "You're destroying my life, my fucking career," he snarled. "You've got to stop it. Stop it now."

"Get out!" she screamed. "You have no right to be here. The judge said so. You'll go to jail if you don't get out right now."

Jack held up his hands again. "Look, we can make a deal," he said. "You can drop the charges—all of them—and I can give you a written agreement to a divorce, with a set amount of alimony."

He took a step forward, and the movement panicked Leslie. She turned and bolted for the carryall, her feet slipping beneath her, causing her to stumble, but she fought forward, hunched over, her hands and feet scrabbling at the floor, keeping her momentum going.

Jack reached her when she was still a foot from the bag, his hand grabbing her wrist, her free hand swinging out for it, but only managing to knock it over, spilling its contents over the floor.

Jack yanked her upright, staring down at the blue metallic glint of the automatic. His eyes widened with sudden rage.

"What were you going to do, shoot me? Fucking shoot me?" His hand swung in a wide arc, backhanding her across the face.

Leslie staggered and fell, but she scrambled up quickly and lunged past him, headed for the door.

Jack grabbed for her but missed, then lurched after her, catching her by the back of her shirt just as she passed through the barn door. He yanked, spinning her, and she fell to the ground again.

Jack saw the other woman for the first time now. She was older, and dressed in a heavy green poncho, and her eyes glared with an inner rage that startled him.

"Leave her alone!" The words were hissed. Each one said singularly, emphatically.

"Get out of here. This is none of your fucking business," Jack snarled.

The woman sprang at him, her hands in front of her like claws, and Jack struck out, his fist hitting her squarely in the chest, stopping her forward movement and driving her back, until she stumbled and fell against a pile of recently chopped wood.

"Electa!" Leslie shouted, seeing the sudden look of pain on the older woman's face.

Jack spun back and glared down at Leslie. "You fucking bitch," he shouted, then lashed out with his foot, catching her squarely in the ribs.

Electa fought for breath and struggled to a sitting position. In a chopping block next to her, a small hatchet lay embedded in the wood. She grabbed for it, using the handle to pull herself up, then twisting her wrist and yanking back, she jerked it free. She staggered forward, her balance uncertain, as she raised the hatchet above her head.

"Leave her alone!" her voice hissed again. "She doesn't belong to you."

Jack spun back to face the older woman, his arm cocked to strike out at her again. He barely saw the axe, barely heard the whisper of its blade, as it drove down into his forehead, cleaving his skull open like a ripe piece of fruit.

Jack's body stood upright for a moment. Then the muscles seemed to stiffen, then shake, until—almost at the same moment of Leslie's piercing scream—they collapsed and sent his body falling in a crumbling heap to the ground.

Electa stood above the body, face white with rage, eyes staring at the hatchet, which had been ripped from her hands and lay embedded in Jack's forehead. On the ground, next to the body, Leslie lay sobbing hysterically. Then her hands and feet began to kick out, pushing her foot by foot, away from Jack's still-twitching corpse. Finally she turned herself and began crawling away toward the house.

Electa stood staring at Leslie's retreating back, then looked again at the grotesque figure of the body. Then she turned abruptly, her face white and shaken, and began an unsteady march across the wide lawn that led to her own house.

Ray Perot pulled his car into Electa Litchfield's driveway, sending up a spray of gravel as he slid to a jolting halt. He climbed from the car and marched angrily to her rear door, knocked once, then again, then finally pulled it open and stepped inside.

"Electa!" he called, the voice harsh and demanding. Where the hell was the damned woman. He started down a long hall, then called again, stopping short when a door at the far end of the hall opened, revealing the woman, dressed in a green poncho.

"What do you want, Ray?"

Her voice seemed shaky to him, and her face didn't hold much color. "You know where I can find McCloud? I've looked all over this damned town for him."

Electa turned without a word and walked back into the room. Perot followed, coming to an abrupt halt as he passed the doorway and found himself in Electa's taxidermy room.

"Jesus Christ," he said. "What the hell is all this?"

Electa's back was to him; she didn't turn. "It's my work-room," she said.

Perot stared about him, at the table lined with various knives and instruments, the walls covered with jars of chemicals and other paraphernalia. There were skins stretched to dry, and on a far wall other jars, these holding what looked like the remains of an explosion in a butcher shop.

"Christ, Electa. I knew you were a strange woman, but this is more than even I would have guessed at."

Electa turned slowly. "You always thought that of me, didn't you? Even when we were children. Someone strange, you could use as you wanted, and then just laugh at with all your friends."

"Jesus Christ, Electa. Are you still harping on that? Christ, we were kids. Only twenty."

"You were twenty. I was only nineteen," she snapped.

There was something strange behind those eyes, Perot thought. Something happening in that mind of hers. He stared at her. God, she's gotten old, he told himself. Old and withered. His mind floated back. She had been quite something when she was a kid. Not beautiful, kinda plain really. But when you got those clothes off you saw what she was hiding under all that bulky stuff she always wore. And she did everything you asked her to. Christ, everything.

"Look, Electa. We were just a couple of horny kids. We were just—"

"No, Ray!" Electa's voice was like a gunshot, cutting his words down. "I thought you were special. Oh, I thought Ray

Perot was so, so special. I gave myself to you in every way you wanted. I made myself a little slut for you. And you went around and told everybody. Told them every little thing we did. And you laughed about it. About ugly Electa, who you could get to do whatever you wanted."

"Shit, woman. All boys do that. It's just part of growin' up. Tellin' the other guys how you were able to get yer dick wet. That's all it was." He shook his head, shook it at her stupidity. "Now just tell me where McCloud is and I'll get the hell out of here."

"It wasn't like that for me, Ray." Her voice was higher now, almost a controlled hysteria. "It's not like that for a young girl. It's a way to get love, to know that someone doesn't think you're ugly, or stupid, or worthless. It's a way to know that somebody wants you for what you are. Bare, naked, not covered by any veneer or make-believe of what you've been told you're supposed to be. You give it all, Ray. You give it and you pray to God that it will be seen as something good, something worthwhile. That you won't be laughed at as something useless, something stupid."

Her eyes were blazing with something, Ray now saw. It was slightly frightening, unnerving, and it annoyed him that it made him feel that way.

"Shit, you got a stiff dick, and that's all you had a right to expect. Just two kids in rut, that's all. And if I told people, you shoulda expected that. Shit, for all I knew, you were tellin'—"

Electa stepped quickly forward and struck out with her hand, catching him solidly in the face, rocking his head back.

Perot reacted instinctively, grabbing her shoulders and forcing her roughly back until she hit the long work table in the center of the room.

"You fucking cow! You silly bitch!" He was holding her at arm's length, pinned against the table, and his face was swollen with anger now, the eyes bloodshot and glaring. "Yeah, I told 'em. I told everybody what we did in the backseat of my car. I told 'em how all I had to do was ask you and you would—"

Electa blocked out the words, filling her head with white noise so she couldn't hear the brutality of each verbal blow.

Her hand fumbled along the table behind her, searching for something with which to strike back, finally finding it as her fingers closed over the handle of a long, thin-bladed skinning knife.

Perot's eyes were blazing now, and his mouth was working in a twisted snarl, spitting out words Electa no longer heard. Her hand swung from behind her back, the cutting edge of the long blade pointed up, the tip rising at a 45 degree angle, and she brought it forward with a force that made Perot's eyes bulge and mouth gape as the blade sliced into his stomach just above the belt line.

He let out a gasping grunt, spittle oozing from the corners of his mouth, and his hands tightened on Electa's shoulders as she grasped the handle with both hands and began to jerk it up in a staccato, slicing motion until it lodged in the cartilage of the sternum, cleaving a section of his heart in two, and sending a spray of bright red blood across the front of her poncho.

Perot's body sagged to one side, his feet beating a tattoo on the floor, and Electa turned with him, until his back was against the table. His body fell back, eyes staring with disbelief at the ceiling, and his throat emitted one long, shuddering breath that came out as the drawn-out word *Youuuuu.*

Electa stared at his dying eyes. "Yes, me, Ray. Always me," she whispered. "Now you know. Now everyone will know."

She released the handle of the knife and staggered back, her eyes roaming the taxidermy room as though seeing it for the first time. She turned and walked slowly from the room, her movements somnambulistic, then entered the main part of the house, stopping at a small table to stroke the breast of a mounted barred owl.

"It's all right," she whispered. "People will understand. Oh, they'll talk about me again. But they'll understand. They'll understand how I had to stop it all from happening again."

Electa's hand dropped from the bird's breast, and she slowly climbed the stairs to her bedroom. Once there she looked about, noting that everything was neat and clean and straightened. She thought about her kitchen, recalling that everything had been washed and put away. The house was clean. Neat as a pin. No one would say Electa Litchfield left a mess behind.

She walked to the mounted cat on her dresser and stroked it gently. "No, they won't, will they, kitty? Oh, I suppose they'll complain about Ray and that man in the yard outside. But I can't be expected to pick up after that trash, can I, kitty?" She stared at the cat as though it was speaking to her. "The other thing? Well, I suppose they'll talk about it. People do like to talk. But I was innocent when I did those things. So very innocent. Just like now."

Electa turned away from the cat, then glanced back over her shoulder, giving it one final look, and walked to the corner where her shotgun was propped against the wall. She broke it open with steady hands, assuring herself it was loaded, then walked to a chair before the window and seated herself. She stared out at the lawn and watched a robin hop along the grass, then stop and tilt its head to one side, listening for sounds that would signal food. Carefully, she positioned the butt of the shotgun on the floor between her legs and lowered her chin until it rested against the upturned barrel. She held the stock firmly with her left hand, then, reaching down with her right, placed her thumb against the trigger. A faint, distant smile played across her mouth, and she pressed down against the trigger.

Jubal entered Electa's rear door. He had been near the edge of the wood, and he had heard a muffled thudding and had immediately known what had made the sound.

He went first to the taxidermy room and stared dispassionately at Ray Perot's splayed body, then turned and hurried into the main portion of the house, first searching the downstairs rooms, then taking the stairs three at a time.

He staggered to a halt as he entered Electa's bedroom. She was slumped sideways in the chair by the window, as though tossed there like a rag doll, and the top of her head was blown away, the remnants of what had been there now spread in a grotesque pattern of bone and blood and brain on the ceiling above her. The shotgun lay at her feet.

Jubal walked to the body and knelt beside it, staring at what remained of the face he had known for so long.

"Why, Miss Electa?" he whispered. "I woulda helped ya. I wouldn'ta told nobody. Why'd you gone an' do this now."

Tears began to course down Jubal's cheeks. It had been a

long time since he had cried. Almost 20 years now. But he needed to. Now he needed to again.

Devlin and Quint found Leslie seated on the steps of her back porch as they climbed out of Devlin's car. She just sat there, every inch of her shaking, and she looked at Devlin, unable to speak, and just pointed with her hand toward the barn.

They found Chambers' body just as Electa had left it, the hatchet embedded in his forehead, a look of utter disbelief still on his face.

"Jesus," Quint said. He shook his head, as his training took over. "It went halfway into his head. The force of the blow must have been awesome."

Devlin's head snapped toward him. "Something a woman couldn't do? An average-sized woman?"

Quint recognized what he was doing and shook his head sadly. "Afraid I can't say that, Paul. With enough adrenalin pumping, any sized person could do it."

Devlin turned and started back toward the house, surprised by his own gut reaction, the immediate need to protect Leslie. "You better check Leslie, make sure she's okay," he said.

When Quint had finished and pronounced her unhurt, Devlin knelt in front of Leslie and took one of her hands in both of his. "Tell me how it happened," he said.

Leslie seemed dazed, not fully coherent, and her eyes blinked repeatedly as though trying to focus on her own thoughts.

"I was in the barn," she said at length. Her eyes widened as if remembering. "There were roses," she said. "Dozens of them. Someone had put them there, on the freezer, under the tarp. And on the table. But only one there."

"Take it easy," Devlin said. "Did Jack put them there?"

Leslie shook her head. "I don't know. I don't think so. He came in right after I found them and . . . and he attacked me. Hit me. Knocked me down." She drew a breath, fought to hold it. "I ran outside, but he caught me and knocked me down again. Kicked me. Oh, God. Oh, God."

"Is that when you hit him? Hit him with the hatchet?" Devlin asked.

Leslie shook her head wildly back and forth. "I didn't. Didn't hit him." She fought for breath again. "Electa hit him. She came to help me and he attacked her too. Knocked her down too. Then she grabbed the axe and hit him." She closed her eyes, then covered them with her hands, as though driving the vision away. "Oh, God," she said again through the muffling of her hands.

"Where's Electa now?"

Leslie shook her head again, her face still covered. "Don't know. Her house, I think."

Devlin stood and turned to Quint. "Take her in the house and do what you can for her," he said. "And call my office and get me some backup out here. And tell them to call the state cops, tell them we need the crime lab out here quick."

Devlin opened Electa's rear door slowly, thinking of the shotgun he knew she had, thinking he should draw his own weapon, but knowing he didn't want to; wouldn't no matter what. He eased into the house and worked his way toward the open door that led to her taxidermy room.

"Electa," he called softly, not wanting to startle her. "It's Paul Devlin. I'm here to see if you're okay."

Nothing. He called again, louder this time, but again there was no response. He eased himself along the wall to the open door and stepped quickly inside. He gasped at first sight of Ray Perot's body, then, as his professional instincts took over, he scanned the room quickly, and drew his revolver without a second thought.

He paused, looking at the pistol in his hand, then gritted his teeth and moved quickly to the door that led to the main part of the house.

Slipping inside, his revolver held up beside his head, Devlin again called out Electa's name. He heard movement on the floor above, and called again. Still nothing.

Devlin moved up the stairs, his heart beating in his ears, his mind telling him his backup would arrive soon. He reached the door of Electa's room, and again identified himself in a soft, he hoped soothing, voice, then stepped inside. His gorge rose when he saw Electa's mutilated body. His eyes dropped to Jubal, kneeling before the body, and he automatically brought his weapon to a two-handed shooter's stance. As his finger touched the trigger for the first time, his hands began to shake.

Jubal, still on his knees before Electa, turned slowly, his hands raised. "She's kilt herself," he said simply, watching as Devlin lowered his trembling hands.

# CHAPTER
# 19

Devlin led Jubal across the wide lawn, just as Luther Barrabee's patrolcar pulled into Leslie's drive. To his right, he could see that Chambers' body had been covered—by Quint, Devlin thought—and as he reached the rear porch, the doctor emerged from the kitchen door and nodded.

"She refused a sedative, but she seems much better now. She's a strong woman." He glanced at Jubal, his face forming a question.

"We have a murder and suicide over there," Devlin said.

"Who?" Quint asked.

"Ray Perot. Looks as though Electa killed him, then shot herself."

"Oh, God." Leslie had come up behind Quint. Her face went suddenly ashen, and she sagged against the door jamb.

"I better have a look," Quint said.

Devlin took his arm as he started past, halting him. "Perot was cut, very much like the women were. Take a close look at him. I'll need points of similarity."

Shock registered on Quint's face. "Sweet Jesus," he said. "Electa."

"Looks that way," Devlin said. Luther Barrabee had joined them and Devlin turned to him. "You get ahold of Mooers?" he asked.

"Free radioed him and his men soon as you called in. They're on their way here," Luther said.

"Good. I want you to take Jubal to the station. I'll need to talk to him later."

"Cuffs?" Luther asked.

"No," Devlin said. "He's a witness, that's all." He looked at Jubal. "I'll be down to talk to you in about half an hour," he said. "We just need a formal statement, that's all."

Jubal gave him a blank look. His cheeks were still streaked with tears, and he seemed confused, uncertain of what was going on about him. For the first time since he'd known him, Devlin thought, the man looked vulnerable.

Devlin climbed the porch steps and took Leslie's arm. She immediately dropped her head to his chest.

"I'm sorry," he said. "But I need you to come out to the barn with me, and go over everything just as it happened. Step by step."

Devlin was surprised how well Leslie was able to control herself. He was holding her arm, and even as they passed Chambers' covered body, he felt her tense, but her step never faltered. Inside the barn, she explained her movements, stopping at the drawing table where she had found the first rose. It was on the floor now, and Devlin retrieved it, placing it on the table.

He looked down at the drawings there, then up at Leslie. "Did you do these?" he asked, pointing to the women at the sides and corners.

"I must have," she said. "I can tell by the style. They're doodles. I often do them when my mind is concentrating on something else." She stopped; pointed at the flower that had been added to one of the sketches. "But I didn't put this here. It's not the way I'd draw it. Not at all."

Devlin shuffled the drawings, looking at each. "These murders must have been weighing pretty heavily on your mind," he said.

Leslie nodded. "More than I thought, I guess."

Devlin looked toward the freezer, at the clump of withered

roses that lay in a tangled mass in front of it. He walked to it, taking Leslie's arm and drawing her with him. "What made you look under the tarp?" he asked.

"I could tell there was something under it. There was this bulge in the tarp." She hunched her shoulders together, fighting off a shiver. "I had just found the other rose, and the altered drawing, and I had to see what was under there." She shook her head, then added quickly. "It was then that Jack came in, and we fought, and then I ran outside."

She started back toward the door, but Devlin took her arm, stopping her. He was staring at the lock on the freezer. "Do you have a crowbar, or something like it?" he asked.

Leslie retrieved a short crowbar from a workbench against one wall. "Some tools were left with the house," she explained, handing it to Devlin.

He inserted the bar into the new bicycle lock and pulled several times, snapping the hinged clasp that had been affixed to the freezer. "You told me before you didn't remember this lock being here," he said, not really asking it as a question.

"That's right," Leslie said. "And I think I would have. Freezers have always frightened me because of that child I knew who died in one."

Devlin took the lid in both hands and raised it. He stared inside. At the bottom of the otherwise empty freezer were four plastic bags. The freezer was not operating and the plastic on each was clear. Three contained what appeared to be human hearts. The fourth, the small heart of some animal. Leslie's cat, Devlin told himself.

He closed the lid and turned to face her.

"What is it?" she asked. Her face seemed frightened again; her jaw was trembling.

"The hearts that were taken from the women," Devlin said.

Leslie's hands flew to her mouth. "Those women's hearts were taken? And put here?"

A wave of relief went through Devlin. Only the police and the killer knew about the missing hearts. He drew a breath, hating his cop's mind that made everyone suspect.

"Electa must have put them here," he said.

"Electa! Oh, God. No, Paul. It couldn't have been her."

"I'm afraid that's the way it looks. We have more investigating to do. We have to search her house. Check her car for fibers and all, but I'm pretty sure we'll find what we need."

Leslie shook her head back and forth. "I don't believe it. I just can't." She looked up at Devlin. "Paul, the woman saved my life."

"Saved you for what?" Devlin asked. "For whom?"

Devlin left the interrogation room and went into his office where Quint was waiting. He slid behind his desk and rubbed his eyes with the palms of his hands.

"Was Jubal able to add anything?" Quint asked.

"Not a great deal," Devlin said, leaning back in his chair and stretching. "He had a long relationship with Electa. Going back to when he was a kid in school. Used to bring her animals he'd trapped. Spent a lot of time with her. Seems she was one of the few people he could talk to."

Quint held up a small leatherbound book. "I've been reading some of Electa's diary that you got from the house," he said. "She talks quite a bit about Jubal in here. Even about what happened to him in the army. You've glanced through this. Is that what happened to him?"

Devlin nodded. "The first day he'd arrived in Saigon," Devlin said. "He and some men from his unit stopped in this bar to have a beer. Seems this hooker came over to them, plying her trade. She left her purse behind on the floor. Jubal was in the men's room when the bomb went off." Devlin shook his head. "He never recovered from that. Just kept babbling about having to go out and get the Saigon whores. I guess seeing his friends blown to pieces was too much for him. Even with all that violent training he'd had." Devlin laid his forearms on the desk, resting his weight against them. "The people in Special Forces weren't too sympathetic. They hospitalized him, then finally shipped him back, and hustled him through a psychiatric discharge."

"Shameful," Quint said. He shook his head. "Electa seemed to think he was ashamed he never had a chance to fight over there."

"I think that's why he roamed the mountain, acting like he was protecting it from some invading force," Devlin said.

"You don't think he's dangerous, then," Quint said.

"Oh, yeah. I think he's dangerous. I just don't think he did any of these things."

Quint thought about that for a moment. "I also read the parts about Ray Perot," he said at length. "I don't think she ever recovered from the abuse he visited on her when they were kids."

"Well, she sure as hell paid him back," Devlin said.

"Poor, pathetic woman."

"I wonder why she didn't take his heart too," Devlin said, as much to himself as Quint.

"She probably realized there was no point. She knew she'd be caught then. Knew it was over for her." Quint placed the diary carefully on the desk. It contained much of the woman's soul, and he felt it should be treated as such.

"Are you releasing Jubal?" Quint asked.

"As soon as Mooers has a chance to talk to him. He's on his way back from the scene now."

"Who's there guarding things?" Quint asked.

"Gaylord's at Leslie's house, and Luther is at Electa's." Devlin sat back in his chair. "You know I'm still confused."

"About what?"

"Electa. I can understand her killing Chambers and Perot. It was men she was abused by—that kind of man—and I can understand her hatred for them. But why the women?"

"In her diary she made quite a few references about how she let herself be used sexually; about the kind of women who allow that sort of thing to happen. There seemed to be a lot of self-hatred, and hatred for women like that." Quint shook his head. "I guess it made sense to her," he said.

"Seems like Jubal was the only person—man or woman—that she did care about," Devlin said.

"It made sense, I suppose," Quint said. "He was an innocent. And his beliefs weren't very different from her own."

"I guess that's why he covered up for her. Kept his mouth shut about what he knew."

"What do you mean?" Quint asked.

"He told me he saw Eva Hyde killed."

"Jesus."

"Oh, he wasn't really close. But he said he recognized Electa by the poncho she always wore in the woods. And apparently she had a flashlight when she did . . . when she did the rest of it, and he could see the nail polish on her fingers, and her hair blowing out from under the poncho's hood." Devlin slowly shook his head, as if trying to make it all real to himself. "Kept saying she didn't have to kill herself; how he would have helped her hide Perot's and Chambers' bodies."

Quint scratched his head absently, almost as though the nails gently raking across his head might pull some hidden thought from it. "Don't think I ever saw Electa wear nail polish," he said. "Though I suppose most women do from time to time."

"Maybe she fixed herself up before she did these things. Christ, everything else about this case is that strange."

Quint nodded. "You gonna charge Jubal with anything. For covering things up, I mean."

"No. We'd just be wasting the court's time. With his history a charge like that wouldn't stand up."

"What about Mooers?"

Devlin smiled. "There's nothing in it for him now. He's not going to curry any favor with Ray Perot. I think Mooers will be happy just to have it finished. He didn't exactly distinguish himself on this one."

Their conversation was halted as Pop Duval appeared in Devlin's doorway. He looked nervous, almost frightened.

"I heard about what happened," he said. "Is Miz Adams okay?"

"She's fine, Pop. She's out at her house if you want to see her."

"Yep, I'd like that," he said. He paused, shifting his weight nervously. "Like ta see Jubal first, if I kin. You gonna haveta keep my boy locked up?" he asked.

Devlin shook his head. "He's gotta talk to the state cops, then we'll turn him loose." He could see relief wash over the old man's face.

"I was afeared it was him who done those things," Pop said.

"No. He was just trying to help Miss Electa."

Pop nodded. "Always was close to her. All the way back to the time his momma died."

Yeah, Devlin thought. Two battered souls, hanging on to each other for dear life. "We ought to get him some help, Pop. Some kind of counseling."

"That'd be good," Pop said.

"Maybe we could put some heat on the VA people," Quint said.

"Ya think?" Pop said.

"I'll make some calls," Quint assured him.

Devlin led Pop to the interrogation room just as Eric Mooers rumbled into the outer office. He did not look like a happy man, Devlin noted.

"Jubal's talking to his father. You'll want to talk to him, I suppose?"

"Shit. What for?" Mooers said. "Just send me a copy of your report, and I'll handle it with that."

Devlin held back a smile. Mooers couldn't bring himself to offer any kind of congratulations, or any acknowledgment he'd been off base. And the fact that he couldn't made Devlin's day.

"Is the crime lab finished up?" Devlin asked.

"All wrapped up," Mooers said. "Bodies are gone. Everything. I told two of your men to stay there—Gaylord and Luther. One at the Adams' house; one at Litchfield's. Just in case the reporters started nosin' around. McCloud's out there now, but I figured you wouldn't mind. He can feed stuff to anybody else who shows up. Keep those press assholes happy that way."

My God, Devlin thought. The man's actually checking with me to see if what he did was okay. He wished he could have the words bronzed.

"I'll have a copy of my report sent to your office by the end of the day," Devlin said. He could see that Mooers was trying to say something in reply. Somehow the words just couldn't get past his lips.

Leslie sat in her kitchen nursing a cup of coffee, Jim McCloud opposite her at the large harvest table. Through the wide multipaned window he could see Gaylord French standing sentry outside the barn, which was now roped off with yellow crime-scene tape. He had arrived half an hour earlier, expecting to find Leslie alone.

He had seen the crime lab truck and several state police cruisers heading out through town toward the highway and had assumed the police had finished their investigation. The children, he knew, weren't due home from school for another half an hour, and he knew Paul Devlin was in his office interrogating Jubal Duval. But she hadn't been alone; the place still had the feel of an armed camp.

"It will all be over soon," he said. "The cops will disappear and life will get back to normal."

"Normal." Leslie shook her head. "I'm not sure I even know what that means anymore."

"It means you'll have the quiet you came here for. That you won't be looking over your shoulder all the time. Having the police stop by to make sure you're all right."

Leslie stood and walked across the kitchen to the antique mirror that hung on the far wall and began straightening her hair with her fingers. It was the first time she had thought of her appearance since it had all begun. Hours ago now.

And you look like hell, she told herself. The thought hung on. Just like mother always told you when you were a child. *You're not a pretty girl, Leslie. You're plain as dirt. Better pay attention in school, and concentrate on your brain if you expect to get anything out of life.* How hard she had tried to change her mother's mind, to make her think she wasn't some ugly duckling. But it never worked, not with that, or with other things. There was always something wrong. She was always too slow, or too clumsy, or too sloppy, or too fresh, or too eager, or too . . . And God, how she had cried when the woman died. Not because she missed her, but because she had been glad she wouldn't have to hear those hated words any more. Guilty she had felt that way, but glad just the same. Her father had always told her how beautiful and wonderful she was. How special. She had needed so desperately to hear that.

A faint look of self-pity came to her eyes. It's all you ever wanted from Jack. All you ever wanted from anyone to whom you gave your love.

She turned back and offered McCloud a weak smile. "I appreciate your being here," she said. "I thought you'd be running around gathering information."

"I did that earlier," McCloud said. "I was out here, actually— a couple of hours ago—but they wouldn't let me see you. When I saw the state cops pulling out, I decided to come back and see how you were."

How she was. Leslie wondered what the answer to that might be. Perhaps in a few years she'd know the answer.

She glanced at the kitchen clock. It was almost time for the school bus. At least the bodies had been removed. At least the place wasn't crawling with state police, with everyone talking about the grisly details.

"Jim, do you think Tim could stay here with Robbie this afternoon? It might help if he had someone to play with, to keep him occupied."

"Sure. I'll tell him when the bus arrives. Then I'll have to go into town and see Devlin. I'll pick Tim up for dinner. You and Robbie are welcome to come over. I doubt you'll feel much like cooking."

Leslie smiled weakly. "Thanks, but I really think I just need to be alone."

McCloud nodded. There would be children around. And police. It would be some time before Leslie would be alone, he told himself.

"He spent most of the day looking for me. He was at the paper, at my house, and finally he went to Electa's. Apparently Gaylord passed on my message. My wife said he was fuming." McCloud grimaced. "If I hadn't spent the morning in Montpelier—or if I'd at least told someone I was going there—he never would have ended up at Electa's house."

"It's not your fault," Devlin said. "It's nobody's fault."

"I know," McCloud said. "It just feels so strange. So damned strange."

"If Perot hadn't been the kind of man he was, he wouldn't have done any of those things," Quint said.

"Yeah, if pigs had wings," McCloud said. He opened his notebook, preparing to get the answers for which he had come. "Dammit," he said. "I forgot to tell you. Phillipa's at Leslie's house. She wanted Tim to stay and keep Robbie occupied, and when Phillipa heard that, she got off the school bus too. I figured if you didn't want her there you could have Gaylord, or somebody, take her home. I hope you don't mind."

Devlin thought for a moment. Everything was cleaned up; there was nothing the kids could see. "No, it's fine. I can pick her up there on the way home. I was going to stop there anyway." He reached for the phone. "I'll call and let Leslie know."

Before he could call, Gunter Kline burst into Devlin's office over Free's shouted protests. His eyes were wild, and he seemed as close to panic as Devlin had ever seen the man.

"I just heard," Gunter stuttered, as Free came up behind

him. Devlin waved the patrolman off. "Is she all right? Was she hurt?"

"Leslie's fine," Devlin said. "Badly shaken, but fine." He told Gunter what had happened. About Chambers and Perot and Electa. Relief seemed to wash over the man, and seeing it gave Devlin a twinge of anger; jealousy. He wanted to tell him that his damned gun hadn't done her a bit of good, but he held back. "I've got a couple of men out there, keeping an eye on things, so she's being well looked after."

Gunter shook his head, as though trying to force his mind to absorb all the information. "Maybe I'll go out there and see her. See if she needs anything," he said.

"She said she really needs to be alone," McCloud said, feeling a surge of protectiveness. "In fact, she said she might go down to Philadelphia for a while. Just to get away from everything."

"What?" Gunter stared at McCloud not understanding at first. "Oh, yes. She has a grandmother down there. Yes. That would probably be good for her. To get away from all this madness."

And she has a husband to bury, Devlin thought. And a life to begin sorting out.

Gunter stared at Devlin, then shook his head again. "What's happening here, Paul. Nothing seems to make sense anymore."

"It's over now Gunter," Devlin said.

"Is it? God, I feel like I've been living on a roller coaster." He squeezed his eyes shut and drew a deep breath. "Christ, I need a drink," he said.

"Go have one," Devlin said. "Maybe we'll all come over later and join you."

"Jeez. Wait till the other kids hear about this. They're gonna wet their pants," Tim said.

"Don't be gross," Phillipa said, then giggled despite herself.

The children were in the field about 50 yards from the barn and appeared to be playing quietly. Actually they were watching Gaylord French, standing outside the yellow crime-scene tape, and trying to figure out where Jack Chambers' body had been; where all the action they had missed had taken place.

"God, I wish I had been here," Robbie said. "Seen Electa come racing along with that axe. It musta been like something in one of those massacre movies my sister never lets me watch."

"Gruesome," Phillipa said, wrinkling her nose.

"Yeah," Tim said eagerly, despite the small twinge in his stomach.

"I wish we could go in Electa's house, and see where all the rest of it happened," Robbie said.

"I bet there's blood everywhere," Tim added. He watched Phillipa make a sick face. "I bet old Electa was gonna stuff him. Just like all those animals you saw," he said to Robbie.

"That's disgusting," Phillipa said, as she thought she was supposed to, and deep down really meaning it.

"Let's go talk to Gaylord again," Robbie suggested. "Maybe he'll tell us more stuff."

"So there's not much more I can tell you," Devlin said as McCloud scratched away in his notebook. "There was no note; no confession. We have Electa's diary, and in an indirect way it seems to confirm she was the killer. She wrote about the killings; about each of the women, and how she felt about their lives. And she wrote about Perot."

Devlin stopped, and McCloud looked up from his notebook and stared at him. "I find it hard to believe. Christ, I've known her all these years."

Devlin felt his own concerns, his own nervous doubts, resurface. "Even without Chambers and Perot, if I had all the evidence I have now, I'd have arrested her," he said. He watched McCloud shrug agreement. Then why does it make you so uncomfortable, he asked himself. Because there's still one question you haven't gotten an answer to.

Devlin picked up the phone and punched out a number. It was answered on the first ring by a familiar rasping voice.

"Bernie, you skinny hump," Devlin growled. "What're you doing, sitting around the office counting your take from last night's bribes?"

"Who the fuck is this?" the voice of Bernie Peters rasped back.

"Paul Devlin, you sawed-off little shit. How've you been?"

A new stream of obscenities—friendly this time—came across the line, and the two detectives, who had worked together for so many years, exchanged news about the past months.

"Listen Bernie, I'm trying to get a hold of Charlie Moriarty. He was checking some information for me. Is he around?"

"He caught a big one," Peters said. "One of our up and coming designers—got his shit in all the better stores—did in his boyfriend, then hired two assholes to cut up the body in his sunken tub and get rid of the pieces. The clowns left some parts—including a hand that gave us a nice set of prints—on a fucking subway platform, and we traced it back to lover boy while he was still scrubbing down his bathroom."

"Beautiful," Devlin said.

"Yeah, ain't love grand," Peters said. "Anyways, I'll have that tub of lard call you as soon as he drags his fat ass in here. Stay away from the cows up there," Peters warned in closing. "I hear they all got AIDS."

Devlin had just finished briefing McCloud when Moriarty's call came in. He had told the newspaper editor everything. The missing hearts, the pressed roses left behind. There would be no trial now, and no one's rights would be jeopardized.

"Charlie, how are you?" Devlin began. "I hear you caught a sweet one."

"Fucking assholes," Moriarty said. "They couldn't find their dicks with both hands. I'm surprised they didn't leave a fucking trail of breadcrumbs back to the murder scene."

"You're entitled to an easy one every year or two," Devlin said.

Moriarty grunted at the righteousness of the statement. "Listen, Paul, I'm sorry for the delay in getting back to you," Moriarty said. "I had the info you needed yesterday, then all this shit came down on my head."

"No sweat," Devlin said.

"Man, you got a beauty here," Moriarty continued. "There's a juvenile record on one of your suspects would make your hair stand up. No charges ever filed, but that's because the old man wrapped the kid up in a very private institution where nobody could get through. But the circumstantial evidence on the case was pretty heavy."

Devlin listened, all color draining from his face, his hand tightening on the receiver until it too was white. His mind screamed at him that it couldn't be so. Then words spoken to him recently, inflections, hints at instability, all came rushing back.

"Jesus Christ," he said, as he put the phone down and pushed himself up from his desk.

"What is it, Paul?" Quint demanded, his voice burdened with concern.

"It wasn't Electa," Devlin said. "She wasn't the one."

The children were rolling around on the grass, giggling and screeching when the figure came out of the woods. The hood of the green camouflage poncho was pulled up, and a thick strand of long hair hung down over one eye, obscuring much of the face. Robbie stood slowly, watching the figure approach, and he knew immediately who it was. He had seen the figure from the road that day. The day Amy Little's body had been carried into the woods.

A hand reached up, brushing the strand of hair away, the red polish on the fingernails glinting in the afternoon sun.

"Is your sister here?" Gunter Kline asked.

Robbie began to tremble, and he had difficulty getting any words out. "Nooo," he finally managed.

"You shouldn't lie to me," Gunter said. "Children who tell lies have to be punished. Mothers are supposed to punish children who do that."

Robbie's face had gone white, and he knew he had to turn and run, had to get away from the man, had to tell Gaylord, who was still standing by the barn, had to warn his sister. He had to do all those things before the man grabbed him. He knew it, understood all of it, but his legs wouldn't move.

"You saw me that day," Gunter said. "I know you did. Saw me doing what mothers have to do."

The words broke Robbie's spell, that and the sound of Pop Duval's pickup truck pulling into the driveway. He turned and started to run. But Gunter was too fast for him. He moved faster than Robbie would have ever thought the man could move.

Gunter's left arm circled Robbie's throat and pulled him roughly back. There was a long, thick-bladed knife in the hand, and he placed it against Robbie's throat, the razor sharp edge pressed against the flesh.

"Call your sister," Gunter hissed. "I had to come for her. I couldn't wait anymore. There are too many people trying to take her away from me. And she's mine. She needs a mother's punishment too."

The other children began to scream in terror, alerting both Gaylord and Pop, and drawing Leslie quickly to the kitchen door.

Gaylord began moving toward Gunter, his hand instinctively going for his pistol. "Let go of that kid," he shouted. "Right now. Let him go."

Gunter's right hand moved to the pocket of his poncho, then snapped up, extending the long barrel of a Colt Python 357 magnum at arm's length, the sights centered on Gaylord's chest. The quick movement had thrown the poncho hood back, revealing a long, blond wig, which now sat slightly askew on Gunter's head.

Without hesitation, Gunter squeezed the trigger and fired point blank into Gaylord's chest. The impact of the powerful weapon, which could shoot through the engine block of a car, sent the patrolman's body flying into a backwash of blood. He was dead before he hit the ground.

Pop froze at the sight of Gaylord's murder, but only for a second. He had only been a few steps from his truck, and now he raced back to it, pulled his rifle from the rear window rack, and jacked a 30.06 round into the chamber as he ducked behind the open truck door, even though he knew it would never stop a bullet from Gunter's magnum.

Leslie screamed and raced down the back steps, but Pop reached out and grabbed her wrist, pulling her down behind the truck door.

"If you want your brother alive, you come to me, slut!" Gunter shouted. "Come to me, or I'll slice his head off."

Leslie pulled frantically against Pop's grip, but the old man only tightened it, holding her in place.

"Let me go," she screamed. "I've got to go to him. He'll kill Robbie."

"He'll kill both of ya, if ya do," Pop snapped. "You tell him you'll come if he lets Robbie go. Then I kin get a shot at him."

Before Leslie could do as she was told, Luther Barrabee came racing out of Electa's house and started across the wide lawn.

Gunter saw him out of the corner of his eye and pivoted his shooting hand toward the oncoming patrolman, squeezing off two rapid rounds that kicked up the dirt at his feet.

Luther threw himself to the ground, his revolver now out in front of him, steadied by two unsteady hands.

Slowly, Gunter began backing toward the woods, his eyes gleaming hatred, his head darting from side to side, watching for any new, unexpected attack.

"I'm taking the boy with me," he shouted. "Up into the woods. You come to me, slut, if you ever want to see him again."

Leslie screamed for him to wait, but Gunter continued to back away, the knife still pressed against Robbie's throat. The woman would come. As long as he had the boy, she would come to receive mother's punishment. He knew it. He had no doubts at all.

# CHAPTER
## 20

Devlin stood at Free's shoulder as the patrolman tried to raise Gaylord and Luther by radio. Finally, after several minutes, Luther's shaky voice came through. Devlin stood frozen for a moment, his mind ridiculously telling him there was now no point in going to Gunter's restaurant, then he pushed Free aside, assured himself the other children and Leslie were not hurt, and told Luther to tail Gunter at a safe distance, and to use his pocket knife to mark trees so they could follow his route.

"Don't do anything that's going to get that boy hurt," Devlin cautioned. "And watch your ass. We'll be there as fast as we can to back you up."

When Luther signed off, Devlin turned to Free. "Get ahold of Buzzy, and tell him to get out there. Then get on the state police ban, and tell Mooers to get his men back to the Adams' house."

As Free began dialing Buzzy Fowler's home number, Devlin went to the weapons locker and withdrew a sniper rifle equipped with a Leopold scope and headed out the door.

"Come on, Doc," he called. "We may need you."

"I'm coming too," McCloud said, hurrying after the others.

"Damn," Free said, as the door to the station slammed behind the three men. Buzzy's line had been busy. Probably off the hook, Free told himself. Just so he can't be called in for extra duty.

He turned back to the radio when the door to the interrogation room opened, and Jubal walked into the outer office.

Free pivoted in his chair and glared at him. "And where the hell you think you're goin'?" he snapped.

"I heard," Jubal said. "Goin' to my mountain to help 'em."

"The fuck you are," Free growled, heaving his bulk from the chair and moving toward Jubal. "You get your ass back inside there. I ain't got no orders to release you."

Jubal's massive fist hit Free flush on the jaw and sent him crashing to the floor as though his legs had been cut from under him. His head struck the corner of the old wooden desk, and he grunted once, then slipped into unconsciousness.

Jubal bent over him and rifled his pockets, finding the keys to Free's personal car, then checked to see the man was breathing and headed for the door. The state police would not be called by Fredom Sergeant for another hour.

Devlin's jeep cut off the highway and onto the unpaved road that rose along the ridge on which Leslie's house was situated. The rear tires spun, skidded, then righted themselves as the automatic four-wheel drive kicked in. He gunned the engine and fought the thoughts that attacked his mind. If only he had called Moriarty yesterday, or two days ago, Gaylord French would be alive now. Perhaps even Ray Perot. If only he had been the cop he told himself he was. If only. If only.

"What did you find out on the phone," Quint asked, as though reading his thoughts. The question seemed an accusation to Devlin.

"Years ago, when he was only twelve, Gunter killed his mother." He glanced at Quint, saw the incredulity on his face.

"Jesus," McCloud said from the rear seat.

"It was never proven. It's still carried as an unsolved case. And the cops who worked it never had a chance to really interrogate him. His father put him in a very private, very expensive institution. The kind of place the rich go to hide. The doctors claimed he was suffering from mental shock from his mother's murder, from finding her body." Devlin glanced at Quint again. "She was gutted. Pubis to sternum, while the father was away on a hunting trip. The autopsy showed she'd had sex just before she was killed."

"The boy?" Quint asked, even more incredulous.

"No. The investigation showed she'd had a long series of lovers. When the father worked late at the restaurant, or was out of town, her studs were wrinkling his sheets."

"And Gunter knew it." McCloud said.

"Had to, according to the investigation. He had the room next door, and probably laid there and listened to her humping away."

Devlin gunned the engine, keeping up the jeep's speed on a steep incline. "He'd been a troubled kid before that; was seeing a shrink, who never really got to the bottom of everything. But he swore there was no indication the kid was violent, so the courts refused to force the institution to make him available for questioning."

"And, of course, the juvenile records were sealed," McCloud added.

"That's right," Devlin said. "A cop I worked with in New York had a helluva time getting his hands on them. But he did. Yesterday," Devlin added, his guilt resurfacing. "He was tied up on a case, and couldn't call until today." Devlin knew he was trying to mute his own guilt with the others, but he needed that right now.

"Anyway, when Gunter was finally released from the institution, a couple of years had gone by, and his father got him a lawyer, who insisted he couldn't remember anything. Shit, maybe he couldn't. Maybe gutting his own mother like a fucking fish had driven everything so far back that he really had blanked it out."

Devlin took a sharp curve hard, skidded, then brought the car back on line. "There was one other thing," he said. "According to the initial murder investigation, there was a red rose found next to the mother's body."

"Dear God," Quint said. "And he's been leaving them for the other women he's been killing. They've been some kind of surrogates. The poor, sick bastard."

"Well, he's got one to go," Devlin said. "Now he wants Leslie to come to him in the woods, or he'll kill the boy."

"But why'd he suddenly come out in the open like this?" McCloud asked.

"The attacks on her I'd guess," Devlin said. "He was probably afraid someone else would get to her first." Devlin's mind clicked in. "It's probably why he gave her the pistol and taught her how to use it."

The car was quiet for several moments.

"Or maybe it was because I told him she was leaving town. Going back to Philadelphia," McCloud said, feeling his own sense of guilt surface.

Luther Barrabee moved slowly up the tree-filled incline, struggling for breath that had gone the way of too many sedentary hours on bar stools. He was sweating heavily, but not only from the exertion, and he kept thinking about the service revolver in his holster and the shotgun in his hands, neither of which he had cleaned or practiced with in several months.

Gaylord hadn't had a chance against this guy, he told himself. Gaylord, who'd been fit, and who could outshoot him any day of the week. He gritted his teeth. Gaylord, whose back now had an exit wound the size of a fucking grapefruit.

He stopped behind a good-sized birch, took out his pocketknife, and cut a swath of bark from the tree. He glanced over his shoulder. Where the fuck were they? He didn't want to go much farther alone, but he knew if that bastard killed the boy, he'd never forgive himself if he hadn't really tried to do everything he could. Jesus Christ, I just want to get home alive tonight, he told himself.

He started up the incline again, keeping low as best he could, his head darting from side to side, trying to spot any movement, any abnormal contour that might be Gunter in hiding. The sonofabitch's wearing camouflage, he told himself. Gotta watch for that. And the crazy fucker had red polish on his nails, and a fucking blond wig, he reminded himself. What was he, some God damned transformer, or something. Fucking New Yorker, that's what he was. Another fucking faggot asshole from the city.

And he ain't gonna know how to move around the woods like a home boy, he reassured himself, forcing himself to ignore what an avid hunter Gunter had always been. And he's got that kid with him, an' that's gonna keep him occupied some.

Luther stopped again and began cutting another swatch from a tree. He had leaned his shotgun against the tree, and his hand was frozen two feet from it and his holstered pistol, when Gunter stepped from behind a large rock, his own revolver leveled in one hand, the other arm still around the boy's throat.

"Where is she?" Gunter demanded.

Luther's mind raced. He glanced at the boy, seeing the fear in his eyes, knowing it was a reflection of what his own held. What do I tell him that will keep him from killing me? he asked himself. What?

"Where?" Gunter growled.

"She's comin'. I just came ahead, so's she wouldn't lose you."

"Is that why you're marking the trees?" Gunter asked. There was a wild, disjointed look in his eyes. Almost like you can see his crazy, fuckin' brain workin', Luther told himself.

"That's right," he said. "That's why I'm markin' 'em. You want I'll stay put till she comes, then bring her on up. Whyn't ya leave the boy with me?"

Gunter's face hardened, then a small smile crept to his lips. "You're lying to me. Mothers always know when they're being lied to. You should have known that."

Luther started to speak, but the blast of the magnum obliterated his first syllable, even as his body flew back down the hill. He slid and rolled to a stop, his body numbed by the impact, his mind still conscious. He lifted his head and stared at the blossoming red patch in the center of his stomach. Oh God, he told himself. That crazy bastard has gone and killed me.

Leslie and Pop were still by the truck when Devlin and the others arrived. The children were inside the house. Leslie's face looked pale and terrified, and Devlin could see her body trembling beneath her clothing. He went to her and held her close, smoothing her hair with one hand.

"Tell me what happened," he said.

Leslie told him, her voice faltering, the words coming out in a jagged rush. "And we just heard another shot," she concluded. "Just before you got here."

Devlin released her and pulled a portable radio from his belt. "Luther. This is Devlin. Over," he barked into the built-in microphone. He waited, then repeated the call again.

Gunter's voice came back. "Send her up. Send her up now or the boy will have to be punished too."

Devlin stared at the radio, his mind so filled with Gunter's words he hadn't even heard Leslie's anguished cry.

"She's coming," he said into the microphone. "Don't harm the boy. He hasn't done anything. He's just a child."

The voice crackled back. "All children need to be punished. Mothers know that. They're always so bad. So very bad." There was a pause in the transmission, then the voice screamed out of the speaker. "Send her to me! Send her to me now!"

"Shit," Devlin said. He wanted to reach Free, find out when Mooers and his men would be there. But he couldn't use the radio now. Not with Gunter listening. He turned to McCloud. "Jim, call my office. Find out where the hell Mooers' people and Buzzy Fowler are."

He turned to Leslie. "I know you heard what he said, but I don't want you going up there. I just can't guarantee your safety."

Leslie stared at him, the fear gone now, her eyes blazing anger. "I'm going, Paul. Either with you, or after you leave."

Devlin let out a long breath. And what you're not saying is, God help anybody who tries to stop you, short of tying you up and locking you in a closet. "Yeah," he said at length. "I know you are. I just thought I'd try."

McCloud came through the kitchen door. "No answer at your office, Paul. I called the state cops. They never heard from Free. They said they'd get somebody here as soon as they can, but Mooers and his men are already halfway back to Mont-pelier. I told them to stay off the radio."

"Shit," Devlin said again. "Jim, can you handle a shotgun." He watched McCloud nod affirmative. "Okay, you and Pop are gonna be my army." Some God damned army, he told himself. "Doc, we'll send the kids down the road to a neigh-bor's house, and I want you to come up with us until we find Luther. If there's nothing you can do for him, then you come on back down and stay with the kids. Take Gaylord's pistol with you, just in case."

Devlin glanced around, trying to see if there was anything

else left undone. Just getting everyone else killed, he told himself. Shit, he said again. Shit, shit, shit. But this time he said it to himself.

Pop was the first one to reach Luther's body. He then moved uphill to the point where the shots had been fired and checked the ground to see the direction Gunter had taken. Devlin came up beside him, while Leslie, McCloud, and Quint remained behind.

"I think I know where he's headed," Pop said. "Jubal's got a cave 'bout a quarter of a mile ahead. I figure he's goin' there."

"How would Gunter know about it?" Devlin asked.

Pop explained how someone had shot at Jubal outside the cave several days ago; how he was sure now it had been Gunter, even though he'd had no hint of that then.

"Why didn't you report it?" Devlin asked, knowing that he too would have suspected Gunter and would have brought him in for questioning, friend or no friend. And what else might you have found out if you had? he asked himself.

"Afeared to," Pop said. "Thought ya might use it as a reason to lock Jubal up. Fer his own protection, like. Knew Jubal couldn't handle that. Couldn't handle that at all."

Devlin stared at the old man, knowing he was right about that too. He would have used it as an excuse, if for no other reason than to get everyone off his back.

"Tracks go in that direction?" Devlin asked.

Pop nodded. "Won't be able to cover 'em good neither," he said. "Not havin' ta pull the boy along."

The shotgun blast hit Devlin's left shoulder, spinning him and sending him to one knee. The second shot took Pop in the right leg, dropping him flat. Devlin dropped next to the old man and watched as Gunter—a hundred yards farther up the hill, disappeared into the brush, dragging the boy behind him.

He's got Luther's shotgun, he told himself. But he fired from too far away. He looked at his shoulder, pulling his shirt away. Only one of the double O buck pellets had hit him—the shot spreading in a wide pattern at that distance—and most of the velocity had been spent as well. It hurt like hell and was bleeding freely, but it wasn't going to kill him. Next he checked Pop. It too was a flesh wound to the upper thigh.

"You think you can go on?" he asked, knowing the answer had to be yes if he was to have any chance of finding the cave.

Pop looked at his leg. "Ain't bad," he said. "Slow me up some, but that's all. Damn fool oughtta know a shotgun ain't no good from that fer. 'Specially not one a them cut-down kind you police fellas use."

Devlin struggled to his feet, gritting his teeth against the pain. Yeah, it's gonna slow me down a bit too, he thought. Shit.

Leslie, McCloud, and Quint were at their sides in moments, and Quint immediately started tending to the wounds.

"Nothing's broken," he said. "And no arteries were hit. But you're going to have a lot of pain, and the wounds will keep bleeding if you go on." There was no question in his mind, or voice, that they intended to go on. "And that's going to make you weak as hell before long," he added.

"It's not far," Devlin said. "Pop thinks he knows where Gunter's headed. You go back now, Doc. Watch the kids, and let the state cops know where we're headed whenever the hell they get here."

"Paul, you can't," Leslie said.

"There's no choice," Devlin snapped, his shoulder throbbing now with each movement. "And it's not far. Not far at all."

Gunter stopped at the line of trees covering the cave entrance and looked back. There was no one behind him, but he knew she'd be coming now. He had gotten two of the men—Devlin and the old hunter—and now only that drunk McCloud and the old doctor were with her. Now it would be easy.

He grabbed Robbie by the neck and forced him into a small gap between the trees. Robbie had been staring at the patch of ground covered with leaves and fallen branches—the punji trap Jubal had shown him earlier—and he had been searching his mind for a way to get Gunter to it; get him to fall into it and—. The thought sent chills through him, but he knew he had to try, knew it was the only way he could save his sister from this madman.

Gunter pushed Robbie ahead of him, suddenly finding himself inside the cave. He kept his body in front of the entrance to keep the boy from escaping, found a Coleman lantern near his feet, and bent and lit it.

A soft glow filled the cave, and Gunter's eyes roamed the walls and floor, taking in the photographs of Asian women and children, the stockpile of food and paraphernalia, and the weapons. Quickly, he took Robbie's arm, found a piece of rope, and tied his hands behind his back. Couldn't have the boy attacking him with a weapon, he told himself. And he knew how untrustworthy children were. Everyone knew that.

"Sit," he snapped, pushing Robbie to the floor.

The blond wig Gunter wore was twisted even more to the side now, but he didn't seem to notice, and it made him look even wilder, even more terrifying. Robbie wanted to ask him about the wig and the nail polish, but he was afraid of what it might produce, what other uncontrolled madness it might bring out of the man.

"Can we go back outside?" Robbie asked. "Places like this scare me."

Gunter stared at him, his eyes growing wary. He shook his head. "You're not scared," he said. "It's just those bad dreams again, that's all. Sometimes they seem very real."

"It's not a dream, I really am scared," Robbie insisted.

Gunter's eyes glowed with rage. "It was a dream," he screamed. "When I tell you something's a dream, it's a dream. Don't you *ever* tell me it isn't. Don't you tell me something's happening when I tell you it's not. Don't be so stupid. You always say such stupid things. Don't you dare tell *anyone* those things. Not ever. Do you hear me!"

Robbie began to tremble until his small shoulders seemed to be shaking his entire body.

Gunter continued to stare at him. "I know what you'd like. You'd like to take a knife and stick it into me, wouldn't you? You'd like to take that knife and cut my heart out, wouldn't you?" His voice had been rising in pitch, his eyes becoming more manic with each word. Suddenly, the tone dropped; became almost serene. "But you don't have to do that. It was only a bad dream. Just a bad dream. And you are Mommy's favorite, after all. You always will be her favorite."

Abruptly, Gunter turned and walked to the entrance of the cave, then out to the trees that covered it. He parted the branches and stared out at the descending hill.

Robbie sat shaking, not knowing what to do, what to say next. Go outside, he pleaded to Gunter in his mind. Go out and fall in that hole. Fall in and kill yourself on those sharp-ened stakes. Please. Please.

Jubal decided to climb the opposite side of the ridge from the cave, to come at it from behind where the cover would be better and the enemy wouldn't be watching for him.

The enemy. He knew who that was now; he knew who he was hunting, and what he must do when he found him.

It was always better when you could identify the enemy. They had taught him that, and he had listened. It's just that it ain't always easy, he told himself. Sometimes they dress up like they's somethin' else, an' you can't tell. But now you know. This time you know. For sure.

Jubal moved through the trees, gliding silently, like a part of the forest itself. He had heard two shots earlier, the muffled, dull thump of a shotgun, but it had been on the other side of the ridge, and he knew that's where the enemy was. But he still moved silently, each step carefully placed, barely making a sound.

It was like magic, he told himself. Moving this way through the woods. Become part of it, they had taught him. Only make sounds the forest itself would make. And don't avoid making *those* sounds. The absence of any sound is as revealing as the wrong sound, they had said.

So he moved that way. He was part of the wood. He was a tree. He was a bush. He was a bird navigating through the timber.

And the enemy was his. Even without a weapon, the enemy was his.

Gunter returned to the cave and began to pace back and forth. He returned to the entrance and took Luther's radio from his poncho and keyed the microphone.

"Where is she!" he shouted.

Devlin heard the call and debated whether to respond or not. Leslie and McCloud were more than 50 yards ahead now. He and Pop were moving more slowly, fighting the pain and the weakness that seemed to increase with each step. He had told them to stay close, but they had gradually moved ahead, and he had been unable to call to them for fear Gunter would hear.

The demand came through the speaker again.

"She's coming," he said. "Don't hurt the boy. She's coming to you."

Gunter stared at the radio. It was Devlin. He wasn't dead. "Are you coming too, Paul?" he asked.

Devlin's mind searched for the right answer. "You shot me, Gunter," he finally said. "The old man and I are hurt. I don't think we can make it to you."

Gunter smiled to himself. Just her, he told himself. Just her and the drunk. "I'm sorry I shot you, Paul. But you weren't being very nice. You weren't being very obedient."

He returned the radio to his poncho and looked back at Robbie. "She's coming," he said. "At last she's coming to me."

McCloud slipped and fell to one knee, scraping it badly on a small, jagged rock. He touched it gently, feeling the blood already soaking a small circle on his trousers. He could hardly breathe from the exertion of the climb, and his legs were already aching, and his arms felt leaden from carrying the shotgun.

Leslie seemed to be doing better, driven by fear-induced adrenalin, he told himself. She looked back at him, urging him on with her eyes. But he could tell she was uncertain. Not sure they were even going in the right direction. Pop had told them which way to head; what to look for to be sure they were going the right way. But dusk was creeping in, and everything seemed to blend together, each little rise so much like the last, and it was hard to tell if they were even staying on the same course.

At least they were moving uphill, he told himself. But with the small rises and falls that were part of the hill itself it would be so easy to get turned around and not even know it. Dammit, he wasn't a woodsman. He wasn't even a hunter. He didn't even go out to shoot the occasional rabbit.

Leslie stopped and looked back. Paul and Pop were almost a hundred yards behind now, and she could barely make them out through the trees. She wanted them closer. Wanted them leading the way, and it made her angry and frustrated that they were not. But they were hurt and bleeding, and Pop was even using his rifle as a crutch to force his body up the hill. They couldn't keep up, and she couldn't wait for them. Not with Robbie up there. Not with Gunter holding a knife to his throat.

But where was he? She was afraid if they veered too far in any direction they'd miss him; end up behind some outcropping and pass them by entirely. No, she told herself. Gunter will find you. You're the one he wants. You're the one he needs to kill. The idea sent a wave of cold fear through her, and she wanted to turn and run back down the hill. But she couldn't, and not just because of Robbie.

All her life she had been afraid of allowing herself to become afraid. She had forced herself to acknowledge it, and then reject it. And she had done it out of fear itself. It had all come from her mother, she knew. From her constant criticism; her endless harping. She couldn't allow herself to be afraid of being plain, or foolish, or frumpy, or stupid. She was afraid of that fear, knew she would suffocate and die in it.

She looked down at Jim, several yards below her on the hill. The knee of his trousers was torn and blood stained. She felt sudden panic. She needed him to go on with her. She couldn't do it alone. She just couldn't. Yes you can, she told herself. You can do it if you have to.

"Come on, Jim," she urged. "We have to keep going."

"Are you sure we're still going in the right direction?" he asked.

"No," she said. "But we have to keep doing it. We can't stop. Not now."

Jubal reached the cave, but remained far back, along the edge of the tree line that covered the entrance, watching, waiting, for the enemy he could sense inside. He was part of the trees, part of the brush, and he would use that to move closer when he was sure it was time.

He knew who the man, Gunter, was. He had seen him going in and out of his restaurant; had seen him around the town, and had even seen him hunting the lower edges of his mountain. He had not known he was the enemy then, but they had taught him that the enemy was clever. Now he had the boy, so the boy couldn't be the enemy as he had once feared. He wished he had a weapon, but that didn't matter. He had been taught to kill without one. He only had to be close enough to do it. He thought about the boy, and the others he could hear coming toward him, and he hoped none of them would have to die as well. The men who had trained him years ago had called that *collateral damage*, and though the words were strange to him, he knew it meant that innocent people sometimes had to die, and that in a battle it was something you couldn't control. He had a job to do. He had to kill the enemy, had to rid his mountain of the threat. That's what he was meant to do. That's what they had trained him for.

They reached a small clearing facing a row of pines, and McCloud could see there were footprints and scuff marks on the ground, and although he was not a hunter or tracker, he knew it meant someone had been there recently. He held up a hand, warning Leslie to be quiet, feeling slightly foolish at playing the wise woodsman.

Leslie felt immediate panic. She wanted to call out, wanted to let Robbie know she was close. But she wasn't sure it was the right thing to do. She looked over her shoulder, and could just make out Devlin and Pop about a hundred yards down the hill. She would wait until they reached her, wait until they were close enough to help.

Gunter knelt next to Robbie, his lips almost against the boy's ear. He had seen Leslie and McCloud enter the clearing, and he wanted to lure them closer; to trap them without the sound of gunfire that might alert others following them.

"Call your sister," he hissed.

Robbie shook his head, his teeth clenched, his eyes as determined as a 12-year-old's could be.

Gunter held the shotgun out so the boy could see it. "Call her, or I'll go out and shoot her now."

Tears formed in Robbie's eyes, and he began to tremble again. There was nothing he could do. He drew a deep breath.

"Sis," he called, his voice choked.

Leslie stiffened at the sound, which seemed to come from somewhere behind the row of pines. She saw McCloud raise his hand again, and she bit down on her reply.

McCloud moved slowly toward the tree line, the shotgun held out before him, finger on the safety. He wasn't sure what he was doing, what he should do if he were to see where Robbie was. At least he could move into the trees, keep himself under cover, and find out what was going on.

He stepped into the trees, parting the branches with one hand, pushing his head slightly forward.

The butt of Gunter's shotgun struck McCloud's forehead with such force that he never felt himself falling back. The last thing he saw was a blur of motion just before the impact, just before his world went black.

McCloud's body fell back from the trees like a cloth doll, his shotgun clattering to his feet. Leslie instinctively jumped back, stopping herself, as she saw Robbie propelled through the trees to fall next to McCloud. Before she could even step toward him, Gunter emerged from the trees, his own shotgun held out menacingly, not toward Leslie, but toward the back of Robbie's head.

"You should have come alone," Gunter hissed.

"I was frightened," Leslie stammered. "I was afraid you'd hurt my brother."

Gunter reached down and yanked Robbie up by his hair, bringing a yelp of pain and fear from the boy. He pulled him against him, withdrew the knife from his poncho and layed it against his throat.

"You'll watch him die unless you do just as I say."

Down the slope, Devlin and Pop—50 yards back now— could see the confrontation between a narrow gap in the trees. Devlin motioned for Pop to stay low to the ground, to use the hill to keep them out of Gunter's line of sight, then began to crawl forward, ignoring the pain, determined to get close enough before it was too late.

Leslie stared at Gunter, at the knife he held to Robbie's throat. She had the gun he had given her. It was tucked into the waistband of her jeans at the small of her back. She realized now how useless it was. "What do you want me to do?" she pleaded.

"I want you to come with me. Back through the trees." His eyes became wild, cunning. "I know others are coming, and I want you to hide with me until they go by here. We can be alone then, without anyone to interfere." His eyes seemed to lose focus as though his mind was drifting. "They were always protecting you, keeping you from me. I tried to stop them; tried to get them to arrest Jubal, but they wouldn't. I even tried to kill Jubal, so they'd think it was over and leave you alone. Then those others were after you, trying to get to you before me." His eyes sharpened again and he glared at her. "I knew it was never going to stop. I knew I had to come for you now. No matter what happened." His hand began to shake with rage. "Come here!" he shouted.

Leslie felt panic overwhelming her, and fought it back. "Let Robbie go and I'll come with you," she said. She had to buy time, had give Devlin and Pop time to reach her.

"No!" Gunter shouted. "I'll let him go after they pass us. Not until then."

His eyes were wild again, and Leslie was afraid he'd lash out at Robbie, slash open his throat in a moment of rage.

"All right," she said. "I'll do whatever you say. Just please don't hurt him. Please. Just don't do that."

Robbie stood motionless, his back pressed against Gunter, afraid to move, almost afraid to breathe or swallow with the cutting edge of the knife pressed so firmly against his neck. But his eyes were moving. They were darting back and forth between his sister and the covered pit, now only six feet or so to his right. If only he could move Gunter that way, he kept telling himself. But how? How?

"Gunter."

Devlin's voice filled the clearing, making Gunter's head snap toward the sound, eyes searching the ground. There. Only 30 or 40 feet away behind a mound of earth. And 20 feet to Devlin's left, the old man. It was too late. Too late to hide.

"Go away!" Gunter screamed.

"I can't do that, Gunter. You know I can't."

Devlin kept his rifle below the mound behind which he had taken cover. Gunter knew he had it, had seen it before. But he didn't want him to see it now, didn't want the sight of it to panic him into hurting the boy.

And if he moves away from the boy, what do you do then, he asked himself. Do you shoot the poor, sick bastard? Do you have Pop blow him away. His palms began to sweat at the thought. Please, not again, he told himself. Not another killing to live with, to dream about. He was not afraid of doing it. He knew that. He was frightened of the excitement building inside him; the adrenalin he could almost feel pumping through his body.

"It's over Gunter," he called. "No matter what, it's over. Let me help you."

Gunter's head began to dart back and forth between Leslie and Devlin and the old man. The hood of the poncho was up over his head now, and it shrouded his face, making his eyes seem wilder, darker.

"Go away!" he screamed again. "Go away now!" He pressed the knife more firmly against Robbie's throat, forcing the boy's head up and back. One jerk of his wrist and the boy would be dead.

"Let's talk about this, Gunter. We can work it out." Devlin's voice was softer; soothing, he hoped. A flash of movement caught the corner of his vision, and he turned his head only slightly, not wanting to alert Gunter. He froze, then fought the panic that had begun to grip him. Jubal was moving up on Gunter's left, moving within the tree line, then stopping, and moving again. Only a few inches at a time, but creeping closer. If he rushed the man—even if he got to him before Gunter saw him—the boy was dead.

He had to keep Gunter distracted, had to get him to loosen his hold on the boy. And then he had to shoot him, kill him before he had a chance to grab the boy again. He brought the rifle up as much as he dared, still out of Gunter's sight, but enough so he could snap it quickly to his shoulder and kill the man before he could recover. His palms were pouring sweat.

"Let the boy go, Gunter. He's not the one you want." Devlin's voiced cracked slightly, the strain showing through. Gunter's head snapped toward him, his eyes momentarily questioning the words.

"When did you start killing children, Gunter? When did that start?" His voice was shaking now. "Was Phillipa on your list? When were you going to get to her, Gunter? She's only seven. Were you going to wait until she was nine?"

"I don't hurt children!" Gunter screamed. "I just punish the ones like Mother. Just the ones like her." He shook his head confused. "Mothers have to do that. They have to punish. They're supposed to do that. They have to be perfect. And they have to be punished if they're not."

The man's mind was snapping back and forth, Devlin realized—from being a mother who had to punish to being someone—who?—from whom the punishment had to come. And who had to be punished? The imperfect mother, Devlin told himself. And she had to be punished by the child.

"The children are the ones who have to give the punishment, Gunter. The children have to help you." He was urging Gunter on now. Urging him to do what the man's twisted brain had told him he had to do, what the man had already done years before when he was a child. "Punish the mother," he shouted. "Let the child go. Let him help you punish the mother."

Gunter's head snapped violently toward Leslie, knocking the hood of the poncho away, the blond hair flying about his head, his eyes gleaming with renewed rage.

Only 15 feet away, Jubal froze, his eyes riveted on the long blond wig. He began to shake uncontrollably, his mind flashing back 20 years, all his training rendered moot in that single moment.

Gunter dropped the knife from Robbie's throat, gripping him now only by the shirt, with two fingers of the hand holding the knife. He raised the shotgun, held in his other hand, toward Leslie. "Come here," he growled.

"I'm coming, you bastard." Leslie took a step toward him. "Let Robbie go!"

Robbie twisted, pulling himself free of Gunter's careless grip, and fell to the ground. Devlin snapped the rifle to his shoulder, but before he could fire, his concentration was broken by a scream of rage.

Jubal rushed from the trees, his voice filling the wood. "Saigon whore!"

Gunter spun, the shotgun coming up in one hand and firing in the same motion. The blast caught Jubal in the shoulder, turning his body, but his momentum carried him forward, and he crashed into Gunter, seizing him in a one-armed bear hug that drove the breath from his lungs.

"Saigon whore!" Jubal screamed again, his arm closing like a vise on Gunter's spine. "You killed my friends. You killed all of them."

Gunter twisted frantically, but couldn't push Jubal off. His hand, holding the knife, finally pulled free, and he drove it into Jubal's ribs. Jubal's body sagged and slid down, and Gunter reached out, trying to grab Robbie again.

Leslie pulled the pistol from her waistband. She and Devlin

fired at the same time, one bullet ripping into Gunter's neck. His head snapped back, and with a final shout of rage, Jubal grabbed Gunter again, lifted him from the ground, and drove him back until they both fell, crashing through the leaves and branches that covered the punji pit.

# EPILOGUE

Leslie was placing the suitcases in the trunk of a rental car when Devlin arrived. He climbed from the jeep and smiled. His eyes seemed sad, she thought.

Five days had passed since the "battle of the mountain," as Robbie now called it. All the dead were buried—all except Jack, whose funeral would be tomorrow in Philadelphia—and even the newspaper and television reporters had lost interest, all them gone now, seeking mayhem elsewhere.

Leslie went to Devlin and gently hugged him, taking care of his healing shoulder. She still felt beaten and battered by the events she had lived through, and the feel of his body, the strength of it, gave her comfort.

"I thought you'd be here earlier," she said softly. "We're almost ready to leave."

"I would have been," he said. "But there was one more bit of business I had to take care of."

"About . . . about what happened?" Leslie asked.

"Indirectly, I suppose. We arrested Louis Ferris."

"Robbie's teacher?" She stepped back and stared up at him. "For what?"

"A young woman, whom he met in a bar—a student of his from a while back—charged him with sexual assault." He could see the surprise in Leslie's eyes.

"Do you think he's guilty?" she asked.

"There was a similar charge a few years ago, but it never made its way to court." He saw Leslie's surprise turn to disgust. "Not exactly the kind of news to make you want to stay, is it?" he said.

"I'm sure I'll find things in Philadelphia that will make this place seem like heaven." She smiled, realizing what she had said. "Well, almost," she added.

"Our mass murder rate is a lot lower," Devlin said. "And we've got a very concerned police department."

She drew herself against him again. "I know," she said.

He took her arms, wincing slightly at the pain in his shoulder, then stepped back and looked into her face. "Come back," he said.

"I will."

"I don't mean just to sell the house."

She smiled, a bit sadly, he thought. "I just need some time to think. And to get Robbie away from everything."

"The kids will miss him," Devlin said. "Phillipa didn't even want to go to school today. She wanted to come here."

"But you made her."

"I told her Robbie would be back. And I can't stand seeing her cry."

"She's lucky to have you."

"I've got room for more," Devlin said.

"I know."

Leslie looked up at him, her eyes hesitant, uncertain. "Did the information come back? About the bullet?"

Devlin nodded. "Yours missed."

Leslie let out a deep breath, and her body seemed to sag with relief. She looked quickly back at him. "Are you okay?"

"I'm fine," he said.

Robbie came flying out the back door, looking anxious and eager for his next adventure. "Hi, Dev," he said grinning.

He had bounced back well from the horrors that had been visited upon him, although his eyes seemed older, more cautious now. And since that day at the cave, he had treated Devlin as though he had discovered a new friend, one named Wyatt

Earp. Devlin hoped he could show him another side of himself one day.

Devlin ruffled Robbie's hair. "Ready for the bright lights and big city?" he asked.

"Yeah," Robbie said. "But I wanna come back."

"We all want you to," Devlin said.

"How's Pop?" the boy asked. "I haven't seen him since Jubal's funeral, and he looked real sad then."

"He'll be okay," Devlin said. "He knows Jubal finally got rid of the devils that haunted him all those years. And that's something for him to hold on to." He smiled at the boy. "He promised to take me deer hunting next month. I've never been."

Leslie looked at him, holding his eyes. "Will that be all right for you, Paul?" she asked.

He offered a weak smile. "Yeah, I think it will. I think that devil's under control too." He looked at Robbie. "May not shoot anything, but at least I'll march around the woods and kick up some snow."

"You'll have to be more quiet than that," Robbie said seriously.

"Maybe you should come back and go with us," he said.

"Boy, would I like that," Robbie said.

"We'll see," Leslie said. She looked at Devlin. "We really will."

Devlin watched them climb into the car, then leaned in the window and kissed Leslie gently on the cheek. "Drive safely," he said.

"I will."

"And come back."

"I will."

"To stay."

She smiled at him, and he took hope in that smile. It was all he could do.

Devlin watched the car pull out of the driveway and turn toward town and the highway beyond.

He was glad that he had lied to her; glad she didn't know; didn't have to carry Gunter Kline with her for all the years that lay ahead. He knew what it was like—living with someone you had killed. And he knew it was better this way.

"Come back," he said softly to himself.